ACCLAIM FOR SARAH E. LADD

"Beautifully written, intricately plotted, and populated by engaging and realistic characters, *The Curiosity Keeper* is Regency romantic suspense at its page-turning best. A skillful, sympathetic, and refreshingly natural author, Ladd is at the top of her game and should be an auto-buy for every reader."

—*RT Book Reviews*, 4½ STARS, TOP PICK!

"An engaging Regency with a richly detailed setting and an unpredictable, suspenseful plot. Admirers of Sandra Orchard and Lis Wiehl who want to try a romance with a historical bent may enjoy this new series."

—*Library Journal* ON *The Curiosity Keeper*

"Ladd's story, with its menace and cast of seedy London characters, feels more like a work of Dickens than a Regency . . . A solid outing."

—*Publishers Weekly* ON *The Curiosity Keeper*

"A delightful read, rich with period details. Ladd crafts a couple the reader roots for from the very beginning and a plot that keeps the reader guessing until the end."

—SARAH M. EDEN, BESTSELLING AUTHOR OF *For Elise*, ON *The Curiosity Keeper*

"My kind of book! The premise grabbed my attention from the first lines and I eagerly returned to its pages. I think my readers will enjoy *The Heiress of Winterwood*."

—JULIE KLASSEN, BESTSELLING, AWARD-WINNING AUTHOR

"Ladd proves yet again she's a superior novelist, creating unforgettable characters and sympathetically portraying their merits, flaws and all-too-human struggles with doubt, hope and faith."

—*RT Book Reviews*, 4 STARS, ON *A Lady at Willowgrove Hall*

"[E]ngaging scenes of the times keep the pages turning as this historical romance . . . swirls energetically through angst and disclosure."

—*Publishers Weekly* ON *The Headmistress of Rosemere*

"This book has it all: shining prose, heart-wrenching emotion, vivid and engaging characters, a well-paced plot and a sigh-worthy happy ending that might cause some readers to reach for the tissue box. In only her second novel, Ladd has established herself as Regency writing royalty."

—*RT Book Reviews*, 4½ STARS, TOP PICK!
ON *The Headmistress of Rosemere*

"If you are a fan of Jane Austen and *Jane Eyre*, you will love Sarah E. Ladd's debut."

—USATODAY.COM ON *The Heiress of Winterwood*

"This debut novel hits all the right notes with a skillful and delicate touch, breathing fresh new life into standard romance tropes."

—*RT Book Reviews*, 4 STARS, ON *The Heiress of Winterwood*

"Ladd's charming Regency debut is enhanced with rich detail and well-defined characters. It should be enjoyed by fans of Gilbert Morris."

—*Library Journal* ON *The Heiress of Winterwood*

"This adventure is fashioned to encourage love, trust, and faith especially in the Lord and to pray continually, especially in times of strife."

—*CBA Retailers + Resources* ON *The Heiress of Winterwood*

DAWN AT EMBERWILDE

OTHER BOOKS BY SARAH E. LADD

THE TREASURES OF SURREY NOVELS

The Curiosity Keeper
Dawn at Emberwilde
A Stranger at Fellsworth (available spring 2017)

THE WHISPERS ON THE MOORS NOVELS

The Heiress of Winterwood
The Headmistress of Rosemere
A Lady at Willowgrove Hall

DAWN AT EMBERWILDE

A TREASURES OF SURREY NOVEL

SARAH E. LADD

THOMAS NELSON
Since 1798

Published in Nashville, Tennessee, by Thomas Nelson. Thomas Nelson is a registered trademark of HarperCollins Christian Publishing, Inc.

Thomas Nelson titles may be purchased in bulk for educational, business, fund-raising, or sales promotional use. For information, please e-mail SpecialMarkets@ ThomasNelson.com.

Unless otherwise noted, Scripture quotations are taken from the King James Version of the Bible.

Publisher's Note: This novel is a work of fiction. Names, characters, places, and incidents are either products of the author's imagination or used fictitiously. All characters are fictional, and any similarity to people living or dead is purely coincidental.

Library of Congress Cataloging-in-Publication Data

Names: Ladd, Sarah E., author.
Title: Dawn at Emberwilde / Sarah E. Ladd.
Description: Nashville : Thomas Nelson, [2016] | Series: A treasures of Surrey novel ; 2
Identifiers: LCCN 2015044774 | ISBN 9780718011819 (softcover)
Subjects: LCSH: Man-woman relationships--Fiction. | Upper class families--Fiction. | GSAFD: Christian fiction. | Love stories.
Classification: LCC PS3612.A3565 D39 2016 | DDC 813/.6--dc23 LC record available at http://lccn.loc.gov/2015044774

Printed in the United States of America

16 17 18 19 20 RRD 5 4 3 2 1

This novel is dedicated to Martha—in loving memory

Chapter One

*M*rs. Brathay's shrill voice shattered the late-morning silence like a warbler's call unsettling dawn's still mist.

"Miss Creston! Are you in here?"

Isabel Creston froze just inside the door to the kitchen garden. She'd been caught.

Again.

Determined to hide her early excursion from Mrs. Brathay's observant eye, Isabel shoved her flower basket onto the cupboard's top shelf, ignoring the pink primrose petals that showered to the planked floor. With a sharp tug she freed the bow at the small of her back to release the gardening smock from her waist, then she shrugged it from her shoulders.

"Yes, I am here!"

Isabel managed to loop her sullied apron over one of the iron hooks and whirl around just as Mrs. Brathay appeared in the corridor.

"There you are," exclaimed Mrs. Brathay, her lips pinched. "I have been looking for you for at least this past hour."

"I am sorry." Isabel offered a sheepish smile. "I was not aware."

"Obviously." Mrs. Brathay ducked to avoid the entry's low wooden beam as she nodded toward the bloom tucked in the neckline of Isabel's gown. "And what in heaven's name is that?"

Isabel drew a deep breath, attempting to buy herself time for an explanation. "It is a rose. From the south garden."

1

"I know it is a rose, Miss Creston." Impatience increased the volume and pitch of the older woman's terse voice. "What I do not know is why you are wearing it in such a fashion. You know such adornments are not permitted."

Isabel bit her lower lip at the scolding. She was well acquainted with Fellsworth School's stringent regulations regarding uniforms, and she accepted the requirement that she wear a stark black gown day after day without complaint. But being forbidden to adorn it with at least a spring flower seemed excessive.

"I only wanted to see how it would look."

"Well, you can take it off now." The headmistress's pointed gaze traveled up from the bloom and landed on Isabel's hair. "And did you go out with your hair loose like that again? I thought we already had this discussion."

Isabel plucked the rose from her gown's neckline, tossed it onto the shelf above the hooks, and smoothed a flyaway hair into place, immediately regretting her decision to dress her hair so hastily. Hair was to be worn in a tight chignon at the base of her neck, not held up loosely with pins as she now wore it. Furthermore, her hair was to be covered anytime she was out of doors.

She had disregarded both mandates.

Mrs. Brathay clicked her tongue. "La, child. What I am to do with you I'm sure I don't know. But now's not the time to be fretting on such things. Mr. Langsby has asked to see you in his study."

Dread, foreboding and heavy, sliced through Isabel. It was not every day that one was summoned to speak with the school's superintendent, and rarely for a positive reason. "If it is about my hair, I—"

"Don't be silly," hissed Mrs. Brathay, her gray eyes alert. "Mr. Langsby is far too busy to be concerned with such things. It seems I must remind you that regulations, and the adherence to them, develops discipline. I fear you have been allowed far too many passes in that regard. If you hope to obtain a permanent teaching position here at Fellsworth, then it would behoove you to show respect for the rules."

Isabel nodded. "Yes, Mrs. Brathay."

"Now, tidy your hair and then go to Mr. Langsby's study. There is a messenger for you there."

Isabel jerked her head up. "A messenger?"

"Yes, a messenger." Annoyance sharpened Mrs. Brathay's tone. "Mr. Langsby is a very busy man, as is, I am certain, the gentleman who is with him. Your little morning escapade into the garden has kept them both waiting."

In an unmasked display of displeasure, Mrs. Brathay gripped her skirt in one hand, turned, and quit the corridor.

Isabel held her breath at the reprimand, and once the older woman was clear of the threshold, she expelled her air. The meaning of Mrs. Brathay's words settled on her.

A messenger.

Here.

For her.

In her experience, messengers rarely harbored pleasant news, and she doubted this one would be different.

She ran her hand down the front of her gown, pausing only momentarily to notice a slight tremble in her fingers. Without giving herself time to contemplate the reason behind it, she brushed away tiny bits of leaves and grass from her morning outing that still clung to the rough fabric.

Delaying whatever or whoever awaited her would not alter the situation.

The most likely reason for the summons was that she had been offered a position as a governess. It had been her objective for many years—and the endeavor of many young ladies who studied at Fellsworth—to secure such a position. But normally, news of that nature would come from Mrs. Brathay, the girls' headmistress, not from the superintendent, whose duty it was to oversee both the boys' and girls' schools.

Determined to receive the news with calmness, she lifted her chin and swept her hair away from her face. After a steadying breath, she turned on her heel and made her way down the narrow corridor leading from the back entrance to the school's main hall.

The school seemed unusually quiet for the late-morning hour. Had the building echoed with the normal sounds of hushed voices and hurried footsteps, however, she might not have noticed the distant sound of a horse's whinny. She stopped and turned to discover the source. There, through the tall, leaded windows, was a carriage as black as coal, and in front of it stood four jet horses. The sunlight shone on their glossy manes and polished harnesses. One of the horses, a giant, majestic creature, tossed his head, and the high-pitched whinny echoed yet again. The carriage's door boasted an unfamiliar yet vivid crest of red and gold. She stood transfixed by the elegant sight, for such a carriage rarely came to rest before Fellsworth School's humble entrance. The image both incited new questions and returned her to the task at hand.

Tearing her gaze away from the sight, Isabel turned and hastened from the foyer down the hall leading to the superintendent's study. At its end, the thick door stood slightly ajar. As Isabel drew closer to the slim crack, she angled her head just so to glimpse the back of a gentleman sitting in a padded chair. This man could not be Mr. Langsby, for his shoulders were far too broad and his hair too full and light. Even by what little of his clothing she could see, there could be no denying the fabric's richness and the crispness in his coat's high collar.

Growing more curious, she removed the few pins clinging to her locks, shook out her unruly hair, coiled it tightly per protocol, and secured it in place. She had little idea what message awaited her once she passed the threshold, but she would not meet it unprepared.

Once satisfied her hair would not come tumbling about her shoulders, Isabel lifted her hand and tapped on the door.

A voice, deep and solemn, sounded from within. "Enter."

Before pushing the door open with her fingertips, Isabel drew a deep breath in an attempt to calm the possible scenarios swirling through her mind. She stepped into the spacious chamber, her footsteps barely audible on the thin, worn rug.

Bright white sunlight spilled through the freshly cleaned leaded windows and splashed on the contents of Mr. Langsby's modest study. An expansive walnut desk stood anchored in the center of the oblong room, and atop its polished surface sat piles of papers and books so plentiful that Isabel wondered how Mr. Langsby even knew the task at hand.

But it was not the pile of letters or the height of the windows that captured her attention. For as she entered, the messenger stood and turned to face her.

Isabel had not formed a clear idea of what sort of man might bring her a message, but she was certain that even in her wildest imagination, he never would have been like the man before her. She had expected a footman or possibly a tradesman of some sort, but before her stood a gentleman. His status was evident in the cut of his clothes, the arrangement of his hair, and the glossy sheen of his boots. With light brown hair and a strong, square jaw, he was extraordinarily handsome. She summoned courage to look at his eyes. They were warm and deep but large and bright. And they were fixed firmly on her.

It felt as if minutes passed before Mr. Langsby spoke, though common sense whispered it had been but a few seconds. "Miss Creston, good, you are here at last."

She turned to Mr. Langsby as if jolted by his words. He was seated behind the desk. As usual, a crisp black coat adorned his wiry frame, and his thinning gray hair was gathered into a sparse queue at the base of his neck. Compared to the other man in the room, he appeared almost frail.

Isabel found her voice. "My apologies, Mr. Langsby. I am sorry to have kept you waiting."

"Well, you are here now. And not a moment too late, for there is a guest here for you." Mr. Langsby stood and turned to face the tall man standing before her. "I'd like for you to meet Mr. Bradford. Mr. Bradford is the superintendent of the foundling home in Northrop, just south of here."

Mr. Bradford.

Isabel returned her attention to their guest, and he smiled and gave a crisp, formal bow.

She curtsied as elegantly as her nervous legs would allow.

Mr. Langsby continued. "Mr. Bradford is an old friend of mine. I have known him for a number of years now. Imagine my surprise when he arrived this morning with this missive concerning you."

Mr. Bradford finally spoke, his voice deep and rich. "I am always pleased to visit at Fellsworth. And I am even more pleased to make your acquaintance, Miss Creston."

Mr. Bradford's words suggested that he'd visited Fellsworth prior to this occasion, but she was certain she would remember seeing such a gentleman.

Mr. Langsby adjusted the spectacles on his long nose, lifted an opened letter from his desk, and turned his full attention to Isabel. "Is the name Mrs. Margaret Ellison familiar to you?"

Isabel frowned as she searched her memory. "No, sir, it is not."

"Perhaps you think it an odd inquiry, but I assure you, my reason for asking is sound. The missive Mr. Bradford conveyed is from a Mrs. Margaret Ellison of Emberwilde Hall. I have not had the pleasure of correspondence from Mrs. Ellison prior to this interaction, but in this letter she inquires after you by name."

"After me?" Isabel repeated, unable to conceal the surprise in her voice. She had resided at this school for years and had precious few acquaintances outside of Fellsworth's halls.

"Yes." Mr. Langsby nodded. "It appears that Mrs. Ellison is a relation of yours and wishes to open her home to you."

Isabel stared at Mr. Langsby as if he had grown a second head. "I'm afraid you must be mistaken, sir. I have no other relations apart from my sister."

As if sensing her confusion, Mr. Bradford stepped closer. "Perhaps I can explain. Mrs. Ellison has reason to believe that she is your aunt and has sent me to investigate the matter. Mrs. Ellison's sister was Mrs. Anna Creston, formerly Miss Anna Hayworth of Northrop."

At the mention of the treasured name, the room's temperature seemed to rise with each tick of the mantel clock. How long had it been since that name had met Isabel's ears?

"Anna Creston was my mother." Isabel said the words aloud, slowly, as if to remind herself of the statement's truth.

There could be no denying a connection. For how else would such a woman know her mother's name, especially after all of these years?

After a lengthy pause, Mr. Bradford spoke again. "Mrs. Ellison only recently learned of your father's death, and she believes herself and her family to be your only living relatives. Knowing that I have long enjoyed a friendship with Mr. Langsby, she asked if I would deliver this message personally and vouch for her good nature."

Hardly able to believe what she had heard, Isabel extended her hand toward Mr. Langsby. Somehow she managed to squeak out words from her lips, which had suddenly grown very dry. "May I see the letter?"

"Of course." Mr. Langsby pinched it between two long, bony fingers and extended it toward her. She slid her finger under the wax seal, which had already been broken, and flipped open the letter.

Dear Mr. Langsby,

This letter may come as quite a surprise, but such circumstances call for such missives.

My name is Mrs. Margaret Ellison of Emberwilde Hall.

I have just this week learned of the death of my brother-in-law, Mr. Thomas Creston, and I have also learned that my niece, Miss Isabel Creston, has been a resident at your establishment for a number of years. Miss Creston is the only daughter of my deceased sister, Mrs. Anna Hayworth Creston.

In light of her father's death, I should like to offer Miss Creston a home with us at Emberwilde Hall. You must know, Mr. Langsby, what a pleasant surprise it was for us to learn that my own niece was already living in Surrey.

I do not need to tell you how difficult it is for a young woman to make her way in the world, and we should like to welcome her into our family, whatever her situation may be.

In order to show our support for the good work you are doing, please accept this enclosed donation to the betterment of your cause. Have you any questions as to my personal nature or that of my family, please direct them to Mr. Bradford, who is delivering this letter by hand. He is a great family friend and should be able to answer any questions you have.

As you can imagine, we are eager for our niece to come to us. We have sent a carriage for her in the hopes it will allow her to join us immediately.

I am yours, respectfully,

Mrs. Margaret Ellison

The impressive carriage in the drive. The jet-black horses. They were here for her.

Isabel wanted to demand answers, to summon every detail Mr.

Bradford could muster, but even as she wanted more information, her mind craved space to understand what she had just learned.

Isabel stared at the elegant penmanship and even strokes for several seconds before lowering the letter. She noticed how her blood rushed through her at an uncomfortable pace, forced by the sudden pounding of her heart.

"Were you aware of any aunt?" Mr. Langsby asked.

Isabel shook her head slowly, her face growing hot. "No, I was not. My mother died when I was but five, and my father never spoke of her or her family."

Mr. Bradford cleared his throat, and she turned toward him. His expression appeared very kind, his eyes soft and his manner gentle. "I am sure this is unexpected news. You probably need time to consider your decision. Langsby, with your permission, I'll take my leave to care for my horse and will return shortly."

"Of course."

Mr. Bradford bowed toward her, smiled warmly, then took his leave, pulling the door closed behind him as he did.

The room seemed impossibly quiet in his absence. In fact, some part of her wished he had stayed, as if he held the answers to the rest of the questions swirling in her mind.

Mr. Langsby stepped back behind his desk and prepared to return to his seat.

As he did so, Isabel lifted her eyes to the wall in front of her, taking note of everything she could, from the wrinkled maps and faded paintings hanging haphazardly on the papered walls to the heavy emerald-colored curtains flanking the windows, as if looking upon something familiar could ease her into the truth.

Once Mr. Langsby was seated, he nodded to the empty chair. "Be seated, Miss Creston. I should like to talk with you further."

Isabel complied.

Once she was settled, he spoke again. "You have been at our school a long time, Miss Creston, have you not?"

Isabel nodded. "I came here when I was seven years of age."

"And now what is your age?"

"Twenty, sir."

Mr. Langsby reached for the letter, which was still in her hand, and, once securing it in his grasp, tucked it in a drawer. "It is always our hope, as you well know, to prepare our youths to make their own way once they leave our humble halls. You are no different. I do not need to tell you that it is a difficult world, one full of temptation and sorrow, difficulty and sadness.

"You are a gifted educator, Miss Creston, well liked and amiable, and there is not a doubt in my mind that you would make a fine governess. But as you know, several of our young women are currently seeking such a position. There are far more eligible young ladies than available openings. You are blessed, for it seems that you will not need to find employment. It is always preferable for a young woman to remain under the protection and providence of her family, of that I am certain. Do you not concur?"

It was the word *family* that pressed against Isabel's heart. Yes, she had, at one time, a family. But the father she barely knew had died more than two years prior. The only true family she had now was her half sister, Lizzie, who was a student at Fellsworth.

Isabel could only nod.

Mr. Langsby continued, his voice steady, his lanky hands folded primly on the desk. "We are grateful for the work you have done here while waiting for a more permanent position, and had your circumstances not changed, I would encourage you to pursue that path. But now that you have family to return to, I must encourage you to accept the terms of this arrangement."

Her stomach knotted. "Do you mean I must leave Fellsworth?"

Mr. Langsby's eyes were unwavering. "There are several young ladies here who are not as fortunate as you. I hate to put this in terms of an ultimatum, but if you should decide to turn down this offer from Mrs. Ellison, I am afraid there will no longer be a position for you here. It is our job to prepare our students to help them enter the world. You no longer need our assistance, for you have a family that is willing to provide for you."

"And what of Lizzie?" Isabel shot back, scooting to the edge of her chair, emotions coursing through her in waves. "The letter makes no mention of her."

Mr. Langsby's apparent calmness chafed Isabel's heightening nerves. "The letter did say that they will welcome you to their family, whatever your situation may be. And, as it happens, you are a guardian to the child. I know that you and Lizzie share a father only, and the Ellisons have no blood relation. So I leave it up to you whether to take her with you or allow her to remain in our halls. We turn no student away, Miss Creston, as you are well aware."

"Lizzie stays with me." Isabel blurted the words, finding it impossible to suppress the defensive lilt to her voice. "I will not leave without her."

"As you wish." Mr. Langsby stood slowly, the sunlight highlighting every movement. He removed his spectacles and leaned against the desk. "I sense this is not what you expected, Miss Creston. And I understand. You must believe that I do. But I hope you would see this for what it is—an opportunity. You will be provided for. What else could you ask? You may not know much of the estates beyond Fellsworth, but allow me to assure you that Emberwilde Hall is well known for its wealth and grandeur. You should feel grateful for such an advantageous offer."

Grateful hardly seemed the proper word to describe her emotion. Not in this instance, anyway. She did not relish the idea that her future had essentially been decided for her based on the mere contents of a letter, and being told that the opportunity was advantageous heaped insult on an already sore wound. For if she did have a family, why had it taken them so long to learn of her existence? It made little sense.

But she would show no emotion. The superintendent's stiff lip indicated that his decision would prove steadfast, and she would not lower her pride to argue.

She jutted out her chin. "I am grateful, Mr. Langsby."

"Anticipating your agreement to the idea, Mr. Bradford and I discussed the details while awaiting your arrival. As Mrs. Ellison's letter indicates, she has sent a coach, hoping you would accept the offer. Since that is the case, Mr. Bradford will escort you today."

"Today?" Her determination to show little emotion began to dissolve. "That is hardly enough time!"

"I have learned through experience that it is better to not let matters such as this linger."

Panic's heat rushed up from her bodice. This day had been coming. She could not stay at Fellsworth forever in this tidy little cocoon that enveloped her in security. Being forced to make such a decision in a short time seemed unreasonable, especially when the decision affected not only her, but Lizzie as well.

She searched Mr. Langsby's face for any sort of sympathy, but his expression was stony and steadfast. His decision had been made. He believed this the best move for her and for Lizzie. No amount of reasoning would change his mind.

Mr. Langsby remained silent, and as Isabel contemplated her options, she fixed her eyes on the south wall. A broad chimney-piece showcased a healthy fire, its snaps and pops a cheerful song in the otherwise austere silence. Shelves overflowing with books lined the north wall, the breadth of which utilized every inch of space from the planked floor to the plaster ceiling. It looked exactly as it had when she arrived those many years ago. It would likely remain the same long after she was gone.

She let her mind's eye return to Mr. Bradford. In her short interaction with him, he had seemed so kind. So affable. He was the sort of gentleman who would turn many a young woman's eye and bring a flutter to a lady's heart. But Isabel had learned the hard way that appearances were often deceiving.

Yes, she had known this day was coming. It could not be avoided. But she had always thought she would leave to accept the position of a governess.

Not to join a family.

Chapter Two

$\mathcal{B}$y the time Isabel and Lizzie left Fellsworth School, bright, cheery skies had given way to a turbulent storm. The rain fell in thick sheets but did little to slash the oppressiveness of the early spring heat.

Isabel wanted to blame the tightening of her throat and the watering of her eyes on the weather. It was much easier to accept that the stifling mugginess made breathing difficult, or that the morning buds had caused her eyes to itch. But as she watched the school grow smaller and smaller through the carriage window, a tear slipped down her cheek.

She immediately wiped it away. It would not do to let young Lizzie see her show such emotion. It could frighten the child. But like her, Lizzie had spent years calling the old stone structure "home," and in a matter of one day's time, all had changed for both of them.

Mr. Langsby's parting words echoed in her mind.

"The important thing now is that you and Miss Lizzie will be with your family. I sense you are hesitant about this particular arrangement, but this is for the best. You will always have friends at Fellsworth School, but Emberwilde Hall is where you need to be."

And that was it.

Isabel bit her lip as the realization that she might never see the school again resonated. With each new breath a fearful restlessness churned within her.

From this moment on, all would be different.

The tranquil school grounds gave way to the village of Fellsworth, and the familiar buildings and cottages blurred in her vision as a messy mix of browns and grays. It seemed the quaint town that had welcomed her all those years ago was sad—or perhaps indifferent—at her departure.

"I don't want to go." Lizzie's emphatic words rose above the clattering of the carriage wheels and sliced the reflective silence.

Isabel pulled her gaze from the soggy countryside and looked at her eight-year-old sister.

The child had repeated the words a dozen—nay, perhaps a hundred—times over.

With red-rimmed eyes and a tearstained face, Lizzie sat huddled in the corner of the carriage on the opposite side. Her charcoal-gray shawl was tugged tightly around her, clutched in her white-knuckled grip, and a scowl creased her young brow. Her knees were pulled to her chest, and she was ignorant of the manner in which her dirty half boots marred the fine seat.

Once Lizzie realized that Isabel was looking at her, the child hurled words. "Why do we have to go?"

The pain twisting her young sister's expression ripped at Isabel's heart. "We've been through this."

Lizzie mumbled, "We won't have any friends there."

Isabel swallowed her own lump of frustration. If the truth be told, she did not like the idea any more than Lizzie, but what could be done? Mr. Langsby had made his declaration. The plan had been set into motion. With no funds of their own, they had few choices.

Isabel leaned forward, and when her sister refused to make eye contact with her, she rested her gloved hand on her sister's knee. "Listen to me, Lizzie. Father is dead, both our mothers are dead, and we have no other family. It is important that we nurture the relationships we have. The world is a lonely place for women like us who have no real means of support. This will be good for us, you'll see."

"But why now?" Lizzie blurted, the volume of her voice increasing with each syllable. "We've been at Fellsworth a long time. If the Ellisons truly wanted us to live with them, they would have invited us a long time ago."

Isabel hesitated. Had she not wondered that exact thing? She tried to soften the news. "But Mr. Langsby said they only just learned where we were. And he says that Emberwilde Hall is a fine estate, with servants and horses and fields and forests."

"How does Mr. Langsby know? He's probably never been there."

"Be that as it may, Mr. Langsby thinks it is best for us to go."

"Why do we have to do what he says?" Lizzie demanded with all the energy her small body possessed.

"Because he is in charge at Fellsworth. He makes the decisions. As much as we wish it weren't so, we can't always control what is happening to us."

"I hate him."

Isabel drew a sharp breath at the vehemence in her sister's voice. She reached out and clutched her sister's hand to capture the child's attention. "Lizzie, we hate no one. I never want to hear you say such a thing again. Is that clear?"

"But why not? Don't you hate him?" A tear trickled down her cheek. "He must hate us too, otherwise he would not make us leave."

"He does not hate us, but even if he did, we do not hate. We must be kind, even when the world is not. The earlier you learn that lesson, the happier and more pleasant your life will be."

Lizzie turned as far as she could away from Isabel so her shoulders were square with the carriage window and her narrowed eyes were fixed on a distant point outside.

Isabel let her shoulders sag in a rare lack of discipline. Could she fault Lizzie? A small part of her wanted to behave the same—to cry and pout and proclaim the injustice. The other students had been her siblings; the teachers had been her guardians. But sticking out her lower lip and digging in her heels would not help.

Sorrow's sigh rushed from Isabel, and she sat back against the seat. Now, in the heat of her sister's anger, was not the time to discuss such a thing. She had learned the hard lesson of acceptance long ago, but Lizzie was just beginning.

She forced her gaze out the window, where she glimpsed Mr. Bradford riding on his horse not far from the carriage. She leaned forward once again with interest. A brown, wide-brimmed hat was pulled low over his face, revealing only small glimpses of his finely cut jaw and chin. The greatcoat covering his shoulders was slick and shiny with the rain and fluttered in the wind. He did not glance toward her, but instead, his attentions were fixed on the muddy road.

Despite the rain, he had insisted upon riding alongside the carriage. It was a kind gesture, but what struck Isabel the most about this was the way he made her feel. His words had been gentle, his countenance patient. He seemed to understand how difficult it was for them to leave Fellsworth and did not rush them as they said their farewells. Yes, she was heartbroken to leave, but in the carriage's silence she allowed her mind to indulge in new possibilities. For years her path had been firmly focused on becoming a governess or teacher. But her aunt's kind invitation could open new worlds for her—even marriage.

A family of her own.

Security.

Happiness.

Mr. Bradford gave his horse a kick with his black boot, and then the pair ran ahead of the carriage and out of her sight. With a sigh, Isabel leaned back against the seat and adjusted her bonnet's bow beneath her chin. It would never do to think that someone like Mr. Bradford would show her any attention other than kindness, but the change in her circumstances gave her heart a reason to dream.

Chapter Three

*C*olin Galloway shifted the horse's reins to one gloved hand and looked up to the canopy of leaves and branches above him. Fragile buds danced in the spring wind, delighted to finally lift their faces to a warmer sky after a winter riddled with snow and ice.

But he was not here to admire their emerging beauty or bask in the sun's amiable glimmer.

For he faced a much more sinister task at the forest's cool, misty floor.

Charles Ellison, master of Emberwilde Hall, dismounted his chestnut gelding and planted his boots beside another set of footprints in the soft earth. He pointed a thick finger at the ground below. "I want these trespassers off my property."

Colin followed suit and dismounted, his own movements much quicker than the portly gentleman's. He tied Sampson's reins to an obliging tree trunk and surveyed the small clearing.

All around him the forest was alive. Musty scents of mossy foliage and damp earth abounded. Woodpeckers and collared doves swooped between the thick branches overhead, and gray squirrels jumped and played amid the brush. Colin stepped forward, and as he did, his riding boot sank into the soft carpet of leaves and mud.

Colin knelt down to obtain a better view of the prints, but the day's fading light and the long gray shadows made it difficult to identify anything distinctive.

"Someone has been here, that is certain," Colin mused,

straightening to his full height. "Are you sure your gamekeeper did not make these himself?"

"I'm certain." Ellison's gruff tone hinted at frustration. "Harding knows his own shoes. There is something else you must see. It's over this way."

Despite the sentinel trees creating a fortress around the clearing, a breeze, cool and cutting, threatened to unsettle Colin's wide-brimmed hat. He watched with curiosity as Ellison stepped gingerly over the muddy undergrowth. As the magistrate for the village of Northrop, Colin had grown accustomed to the locals and residents of nearby villages seeking him out with every manner of complaint. But typically, the reports he received were of little consequence: a missing goat or an unpaid minor debt.

But something about this particular report was different.

"It's over here," Ellison called, his voice muffled by a sharp uptake in the wind.

Colin followed as bid, unsure of what he was looking for.

"This is what Harding found yesterday whilst clearing the hare traps." Ellison pulled back several low-hanging branches and motioned for Colin to draw near. "Grab the lantern. You'll need it to see."

Colin unlatched the lantern from Ellison's saddle and, holding it out before him, approached the exposed opening. There behind the curtain of brushwood and thicket was a short wooden door propped ajar. He shifted the lantern so the meager light would illuminate the space beyond. For as far back as the light could shine, he saw them—cask after cask. Additional stacked crates lined the earthen wall of the small cavern.

"Do you know what that is?" Ellison's gruff words were more a demand than a question.

Colin nodded. He knew exactly what he was looking at.

Ellison's jaw twitched as he dropped the leafy curtain,

concealing the door. "You and I go back a long ways, Galloway. You know I am not one to be overly concerned with legalistic ballyhoo. Far from it. But I am not so daft that I don't comprehend what is happening here."

For a brief time after serving in the army, Colin had worked on the southern coast as an excise officer, and the sight before him was chilling in its familiarity. Now that the war with France was over, smuggling activity was once again becoming more prominent. Even as recently as a year ago, news of such happenings in their area was rare, but ever since several coaching agencies added routes through Northrop to London, newcomers came to their village daily. While most of the residents were pleased with this increase in local traffic and commerce, Ellison had always been outspokenly against it.

This discovery only added fuel to his fire.

Ellison stepped back to his horse and adjusted the stirrup. "If these rogues and scallywags want to avoid taxes, that is their business. I couldn't care less if they risk their necks for a bit of cheap wine. But my family has been here for almost two centuries. We've fought off poachers and gypsies, and I'll not tolerate blackguards. 'Tis no secret that Emberwilde is facing difficult circumstances, times being what they are, and I'll not allow such shenanigans to mar our name."

Colin drew a deep breath and blew it out. No, he would not tolerate smugglers either, not when he was responsible for upholding the lawfulness of this area. Smugglers were a dangerous lot, cunning and crafty, not easily deterred, and fearless. Nothing could stand in the way of them and their profits.

Colin stepped back. "For now, leave everything as it is. I'll contact the revenue officer and see if there has been any word of smuggling on the Lockton Route. He'd know if anything of this sort has been reported. We can decide how to proceed from there. For now post a guard or two here to keep an eye on things."

Ellison eyed him as if making a decision. "I'll not merely keep an eye on things long," he finally said, returning to his horse. "If you can't help me put a stop to it, I'll find a way to do it myself." He paused, hand on the beast's flank. "I trust you won't give me cause to lose confidence in you, son."

Colin knew Ellison's words were not to be taken lightly. Though kind, even paternal at times, Ellison was also an entitled and ambitious man whose fiery temper often clouded his judgment.

"Whoever put this here will come back for it eventually," Colin said. "We will be ready for them when they do."

Ellison pinned his narrow gaze on Colin. "I'll offer fifty pounds to the man who gives good information on this. Disseminate that offer as you see fit, but I must insist on your discretion. You know all too well that such talk would only aggravate the already jaded view of this forest. As it stands, my own wife will not even set foot in here. I would barely be able to get her out from behind Emberwilde's walls if she thought there was criminal activity in these woods."

"Understood."

Ellison mounted his horse and then turned back to Colin. "Good. Come back with me to the house. You can talk with Harding yourself, and we've other matters to discuss."

Colin mounted Sampson and followed Ellison out of the forest. Rain drizzled from the pewter skies and a sharp wind howled from the north. He was eager to be out of the moisture, but he had little confidence that even getting out of the bitter spring elements would quiet the apprehension building within him. It had been years since he had set foot in the Emberwilde Forest, but based on the evidence he saw, difficult times could be waiting for them. He was hardly one to shirk away from a problem, but if experience had taught him anything, it was that this particular bit of land could be an unpredictable place. Now that he had returned, he could not deny the unidentifiable hold the Emberwilde Forest had on him.

Chapter Four ————————————————

The journey from Fellsworth to Emberwilde Hall was a slow one made even slower by the muddy roads and gusty winds. The terrain evolved from rolling green countryside to heavily forested land.

Isabel and Lizzie broke their journey at a small inn, where they ate a light meal of bread and cheese. Isabel was disappointed that Mr. Bradford did not join them, but he had begged their forgiveness as he tended his horse. Once the driver changed out the coach's horses, they embarked once more.

Shortly after resuming, Lizzie stretched out on the opposite seat and fell asleep. It was a wonder the child could sleep, Isabel thought, for every so often they would hit a rut or stone in the road, causing the entire carriage to lurch.

Without a timepiece, Isabel soon lost track of the hour. With only the color of the overcast pewter sky as her guide, she was beginning to think that they could not possibly arrive at Emberwilde before darkness fell. She did not like the idea of being out after sundown with men whom she did not know.

Isabel returned her attention to the scene at her window, and what she saw made her straighten.

There, beyond the crest of trees, the black spires of a great house jutted toward the sky.

Her pulse quickened in an intricate mixture of uncertainty and excitement. It was the moment she had both dreaded and anticipated since leaving Fellsworth.

The carriage rumbled over a bridge of stone and earth, and the structure once again disappeared behind a thick veil of tall trees. Shadows flitted intermittently across their carriage, flickering between darkness and light. After several moments, the space between shadows lengthened. The carriage slowed.

The sudden change of pace shifted Isabel on her seat, and she reached out her hand to steady herself.

"Why are we stopping?" Lizzie's voice was soft as she woke. She rubbed her eyes with the back of her fist and sat upright. "Have we arrived?"

Isabel did not answer. Instead, she angled herself to get a better view.

As the carriage drew to a halt, she squinted and saw a large man on a brown horse come around from the trees' edge to the carriage. She bit her lip. Tales of highwaymen and vandals manifested in her mind.

But this man, dressed in a sharp black coat and tall shiny boots, was not moving fast enough to hijack them, nor did his movements indicate any urgency. He was of a heavy build, with gray side whiskers and silver hair that hung below his low-brimmed hat.

A second man appeared behind him, much younger and thinner, also on horseback.

The driver and the first man engaged in conversation, but the tones of their voices were so low she could not make out a word. Relief rushed her when Mr. Bradford came around the carriage into her view. Surely these were not miscreants or vagabonds, not if Mr. Bradford spoke to them with such ease. Her heart raced within her at the uncertainty of the moment.

The men laughed, and then the older horseman leaned back to look into the carriage. Light eyes fixed on her. He dismounted, made his way through the mud toward the carriage, and opened the door just wide enough to see inside.

His voice boomed. "Miss Isabel Creston?"

Isabel straightened, the rate of her heartbeat increasing within her. "Yes, sir, I am Isabel Creston."

She moved to exit the carriage, but his protest stopped her.

"Stay put, dear girl, stay put. There is far too much mud, and I would hardly want you to spoil your slippers, for my wife would have my head for it! We've been waiting for your arrival. I am your uncle, Charles Ellison. My, but it has been a long time, child. A long time indeed. I daresay you do not remember the last time you set foot on Emberwilde land."

The words shocked her. She did not recall ever stepping on Emberwilde soil. "I do not, sir."

"Well, it is high time you returned. And you are most welcome here." He looked past her to Lizzie, who had straightened and put her feet on the floor. Her eyes were wide, her lips pressed shut.

"And who is this?" her uncle asked, chuckling at the sight. "Have we a stowaway?"

Isabel forced a smile at his attempt at humor. "No, sir. This is my sister, Lizzie Creston."

Uncle Charles jerked his head up, his jowls shaking at the motion. "Sister, you say?"

"Yes, sir."

He huffed under his breath and looked at the men behind him. "Well now, this is most interesting. We did not know of a sister. But of course, you are both welcome, and we shall sort out the details. Family is always welcome within Emberwilde's walls. How do you do, Lizzie?"

Lizzie's words were impressively polite. "I am well, thank you."

He smiled, amused, then stepped back out of the way. "Allow me to introduce my colleague, Mr. Colin Galloway. He is the local magistrate. He will be the first of many of our friends and neighbors that I've no doubt my wife will introduce you to in the coming days."

Isabel turned her attention to the man atop the horse. He did not dismount, but tipped his hat and lowered his head in a bow. She noted how young he appeared to be a magistrate, but then again, she had never met one. None, anyway, besides old Mr. Newgate, Fellsworth's magistrate.

"It is a pleasure to meet you, Mr. Galloway," she said in her most confident voice.

"The pleasure is mine, Miss Creston."

Her uncle shifted to the side. "And you, of course, are acquainted with Mr. Bradford."

She looked past him toward Mr. Bradford, whose bright smile and direct gaze made her feel almost as if they shared a secret, although she had no idea what such a secret would be. She hoped a flush did not color her cheeks. "I am, Uncle."

"Well then, I shall have the driver convey you on, for I do believe more rain is imminent, and I am sure you would like to arrive before the heavens break free. Your aunt and cousin are both eagerly awaiting your arrival, so it will not do to keep them waiting. They have become concerned one of the horses went lame or a wheel was broken and asked that I send a rider out in search of you. So you'd best be off before my wife is quite overtaken with the fits."

Isabel smiled at her uncle's words. She could not help but like him. "I hope we have not caused her too much distress."

"You will soon learn my wife is easily distressed, but my daughter calms her quite well."

"So we are almost there?" Lizzie piped in. "We've been riding forever!"

Isabel reached back and touched her sister's leg in an effort to keep her from saying something inappropriate, but to her surprise, her uncle laughed.

"Forever, you say? That is a long time. Well then, I ought to let you get about your travels." He turned and pointed toward a distant place in the sky. "You cannot see it for the trees, but once you emerge from this section of the woods you will see Emberwilde. I daresay you will arrive in no more than five minutes." Her uncle signaled to the driver that it was time to proceed. "I will see you at the house, I am sure."

"Thank you, Uncle."

But when he pushed the carriage door closed, it did not latch all the way, and even though she did not mean to eavesdrop, she could not help but overhear her uncle's rough voice.

"Not one, but two, gentlemen! Ah, but what is another mouth to feed. She's a pretty lass and will catch herself a husband in record time, if I am a judge of such things. What say you, Galloway? A man in your situation needs a wife."

At the words, Isabel's heart sank and she leaned back against the seat. The blood rushing through her ears and the howling wind prevented her from hearing more. Her uncle's welcome had seemed genuine, or so she had thought. Was he jesting, or did he resent their presence? Had he really just spoken to the other man about marriage?

The carriage was set into motion once more, swaying both Isabel and Lizzie, and Isabel made certain the door was secure. As the scenery began to flicker by, her uncle's final words echoed mercilessly within her. She had always wanted to marry one day. What young lady would not? But to hear her uncle speak of it with such enthusiasm, and on the very day of her arrival, made her ill at ease.

Within moments, Lizzie scrambled to her knees once more. "I see it! Look, Isabel, there it is!"

Despite a sudden jolt, Isabel steadied her position and craned her neck to glimpse the majestic spires reaching into the stormy sky. *Emberwilde Hall.*

Like a bolt of spring lightning, a haunting sensation streaked through Isabel's limbs as she took in the ancient structure of gray stone and glass through the pockets of trees and brush. The sight pushed her uncle's words aside, and she squinted to better make it out through the drizzle and fog. As she did, a vague recollection emerged from the recesses of her mind, scratching, pawing for recognition.

But the shifting memory would not take full form. She thought she remembered being told that her mother had come from wealth. That memory, at least, must hold merit if Emberwilde was associated with it in the slightest.

Isabel leaned back against the seat, blowing out her breath and drawing another deep one. Lizzie pressed her fingertips to the clean window, the angst and frustration replaced with expectant enthusiasm for the unknown. Even as Lizzie's excitement intensified, Isabel's nerves tightened. In a matter of minutes she would come face-to-face with the pieces of her life that had for so long been a mystery.

Whatever her father's reasoning for keeping her aunt a secret, it could not matter now.

"It looks just like a castle." Lizzie's breathless words of awe pulled Isabel from her thoughts. For the first time all day, the little girl's cheeks boasted a rosy hue, and her brown eyes were wide with wonder. "Do you think it has a ghost?"

"A ghost?" Isabel repeated with a quick laugh. "Now what would give you that idea?"

"Jane said that all castles have ghosts."

"Well, it isn't a castle," Isabel corrected, but even as she leaned forward to assess the building rising over the treetops, the beauty of it caught in her throat. "And there are no such things as ghosts."

Isabel rested her head back on the cushion and closed her eyes. In a few minutes, all would be different. There would be no going back—ever.

Chapter Five

*Y*ou've arrived at last!"

A woman clad in lavender satin met Lizzie and Isabel when they arrived in Emberwilde's front hall. She had rushed from an adjoining room, the suddenness of her appearance almost taking Isabel by surprise.

The woman was the epitome of elegance, or perhaps frivolity. Black lace trimmed every inch of the gown's hems and patterned the ample bodice. Her light gray strands of hair were piled high on her head and covered with an intricately woven black cap. Isabel knew little of fashion, but her sense of propriety suggested that the ensemble was far too ornate for an evening at home. The stranger's face flushed pink as she rushed toward Isabel, arms outstretched.

"Oh, my dear, my dear! I am so pleased you've arrived!"

She crushed Isabel in a tight embrace.

Unprepared for the display of affection, not to mention the woman's overwhelming scent of lily of the valley, Isabel stiffened and resisted the urge to step backward. Lizzie's hand slid from her own as the woman squeezed her tighter.

The woman had to be her aunt. Who else could she be?

After several uncomfortable moments, Margaret Ellison held her niece at arm's length, her eyes wide as she made little effort to hide her assessment of Isabel's person.

"Beautiful," her aunt exclaimed with a sharp shake of her head, her eyes bright. She cast a glance over her shoulder at a younger woman. "Did I not tell you that she would be beautiful?"

Aunt Margaret turned back to Isabel, surprising her by reaching out to touch a piece of hair that had escaped Isabel's modest pins. "The exact same hue. So very blonde. I would have known you anywhere. You look exactly like your mother did at your age."

She embraced Isabel again, and when she released her this time, tears brimmed in her eyes. She hastily wiped at them with the back of her hand. "I must say, I never thought I would see this day."

Several awkward moments ensued. The older woman studied her as if she were a statue on display.

Isabel took the time to assess her aunt as well.

There was no denying the relation. Ice-blue eyes so like her own studied her with unmasked approval, but the long, straw-blonde eyelashes served as the true likeness that bound them together.

And then her aunt's gaze landed on Lizzie. She appeared almost alarmed, and her hand flew to her bosom. "And who is this?"

Isabel put her arm around Lizzie's shoulders, noting the resistance as she tried to urge the child forward. "This is Lizzie, my sister."

"Your sister? No, no. You do not have a sister." The authority in the older woman's voice was jarring. She shook her head in emphatic disagreement, her eyes fixed on the child.

"Lizzie is my father's daughter," Isabel hurried to clarify, fearing that her aunt's reaction would echo her uncle's parting comment. "He remarried several years back, and Lizzie's mother died. It was then Lizzie joined me at Fellsworth, and now that our father is dead I am her guardian."

Isabel pulled Lizzie to her side. She feared her aunt's response, for even though she had only just met her aunt, the older woman certainly had no qualms about sharing her opinions.

Isabel felt the need to fill the empty silence. "I do hope it is all right that she accompanied me. The letter said I was welcome whatever the situation."

The tension in the air increased by the moment, but then her aunt relented. "So it did."

The young woman waiting in the hall stepped forward. She was a vision of femininity in pink printed muslin and a gauzy cream chemisette. She stooped in front of Lizzie and gathered the child's hands in her own.

"Oh, how delightful. It has been so long since we had a child in the house, hasn't it, Mother?" She knelt down to be eye level with Lizzie. "Hello, Elizabeth. It is a pleasure to meet you. My name is Constance. You and I are cousins."

Lizzie's tense shoulders slackened, and she gave an awkward curtsy. "How do you do?"

"Oh, you are delightful!" Constance giggled. "Mother, isn't she? I know for a fact that Cook has made fresh tarts just this morning. Would you care for one? I bet you are hungry after your journey."

Lizzie cast a shy glance up toward Isabel before nodding.

With an elegant wave of her hand, Constance motioned toward the silent footman at the room's entrance. Within seconds he bowed and disappeared through the door.

She then straightened and looked to Isabel. "Such a pleasure to see you, Cousin." The pretty girl with honey-gold hair and hazel eyes gave a practiced curtsy.

Isabel returned the greeting. "It is a pleasure to meet you."

Constance's eyes grew wide. "Oh, but we have met before, do you not remember?"

Isabel searched her memory, but no recollection of her cousin glimmered. "I am sorry, I do not."

Her aunt raised a hand impatiently. "Well, never mind that now. It was very long ago. There will be plenty of time to get reacquainted after we have gotten you both settled. Sadly, you will have to wait until another time to meet your three other cousins. They are all married and live quite a distance away, I am afraid. And you shall never meet Freddie, your only male cousin, my dear, for he died in battle several years ago. Oh, I do wish your uncle was here to greet you, but estate business keeps him very busy this time of year, and I fear it may be quite late before he returns from his duties."

"Actually, we met him on the road as we approached," Isabel offered. "He stopped the carriage to introduce himself."

"Well, that is fortunate. You will find that Mr. Ellison's responsibilities keep him very engaged."

Isabel looked over her shoulder to the corridor as men carried in their meager belongings. "I am very grateful for the invitation. Lizzie and I are pleased to be here."

"I am only sorry the invitation came so late. I received word of your father's death from one of my distant cousins, who lives in London, just a month ago. After your mother died, I offered to let you live here. After all, your father's occupation consumed all of his time. How could a man without a wife care for a child and properly see to his occupation? He would hear nothing of it, though, and much to my dismay we soon lost all contact with him."

Her aunt's light eyebrow arched as she assessed the front of Isabel's gown. "But now, all that is in the past. I see you are still in mourning for him."

Isabel ran a hand down the rough fabric. It would be an easy mistake to assume by her attire that she was in mourning, for the black, unadorned linen would certainly suit such an occasion, but she only had two dresses, and they were both exactly the same. "No, ma'am, I am not. This gown is the teacher's uniform. All the teachers at Fellsworth wear them."

"A teacher?" Aunt Margaret's expression pinched in obvious disapproval, and she nodded toward the charcoal-gray pinafore that Lizzie wore. "And your sister's gown?"

"All the students her age wear a similar gown."

"Well, at least that is something we shall be able to remedy quickly. Those gowns will never do here. We shall have a suitable seamstress come right away. All that can wait until later, though. First, you must eat." She glanced at Lizzie and waved her hand in front of herself, as if to shoo the matter away. "We always have plenty."

Isabel took Lizzie's hand in her own once more and allowed her aunt to lead them into the drawing room. As her boots tapped on the stone floor, she only half listened to her aunt's descriptions of the home and the opulent furnishings. There would be time for all of that later, for she could barely hear the words above the doubts and fears swirling about in her head. She never considered herself to be shy or overcome by timidity. In fact, her manner was often so outspoken that she was frequently reprimanded. But this home and these people—her relatives—were unlike any she had interacted with before. She drew a deep breath to calm her taut nerves. She was grateful to her aunt and uncle, but a small voice in her head whispered words of caution. She and Lizzie were definitely far from Fellsworth, and very far from home indeed.

Night fell quickly over Emberwilde, bringing with it harsh winds and spring rain accompanied by startling lightning strikes and cracks of thunder.

The raindrops pelted the stone walls and crashed against the leaded glass windows, resulting in a racket unlike any that Isabel could recall.

It was a wonder that Lizzie had fallen asleep so quickly. Isabel had expected the evening hours to upset her sister. Her aunt declared they should not share a bedchamber. Lizzie had never slept alone in a room of her own, but the journey had been so tiring, the excitement so exhausting, that she fell asleep almost the moment her head rested against the pillow. She now slept in a bed as wide as three of Fellsworth's narrow beds pushed together.

Isabel was hesitant to leave Lizzie alone. She lingered in the doorway, watching the child as if she might wake at any moment. Lizzie would be frightened to wake up alone in such a room, but Aunt Margaret had expressly instructed Isabel to join her and Constance in the music room. Isabel longed for sleep, but she did not dare to refuse her aunt's request.

Isabel took up a candle, and upon quitting Lizzie's chamber, she quickly became lost in the maze of small rooms and shadowed, crooked corridors. The halls seemed to lead to nowhere, and because the doors and walls alike were paneled, discerning where to go was difficult. Intricate tapestries and innumerable portraits lined the walls, each one looking very like the last. Even with her candle's aid, darkness shrouded all.

She was able to find her way only with the assistance of one of the housemaids.

Once in the music room, the cool shadows gave way to a warm yellow light. As cold and unwelcoming as the rest of the house was, this room was every bit as inviting. The glow from the vibrant fire chased away the stormy evening's pulsating chill, and the soft strains from the pianoforte covered the sounds of the howling gusts and biting downpour.

"There you are!" exclaimed Aunt Margaret when at length she took notice of Isabel standing in the doorway. A seemingly genuine smile graced her round face. She stood from her perch on the small settee next to the fire, which glimmered in the pearls about her neck and in the silver strands of her hair. "We were beginning to wonder where you had gotten to. I trust your sister is asleep."

"Yes, Aunt Margaret. She is, thank you."

Constance, the musician responsible for the instrument's

haunting strains, ceased playing and turned her head. She was seated at the gilded pianoforte, the case of which was intricately painted with cherubs and vines. Constance's long white fingers splayed in easy elegance over the keys. Her light hair and the metallic threads woven into her dress shimmered in the candlelight.

Constance lowered her hands to her lap. "You found us! I was about to search for you, fearing you'd become lost."

The gentleness of her cousin's tone set Isabel at ease. "I did find my way, but I must confess I had to seek assistance."

Her aunt leaned forward, an earnest expression tightening her face. "This is a very old home, as I am sure you can tell. So much of it has been built and rebuilt throughout the decades that at times the layout does not make much sense. But you will adjust to it soon enough."

Constance turned to face her fully. "Tell me, Isabel, how do you like your chamber?"

Isabel considered the question. Never had she had an entire room to herself. "It is lovely."

"I've always been fond of that room," Aunt Margaret said. "The Lilac Room, it's called. Apparently, years before my arrival lilacs used to grow beneath the window, and when the windows were open the scent would perfume the entire chamber. It has a lovely view of the Emberwilde Forest. I had planned to give you the Bluebonnet Room that overlooks the gardens, but learning of your desire to stay close to Elizabeth, I thought you would prefer the one that adjoins with hers."

"That is very thoughtful of you." Isabel turned to her cousin, who was still seated at the keyboard. "You play beautifully."

A pretty smile colored her cousin's face and her eyes flicked up from the keys. "You are too kind. But I ought to play much better than I do, considering how earnestly my governess tried to teach me the art."

Isabel smiled. She found her cousin endearing. The girl's sweet tone and easy smile put her at ease.

"Tell me, Isabel, do you play any instruments?" Constance inquired.

Isabel pressed her lips together. She was not quite eager to share the nuances of her life at school. Even though these ladies were family, they were still strangers. "No, I do not."

"Surely you sing, at least," Constance probed.

"I am sorry to disappoint you, but no. Music was not encouraged at Fellsworth."

Her aunt's mouth fell open. "Not encouraged? Why, that is unheard of!"

Isabel had anticipated her aunt's surprise, for Fellsworth was not a typical school for young ladies. The school did not even own a pianoforte, or any other instruments. Instead of French and dancing, which were taught at many girls' schools, she learned arithmetic and cooking. Instead of elegant embroidery and decorative needlework, she learned the more practical aspects of sewing. And while needlework was encouraged, it was likely very different from her cousin's exposure to the art. No doubt her aunt would be shocked to learn the specifics regarding Isabel's education. Emphasis had been placed on activities and skills that would benefit her as she entered the world, not on fine arts.

"Sit down, Isabel. Constance will play another song for us. It is so important to keep such skills in good practice, even though her match has already been made and she is betrothed. A lady must never become lax in her disciplines." Aunt Margaret motioned Isabel to a padded chair next to the fire.

Her cousin began to play a melancholy tune that filled the vaulted room from the plastered ceiling above to the polished floor beneath. The notes were mesmerizing despite how they clashed with one another, the angst and emotion strong. It was unlike any sound

Isabel had ever heard, pure and soft, and yet exuding strength and control. It was a wordless poem, perfect in its rhyme and rhythm.

"'Tis a shame you do not play," her aunt said as the music concluded. Then she stood and took a few steps toward the hearth, leaving a floral scent in her wake. "Of course, your mother was quite the musician. Her talent rivaled that of any in the county."

Isabel jerked her head up. Time had dulled the pain associated with her lingering memories of her mother, but being in this space piqued her curiosity.

She was finally in the presence of those who could answer questions that had long simmered within her. There was so much she wanted to know about her mother, and yet she was torn. For what if she heard something she was not ready to hear? And yet, she desired to know everything. Absorb everything. She had entered a new life, and there could be no turning back.

"Your mother used to play that very song that Constance just finished. Oh, how I miss her." A far-off expression flashed on the older woman's face before she nodded to the wall behind Isabel. "There, that is her portrait."

Isabel stiffened, and she realized she was holding her breath. Time had erased so many memories. She had only vague recollections of blonde hair. A soft smile. A gentle touch. But all other specifics had been lost to time's firm grip. She turned, and her gaze landed on a small yet ornately framed portrait tucked in the room's distant corner.

"That is my mother?" Isabel asked, uncertain she could trust the words.

"Why, yes, child. Do you not recognize her? This portrait was painted when Anna was seventeen, I believe. It hung at Heddeston Park, our parents' home for many years, but after they died I had it moved here."

Isabel stood and stepped toward the painting cautiously,

fighting to keep an unexpected rush of emotion at bay. How often had she tried to remember what her mother looked like? The gilded frame flashed in the firelight. The thick lacquer sparkled like a priceless treasure. The painting's details were too fine to be seen clearly from the distance across the room, but Isabel could identify fair hair. A narrow face.

Isabel attempted to swallow the emotion swelling in her throat, but it would not be dispelled. The portrait drew her to it, taunting her with the truth that once she soaked in the sight, it could not be forgotten.

As she moved closer, hazy recollections seeped through her memory's wide gaps. She wished she could force thought into sharper focus, but it was impossible, for her memories had been neglected to the point of wasting away.

She stopped several feet before the artwork. Clear, light blue eyes stared back at her from a narrow face. Pale skin, every bit as fair as her own, was highlighted by the painter's stroke, and a pert nose and high cheekbones almost made it seem as if Isabel were beholding her own reflection.

But it was the expression in the eyes and the set of the mouth that struck her. The countenance was pensive, almost sorrowful, and it called a heavy feeling to her heart.

"You look just like her." Aunt Margaret drew close behind her, the tip of her walking cane tapping the polished floor.

Isabel did not avert her gaze.

The picture held her steadfast focus, as if by a supernatural command.

"See the eyes?" her aunt continued. "So unusual. Icy and pale in the center with the vibrant blue outer rim. Such a mark of the Hayworth name. A mark you possess, my dear."

Isabel stiffened as her aunt rested a hand on her arm.

She was not used to being touched.

"Everything seems right now that you are here with us at Emberwilde. This is the life you were destined for, not wasting away at some school." Aunt Margaret fairly hissed the words, as if to display her disgust. "You have Hayworth blood running through you. You belong here. This is your heritage."

Isabel bristled at the suggestion that her life had, thus far, been misspent.

Her aunt continued. "Believe me when I say that it is a shame to turn one's back on such a rare gift. You have beauty. Breeding. Gifts, Isabel, do not deny them. Your mother possessed these gifts and yet did not respect them when she went against our father's wishes and married your father. And such a price she paid. It is my sincere desire that you will allow me to help you navigate the waters so you do not repeat your mother's mistakes."

Isabel closed her eyes as if to muster strength. Too many thoughts swirled within her to be able to focus fully on only one. The words and information were coming at her with such haste she was not sure she could bear to hear more. Her uncle seemed ready to marry her off. Her aunt seemed determined to handpick her future husband. And she had been at Emberwilde but a few hours! She did not trust her aunt—not yet. Yes, she supposed the woman to be kind, but insufficient time had passed to ascertain the truth of her nature.

No, she was unprepared to learn more about her mother at this moment.

Isabel shifted in her mounting discomfort, but if her aunt took any notice of Isabel's uneasiness, she shielded it with fast words.

"I know what you must be thinking, Isabel. You must not consider me insensitive for speaking so of your father, but if you are to live here you might as well know the truth behind your circumstance, for you probably never learned it. 'Tis no secret that I was not fond of your father, nor he of me. That is evidenced by our estrangement these years since your mother's death. I suppose there are kind things I can say of him, however. He was exceedingly handsome in his prime. Fair haired with a chiseled chin. He and your mother made a striking pair, to be sure. He was a man of strong convictions, and exceptionally well spoken for a man of his background. But these things are not enough to secure a proper future. Anna did not understand this. Hopefully, I can help right her wrong as far as you are concerned."

Isabel did not understand her aunt's meaning. "As far as I am concerned?"

"You are beautiful, as was your mother. But instead of using her assets as a means to secure a future for herself and her children, she allowed herself to be swayed by selfish pursuits. I humble myself to think that perhaps I can help guide you as you continue down your life's path."

Defenses bubbled within Isabel.

It was true—she had not understood her father. She could not remember her mother. But Aunt Margaret seemed intent upon pointing out their flaws.

"But they loved each other, did they not?" reasoned Isabel. "Surely that was enough?"

Her aunt laughed, a dry, condescending burst that only served to agitate Isabel further.

"My dear, love is a fickle fancy. How enticing it is to read stories and fables of romance that stands the test of time and situation, but it is not always so. I have the benefit of time on this earth. It is my hope that you will take the advice of those who have much more experience than you, unlike your mother, who turned her back on those who loved her."

Isabel bit back a sharp retort and a defense of the parents she barely knew. She turned her attention to the painting.

"I love my daughters," continued her aunt, stepping next to

Isabel so they stood shoulder to shoulder as they looked at the painting. "I desire nothing more than for each of them to be happy as they mature into adulthood. But in order to show my love, I had to make decisions for them. Now they are secure, each one in a certain future. This, my dear, is love. You love Elizabeth. I recognize it in your interactions with the child. But with love comes responsibility. You will do what is necessary to see her well taken care of, and now she is part of our family. It is time for you to accept assistance and guidance from those who care for you."

Isabel did not mean to be wary. Her aunt's words were kind, but Isabel heard the veiled warning in the somber tones. She cast a glance back at her cousin, who was now standing behind them. A pleasant, if not contemplative, expression colored her face. She remained silent. Isabel could not help but wonder why.

Her aunt's countenance brightened. "Speaking of guidance and responsibility, I have a fun outing planned for the morrow. Oh, I know you've just arrived, but tomorrow I should like to take you to visit the local foundling home."

Isabel was not sure she had heard her aunt correctly. "A foundling home?"

"Why, yes. As one of the most affluent families in the area, it is our duty to see to the less fortunate, is it not?"

Isabel did not disagree. It only seemed a strange shift in topics. "Yes, Aunt."

"Then it is settled. Constance and I spend a great deal of time and effort on the foundling home, and I think you will find it quite interesting. You, Constance, Elizabeth, and I will call there in the morning." An expression akin to a grin crossed her aunt's face. "I think you will find Mr. Bradford, the superintendent, to be a very agreeable young man."

Isabel straightened at the recognition of the name, her interest piqued. "Mr. Bradford?"

"Yes, Mr. Bradford. The very one who retrieved you and your sister from Fellsworth. Knowing I was eager to find you, he was most helpful in making the connection with your Mr. Langsby. As a show of our appreciation, it is only fitting that we should pay him a visit to show our gratitude."

After the heavy conversation concerning her parents, this news was a welcome relief. In all of the day's taxing events, her introduction to Mr. Bradford did seem to be the one bright moment. The memory of his kind smile and easy manner warmed her.

Perhaps there was something to anticipate after all.

Chapter Six

$\mathcal{C}$olin followed Ellison in through Emberwilde's main door.

Normally, his business at the great house would take him to the tradesmen's entrance, which was closer to the steward's office and Mr. Ellison's private chambers, but the falling darkness and relentless rain made the long walk seem excessive.

Within moments of entering, Beasley, the butler, was at the door to take their things.

"My apologies for keeping you waiting, sir." The butler's gruff tone was barely audible above the storm raging outside.

"Don't give it a thought, Beasley," responded Ellison in his customary good nature, turning to allow the butler space to help him out of his greatcoat. "No doubt you were expecting us to come round to the back."

After seeing to his master, Beasley turned to Colin, ready to take his coat.

It always felt odd to Colin to have another grown man tend his coat, a task that he was capable of himself. Despite the fact that he owned an estate, he had not grown up with corresponding luxuries. His parents died when he was a young child, and his aunt and uncle had taught him to care for himself from a very early age. When he was a boy and would come to spend the days with Freddie, the Ellisons' deceased son, he would try to follow the rules of behavior, but to this day it felt contrived.

Ellison turned to Beasley. "Are the ladies awake?"

"They are in the music room."

Colin listened with interest as he removed his hat from his head, careful to keep the rain clinging to him from splattering on the floor. He had only glimpsed the new arrivals when they had encountered the carriage arriving earlier that day. He had to admit, he was curious about Isabel Creston. Typically, Colin would not concern himself with a visiting niece, but his curiosity had been piqued when he glimpsed her through the carriage window. He'd noticed blonde hair. A black cloak. An elegant profile. The sight, fleeting as it was, had latched onto his mind and would not release it.

It was not every day an attractive young woman arrived in Northrop.

"If the ladies are still awake, there is no need for me to stay," Colin said. "We can discuss this another time. You've family matters to tend to."

"Nonsense, Galloway. We've business at hand that cannot wait, and you'll need to meet her sometime anyway. My wife has declared that she is to live here with us. Goodness knows how she thought that to be a good idea with Emberwilde in its present state, but you know my wife."

Colin nodded. Yes, he did know Mrs. Ellison's tendencies. Whereas Mr. Ellison was practical and open about his financial situation, Mrs. Ellison was determined to continue to project an image of wealth.

Ellison continued. "Besides, the best outcome would be for her to marry, and marry quickly." He slapped Colin on the shoulder and a grin cracked his usually austere expression. "You are one of the most eligible young men I know."

Colin shook his head and handed his hat to Beasley.

Outside, thunder roared and a fresh wave of icy rain slammed the ancient walls of Emberwilde. The wind whistled through the uneven crevices and window spaces. Beyond his present curiosity about the new visitor, Colin had no wish to walk home in the rain.

So he complied with Ellison's request and did as he was bid. He handed his things to Beasley and followed Ellison through the foyer.

"Mind your steps, Galloway," Ellison instructed. "This floor can get mighty slippery if your boots are still wet."

Colin glanced down. Even the floors in the massive house were elegant. Not a single item was out of place. Even though spring had just begun, blooms from the hothouse adorned tables and mantels, filling the painted Chinese vases and crystal bowls.

Strains of soft, delicate music met his ears and grew louder with every step he took. No doubt it was Miss Constance Ellison playing, for her musical talents were praised throughout Northrop. He waited for Ellison to open the door.

"Father! You are home at last!" The melody came to a sudden stop, and Miss Ellison stood from the pianoforte, a vision of perfection and elegance, and hurried to her father. She reached out, placed a hand on his arm, and kissed his cheek. "We have been worried about you, out in that rain. You must be freezing. Just look at you. You are all wet."

Ellison chuckled and patted her hand. "And aren't you just like my pet, always concerned for me? I shall miss it immensely when you marry your young man and move away from your old papa. For who shall care for me then?"

"Oh, Father, you know that is months away." She waved a hand dismissively, her eyes brightening under her father's praise. "And of course, Mother will care for you."

It was then that Miss Ellison noticed Colin. She turned her eyes toward him. "Good evening, Mr. Galloway. I trust you are not too wet from being out on a night like this. Honestly, I don't know what you have been about!"

He returned the greeting with a bow. He exchanged glances with Ellison, interpreting his silent stare as a reminder to say nothing of the events in the Emberwilde Forest. He turned his attention back to Miss Ellison. "I am quite well, thank you for your concern. It's only a bit of a spring rain, nothing to worry over."

"Only a bit of spring rain!" she exclaimed. "Just listen to that thunder. Why, it hasn't stormed like this in ever so long."

Colin had always been fond of the young Miss Ellison. Of all of the ladies to grace the halls of Emberwilde, she had always been the most agreeable.

He lifted his gaze toward the blazing fire. Her mother, Mrs. Ellison, an older, stouter version of her daughter, had moved from the far edge of the room and was approaching her husband. Her countenance lacked her daughter's warmth and hospitable nature, but he had expected nothing else. She did not look at him, nor did she offer a greeting. Her attention was fixed firmly on Ellison. After all these years of living in such close proximity, Colin found her obvious snub somewhat amusing.

He looked past Mrs. Ellison's plump form, and then he saw her. Miss Creston.

The newcomer with impossibly bright blonde hair stood next to a painting. A severely cut black gown clung to her slight frame.

Was she in mourning?

Miss Ellison's bright tone drew his attention. "But look, Papa, I hear you have met my cousin."

A fatherly smile spread across Ellison's round face. "Yes, I met Isabel earlier this day."

Miss Creston stepped forward as her name was spoken. Colin had never considered himself prone to romantics or apt to have his head turned by a pretty face, but something about her made all noise dissipate and sharpened his focus.

There could be no mistaking the family resemblance. His eyes mapped the distinct features that linked Miss Creston to the

Ellisons. Fair hair and skin. A straight nose that tipped up ever so slightly. Light—almost white—eyelashes and brows that framed a narrow face. If he didn't know otherwise, he would declare Miss Creston and Miss Ellison sisters, so similar was their likeness. But Miss Ellison's coloring was slightly deeper, her eyes more hazel than blue, and her hair more the color of honey than summer wheat.

The young woman finally stepped forward and spoke. "It is a pleasure to see you, Uncle."

"So formal! So polite," exclaimed Ellison as he stepped toward her. He placed his hands on her shoulders and kissed her forehead. "And where is the little one? I was quite surprised to see her. No doubt she will keep us on our toes."

Miss Creston smiled. "She is asleep. She is not used to travel and was quite tired."

"Well now!" Ellison beamed. "Can't say as I blame her. Traveling is exhausting business. We shall see her in the morning."

Miss Creston remained controlled. "Yes, sir."

"Now, Isabel, we are family," Ellison said. "I insist you drop this sir business at once."

At this Miss Creston smiled—a beautiful smile that both pricked and unsettled Colin in its natural delicacy and allurement.

He was lost in his own silent musings until he heard his name mentioned.

"I know you were introduced to Galloway earlier, but it was hardly a proper introduction." Ellison pivoted toward him. "Isabel, this is Mr. Colin Galloway. He is the local magistrate, a local solicitor, owner of Darbenton Court, and a very great friend of the Ellisons."

It was then she turned and let her full gaze rest on him. An eerie sense of understanding rushed him, as if some underlying thread invisibly connected her to him. Despite her likeness to her cousin, one quick glance displayed the differences with equal clarity. For she was controlled and demure. He sensed her to be the sort of woman whose eyes spoke louder than her words, her expressions more descriptive than any phrase she could utter.

In turn, he gave a bow and found his voice. "A pleasure, Miss Creston."

She returned his greeting with a curtsy. "I am pleased to meet you, Mr. Galloway."

He liked the sound of his name on her lips, soft and sweet. And familiar.

"I am sure that Mr. Galloway has somewhere he needs to be." Mrs. Ellison's interruption rang sharp and cool, slicing through their gentle conversation. "We've no desire to keep you from your important duties."

Colin finally locked eyes, firm and unwavering, with Mrs. Ellison, the woman who at one time had been almost like a second mother to him. But circumstances and events had severed him from her motherly tendencies. He adjusted his stance, the floorboards creaking as he did so.

"Quite the contrary." Ever the middle ground, Ellison stepped forward. "Galloway and I have business of our own to tend to."

Ellison looked to his daughter and niece. "Such a pleasure to have you at Emberwilde, Isabel. I look forward to catching up with you all over breakfast. But for now, I cannot waste Mr. Galloway's time, and no doubt he is eager to return home. So we will leave you now."

Colin followed Ellison from the comfortable music room to the hall. As he did, he could feel the stares burning holes in the back of his coat.

Things were changing at Emberwilde. Changing, indeed.

Colin was glad to be free of the confines of the music room. He shook his fingers through his hair and pushed it off his face. It had been a long day, and something told him it was about to get longer.

The men made their way to Ellison's office, a large room toward the back of the great house. Ellison was adamant about tending to his business personally. He employed a steward and a bailiff, but he was integrally involved in Emberwilde's everyday details. Even with his busy day-to-day commitments, he had always taken time to teach Colin what he knew, especially after his own son died and Colin returned from war. A trust existed between the two men, and Colin trusted very few.

It was comfortable in Ellison's study. Dusty books lined the room's south wall from floor to ceiling, and ancient maps and land-scape paintings cluttered every other inch of wall space. The room's furnishings were sparse, save for a desk, a table, and four chairs scattered about. In anticipation of the master's arrival, a cheery fire had been brought to life in the grate, and several candles were positioned around the room, lighting the space with their soft, flickering light.

Without waiting for an invitation, Colin sank into one of the padded chairs by the fire and extended his booted leg. The fire's warmth was welcome after a day spent in the dampness.

"She is a lovely thing, isn't she?" Ellison exclaimed as he dropped into the chair opposite Colin, glass of port in hand.

Colin knew exactly whom he was talking about. There could be no denying it, but the less said on such matters, the better. "Indeed."

"She'll make a fine wife for someone someday." Ellison gave a sharp nod before tossing the amber liquid down his throat. "No doubt that is Mrs. Ellison's intention. Now that Constance is spoken for, my wife will need something of the sort to occupy her mind, and seeking and selecting Isabel's future husband should do just that."

Colin chuckled. Mrs. Ellison had made quite a production

of finding the most suitable husbands for her four daughters. But whereas Mrs. Ellison was often perceived as light and carefree by the townsfolk, Colin was well acquainted enough with the family's situation to know that a more selfish reason fueled her motives. Emberwilde Hall was entailed, and as such should have passed to Freddie upon Ellison's death. But with Freddie dead, the property would pass to Mr. Ellison's nephew, leaving the ladies adrift. Now that all her daughters were married or betrothed, Mrs. Ellison should have been able to rest, but it was not her nature.

"I was only partly joking about your taking a wife, Colin. It's high time, a man like you in the prime of life."

Colin shook his head and gave a little chuckle. He was no stranger to the pressure to marry. He was just not accustomed to it from Ellison. "I am in no position to marry. Not now."

"Oh, I disagree. You have an estate that needs tending. You can't continue to live in that boardinghouse forever. Unless, that is, you've taken a liking to old Mrs. Daugherty."

At the thought of his miserly landlady, Colin huffed. "Not likely, sir."

But Colin could not argue Ellison's point. He did own land, and quite a bit of it.

When he was young, a fire not only claimed his parents' lives, but destroyed the estate's family house and immediate outbuildings. His aunt and uncle became his guardians, and because Colin was too young to inherit, his uncle served as the estate's agent. His uncle's own business had taken priority, however, and during Colin's boyhood the main house and properties were never rebuilt. The estate continued to reap an income from its tenants, but the great house and its fields were never leased or repaired. Since returning from the war, Colin had made steps to provide for and establish relationships with his tenants, but he had not amassed the funds to rebuild the great house and reclaim the damaged land. Between managing his tenants and his work at his cousin's solicitor's firm, he had scarcely a free moment to entertain such a notion.

"There is great opportunity there, indeed. But a great deal of work to be done as well."

"Never known you to shy away from work, Galloway."

It wasn't the work that intimidated him. In fact, far from it.

"Houses can be built," Ellison continued. "You've a great deal to your name, and you are well respected. It is time you put your land to work for you in a more effective manner."

Colin adjusted the cuff of his coat. "Capital is required for such a venture. Capital I do not have at the moment. And if I am to look to the rents I receive and my wages in my cousin's office, I am in a sore state."

"I understand that quandary all too well. Ah, money. Were I able I would cut down every tree in that bothersome Emberwilde Forest and sell every last bit of timber. That would set my financial troubles right, to be sure. But the forest cannot be touched. It must remain in place for future generations. So I will prevent it from becoming a hub for illegal activity instead of using it to keep the estate afloat. But you, on the other hand! Timber abounds. Mark my words. You have capital in the form of raw materials. Sell that timber, my boy, and see what kind of home you can set up for yourself."

The words simmered. Had he not entertained those very thoughts? Of turning his humble birthright into a thriving estate in its own right?

Ellison continued. "Then you will be in a position to marry, and your wife would be a very fortunate lady. I am, at the moment, out of daughters to marry off, but I can think of no one I would trust more with my niece."

Colin chuckled. It would not end, he knew. Once Ellison got a notion in his head, it was not easily dislodged. "You sound just like my aunt. She has taken a sudden interest in my romantic pursuits."

"And your aunt is a wise woman. She is right to urge you toward such things."

"You do not even know your niece."

"Bah. That is not needed. In fact, the less you know prior to marriage, the better. It would unite our family, much to my pleasure."

"And Mrs. Ellison? She would hardly share your opinion."

"No, she would not. But that would be on her, now, wouldn't it?"

Ellison leaned over to pour himself another glass of port, then extended the glass to Colin. When Colin refused, Ellison poured the liquid down his own throat, then balanced the empty glass in his hand. "You have the benefit of time on your hands. I do not. I grow older by the day. But you, take advantage of these years."

Chapter Seven ―――――――――――――――

*T*he wind swirled outside Isabel's chamber window, slamming bits of rain against the wavy glass. The storm had intensified as the evening progressed. Now, icy blows shattered the night's usual silence, its whistles and howls inviting her mind to every manner of distraction. Despite her body's cry for rest, she was sensitive and jumpy after her talk with her aunt, and she doubted her ability to calm down enough for sleep to rescue her.

In her chamber's hearth, a dying fire hissed and popped as its flames licked the dry wood, perfuming the air with the scents of heat and earth. She'd never enjoyed her own fire in her own chamber. She should enjoy the luxury and let herself be wrapped in its obliging warmth, she thought, but instead, her tired eyes stared unblinking at the light. Isabel sat beside the fire, brushing out her hair.

Her awareness shifted to the statuesque goddesses carved into each side of the marble chimneypiece. The face of the goddess on the left was serene and angelic, her eyes downcast, in peaceful reverie, her gently curved smile frozen. But the goddess on the right, with her eyes fixed toward the heavens, appeared sorrowful, if not fearful. No doubt one more educated in Greek mythology would be able to ascertain the goddesses' identities. Isabel ran her finger over the smooth curves of the frightened statue, marveling at the detail in the hair. The face.

Burns, the lady's maid, cleared her throat. "If there is nothing else you need, miss, I will leave you to retire."

Isabel had met Burns earlier that evening. Their exchanges were awkward at first. Isabel had never relied on anyone for daily assistance, with the exception of one of her chamber mates, who helped with her stays. It would take time to get used to having another person waiting on her in such a manner. This evening Burns had been so quiet tending to Isabel's gown that Isabel had almost forgotten she was in the room.

Isabel stood. "Actually, there is one more thing. Do you think you could show me how this window opens?"

Burns's eyebrows drew together in question. "But it is raining, miss."

"I know, but the air feels a bit heavy, do you not think? It will be nice for the morning, when it stops. My aunt said you could smell the lilacs from here. Do you know if they are in bloom? I tried to open it earlier, but it was stuck."

Burns fixed her small eyes on Isabel. "You'll not be able to get that window open, miss. It's been nailed shut."

"Nailed shut?" Isabel frowned, turning to assess the window. "But why would someone nail a window shut?"

Burns draped Isabel's black gown over her arm and smoothed the fabric. "It isn't my place to say."

Isabel's curiosity was piqued. "Can we remove the nails?"

Burns averted her eyes, gathered Isabel's discarded stockings, and laid them over her arm as well. "I'm not so sure you would want to do that."

"But why?"

As if admitting some sort of defeat, the lady's maid stepped toward the window and lowered her voice. "Mr. Ellison's mother had this window nailed shut well over thirty years ago, and it has not been open since."

Isabel frowned. "But that doesn't make any sense."

"After you have been here awhile, it will make sense," Burns stated matter-of-factly.

"I . . . I don't understand."

"I've said too much." Burns inched backward. "Forgive me, Miss Creston."

She turned to leave, and Isabel called after her. "Wait, please don't go. Why would Mrs. Ellison have these windows nailed shut?" If she was going to spend the night in this room, she needed an answer. Was there danger?

Burns stepped back and cast a glance over her shoulder, as if she expected someone to be watching her, then lowered her voice. "She had all the west-facing windows nailed shut, for she feared the ghosts."

At the word, a tiny chill traveled down Isabel's spine. Lizzie's innocent question from the carriage leaped to the forefront of her mind.

"You know that forest out of your window?" asked Burns.

"The Emberwilde Forest?"

"Some call it that, but most folks around here and in town call it the Black Wood Forest."

Isabel brushed her hair from her face. "It looks like such a beautiful forest. Why would they give it such a gloomy name?"

Burns narrowed her eyes. "Beautiful places can be deceptive. Perhaps you've not heard the legend."

"I haven't."

"Horrible, sad story." Burns lowered the garments she was holding and looked out the window into the black night. "The better part of a century ago, gypsies took up residence in these woods. Your uncle's ancestors tried everything to be rid of them, but they were unsuccessful. Legend has it that the gypsies threatened to put a curse on the land. But then there was a massive fire, and several gypsies died."

"How terrible!" exclaimed Isabel.

"Lost a good section of the forest. The fire scorched many a tree in the rest of it, and they were black for decades. Some said it was the souls of the trees dying.

"Places have memories, Miss Creston. Do not doubt it. Ever since then, stories spread like wildfire. Odd things happen to folks who go into the forest. Some blame it on the ghosts of the gypsies, seeking their revenge." She tilted her head, her eyes bleary in the firelight. "Still want the nails removed?"

Isabel couldn't resist the little chuckle that escaped her lips. "There are no such things as ghosts, Burns. Surely you know that."

"I *don't* know that, Miss Creston. In fact, many would agree with me. Stay within Emberwilde's walls long enough and you might change your mind."

Isabel swallowed and met Burns's gaze purposefully. "I do not believe in ghosts, or curses, or anything of the like."

"Well then, you'd best take that request to have the nails removed up with your uncle. I doubt your aunt will allow it. She's a superstitious woman. I doubt that many around here would willingly be letting the ghosts in."

With that, Burns curtsied, adjusted Isabel's gown in her arms, and quitted the room, leaving an eerie silence in her wake that seemed to quiet even the pounding rain.

Isabel looked out the window. She knew the lawn below met up with the forest's edge. She had seen it when first shown to her room. Now the landscape was black—pitch black—for clouds blocked the stars and shielded any light from the moon.

As she stared into the darkness, though, something caught her eye. It looked like a bit of light coming from the ground. The opaqueness made it impossible to judge the distance, and the falling rain made the light jump. She squinted, but soon gave up trying to get a better view. In all likelihood it was simply the light from her fireplace bending and reflecting on the window's warped glass.

She moved to her bed and fell backward onto it. A canopy

blocked her view of the ceiling. She squeezed her eyes shut, hoping for sleep. How the muscles in her back and shoulders ached from the jostling in the carriage, and a slight pain resounded in her head.

A good night's sleep was the remedy for both.

But sleep eluded her.

Unable to find solace, she stood, shook out the folds of her nightclothes, did her best to ignore the wind's mournful howling, and crossed the room. Her valise, along with her other possessions, had been placed inside the wardrobe. She opened the heavy oak door and retrieved her valise to unpack her few items.

As she reached inside the bag, her hand brushed a piece of cloth. She paused and stared at the small bundle of rough linen for several seconds. It was secured with a length of twine and nestled neatly among her belongings. She lifted the bundle and returned to her bed. Holding her breath in anticipation, she released the twine. The fabric fell to the side, revealing a folded letter atop the unfinished piece of needlework.

Tears sprang to her eyes, for she recognized the handwriting and the needlework immediately.

It was from Mary, her dearest friend and confidante at Fellsworth.

She pushed a lock of hair from in front of her eyes before unfolding the letter.

Dear Isabel,

It is with mixed emotions I write you. How my heart is pained to bid you farewell. You are my dearest friend. How shall my days ever feel the same without you in them? Not knowing when we will meet again brings such sadness.

But at the same time, my heart rejoices for you and Lizzie! How many times have you and I daydreamed about how wonderful it would be to join our families? To not be bound by the restraints imposed upon us by our situations and to escape the inevitable paths that stretch before us? I know you well enough to suspect your apprehensions to leave Fellsworth, but heed my words! This opportunity is a gift. Please consider it as such. Embrace your new world. Find your home and where you belong.

Who knows what the next days will bring, and who will cross your path. But it is my prayer for you that you embrace this opportunity. Be an example for Lizzie and for all those you may meet. We do not find ourselves in new situations by accident. Oh, no! Remember, with each dawn seek guidance, and with each night give gratitude. For there is a divine plan for each of our lives, and a journey, and you have started yours.

Please write to me, and I shall return your letters as often as I can. You will be in my prayers each day, as I know I will be present in yours. True friendship will span time and circumstances.

Till our paths cross again,

Mary

Isabel lowered the letter to her lap. Homesickness bit at her tender, tired heart, its harshness bringing tears to her eyes and a shaky breath to her lips. With an unsteady hand she lifted the fabric for closer inspection. Mary's even, straight stitches adorned the piece. *My voice shalt thou hear in the morning, O Lord; in the morning will I direct my prayer unto thee, and will look up.*

Isabel traced her finger over the smooth stitches. Each girl at Fellsworth created such samplers as part of their education and spent time every week working on the craft. But it was not the stitching that gave her reason to pause.

Every morning at Fellsworth, students, teachers, and staff would rise at dawn and spend time alone in contemplation before tending to their responsibilities. They would begin their days in prayer and end their days in the same manner. Isabel had struggled with the practice at times. Her mind would wander. But Mary never wavered.

In her mind she could hear Mary saying the same words. Encouraging her.

She managed a small smile as she placed the tiny sampler on the side table and propped it up so she could see it.

She had not spent even one night away from Fellsworth in over a decade, and now she was in a room fit for a lady.

But she was not a lady, not compared to her aunt's elevated diction or her cousin's effortless elegance. She looked at her rough nightdress and ran her finger over the uneven hem. She doubted she would ever be.

A creaking sound behind her drew her attention, and she turned.

Footsteps sounded near the door that adjoined her room to Lizzie's.

A sudden jump in her pulse brought her to her feet, and she looked toward the door.

There it was again. The scrape—a mournful sound, like the cry of wood against wood—sounded again from the gilded chamber.

The door was beginning to move.

The hour was late. No one else should be awake.

She chided herself. The talk of ghosts and folklore made her jumpy, in a ridiculous sense.

"Who's there?" Isabel called, her voice thin.

Her imagination half expected a monster, or at the very least a mysterious stranger.

Instead, it was a small hand that gripped the edge of a door.

Relief rushed from Isabel in the form of a sigh.

Lizzie's voice was small compared to the roar of the angry wind. "Isabel?"

Isabel placed the letter on the bureau. "Lizzie! You gave me a fright. What is the matter?"

Lizzie rubbed her face as she spoke. "I can't sleep."

Isabel reached her arm out to the child, bidding her to come closer. Lizzie closed the door and ran over to the chair, her bare feet padding the wooden floor.

She should send the child back to her own room. It was important to set a boundary, for they were in a large house now and probably would be for some time. Lizzie needed to be able to sleep alone.

But how could she fault the child when she herself struggled to find solace?

Isabel sat and pulled her sister onto her lap. The girl's small feet were cold against Isabel's legs.

Once Lizzie was settled and the popping of the fire and the roar of the wind the only sounds that remained, Isabel whispered, "And why can't you sleep?"

Lizzie wiggled. "The wind is scary."

"Scary?" Isabel paused. The panes shivered in their leading, and then a blast of rain pelted the surface. "No, it isn't scary. 'Tis only noisy. The same wind blows during the day."

Lizzie shivered against her. "It sounds like an animal. A mean animal."

Not so long ago, such sounds used to give Isabel a fright. But now her duty as caretaker prevailed. "I promise you, there are no animals in here. You are quite safe. Tomorrow, if the weather is fine, we shall take a walk around the grounds and you will be able to see for yourself how lovely Emberwilde is."

Lizzie made no response; her silence on the matter was evidence of disbelief. The child dropped her head to Isabel's shoulder, and for several moments they were silent. Isabel thought her sister had drifted off, so still and quiet was she, but after several minutes of slow, steady breaths, Lizzie whispered, "I want to go home."

The words, tiny and quiet in the stillness, tugged at Isabel. The concept of home had always been an abstract one. Even though her father lived in London and had a home there, Isabel had never returned to it after leaving for Fellsworth. The demands of his occupation prevented him from seeing her, and after he married Lizzie's mother, her stepmother was very clear that Isabel was not welcome in the home. Isabel often felt as if she were an orphan, alone and forgotten. When Lizzie's mother died, their father sent Lizzie to Fellsworth as well, and Isabel welcomed Lizzie, eager for even a bit of family to call her own. By the time her father died, she'd grown to consider Fellsworth home, and clearly Lizzie did as well.

Isabel stroked the child's wayward locks. "It is different here than at the school, is it not?"

Lizzie only sniffed.

"But do you not think it will be lovely to have a family around us? To have an aunt and uncle? And cousins?"

Again, no response passed Lizzie's lips.

Uneasiness crept over Isabel and frightened her much more than wind against the windowpane could. She had tried to push her uncle's words from her mind, but his words about feeding extra mouths and finding a husband for her would not leave her be. They echoed in her mind like a noisy blackbird, giving her mind yet another reason for caution and trepidation.

"All that matters, that *really* matters, is that you and I are together. Now, if the two of us are together, is there anything that can truly make us sad?"

Lizzie shook her head.

"No matter what happens while we are here, I promise you that I will never leave you. We shall never be separated. Do you believe me?"

The little girl nodded sleepily.

The words in Mary's letter flitted through her mind.

For there is a divine plan for each of our lives, and a journey, and you have started yours.

"We are on a journey, you and I." Isabel squeezed her sister. "And I don't know about you, but I am excited to see what adventures are waiting for us."

Chapter Eight

"Mr. Galloway!"

Mrs. Daugherty's sharp voice echoed throughout Colin's small chamber on the second level of the boardinghouse.

"Mr. Galloway!" she barked, sharper this time. Knuckles rapped on his closed door in barbed persistence. "You are needed downstairs at once. The girl from the Holden farm is here and needs to speak with you."

Pushed by the urgency in the voice, not to mention the desire for her to curtail the insistent knocking, Colin shoved his blanket away and jumped from his bed. He shook his fingers through his tousled hair and turned to the room's only window to gauge the hour. The gray light of early dawn crept in around the fabric covering the narrow pane.

Why would someone from the Holden farm want to speak with him?

The image of James Holden flashed in his mind. The short man with thinning gray hair and a round belly was a most capable fellow. A stolen chicken or missing cow was the likeliest reason the farmer would contact the magistrate. But at this hour of the day?

He called back through the closed door. "Be right down."

As he reached for his buckskin breeches slung over the back of a nearby chair, he could hear Mrs. Daugherty muttering on the other side of the door.

Colin, too, muttered under his breath, not so much bemoaning the earliness of the hour as the impatience of his sharp-tongued landlady. No doubt Mrs. Daugherty's razor-edged voice and intense knocking had woken the four other gentlemen who boarded here, including Henry, his own cousin, who let the room on the other side of his wall. Eventually, her footsteps retreated down the hall.

The previous day's conversation with Ellison echoed in his mind. Perhaps it was time to give more consideration to restoring his property and moving away from the boardinghouse. But with his heavy responsibilities as a solicitor and magistrate, it made little sense to move so far out of town.

He straightened, tucked his shirt into his trousers, and pulled his heavy black riding boots over his stockings. Before going out he paused to check the small looking glass hanging next to his door. Anyone calling at this hour, regardless of the reason, would have to accept his hasty dress as good enough.

Colin punched his arm through the sleeve of his coat, unlocked his door, and swung it open.

The scent of salty ham and baking bread met him in the hall—a familiar morning scent. He made his way down a stairwell so narrow his shoulders nearly brushed either side as he descended.

Cool air rushed him as he reached the bottom. The half door to the kitchen garden stood ajar, and windows were high in their sashes, letting the early morning's cool, fresh air into the low-ceilinged room. He filled his lungs with it before turning the corner.

There, just inside the main door, stood Mrs. Daugherty. Next to her stood a young girl with her arms around a woven basket.

Colin forced a smile to his face. "Good morning, Mrs. Daugherty, Miss Holden. How can I be of service?"

Thin arms folded over her chest, Mrs. Daugherty jerked her head in the girl's direction. "This young lady would like a moment of your time."

At second glance, Colin recognized the girl as Becky Holden, the farmer's eldest daughter. He was not good at judging the age of children, but she looked like she might be eleven or twelve. A roughly fashioned cape of gray felt was around her shoulders, and her hair was pulled into two tight plaits that fell down her back.

Becky cut her eyes toward Mrs. Daugherty, as if seeking approval, before turning her attention fully to Colin. Her voice was thin, almost a whisper. "We found her at our farm this morning."

He was about to ask her to repeat herself when the girl thrust the basket toward him. He reached out and touched the blanket covering the basket's contents.

There, tucked beneath the blanket, was a baby. Judging by the color of its skin and its size, it was brand new to this world.

He jerked his hand back. He didn't know the first thing about babies, and the last thing he wanted to do was disrupt it. But at his motion, the infant's eyes flew open, and this was followed by a wail, feisty and angry. The child's face deepened to crimson in mere seconds and a tiny fist flailed into the air.

The girl shoved the basket toward Colin. "It was on the doorstep. Our hired hand found her there when he went to tend the sheep."

Colin scrambled to keep the child from clattering to the floor. Once he had control over the basket, he held it to his chest, the baby wailing even louder.

The girl's face blanched and tears gathered in her eyes. She inched backward, and her eyes grew wide. "Mother said to bring her to you. She said we don't want any trouble and that you would know what to do."

As magistrate, Colin felt responsible for seeing to the orphans, widows, and the poor. The number of abandoned infants had increased over the past year or so, ever since Northrop's foundling home had declared that they would accept any child into their care. Word had spread through the neighboring villages, and now, every so often an unwanted child would be left in some conspicuous place.

Several months ago a baby had been left on the vicar's stairs, and about a year ago one had been left at the inn. They were rarely left at the foundling home itself, because of the large gate surrounding it.

Colin set the basket on the table gingerly and blew the air from his lungs.

"For heaven's sake, Mr. Galloway," exclaimed Mrs. Daugherty, taking the baby from the basket and cradling it in her arms. "She'll not bite. 'Tis but a babe, and you are acting as if you have never seen one."

Colin cleared his throat and regained his composure. He looked to Becky, who was kneading the edge of her cape with her fingers. "Tell your father I'll be by his farm this afternoon."

"Oh, but he hasn't done anything!" Becky's dark eyes widened, and her head shook slowly from side to side. "The baby was just there, it was just—"

"I know he's done nothing wrong," clarified Colin, attempting to alleviate the girl's anxiety. "I need to speak with him just the same."

Becky nodded, stepped backward, and ran out through the door.

"Tsk." Mrs. Daugherty rocked the baby from side to side as she turned to watch the girl's retreating form. "You can go out to the Holden farm all ye like, but you know as certain as the sky is blue that he won't know nothing. You ought to keep regular hours, Mr. Galloway. That way folks would stop coming here like they do. I run a boardinghouse. Not an office."

Mrs. Daugherty always feigned annoyance when Northrop's residents would visit the boardinghouse seeking assistance, but Colin knew her fascination with gossip. Because he lived here, she was often the first in town to know what was happening with her neighbors, and she liked it that way.

A landlady like her was both a blessing and a curse.

She clicked her tongue. "You must find a way to put an end to this before we have more babies than we know what to do with. If people think that they can bring all their unwanted babes to Northrop, then we'll find ourselves in real trouble."

It was true, Colin knew, but what could be done at the moment? "I will take the baby to the foundling home this morning."

"You'd best hurry then. Poor thing's probably half-starved already." Mrs. Daugherty returned the baby to the basket, inciting yet another cry. "Been a long time since I cared for a wee babe like that, but I do know babes are hungry all the time."

He pressed his lips together in contemplation as he looked at the tiny wriggling figure.

The perfect light eyelashes. The tiny hand that waved in the air.

So very young.

So very innocent.

Mrs. Daugherty turned to leave, and Colin opened his mouth to stop her. The idea of being alone with the baby unnerved him. But then his cousin Henry came lumbering down the steps, awakened no doubt by either their landlady's incessant pounding or the baby's shrill cry.

"What in blazes is that?" Henry grumbled, his hair in disarray and his face creased with sleep lines.

Colin stepped aside so that Henry could see the basket, and the child released another wail.

Henry wrinkled his nose. "Cute little thing. Where'd it come from?"

"The Holden girl just brought it," Colin explained. "Said it was left on their doorstep."

Henry leaned over the basket, his neck cloth hanging undone around his throat. "Hmm. Any note or anything?"

Colin assessed the basket. Normally no note accompanied these abandoned children, but he ought to check. The baby fit tightly in the basket. He felt around the thin blanket to see if he could find anything.

"Egad," exclaimed Henry, an amused expression brightening his sleepy face. "Just pick it up and look."

Colin set his lips in a firm line. He reached into the basket, tucked his hand beneath the baby's head and body, and lifted. The baby let out a mighty wail, one so loud it rivaled the cries he had heard on the battlefield.

He held the child out in front of him, angling it uncomfortably.

"Quick," Colin called to Henry and nodded to the basket. "Look in there. Is there a note?"

Henry lifted the blanket and shifted the small cloth at the bottom of the basket. "No, nothing."

Colin looked at the baby in his hands. "I suppose it's best to take it to Bradford at once. He'll know what to do with it."

"Best stop by and see if Mother will go with you. You know how she adores children and the sort, and besides, she will know what to do about the crying. I'd go with you, but I am due out this morning at Heddeston Park. Meeting with the steward. It seems they are getting close to identifying the heir, and I have offered to work with their solicitor to finalize the details as soon as possible. I'll fill you in later when you come into the office."

Colin nodded. He attempted to return the red-faced, angry baby to the basket but could not get the angle right.

Yes, Aunt Lydia would know what to do.

By some miracle, the baby fell asleep on the short walk from the boardinghouse to Lockert Cottage, his aunt's home, which was situated on the outskirts of the village. With the baby quiet, it was actually a pleasant spring walk, despite the knot in the pit of his stomach caused by the fact that this little one had been left alone.

It was a sobering—and personal—contemplation.

Colin's own parents and siblings had died when he was two in a fire on their nearby estate, leaving him alone in the world. But unlike this child, his abandonment had not been by choice. Fortunately, his aunt Lydia and uncle Richard opened their home to him. His cousins, Henry and William, had become like brothers to him. The family loved him. Taught him. Cared for him. Treated him as their own.

This poor child may never have the same good fortune.

He approached the cottage gate, taking a moment to study the modest dwelling. The thatched roof and white exterior were burned into his memory. He could call every detail to mind at any time, from the beams that ran across the front to the shutters that flanked the window.

This was a visit he made nearly every day. Ever since his uncle died three years prior, either Colin or his cousin Henry would visit daily to see to the home's maintenance and assist his aunt with tasks that she or her aging staff could not tend to themselves. She had invited both men to live with her at Lockert, but William's widow, Miranda, already lived there with her son, Charles, and Colin and Henry kept odd hours.

Colin opened the gate and passed through, careful not to let the basket hit the stone sidewall. The sound of laughter rang from the cottage's far yard, then a black-haired boy came running around the corner.

"Uncle Colin!"

Charles flew with all the energy his small frame could muster. "I didn't know you were coming so early!"

Colin could not help the laugh that escaped him as the boy rushed him, his curly hair flopping about his face as he ran, his cheeks flushed pink. How the boy reminded Colin of William when he had been a boy. Dark hair, laughing eyes, and a smattering of freckles.

"What's in the basket?" Charles asked, stopping abruptly a few feet away, but then he quickly changed his own subject. "Have you come to take me fishing?"

Colin adjusted the basket in his hands. "I wish I could, but not today."

The boy pouted. "But why not? It isn't raining, and Mother never lets me go alone. Not ever."

Colin was about to respond when a feminine voice interrupted. "Who's there, Charles?"

The voice, familiar as it was, still had the power to stop him in his path, derail his mind of whatever it was previously focused on.

There, in the threshold, stood William's widow, Miranda Galloway.

She was every bit as lovely as she had ever been. The sun's white morning light highlighted her glossy black hair, and her eyebrow arched with an air of entitled amusement. Even in her practical dress of pale blue and a woven apron, she managed to present herself as attractive.

He held eye contact with Miranda for but a second before turning his attention back to Charles and rustling his fingers through the boy's hair.

This was the time of the visits he always lamented. One would have thought the span of nearly a decade sufficient time to erase poignant feelings and emotions. *Time may help the mind erase past wrongs; the heart is another matter entirely,* he thought.

Miranda swept toward him in the cottage courtyard, bringing with her the scent of lavender—a sickening-sweet scent that she had worn since adolescence.

A scent he had grown to despise.

"Colin," Miranda exclaimed, as if his presence were a wonder as opposed to an everyday occurrence. "What a pleasure. We weren't expecting you this morning."

"I had a bit of an unexpected surprise. Is my aunt at home?"

"How intriguing. Of course she is here. She is in the kitchen with Cook discussing the day's meals." Her gaze fell on the basket. "So you've a surprise, do you?"

Without invitation she leaned toward it and pulled back the cloth. "A baby! How lovely! Wherever did it come from?"

He drew his breath in preparation to respond, but to his relief, his aunt appeared on the front threshold, her timing, as usual, impeccable.

She crossed the yard, wiping her hands on her apron. "Colin, you're early! I saw you from the window." She stepped forward, but then stopped when she saw the baby. Instead of sharing in her daughter-in-law's amusement, she drew her eyebrows together in concern. "Merciful heavens. Another one?"

Colin nodded, pulling the blanket back farther. "She was left at the Holden farm last night."

Aunt Lydia frowned. "Such a pity. And such a beautiful babe too."

She reached for the baby and lifted her from the basket with the ease of a longtime mother, and she clicked her tongue in a soothing manner and gently rocked the child from side to side.

With her presence, the tension in Colin's shoulders subsided. He could deal with hoodlums and vagabonds all day long, but babies were beyond him.

"Are you going to take her to the foundling home?" Aunt Lydia asked, adjusting the child in her arms.

He shrugged. "I see no other option."

"She needs to eat. And no doubt her clothing could stand to be changed. Why, she is in nothing but rags! This will not do."

"Would you care to accompany me to the home? I think she prefers your arms to this basket."

"Of course she does. What child likes to be in a basket? Why, the idea! And yes, I shall accompany you." She turned to Miranda. "You can go over the menu with Martha, right? I won't be long. I will get my cape and be back presently."

His aunt put the child in Colin's arms. Initially he stiffened, but for the first time, as he held the child, she did not protest.

The tension in his arms began to slacken, and he let the baby rest against the wool fabric of his coat.

Miranda cut her chocolate eyes to him. "I must say, you appear very natural with a child in your arms."

He did not meet her gaze. Instead, he fixed his eyes on the wee babe's head.

Perhaps Miranda could dismiss the history that separated them and could pretend as if the betrayal had never happened.

He could not.

"If you would be so kind, please tell my aunt I will wait for her by the gate."

He saw the flash of disappointment on Miranda's face before he turned to the road. He knew what she wanted—to erase the cloak of time.

But what she should not forget was that he knew her too well.

Chapter Nine

The following morning Aunt Margaret remained true to her word—the ladies of Emberwilde embarked for a short journey to the foundling home. Isabel had hoped for a quiet day to allow her and Lizzie to get their bearings in the sprawling house, but perhaps it was best not to have too much time for solitary contemplations.

If she were honest, the thought of encountering Mr. Bradford once more intrigued her. Their interactions the previous day had been limited, but something in his manner put her at ease. Instead of allowing her mind to be engulfed in some of the heavier thoughts pressing her, she resolved to enjoy the morning.

Once in the carriage, Isabel sat next to Lizzie and across from Constance. They were waiting on Aunt Margaret, who was engaged in a conversation with the housekeeper.

As they waited, Constance leaned forward as if taking Isabel into confidence. "Mother is quite proud of the foundling home and the endeavors associated therein, as you will see. She devotes a great deal of her spare time to it. It is quite close. The building is on Emberwilde's property. Mother and Father donated the use of the building to the cause, and they continue to provide a great deal of financial support. Of course, Mr. Bradford is responsible for the institution, but he relies on Mother's expertise."

Isabel fidgeted with the cuff of her gown and looked back at Emberwilde, wondering what expertise her aunt could have with a foundling home. After all, her aunt was a privileged woman, and had been since the day she was born.

Her cousin continued. "Mother pours a great deal of consideration into it. Especially now that I have a successful match, I think it is a way she manages to occupy her time. Without it I think she would be driven to distraction."

"That is very kind of her to spend her time in such a fashion," noted Isabel.

"She did say that she is most interested in your take on the facility. After all, did you not come from a situation similar to a foundling home?"

Isabel cast a glance down at Lizzie to see if she was listening to the conversation, but her sister's attentions were fixed on a horse being led across the yard. She looked back to Constance. "No. Not exactly. We were at a school."

"I see." Constance leaned back and adjusted the white glove on her hand in a manner that suggested she did not see the difference.

In this new, opulent world that now surrounded her, it would be nice to return to something more humble, more like what she was used to, even if for a short visit. Emberwilde was beautiful, but Isabel had been there only one morning and was already wondering how she was going to pass the long afternoon hours. Perhaps with the foundling home in such close proximity she could offer her assistance in some way.

At length Aunt Margaret joined them. Obvious care had been taken in her preparations. She was dressed in a gown of pristine brocade the color of cornflowers and trimmed in gold beadwork. A white fichu was tucked into the bodice and framed her neck elegantly. An ornate bonnet with flowers and feathers covered her silver curls. As Isabel was assessing her aunt's gown, she could sense her aunt assessing her own black dress. The corners of her aunt's mouth turned downward.

Once her aunt had settled into the carriage, she leaned forward and placed her hand on Isabel's arm. "Do not be uneasy about your appearance, pet. For I have already sent word to the dressmaker to come to us as soon as possible to have you and your sister fitted for new gowns."

The comment amused Isabel. "I am not uneasy, Aunt. I am quite comfortable with this attire."

"But to be in such somber colors while not in mourning? It is not to be tolerated. You are far too young for such a hue. Youth deserves beauty, and in my humble opinion, a lady with your gentle complexion should be in soft colors."

The ride to the foundling home was very short. In fact, it seemed silly that they went to the trouble of taking the carriage, for the building was just on the other side of the large iron gate that marked Emberwilde's main entrance. But her aunt had insisted upon the carriage, declaring that it was imperative that they enjoy their outing fresh and free from the effects of the day's hot sun.

As they traveled down the main drive, Isabel recognized the scenery from her and Lizzie's arrival. Unlike yesterday, the sun's glow fell on the landscape. The Emberwilde Forest was beautiful—dark and dense, full of lush greenery. It exuded a peaceful ambience that had Isabel wishing to explore the beauty. She had not given credit to Burns's story, which could be little more than a tall tale. And yet, she was somehow intrigued. Burns had mentioned that Aunt Margaret would not allow the nails to be removed from Isabel's chamber window. Surely her aunt did not fall prey to such nonsense, but Isabel decided to wait and inquire about it another time.

Once free of Emberwilde's front lawn, the forest lined the drive and the expansive curving road. They passed through the main iron gate, and just on the outside of the gate sat the found-ling home.

Isabel had seen the home the previous day as they passed into Emberwilde but thought little of it. It was small yet charming. She guessed the building to be almost as old as Emberwilde Hall itself, for it boasted the same gray stone and the same diagonally leaded windows present on the main house. A heavy wooden door with a black iron handle marked the main entrance.

As the carriage drew to a halt, butterflies fluttered within her. In all likelihood, Mr. Bradford's kindness stemmed from the fact that he was friends with the Ellisons, and not because he thought she was deserving. While at Fellsworth she rarely was introduced to new people, especially gentlemen, and the idea appealed to her. Now that the shock of the change was slowly dissipating, she was looking forward to finding a place in the society in which she now dwelled.

"Look, Isabel!" cried Lizzie, leaning toward the window. A bright smile lit her sister's face for the first time since their arrival. "There are children playing! There, beyond that gate."

"Of course there are children, Elizabeth," responded Aunt Margaret quickly. Terseness colored her formal tone. "This is, after all, a foundling home. But I must caution you, limit your excitement, for these children are not your equal, my dear."

Isabel stiffened. The words flattened any excitement surrounding the visit. She and Lizzie had come from a school, yes, but it had been a school that would turn none away. None of the families came from wealth, and many of the children came from poverty. According to the values they had been taught, values that both she and Lizzie believed without wavering, all children were equal and deserved equal opportunity.

An expression of confusion crossed her sister's face, and Isabel placed her hand on Lizzie's arm.

Once the carriage was fully stopped, the women exited. The scent of roses wafted from a nearby garden, and the sunlight warmed Isabel's shoulders and back. Sounds of the children playing and laughing rose about the rustling of the nearby forest, a sound that Isabel decided was a positive mark for the home.

They were greeted at the main entrance by a young woman

in a white apron and cap. She said nothing, and Aunt Margaret pushed her way past the servant without acknowledging her. Isabel cringed at the brashness of the action, but Constance seemed unaware of any breach of etiquette. Isabel reached for Lizzie's hand as they passed through the door and into the narrow foyer, casting an apologetic glance toward the young woman.

From the foyer Isabel followed her aunt as she turned left through a door and stepped into a bright, cheery office. It was not an elegant room like those at Emberwilde. It was sparsely furnished, but tidy and clean. The walls were paneled in dark wood, and her boots trod a planked wooden floor. Several tall, narrow windows lined the front and side walls, and a broad fireplace of brick and stone was situated behind the oak desk surrounded by modest oak chairs. To the left of the desk was a closed door. Between the desk and the fireplace stood a tall, impressive man. Mr. Bradford.

He adjusted his coat and cravat, a broad smile flashing against fair skin.

He was attractive—no, handsome. The seaming of his coat accented his broad shoulders and tapered waist. In fact, the cut of his clothing was impeccable, which surprised her. One would not expect a man in his position to possess such fashionable attire. But then again, knowing her aunt's tendency toward elegance and appearances, and knowing that she financially supported the institution, Isabel could only assume that her aunt saw to Mr. Bradford's clothing.

"Mr. Bradford, I do hope you can spare time for some old friends." Not waiting for an invitation, Aunt Margaret settled her cane on a small chair next to his desk.

An arresting smile curved his lip and he gave a sharp bow. "I always have time for the Ellisons and now both of the Miss Crestons. It is a pleasure to see you again. How do you find Emberwilde, Miss Creston?"

Isabel flushed under the directness of his attention and curtsied in greeting before speaking. "I find it to be lovely indeed."

He leaned against the desk and hunched over toward Lizzie. "Miss Elizabeth, the young ladies are currently taking fresh air out in the garden. Perhaps you would like to join them while your sister and aunt visit."

At this, Lizzie gave a little hop and whirled to Isabel, seeking permission.

Isabel hesitated. Her aunt's words from not even ten minutes prior flamed in her memory. In this new world, who knew what her aunt would deem appropriate?

Before she could respond, her aunt said, "Of course, child. We shan't stay long, but a few moments of outdoor air will be beneficial."

Isabel was shocked by her aunt's change in attitude. It was becoming clear that she understood little about the behaviors expected of the wealthy.

Mr. Bradford opened the door opposite the front windows, which seemed to lead to another corridor. He disappeared through the door, then reappeared with another young woman in a black gown and white apron. She could easily have fit in as a teacher at Fellsworth with her dark attire and tightly bound hair. She gave a curtsy as she entered.

"Miss Trendle, please escort Miss Elizabeth to the side garden where she may take in the air with the young ladies."

Miss Trendle nodded with a sweet, kind smile. Lizzie cut her eyes toward Isabel one last time, and after Isabel's encouraging nod, Lizzie followed Miss Trendle out.

"Do not worry about your sister, Miss Creston." Mr. Bradford's voice reverberated with unmasked kindness. "You can see the side garden through this window."

Isabel assessed the window he indicated and saw he was right. Through the opening, the sunlight beamed down on several girls clad in gowns of light blue. Giggles and soft voices were carried in on the late-morning breeze. Her shoulders eased when she saw Miss Trendle lead Lizzie out to the girls, who stopped their play in interest of their newcomer.

Aunt Margaret motioned for Isabel and Constance to be seated. When Mr. Bradford noticed there were not enough seats for all of the ladies, he crossed the room and retrieved another wooden chair next to the room's main entrance. The ease with which he lifted it was admirable.

"You are always thoughtful, Mr. Bradford." Aunt Margaret adjusted the glove on her hand as she watched him. "As I mentioned earlier, our visit will not be a long one. I was singing the praises of our foundling home, under your direction, of course. Since my niece will be living with us, I wanted her to witness the endeavor firsthand."

He seemed comfortable as the recipient of her aunt's praise and smiled at Isabel. "You are most welcome here, Miss Creston. I only hope that we can live up to your aunt's high esteem."

Isabel was about to respond, but her aunt cut her short.

"I did not have a chance to thank you personally for your assistance in retrieving the Miss Crestons from Fellsworth. You left in such a hurry yesterday after delivering the ladies that we were unable to thank you properly."

"Please forgive me on that account. The rain had been strong, and I had no wish to bring it into Emberwilde with me." He looked at Isabel. "I must say I am quite impressed by Mr. Langsby, and have been since I met him several years back. He runs an extraordinary establishment. I am always inspired by him."

At the mention of Mr. Langsby, homesickness unexpectedly pinched. Why the reference to the wiry man should have such an effect, she did not know.

Mr. Bradford turned his full attention to Isabel. "And how long were you at Fellsworth, Miss Creston?"

"Recently I have been training to become a teacher while waiting for a governess position or a proper teaching position to become available, but I have attended the school since I was a child—younger even than Lizzie."

"I hope you know you are always welcome to visit here, should you be so inclined. In fact, I would be grateful for your expertise. I aspire to follow in Mr. Langsby's footsteps. How great would it be to run a school one day."

Her eyebrows rose with interest. "Are you considering transitioning the home to more of a school?"

Her question seemed to take him off guard, and Isabel immediately regretted her words. It dawned on her that his comment was likely polite rather than earnest.

He exchanged an uncomfortable glance with Aunt Margaret before smiling at her once again. "That is a lofty ambition. We do what we can by way of education, but of course I would be grateful for your views."

Isabel looked to the children outside. So many young people. And what future did they have? An idea budded within her. Mr. Bradford may or may not relish the idea of transitioning the home into a school, but the idea of spending hour upon hour at Emberwilde seemed a bit overwhelming—and dull. "I am used to spending my days teaching and working with children. Perhaps you would permit Lizzie and me to visit to read to the children. I believe children need other children, and I should enjoy it very much."

Her aunt's mouth fell open.

Isabel had said too much. Assumed too much. She realized her indiscretion as soon as the words escaped her mouth. She had only been here one day, and already her tendency to act before fully considering the consequences had reared its head.

But whereas her aunt seemed mortified, Mr. Bradley seemed amused. His smile broadened. "If you can help improve the educational status of the children here, I would be most grateful. I've no wish to overtax you, though. Surely your duties at Emberwilde will keep you far too occupied for such actions."

Her mind raced with the possibilities. As she wrestled with her thoughts, the main entrance behind them creaked.

The heavy wooden door scraped the floor beneath it.

Mr. Bradford straightened and turned his attention to the sounds. "It appears we have another guest."

All three women followed suit and looked toward the doorway.

Within moments two people appeared there: a tall man with striking blue eyes—her uncle's friend from the forest—and an older woman who had a baby cradled in her arms.

It was Mr. Galloway, the man her uncle spoke to about marrying her. At the very thought, the heat of embarrassment crept up her neck. She stiffened, feeling fresh resentment toward the uncle she knew so little. And did this man share Uncle Charles's opinions?

The amiable atmosphere in the room seemed to chill, and she, along with the rest of those in the room, turned to the intruders for an explanation.

Chapter Ten

*C*olin glanced around Bradford's study. It was hardly the first time he had been in the chamber, nor was it the first time he had arrived when Bradford was entertaining guests.

He had not expected to see Mrs. Ellison, but he was not surprised by her presence. It was no secret that the foundling home was the wealthy woman's pet project and that she took great pride in being its main source of financial support. Nor was he surprised to see Miss Constance Ellison with her mother. But the young woman accompanying them made him momentarily forget why he had come and what he needed to say.

Isabel Creston.

When he first met her in the carriage the previous day, she had been attractive, yes, but here, by the bright light of morning, her hair was so blonde it appeared purer than gold, and her eyes were impossibly pale.

In an effort to compose himself, he gave a bow in their direction, surprising himself by remembering that act of etiquette, then focused his attention on Bradford.

The man stepped forward and offered a bow to Colin's aunt before turning his attention on Colin. "Mrs. Galloway. This is a surprise. Mr. Galloway."

Colin swiped his hat from his head. "Surprise, yes, Mr. Bradford, but scarcely a social call."

Bradford seemed to ignore his words—and his aunt and the baby. "You remember our new neighbor, Miss Creston?"

Colin took the moment to look fully at the young woman. "I do. Good day, ladies." He bowed.

Bradford did not give the women a chance to respond. Instead, he stepped closer to Aunt Lydia and looked down at the child, then propped his hands on his hips. "So, I see you have another visitor for me."

Colin cleared his throat. "This child was left at the Holden farm. She was found this morning."

Bradford lifted the blanket from the child's face. His tone was matter-of-fact. "Newborn?"

"It would appear so, but I am hardly an expert on such things. She was left in a basket, no note or letter."

"You were right to bring her here. We will see she is cared for." Bradford stepped back, ducked his head out of the open window, motioned to someone, then returned.

Colin was surprised when Miss Creston, light eyes wide, stepped forward. Her full lower lip dipped in a frown, and concern creased her brow. She directed her question directly to him.

"Someone abandoned her?"

Colin glanced up, surprised by how she interjected herself into the conversation. This trend of abandoning children was becoming sadly commonplace, and it was refreshing to see that it bothered another in the same manner it bothered him. "Yes. Some are finding it easier to turn their children over than to raise them."

She stepped forward again. "But surely you will look for her mother? Can it be right for a child to be thus abandoned?"

His eyes met her gaze—a strong gaze. She seemed not the least bit intimidated by speaking to a man she did not know on a matter that did not directly involve her.

"Of course I will be traveling out to the Holden farm this afternoon to ascertain what I can, but I fear we will not find much to go on."

Bradford stepped between Colin and Miss Creston. "Sadly, times are hard in this part of the country, Miss Creston. The crops were poor last year, and poverty is high. Some women and families believe they have no options. It is not the first child to be brought to my doorstep in such a manner, and I daresay it will not be the last."

Miss Creston did not seem satisfied with the answer. Her chin lifted as she spoke. "And what will happen to her now?"

Bradford reached out his arms to take the child. "Do not fear, Miss Creston. I shall register her in our ledger, and she will be taken to a wet nurse not far from here until she is old enough to return. That is, unless someone with a valid claim on the child should come to collect her. Although I must say I expect nothing of the like. Do you, Galloway?"

Colin watched the interaction with interest. "I do not."

Bradford adjusted the baby in his arms. "I doubt riding to the Holdens will do you much good, but I suppose it needs to be done. But of course it matters little now that the child is here. I do not concern myself with the parents in a situation such as this, but with the child."

Miss Trendle once again appeared, her expression downcast, and bobbed a curtsy. She took the child from Bradford, then left swiftly.

A strange tug jerked at Colin's heart as he watched the child being carried away—a new number to be logged for the foundling home, a new charge who needed care. The tiny child did not even have a name to her person. She had burst into his life but a few hours ago, and yet now he felt hesitant to leave her.

Mrs. Ellison tapped her cane on the floor, as if determined to be included in the conversation. She leaned heavily against the staff and, with the assistance of her daughter, stood, demanding the attention of the room's occupants. She moved toward them.

Her expression was smug as she cut her eyes in Colin's direction before turning them fully to Bradford.

Her voice rang loudly—too loudly—in the small space. "This is why this work here is so important. You must not forget it, Mr. Bradford. But I know you shan't."

Colin could sense his own aunt stiffening next to him, and he sneaked a glimpse at Miss Creston. She did not appear to be listening, nor did she appear to share in the satisfaction that all was well. Her fair brows were still drawn together, and she looked over her shoulder at the empty doorway that had accepted the baby.

Colin forced himself to avert his gaze and look down at the toes of his boots, dusty from the morning walk over. He had done his duty. It was time to leave. With the baby safely delivered to the proper hands, there was no reason for them to stay.

He was about to bid the party good day when a commotion from the front garden drew his attention.

Within moments, two adolescent boys ran into the room, huffing for air. Their clothes were smeared with mud, and their faces were pale.

Mr. Bradford transformed before Colin's eyes. Gone was his customary easy smile. His countenance darkened, and his eyebrows furrowed.

Bradford thundered, "Gentlemen! What is the meaning of this?"

The youths, their eyes wide, pranced from foot to foot. Unrefined words spewed from their mouths at a frantic pace, each vying to be heard and thereby making it impossible to hear either one.

After pressing his lips into a firm line, Bradford spoke with such severity that even Colin flinched at the sharpness. "Stop this minute! This is quite enough!"

Immediately both boys snapped their mouths shut. With

determined steps, Bradford approached them, arms folded across his chest. He towered over their smaller statures and nodded at one of them. "You. Tell me what happened."

The boy sniffed and wiped his hand across his face. "There was a man, and he had . . . he had a knife! He did! We saw it."

Bradford drew a deep breath and straightened. He cut his eyes toward Colin before focusing back on the boys. "And where did you see this?"

The youth dragged his hand across his nose. "The Black Wood Forest."

Colin lifted his gaze from the boy to Mrs. Ellison. She sighed and lifted her eyes heavenward. It was no secret that the locals often referred to the Emberwilde Forest as the Black Wood Forest—a name that Mrs. Ellison detested.

Bradford must have noticed Mrs. Ellison's displeasure too. The color of his face deepened. "I am sure you were mistaken."

"But we weren't!" the boy protested, the volume of his voice increasing. "He told us to be quiet or else."

This caught Bradford's attention. "You spoke with him?"

"Yes, sir. And he—"

Bradford's tone shifted subtly, as if he was not prepared to hear what the boy would say in front of others. "And what were you doing in the Black—in Emberwilde Forest?"

At this, the adolescent shrank back.

"You are not to be in the forest. I have made that clear on numerous occasions."

The boy fidgeted under the weight of so many stares. "But the man, he said—"

"We will discuss this at another time." Bradford clipped him short. "You will return to your chamber until I summon you."

The taller boy ducked his head, looked at the other, then turned to leave. The smaller one followed, and the room once again fell silent.

"I apologize, ladies." Bradford's chuckle was nervous as he slid his finger between his neck cloth and his throat. "Such an interruption is disruptive."

Alarm covered Mrs. Ellison's face. "Why, the idea of such men in our forest! I agree with you completely, Mr. Bradford. The idea is ludicrous."

Bradford stepped toward the older woman. "I assure you, these young men are prone to the dramatic. My history with the both of them, and others like them, has taught me to heed their words with caution."

Colin shifted uncomfortably, resisting the urge to interject. Bradford may have been able to overlook an odd outburst, but he could not. He reminded himself that he was one of a couple of men who knew about the smugglers' hideaway. The odd sensation that the two events were somehow related plagued him. But it was too early for him to make judgments. Not until he had more facts.

"I'd be willing to take a look, to put your mind at ease," Colin offered. "We don't need any men around here wielding knives, for certain."

Mrs. Ellison's hand flew to her throat, her expression insulted. "Of course there are no men wielding knives in our forest, Mr. Galloway. Mr. Bradford is an excellent judge of character, and he knows these boys better than we do."

Bradford looked from Mrs. Ellison to Colin. "It is not necessary. I run a very tight ship here, and believe me when I say I know these children well. I shall speak with them in more detail and contact you if I suspect anything untoward. Do not trouble yourself." It was then he turned toward Miss Creston. "I am only sorry that Miss Creston's introduction to our establishment was so marred."

Miss Creston offered a pleasant smile. "You forget, Mr. Bradford, that I have spent the last years at a school with a great many children. I am surprised at very little."

Colin returned his attention to Bradford. "I will be visiting Mr. Ellison later today on other business. I will advise him to have his gamekeeper be observant of any suspicious activity. I know Mr. Ellison is on constant watch for poachers and would find any information helpful."

It was a direct rebuttal, he knew. His comment was not well received by either Bradford or Mrs. Ellison, but he had not expected it to be. Mrs. Ellison did not care for him and believed—or desired— the Emberwilde Forest to be above its jaded reputation. Bradford and he had not been on friendly terms since they were young men. But his responsibility was to keep the townspeople safe. And that he would.

Chapter Eleven

*F*rustration fueled Colin's steps away from the foundling home. He turned and lifted his eyes just past the building. The Emberwilde Forest was a majestic backdrop. Thick-trunked trees and deep green foliage were the hallmark of the forest that had stood for hundreds of years. Perhaps the boys had overactive imaginations as Bradford claimed, or perhaps they had seen Ellison's smugglers. Had Aunt Lydia not been with him, he would have investigated immediately. He would see her safely home and then call on Ellison.

His aunt, on the other hand, seemed undisturbed by the recent interaction and even a bit amused.

"Well, that was unexpected," she exclaimed as they cleared the gate and headed back to the village.

"To which part are you referring?" Colin fell into step with her and adjusted his broad-brimmed hat to guard against the rising morning sun. "The fact that the Ellisons were there, or the boys' odd outburst?"

"Neither," she responded. "I was referring to Miss Creston. My, what a beauty she is. Seeing her there was quite a surprise. I had no idea she was in the county. Did you?"

"I did," he responded, squinting toward the sun as he looked away from the forest and across a hay field.

Aunt Lydia stopped short. "And why did you not tell me? You know how I would be interested in such news."

"I do know you are interested in such things." He smiled.

"But I only learned of her presence in Northrop late yesterday. Mr. Ellison and I encountered her carriage as we were returning to Emberwilde."

His aunt resumed her steps and adjusted the bonnet atop her graying head. "Miss Creston's mother was a great friend of mine, a very great friend."

"Oh?" Colin was hardly one to find interest in local gossip, but he was grateful that she wanted to talk on a topic other than the boys' outburst or Mrs. Ellison's coolness.

His aunt continued. "You are probably too young to remember her. Anna Hayworth was her name prior to marriage."

"I am not familiar with the name."

"Oh, I do not doubt it. She died very young, when Miss Creston was but a child. She died on Emberwilde property, in fact. Do you not remember that scandal, Colin? She took a fever while a guest at the home and passed quite suddenly. Miss Creston was with her at Emberwilde when it happened. Anna's husband was not. He was never welcome at the estate, for they had eloped under mysterious conditions, but when he learned of her demise, he traveled to Emberwilde to claim his child. Then he simply vanished. To my knowledge, the Ellisons did not know his whereabouts for years after Anna's death."

Colin searched his memory as they walked down the road. He vaguely recalled a story of a woman dying on Emberwilde property. He had been a boy then, and he recalled Freddie sharing a bit of the tale. He did not remember specifics, but neither did he recall Freddie ever mentioning a female cousin. "I wonder what brought her back after all this time? Surely there is a reason."

"I daresay there is, but you know how the gossips of Northrop will sniff out a story as fast as anything. One thing is certain, though: Miss Creston is a stunning young woman, I will say. Do you not agree?"

Colin could feel his aunt's gaze shift in his direction, anticipating a response to her leading comment. Aunt Lydia made no effort to hide her desire for him to marry. Ever since he returned home from the war, she had tried unsuccessfully to match him with any lady who might catch his eye.

When he did not take her bait, Aunt Lydia continued. "Miss Creston is the very likeness of her mother—that flaxen hair and those icy eyes. How envious I was of Anna's beauty. Imagine how I felt as a girl, her with her long blonde curls and me with hair the color of a common field mouse. But as it turns out, beauty does not guarantee a happy life."

He chuckled at his aunt's comparison. "Aunt, I would hardly compare your hair to that of a field mouse."

"You are kind, Colin. Too kind, in fact, to this old woman. But if you truly want to be kind, you will put my mind at rest and marry. It will do my aging heart good to see you cared for. I do not understand your delay. You still have Darbenton Court and the living there. Of course the house is gone, but you can rebuild easily enough. Any young woman would consider herself fortunate to be the mistress of such an estate. But here you are, a landowner, living like a pauper in a boardinghouse."

"Do not forget Henry lives there," he reminded his aunt.

"But that is different. Do you not see?" she explained. "Henry will have to work to make his way in the world in a different way, just as his father before him. And the law is a noble profession, do not doubt it. But you have the opportunity to do something greater."

He inhaled the scents of the damp earth as they passed a field being turned. It was their age-old conversation, and he could guess the direction it would take next.

"One must wait to meet the right lady," he said.

"If that is your argument, then you have the perfect lady in front of you. One who knows your faults and cares for you anyway."

Colin sobered. He did not want to have the conversation he knew was forthcoming and tried to change the subject. "And what faults would that be?"

"This is no joking matter, Colin." Aunt Lydia's tone grew pensive. "What of Miranda?"

His cousin's widow.

He had known her most of his life, and she had always played a role in his. When they were children she was a neighbor and friend, then as they grew, their relationship deepened. He had loved her and believed that she shared the sentiment, but when he returned from university to learn that she had formed an attachment with his cousin, a deep rift formed. He was blinded by rejection's pain, and instead of facing his responsibilities at Darbenton Court as he should have, he found it easier to abandon the situation, and he and Freddie joined the army.

The urgency of war masked the agony of betrayal, and by the time he returned, he had grown callous to the fact that William and Miranda had not only married but had a child. War had matured him, and he was able to see past the actions of both. But when William died suddenly, leaving Miranda a widow and young Charles fatherless, Colin felt the pressure to care for his cousin's family. It was impossible for Henry to marry Miranda, for by law they were now considered siblings. But as William's cousin, Colin felt it was almost expected of him to care for the family. Guilt was a strong persuader, but something deep within him cautioned him to leave the past in the past, despite Miranda's obvious interest in rekindling their past love.

But his aunt thought otherwise.

"Miranda is quite fond of you. And that boy of hers idolizes you. Do you want to spend your days in that boardinghouse? La. I should think not. Ever since William's death, Miranda has been searching for peace, and she is understandably eager for a home of her own. And you have been searching for peace ever since you returned from the war, do not deny it."

Yes, he did want to marry. Yes, he wanted someone to welcome him home at the day's end. He longed to call somewhere other than that tiny room home. Miranda was beautiful, full of abundant charm and a pleasant nature. His heart had belonged to her at one time. Could he trust her with it again? Betrayal, though distant, still stung. Their romance had been long ago, but time cast long shadows.

He would not marry out of guilt, but perhaps it was time to reconsider his position. He thought of Ellison's words. The man was right, of course. A wife would undoubtedly be a part of both his future and Darbenton Court's. Ellison's suggestion held merit. Miss Creston. Whether the older man's words regarding marriage to his niece had been in jest or in earnest, they weighed on his mind. She was mysterious and new, lovely and charming. Was she his path to pursue, or should he repair what was once whole?

Time would reveal the best course, he was certain, and he would not marry until he, in his heart and mind, felt at peace with the idea.

His aunt's hand was resting on his arm, and he patted her hand encouragingly. "I assure you, my dear aunt, when I find peace, you will be the first to know."

Chapter Twelve

$\mathcal{I}$sabel stood as still as possible in the middle of her bed-chamber, chewing her lower lip, studying her reflection in a narrow mirror.

She did not move a muscle, fearing that any movement might disrupt the seamstress's work.

Mrs. Tindan, the seamstress hired to fashion her gowns, held fabric up to Isabel's chin and pivoted to assess the colors in the reflection—first a pale raspberry muslin, then a pale yellow silk. They had only just returned from their visit to the foundling home, and the seamstress was already waiting for them.

From the corner of her eye, Isabel noticed Constance stand from the nearby settee and step closer to the dangling fabric. Her cousin ran the delicate cloth through her long, elegant fingers. "Definitely the muslin, do you not agree, Mother?"

Isabel cast a glance back over her shoulder at her aunt, who remained seated on the room's only sofa.

A conversation ensued about the benefits of one fabric over the other, but Isabel was too preoccupied with her own thoughts to hear it. The morning outing had tired her, and her heart was strangely heavy. It had been pleasant to see Mr. Bradford again. He was handsome. Gracious. Well-spoken. Just as she thought he would be. But the rest of the morning's events left a chill over her. The sight of the unwanted infant being handed over haunted her, and she did not care for the manner in which Mr. Bradford dismissed the boys' concerns and fears with such condescending haste.

For should he not consider that they had encountered a man with a knife?

Now the Ellisons chatted about fabrics and embellishments and colors and sleeve lengths as if nothing unusual at all had occurred.

If Isabel was honest, part of her was giddy at the notion of new gowns. At Fellsworth, she possessed no more than two at any given time, and never had she owned a gown that had not been worn by someone else.

But as excited as she was, she could not help feeling a bit guilty. For she did not have the funds to pay for new stockings, let alone new gowns.

Her aunt insisted that the gowns were a gift. Now that Isabel and Lizzie were residents of Emberwilde, they must look the part. But Isabel was not so sure, for her uncle's words about more mouths to feed weighed on her. She did not want to be a burden.

No, Isabel did not like relying on the kindness of others. For so many years she had strived to achieve self-sufficiency. And she had been doing so successfully. Or so she had thought.

As Mrs. Tindan began to drape a length of pink poplin over Isabel's shoulders, Isabel turned. "Really, Aunt, you needn't go to all this trouble. My gowns are fine, and I—"

"Your gowns are most definitely *not* fine!" Aunt Margaret exclaimed, her expression insulted. "Your mother was a Hayworth, and you are a Hayworth. No Hayworth should be seen in such a gown as yours. I mean no offense, for it was not your fault that you should find yourself in such a situation. It is one thing to wear it indoors, where no one but the servants will see you. It is another to be seen in public. It is bad enough that Mr. Bradford saw you, but that could not be avoided. No, no, no. It will not do."

Isabel swallowed her surprise and scarcely heard the second half of her aunt's rant. "What situation do you mean?"

Aunt Margaret stood and approached Isabel with an uneven

gait, and when she was about a foot away, she reached out and took Isabel's cheeks in her hands and forced Isabel to look her in the eye.

Isabel stiffened.

"Your situation is a very serious one, and one that must be handled with great care, for the decisions you make in the coming weeks could very well shape your future. You are a beautiful young woman who will no doubt turn many heads. It is my duty to properly introduce you to society, to eventually find you a secure match, but above all to protect you from repeating the errors your mother made. I confess I do not know what you have been exposed to up until this point, but I will do for you what I could not do for my sister: shelter you from the predators who would steal you away from us again."

Isabel's heart pounded in her chest, and she remained perfectly still until her aunt released her cheeks and was once again seated. The words were strong. Her aunt was clearly emotionally invested in her, but why with such forcefulness?

Ears still ringing with disbelief, Isabel straightened as the seamstress approached her with another length of yellow fabric and held it before her.

"Is this more to your liking?" the dressmaker asked, looking past Isabel to Aunt Margaret.

"Very much so," her aunt replied, as calmly as if no discussion had taken place. "Let's use that to fashion an evening gown. Won't that be perfection?"

Isabel remained silent as she assessed the fabric with its shimmering lemon hue. Clearly, her opinion did not matter. This was her aunt's choice. Her aunt's game. Isabel was but a token to be played, a pawn to be moved about at will.

She could almost choke on the irony of her situation—for the most part she had been content at Fellsworth. But had not a part of her dreamed of living in such luxury? And now that she was here, was it preferable? Was she happier surrounded by such advantages?

She let her mind drift back to the foundling home. Seeing the children in the yard did touch her. It reminded her of Fellsworth and what she had been trained to do for the students there. Her offer to help at the foundling home had obviously shocked her aunt, and even Mr. Bradford. But at least she had made her desires known. Her aunt might be a strong, persuasive woman, but Isabel was strong too. Just because she had accepted the offer from her aunt did not give her aunt control over Isabel's life. And she would not give that away freely.

The seamstress gave the fabric to Isabel to hold, then turned to her trunk to fetch another sample.

Aunt Margaret motioned for Isabel to turn around. "While we are on the subject of evening gowns, there is something that I would like to discuss with you before the upcoming dinner party at the Atwells'."

Isabel shook off her feelings of mistrust and faced her aunt, bracing herself. "Yes?"

"It is regarding your dowry."

Dread soaked Isabel. This was a personal topic, one she was not ready to discuss.

But her aunt was determined. "Normally I would never encourage a lady to speak of such things so practically, but as we move forward, I must know the extent of your assets. Have you any?"

At this, Isabel could feel her chin drop. "No. I have saved a small amount from my wages at the school, but it is nothing of significance."

"Do you have any other resources? Any property or possessions to your name? Or Elizabeth's name?"

Isabel shook her head.

"I thought not, especially knowing your father."

The stab pained Isabel. Did her aunt even realize the curtness of her tone?

The air in the room grew heavy, thick, like the skies prior to a storm.

"Your uncle and I should be able to assist you in that regard. No niece of mine will be without a dowry. But I must remind you—you have been blessed with beauty. Hopefully you will have better sense of it than your mother did and use it to your advantage."

Isabel was growing warm. Too warm. This conversation had taken a turn. No longer was this fitting a fun way to pass the afternoon.

Constance, as if sensing Isabel's mounting frustration, stood and crossed the room. She waved the dressmaker away and took the fabric from Isabel.

"Oh, Mother, she has not even met any of the young men in Northrop. There will be time enough to talk of dowries and such."

Aunt Margaret did not seem to share the lighthearted tone. "She must be prepared, as must we all, if she is to need assistance."

"Of course you are right, Mother. But there is no need to make such decisions today, especially when there are so many other things for her to focus on." As Constance pivoted toward Isabel, a teasing smile graced her features. "Isabel, you showed interest in helping at the foundling home. Perhaps that would be a good use of your time. It is, after all, dear to all of us. Do you not agree, Mother?"

Encouraged by the fact that her cousin had heard her suggestion and seemed to have taken it seriously, Isabel seized her opportunity. "I know I could make a difference, and I would welcome the chance to contribute to a cause that is so dear to the Ellison family. I do not wish to be a burden, Aunt. I would be grateful to assist in some manner, regardless how small."

Her aunt eyed her with suspicion, then seemed to relent. For how could she deny the importance of the foundling home? "I have always encouraged my girls to look beyond themselves. We shall discuss it in further detail at another time."

As if signaling her desire to be done with the conversation, Aunt Margaret stood. "I do not know what this seamstress is about. I have asked several times now to see something in green. I suppose I must inspect the fabrics myself."

Isabel's discomfort melted as her aunt retreated. She stepped off the dressing block and sat next to Constance. The late-afternoon sun slanted through the windows. Constance had such a calming effect. Her ability to defuse a situation was likely a result of a lifetime of practice—of being placed in a dozen such situations and having to handle them with grace.

Isabel turned to her cousin, eager to remove the focus from herself. "If I may ask, how long have you been engaged?"

"Of course you may ask!" Constance clasped her hands in front of her. "It is perhaps my favorite topic of conversation. The announcement was made a few months ago, but my fiancé is spending the spring months in Scotland at his family estate."

"When will you marry?"

"As soon as Mr. Nichols agrees to a date. Mother says the sooner I am married, the better it will be. It is always best to secure a man before he has the opportunity to lose interest. Who knows what misfortune may fall to cause a gentleman to change his mind? But of course, you did not hear that from me."

Her cousin spoke so matter-of-factly about the arrangement that Isabel wondered if she loved her intended.

Constance pinned her gaze on Isabel. "Are you not eager to marry?"

Isabel relaxed, finding it much easier to speak of such things now that her aunt's scrutiny was elsewhere. "I suppose I always wanted to marry. I guess it just never seemed like an option."

"Why, that is the silliest thing I have ever heard! Mark my words, Isabel. You are so lovely, you will turn every head. If I were not already engaged I should be extremely jealous, but because I am so happily situated, I think I shall throw all of my efforts into helping Mother find you a suitable match."

Isabel gave a little laugh. "A suitable match does not sound very romantic."

Constance threw her head back and laughed. "Romance is all very well, but hardly practical. We must each think of our own future. And yours, I believe, will be bright.

"So tell me." Constance nudged Isabel's shoulder. "What did you think of Mr. Bradford? And be honest. My mother is too engrossed in the fabrics to listen."

Isabel drew a deep breath. In truth, she had not been in his presence long enough to form an accurate opinion. "He seems very kind."

"I feel he did not give a fair first impression, what with Mr. Galloway arriving as he did."

Isabel recognized her chance to get the answers she was most curious about and lowered her voice. "Is that common, to have children just left about?"

Constance shrugged. "Common? Oh, I wouldn't say common. I think there have been a couple of children abandoned over the course of the year or so. Fortunately, the foundling home will see they are well cared for."

Isabel cast her cousin a sideways glance. "And what of the Galloways? Are they friends of the family?"

"That is difficult to say. You will find we are a family divided on the Galloways. You see, Mrs. Lydia Galloway, the lady who accompanied Mr. Galloway today, was at one time one of my mother's dearest friends, although you would hardly know it from their interaction. And Mr. Colin Galloway was my brother, Freddie's, best friend. They spent every waking hour together when they were boys, and when it was time for them to go to university, they did so together, and then they joined the army at the same time. He was quite a member of our family. Mr. Galloway has a bit of an interesting past. His father owned Darbenton Court, a small estate just on the outskirts of Northrop. The main house burned to the ground when he was but a child, and he was the only survivor."

"Oh, that is terribly sad!" exclaimed Isabel.

"I would not feel too sad for him, for he has had an otherwise happy life in the care of his aunt and uncle. Even though they enjoy a lower status than his parents, he is the owner of all the land that once belonged to his father. He is actually one of the largest landowners for miles, but you would never know it. He lives in a tiny boardinghouse in town and is considered a little odd in his ways."

Isabel frowned but did not ask her cousin to elaborate. He was not quite what he appeared to be, and this fact intrigued her.

Constance lifted a ribbon and studied it as she spoke. "Because of his status and the land he inherited, he was considered a suitable playmate for Freddie, and so he was here quite often."

"If he was as a member of the family, why does Aunt Margaret stand in such judgment of him?"

"My mother blames Mr. Galloway for convincing Freddie to join the army, and she will never forgive him. You are probably not aware of the specifics, but Freddie was killed in a battle. My father does not share Mother's opinion, and you will see that Mr. Galloway and my father are still quite thick. After all, he is the magistrate and a strong figure in our small community. You can understand the dilemma."

Constance's countenance brightened. "But now, let's not think of that. It was all a long time ago. The seamstress is almost done with her work. What do you say to a walk near the village? I am sure you are anxious to learn more about your surroundings, and it is a pleasant afternoon to be out of doors."

Isabel could feel her shoulders relax. A few hours away from Emberwilde was just what she needed to clear her mind.

Chapter Thirteen

The hour was quite late by the time Colin trudged over the High Bridge toward the Pigeon's Rest Inn.

The day had been a long one. After escorting his aunt to her cottage, Colin returned to Emberwilde. Ellison had been otherwise engaged, so Colin and the gamekeeper Harding had investigated the boys' claims of a man in the forest. They discovered nothing, but still, he was uneasy. From there he paid a visit to the Holden farm, to one of his tenants, and then to his cousin's office.

A late chill had settled over the village of Northrop, and a fine drizzle made it feel more like late November than early April. Colin repositioned his coat's soggy collar closer to his neck and pulled his wide-brimmed hat low over his eyes.

His rumbling stomach reminded him that he had missed Mrs. Daugherty's evening meal.

Again.

His landlady was particular about the hours she kept. She held the evening meal for no one. If the hour had not been so late, he would have been tempted to visit his aunt's house for a warm meal, but she would undoubtedly be asleep by now.

No, best stop by the Pigeon's Rest Inn. Besides, he was going to need help finding the parties responsible for the contraband hidden in the Emberwilde Forest, and the inn's proprietor, Robert McKinney, served as a constable.

Colin pushed open the door, and the familiar sounds of the village's only inn and public house rushed him. The abundant fire blazed, its light filling the large room with a yellow glow, and the welcoming chatter of patrons and the clicking of pewter dinnerware filled the timbered space. Scents of burning wood, beef stew, and ale all battled for dominance. Not even a year ago the inn would have been empty at such an hour, but ever since a large carriage agency had reassigned its routes through Northrop, the public house enjoyed an endless stream of new customers.

Colin allowed his eyes a moment to adjust to the room's flickering light, then spotted McKinney near the back wall.

McKinney was an easy man to find in a crowd. He was a massive human, by far the tallest man in the village, and his stocky build made him appear much more suited for tending the fields than managing an inn. More than once his brawn had aided him well in his role as constable, and lately, he often utilized his imposing stature to break up brawls between rowdy patrons.

Colin wove his way between the benches and roughly fashioned tables toward his friend.

McKinney looked up from the dishes he was carrying. "Galloway! What brings you out in this weather?"

"Missed the evening meal." Colin grinned, swiping his hat from his head and shaking the dampness from his hair.

"Missed your meal, eh? Haven't seen you in here in a couple of days. Did you take a dislike to my food?"

"Not at all." Colin removed his coat and hung it on a hook to dry next to the fire. "If not for the Pigeon's Rest, there would be plenty of days when I would not eat at all."

McKinney took off his apron and rolled his sleeves. "That aunt of yours would feed you. Not like her to let a man go hungry."

"True, but the hour's late now. I've no wish to wake her."

"Late, he says," repeated McKinney, amusement adding a comical lilt to his rough tone. "Never mind, good company is always welcome."

McKinney motioned to a young woman with black hair and a stocky build, then he ushered Colin to an empty table. "Nice to see a familiar face for a change. This lot in here tonight is a rowdy one."

Colin took the offered seat and leaned against the roughly shaped table with his elbows. He glanced around at the proclaimed rowdy lot. Not a single familiar face lurked in the space. Two infantrymen kept to themselves in the far left corner, and another cluster of men sat closer to the fire. Their clothes were not ragged, but it was clear that theirs was not a table of gentlemen. Colin turned his attention back to McKinney. "Place is full."

"Humpf," grunted McKinney, rubbing a thick hand over his unruly beard. He jerked his head in the direction of a thin man sitting alone against the back wall. "That one over there told me the company added three more coaches to this route, so we expect more overnight guests en route to London at least three nights a week. Only have one open bed as it is. I'll be turning folks away if this keeps up."

"That's good for business."

McKinney frowned, annoyance furrowing his wide brow. "Got enough business, don't need any more. But I know you didn't come to see how business ha' been."

Colin leaned back as a young woman with a white cap placed a bowl of stew and a pint of ale in front of him, and the same in front of McKinney. The pungent scent of stout ale and hearty broth warmed him.

"So what business of yours has been keeping you so occupied?" inquired McKinney, leaning back in his seat to let the girl serve him, then spooning the stew into his mouth.

The two men had been comrades for years, their roles in the community intertwined. Colin kept the peace, and McKinney observed everything about everyone. All the village came through the Pigeon's Rest at some point or another.

"I do have a little incident that I could use your help with."

"Aha, now we're getting to it." McKinney raised a bushy auburn eyebrow and leaned toward Colin as if not to miss a word. "Help as in my cow got loose and I can't find it, or as in I am the magistrate and need you to keep an eye out for me?"

"I don't have a cow."

"Then it must be t'other." McKinney propped his thick forearms on the table, the room's faint light sparking in his eyes. His expressions might be difficult for a newcomer to decipher, for deep-set eyes and a firm jawline masked any hints. But Colin had known the man all his life.

Colin cleared his throat, taking a moment to weigh exactly how much he should share about the happenings in the Black Wood Forest. In all the years they had worked together on this project or that, he had always found McKinney trustworthy and, furthermore, silent when necessary.

"Had an interesting visit out to Emberwilde Hall yesterday."

"Ah. Every visit with Ellison is an interesting one, him and his hotheaded ways."

"Well, this one was different," Colin clarified.

McKinney indulged in a swig of ale and returned the mug to the table with a thud. "Don't see how."

"Seems there is some smuggling afoot in the Black Wood Forest. Or at least, activity that looks like smuggling."

McKinney sobered but remained silent.

Colin cut his eyes toward the loud group of men before turning his attention back to McKinney. "Do you recall the caverns by the Hearne Pond?"

A sharp laugh burst from McKinney. "Bah! You know me, I'll not set a toenail in the Black Wood Forest. Never have, never will."

Colin lowered his fork, amused by his friend's response. "Oh, come on. Surely you do not believe all that nonsense."

"'Tis not nonsense. I've seen 'em myself, the black shadows. Conley's best pointer ran into that forest and died the next day. Do you think that is coincidence? I don't." McKinney pointed his spoon in Colin's direction. "That forest is haunted, and if I were you I would stay away from it."

"It's not haunted," reasoned Colin. "No such thing."

"Say that all you like, I know what I've seen."

"Do you remember Harding? Emberwilde's gamekeeper?"

"Yes, and he's as odd as they come."

"Whatever you think of him, he's the one who discovered the evidence. Seems someone is counting on everyone's fear and using the caverns to hide contraband."

McKinney leaned forward. "What sort of contraband are we talking about?"

"Not sure." Colin pushed the stew away, his appetite fading. "Several casks—at least eight or nine—wine or rum or something of the sort, and a dozen or so crates. That is what we could see, anyway."

McKinney folded his burly arms over his chest and frowned. "Sure it's smuggling? Haven't heard of that sort of activity going on around these parts. Farther south, sure. But not here. Anyway, I've said it before, and I'll say it again. Ellison and his lot get what they get."

"I suppose in the grand scheme of things it doesn't seem that significant, but I thought you would be interested."

"Me? Interested?" He chortled. "Nothing about the Ellisons interests me."

Colin leaned his elbows on the table and lowered his voice. "He's offering a reward for information. A hefty sum."

"A hefty sum?" McKinney lifted his head. "'Course he is. Just like the Ellisons to throw their purse around, making sure everyone knows of it. But come out with the amount, because what you think is a hefty sum and what I consider to be a hefty sum could be two different things."

"Fifty pounds to anyone providing information that leads to an arrest, and one hundred pounds to the one who delivers the man."

McKinney leaned against the back of his chair and fixed his eyes on a far point in the room. "Come to think of it, there's not much more satisfying than getting a bit of the money. What I can't figure is why Ellison would care about a little smuggling going on. I still say he's no stranger to walking both sides of the law. You know that as well as anybody. Besides, I heard that Emberwilde is facing hard times—in a bit of financial trouble over a deal gone bad. Seems to me this must be pretty important to Ellison if he is willing to part with any amount, little or great."

Colin stared at the rim of his mug. Yes, he had heard the rumors about Emberwilde. Ellison was well known for making risky investments and for his passion for gambling, and based on Ellison's comments regarding finances, he had to believe it to be true. "I only know what I saw, and that was contraband on Ellison's property."

"And that doesn't strike you as odd?"

Colin raised an eyebrow. "What are you suggesting?"

McKinney shrugged and rubbed his hand over his beard. "Men do strange things when they are desperate."

"I don't think Ellison is desperate. You need to stop listening to the chatter that goes on in here."

"Stop listening? This is where I hear the best news!"

Colin took the last bite of his stew and leaned back in his chair. At last, the rumbling in his stomach had dissipated, and after speaking with McKinney he was more eager than ever to get to the bottom of this case. "I wrote to the excise officer to inquire about smuggling in other areas, but until I get a response, watch for odd sorts. 'Tis likely that with all the travelers along the Lockton Route, someone might show up who knows something."

"True." McKinney nodded. "And nothing will get a man to talk like a bit of ale. I'll find out what I can."

Colin stood, preparing to take his leave.

McKinney rose to his full height. "Heard earlier today of a boxing bout that will be taking place over at Foster's Field sometime in the next couple of days. Those draw folks from every corner, all looking to win a bit o' change. Probably find all sorts there, and what sorts would be enticed into the smuggling game."

"Good. Can't hurt to go and see what we can find out. Let me know when it is." He finished his stew and dropped some coins on the table. "Keep this as quiet as you can for now, all right? Ellison doesn't want news of this spread about."

"Humpf. Figures. The man wants help and wants no one to know it. That's an Ellison for you." McKinney joined a sudden outburst of drunken laughter that rose from the corner of the room.

"Ellison's pride might be your financial gain," Colin said. "Best not be too hard on the man." Without another word, he stepped out of the stuffy tavern into the night air.

Chapter Fourteen

everal days after being fitted for new gowns, Isabel overslept. Normally when she woke, dawn would just be breaking, and the white light of early morning would stretch long fingers over the emerald lawns and Emberwilde Forest. But today, without even consulting her timepiece, she could guess the hour by the brightness of the sun pouring through the space between the glass and the curtain. She bolted upright in bed and allowed the soft blankets covering her to slip to the side.

Her night's sleep had been fitful at best. Thoughts of an uncertain future and fears and anticipation of the unknown wrestled in her mind. Her body had been tired, yes, but her mind was engaged in an intense battle, refusing to stop for even a moment.

Undoubtedly she had needed the extra hours, but it was unnerving just the same. For it was her practice to rise every morning at dawn for time alone. Today was the first day she had missed it in a very long time.

It was taking much longer to adapt to Emberwilde's ways than Isabel had expected. She wished it were easier to blend the two worlds she knew. She wanted to embrace the new ideas she was being exposed to here, yet at the same time she wanted to preserve the aspects of her previous life that she valued.

Everything was different. Even the schedule was quite different. And her body—not to mention Lizzie's—was adjusting.

At Emberwilde, there was no urgency to get the day under way.

Even though the servants were up before dawn, Isabel never heard them. The late, unproductive morning made her feel sluggish, but then again, what was there to accomplish here? Servants tended to all responsibilities. She missed the daily sense of purpose and accomplishment.

Her old way of life was slipping from her. But today was a new day. Even though she had overslept, there were still hours left in the morning. She reached for the small table next to her bed and lifted Mary's unfinished needlework and let her eyes rest on the words. How she missed her home.

At least here she had Lizzie's studies to tend to.

Yes, Lizzie.

She wriggled her legs free from the bedding, shook out her nightdress, and stood. With a swipe of her hand, Isabel whisked disorderly wisps from her face and moved to the door that separated her room from Lizzie's. She pushed it open and scanned the space, but her sister was not there. In fact, the bed had already been made and her night things returned to their spaces.

Isabel turned back to her room, grabbed her robe, and rang for Burns.

Within minutes the lady's maid appeared. "Good morning, miss. You have slept late! Are you ready to dress?"

"Good morning, Burns. I am ready, thank you." Isabel untied the bow from her braid and shook out her long hair. "Have you seen Lizzie yet this morning?"

"Yes, I have."

Isabel frowned in concern. Normally her sister would run into her room to say good morning, even before Burns would help her dress.

"Do you know where she is?"

"I saw her out on the south lawn earlier, I believe."

Isabel took little notice of the woman's fidgety response to her question. With Burns's help, she quickly donned one of Constance's older gowns that had been taken in for her to wear until her own new gowns were ready, dressed her hair, and cleaned her teeth before heading downstairs. She found her aunt and cousin in the breakfast room, still sitting over their morning tea. Her aunt was writing a letter at the desk by the window, and Constance was reading a letter.

"Good morning," exclaimed Isabel as she entered the room.

"My goodness, if you did not sleep late!" exclaimed Constance, looking up from her letter. "I believe some of our habits may be rubbing off on you. Do come and sit down. We've good news this morning. The seamstress has finished the first of your gowns, as well as one for Elizabeth, and she will be arriving later today for the fittings. Will that not be entertaining?"

"She certainly took long enough," sniffed Aunt Margaret. "The gowns had better be pristine with this length of time! But, in consolation, I've not seen a finer seamstress than Mrs. Tindan, and at least you will finally have something appropriate to wear. We might attend church service this Sunday, not to mention the dinner at the Atwell house this coming week."

A flutter danced within Isabel. She had to admit she was looking forward to church and the dinner. She had been here well over a week already and had only been to the foundling home.

Isabel was about to take her seat at the breakfast table when something out the window caught her eye.

Isabel's jaw dropped open at the sight.

She hurried to the glass and rested her hands on the ledge to get a better view, for there, sitting atop a brown pony, was Lizzie.

Panic surged through Isabel. "What is Lizzie doing?"

Her aunt turned to the window as if distracted. "Why, Elizabeth is taking her riding lesson, of course. I am on the hunt for a proper riding master, but the sooner we start, the better. We are so far from London that I fear it might take awhile to find a suitable riding master, but there is a price for everything, is there not?"

Her aunt's matter-of-fact tone grated Isabel's nerves. "I know what she is doing, but who gave her permission to do so?"

"Why, I did, of course."

"I wish you would have asked me first. She is frightened of horses. She is—"

"Nonsense. The child was beyond excited by the idea. Besides, we have lost precious time already. In order to raise a proper lady, one must start young. Best to steer her interests to proper feminine pursuits."

With every word her aunt uttered, Isabel's defenses rose. Lizzie was her responsibility. She was the one to oversee her education and to provide permission for activities, regardless of their nature.

Isabel fought hard to keep her voice level. "I appreciate your generosity, Aunt, but truly, I think she does not need this. She—"

"Now, now, I know what is best." Aunt Margaret waved a hand dismissively in the air. "I have raised four daughters of my own. I recognize that certain wildness of spirit, and it must be tamed. Riding is the perfect outlet for such energies."

Alarm swelled within Isabel's chest, pressing against the confines of her rib cage and shortening her breath. First and foremost, Lizzie was not Aunt Margaret's daughter. *Isabel* was Lizzie's guardian. She should be making such decisions on her sister's behalf.

It was a battle that she had suspected to be brewing since the moment they arrived. Her aunt intended to raise Lizzie as she had raised her daughters, with the same values, goals, and hopes for the future.

Isabel's attention fell on the man leading the pony with a rope. "And who is that with her?"

"That is Carter. You can place great trust in the man. All of my daughters ride, and he has been instrumental in their achievements."

Isabel's frustration was fuming into anger. Anger at herself for oversleeping and not seeing to Lizzie properly. Anger at her aunt for making such assumptions. And anger at the situation in general.

Isabel had a choice. She could storm out and demand Lizzie get off the pony, but the child was smiling and looked so happy. Fighting with her aunt would not be productive, for were they not guests in her home?

She shook off the frustration, then sat down next to her aunt. "Perhaps you are right, Aunt Margaret. It is time we pay more attention to Lizzie's education, especially now that we are settling into a routine."

Aunt Margaret lifted her chin in righteous triumph and cut her eyes toward Constance.

Isabel drew a deep breath. If she was to get anywhere with her aunt, she had to modify her approach, regardless of how difficult it may be. She forced a smile. "Thank you for your advice on Lizzie's riding. I am sure she will enjoy it."

"All children enjoy riding, Isabel." Her aunt's words seemed almost condescending.

Isabel bit her lower lip before speaking again. If she gave in to some of her aunt's requests, perhaps she could make more headway with her own. She breathed deeply, taking a moment to quiet her nerves and regain her composure. "I am sure you are right. I have also been giving more consideration to Lizzie's education. I plan to resume her lessons this week to their normal intensity. She grows more accustomed to Emberwilde by the day, and I think it is time to reestablish expectations."

The previous day they had paid yet another visit to the foundling home, and Isabel seized the opportunity to advance her case. Aunt Margaret had continued to object to the sisters spending time with the children, so Isabel spoke before Aunt Margaret could interject. "I have also been thinking a great deal about the Ellisons' commitment to charitable causes, and I believe Lizzie and I should continue to become more involved. As you know, yesterday during our visit to the foundling home, Lizzie and I read with some of the younger girls while you spoke with Mr. Bradford. Such a lesson in charity and selflessness is important, do you not agree? It was a common practice at our school for older children to assist the younger, and seeing that you strive so to improve the foundling home, it would be a positive step."

Isabel did not give her aunt a chance to respond. "The day is fine, is it not? I think I will go for a turn about the gardens before the sun grows any warmer."

"But what about breakfast?" chimed Constance, lowering her fork to her plate. "You must eat."

Isabel looked at the spread of breads and rolls, hot ham, and poached eggs. The thought of eating made her stomach turn.

"Perhaps later," she said.

"Would you like some company?" Constance asked.

"No, thank you." Isabel's reply was much sharper than she had intended. "I've no wish to take you away from your morning activities, and I will just be out a short time."

"Very well." Constance called after her, "Do not forget your bonnet!"

Isabel returned to her chamber, snatched her straw bonnet, then hastily donned it and tied the bow beneath her chin.

As she did, she caught a glimpse of herself in her looking glass.

She stopped and turned, her breath slowing.

She looked like a lady.

This was the first day she had worn one of Constance's dresses, at her aunt's insistence. She had been in such a hurry to get to Lizzie that she had not paid much attention when Burns helped her dress.

Gone was the tight chignon at the base of her neck. A softer, more polished style replaced it, thanks to Burns's talents. Isabel's hair was allowed to curl and was coiled softly against the crown of her head. The flowing gown of buttery yellow silk with a filmy white fichu at her neckline replaced the severe, high-necked black frock. The mere change of colors made her lips and cheeks appear pinker, her eyes brighter. She thought back to that morning when Mrs. Brathay summoned her to Mr. Langsby's study.

She was different on the outside. Was she changing on the inside too?

Deciding to push the thought to the back of her mind, she hurried from the great house and into the bright sunshine.

She found her sister on the other side of the front garden, still on the pony. Lizzie noticed her, for she waved wildly in Isabel's direction.

Isabel lifted her hand and returned the greeting. From where Isabel stood, Lizzie looked quite safe. And now that she had a little distance to think on it, perhaps this was a positive thing.

Isabel allowed her shoulders to slump slightly.

Her sister was smiling—genuinely smiling. It was a wonderful sight, for since their arrival, homesickness and loneliness had plagued Lizzie.

Now that she saw Lizzie enjoying herself, Isabel sighed. Perhaps letting go of some of her expectations would make it easier to adjust. Only time would tell.

As Colin turned the bend, he saw her.

Miss Creston.

He almost missed her, so lost in his thoughts was he.

He'd grown frustrated over the past couple of days. After writing twice to the excise officer about his suspicions of smuggling, he received word that they were too busy to investigate the matter at this time. To make matters worse, he had revisited the cavern deep within the forest, only to find the contraband had been reorganized. Some sort of activity had taken place, and they were no further along in finding the answer than they had been that first day.

Now he was walking down the path adjacent to the forest, leading Sampson as he did so. It was the road he often took to speak with Mr. Ellison, for he had long since forgone entering Emberwilde through the main entrance, as he had when he was a boy. This path was the most direct route to the tradesmen's entrance and to Mr. Ellison's study, but today Miss Creston had found reason to take it. She was walking toward him.

At the sight of her, his interest piqued.

Something about her was different. It was her gown. Gone was the harsh black and shapeless dress. The one she wore adorned her slight figure attractively. The sleeves came to just below her elbows and flared out in lace trim. It displayed her arms. Her neck.

Her bonnet had slipped loose and hung down her back, leaving her blonde hair uncovered and glowing in the sun's bright light. The bonnet's white ribbons were still tied at her throat. She tugged at the bow and then wiped her face with her hand.

His steps slowed. She had not taken notice of him yet.

She seemed agitated. Her arms were now folded across her chest, and her steps were determined. Fast. Her gaze was fixed firmly on the dirt path in front of her.

She turned at the black iron gate and began walking directly toward him. The breeze caught her skirts and they billowed behind her, the soft yellow hue striking against the green background of the trees. Even from the distance her cheeks appeared flushed. He admittedly was not one to pick up on any lady's subtle moods, but something was wrong. In a matter of a few seconds she looked over her shoulder more than once. Following her gaze, he saw a small child, presumably Miss Elizabeth, whom he had yet to properly meet, atop a pony.

At length she glanced up to look where she was going, and then she stopped short.

"Miss Creston," he offered as a greeting, bowing his head.

"Oh, Mr. Galloway." He had surprised her. A muscle in her jaw twitched, and she expelled her breath in a sharp swoop. "I . . . I didn't think anyone would be here. I hope I am not intruding."

"How could you be intruding?" he asked. "This is your home, not mine."

She did not respond. Instead, she looked past him to Sampson, then cast one more nervous glance over her shoulder.

He nodded toward the child. "Is that your sister?"

"Yes. It is. That is Elizabeth."

"I see she has taken to riding."

"Taken to riding?" she repeated, her eyes not leaving the girl. "I don't know for sure. My aunt has decided that my sister should learn to ride a pony, and, well, she seems to enjoy it."

"Your aunt has decided? You do not agree?"

She looked back at him and gave a little shrug. "I don't know."

It was the first time in their brief encounter that she made direct eye contact with him. He had been around beautiful women before, but never could he recall the sensation that overcame him at that moment. It was as if he'd been on the receiving end of a man's fist, but instead, it was only her, small and demure, and all she had done was to cast her glance in his direction.

He found his voice. "And why don't you know?"

"Horses are dangerous."

He laughed at the simple response. "Dangerous? Oh, I don't know about that. If it is any consolation, your sister is in very safe hands. The pony she is riding is Caesar. He has to be approaching thirty years of age. And I know this because I rode that pony when

117

I was a boy. I do not think you need to worry that he will take off on a wild romp across the field."

The pretty smile that ensued pleased him. She cast her eyes downward. "I suppose I am being foolish."

He adjusted his stance. "Your sister is in very capable hands with Carter, there. He is the most adept horseman for miles. If anyone can teach her to be safe around horses, it is he."

She sighed. "I suppose it is obvious that I have very little knowledge of horses or ponies. I've never ridden either."

"When it comes to horses, the danger lies in not knowing how to handle them. In not understanding their power."

She pressed her lips together and looked at Sampson. Her eyes traveled from the top of his ears to his eyes and then to his muzzle. At length, she spoke. "It is that power that frightens me. Lizzie could fall off, she could—"

He shook his head, eager to calm her fear. "There is an art to that too."

"An art to falling off?" She dipped her head forward, her eyebrows lifting in disbelief, as if she did not believe him.

"Indeed. You must fall away from the horse so you don't get trampled. Yes, an art. And Carter will teach your sister these things, do not fear."

But she did fear. He could see it in her face. It was written in her wide eyes and the manner in which she chewed her lower lip as she contemplated what he said.

It was easy to tell someone these things. She needed to experience them. How different she was from the woman he had encountered in the foundling home office, whose words came so freely. "Take Sampson, here. He is a bit fidgety, but all in all, I trust him more than I trust most people."

"Really?" She eyed his horse warily. After several seconds, she lifted her ungloved hand. "May I?"

"By all means."

She reached her hand toward Sampson.

The horse lifted his head to sniff her, and she jumped back. She laughed with relief. A pretty, controlled laugh.

"Try again," he urged.

She fixed her pale eyes on the horse, lifted her hand. Colin held the reins taut, giving Sampson no room to pull back.

Her fingers grazed Sampson's muzzle.

"See?" he asked. "Harmless."

She smiled as if surprised all of her fingers had remained intact. "Harmless," she breathed.

Her transparency was refreshing. She reached out to the horse again, and this time her hand moved from his muzzle to his cheek.

Colin fixed his eyes on her, on the smoothness of her skin and the gentle curve of her cheek. His eyes lingered on her fair hair, her gold eyelashes, and the slope of her nose as she petted the horse. True, he had been curious about her from the day they met, but now it was as if a gateway had been opened. He found himself wanting to know everything about her. Why did she not have experience around horses? Why was she out alone with her bonnet off her head and her hands ungloved? He knew the Ellison women would never make an etiquette misstep like that. And yet she seemed wholly unaware of such propriety.

She looked up at him from the horse and caught him staring.

He immediately looked down at his boots, and she pulled her hand away from the horse.

"Have you any news of the little girl you dropped off at the foundling home the other day?" she asked.

He was impressed that she thought to ask. "Unfortunately, I do not."

"It is a sad thing," she exclaimed. "The poor child, abandoned. I spoke with Mr. Bradford early yesterday, and he said that she had been sent to the country already until she gets older. I wonder what will become of her. He said they gave her the name Jane."

Colin could only stare for a moment. He had been around the Ellisons a long time, and while they had claimed great interest in the less fortunate, he had always wondered about their sincerity. But Miss Creston seemed different. Vastly different.

"I should be going, Mr. Galloway." Her words were hesitant, and she took a couple of steps backward. "Thank you for introducing me to Sampson."

"Of course." He gave a slight bow.

She curtsied in return, then turned back down the path in the direction from which she had come.

He captured one last look as she walked away. Then he turned to Sampson, patted the horse's dappled neck, and continued on his way to Ellison's office.

Chapter Fifteen

*A*fter leaving Mr. Galloway, Isabel headed to Emberwilde's east rose garden. She could still see Lizzie from where she was as she rode the pony. But at least now Isabel felt calmer. The tension that had gathered in her neck and shoulders was dissipating, and the pounding in her heart was starting to subside.

In fact, a smile tugged at the corner of her mouth. Yes, she was worried about Lizzie, but Mr. Galloway had helped calm her fears.

She liked Mr. Galloway. He appeared to be a bit older than she, but he seemed less pretentious than her family here at Emberwilde. Even compared to Mr. Bradford, whom she had encountered a handful of times in the past several days, he seemed calm and observant.

It had been pleasant to speak with someone outside of Emberwilde. Yes, the great house was luxurious. She had more books than she could ever read in a lifetime, gardens to walk in, and every other manner of diversion. But after living in a school full of girls, she missed the busy noise of others.

Her aunt rested a great deal, and her uncle was rarely home. They did have guests, but Isabel was rarely invited to participate in the visits. Be it intentional or otherwise, her aunt seemed content to keep her hidden away. She could, of course, always count on Constance for conversation, and the previous day's visit to the foundling home was a step in a positive direction.

But for the time being, the memory of her short interaction with Mr. Galloway brought a smile to her face.

She could almost even laugh at the trepidation she felt when she first saw her sister on the pony.

She tugged her bonnet ribbons free and removed her bonnet completely as she stepped toward the garden gate, but the sound of her name stopped her.

"Miss Creston."

Isabel stopped on the first step and turned. There in the garden stood Burns. "I am sorry to interrupt your walk, but your aunt has requested your company. She and Miss Ellison are in the music room."

Isabel frowned. It was unlike her aunt to send for her this time of day, for normally Aunt Margaret retired to her room during the later part of the morning to rest or to write letters.

"Of course," Isabel responded.

She swung her bonnet at her side as she followed Burns. The air was cooler inside Emberwilde's stone walls, and whereas Burns headed down to the kitchen, Isabel made her way to the music room.

As she approached, hushed yet fervent whispers could be heard coming from the chamber. She did not wish to eavesdrop, but the intensity in the voices piqued her interest. There could be no doubt that the voices belonged to her aunt and uncle. Her uncle's presence surprised her. Normally he was either gone from dawn until dusk visiting tenants, or he was in his study. It seemed a constant stream of people would come in to see him when he was present, from friends to tenants to tradesmen. Even Mr. Galloway had been on his way to visit her uncle. Isabel once asked her aunt who all the people were and was told that it was not ladylike to show an interest in such happenings.

She paused to listen.

Her uncle's voice met her ears first. "This sort of extravagance needs to stop."

"I do think you are overreacting."

"Times are changing, Margaret. We need to economize, and we will never right ourselves with these sorts of indulgences."

"Indulgences? I hardly consider such things indulgences."

The tone of her uncle's voice sharpened. "I warned you of this before Isabel and Lizzie came to live here. We barely have the funds to continue our lifestyle as it is, let alone—"

"So you would have us live as paupers?" Aunt Margaret shrieked. "We have an image to uphold. Others count on us to remain stable when everything around us shifts."

"Contrary to what you may believe, we do not live as paupers, Margaret, and that image you believe needs to be upheld is of your own making."

"I've heard enough." She clipped his sentence short.

"No, you will stay here until I am finished talking."

Isabel's breath froze in her throat. Could she be hearing her uncle correctly? Were funds a concern at Emberwilde? Everything around her screamed of prosperity and abundance.

"And what of Isabel?" Uncle Charles continued. "You were so set upon making matches for your daughters. You said before she arrived that your interest was in helping her secure a match, and yet now you refuse to speak of the idea."

"She has only just arrived!" her aunt screeched.

"No, something is different. I am not certain what you are up to, but I expect you to follow through with the arrangement we discussed prior to her arrival. Have you learned whether she has a dowry?"

Aunt Margaret's muffled reply was soft. "She does not."

"Well then. Her options will be limited, but she is attractive, so all is not lost. I have mentioned the idea to Galloway, and I shall suggest it again. At this point, he is our best option."

Isabel's breath caught in her throat. Mr. Galloway. So she *had* heard her uncle correctly that first day. Was that why he had been in the garden? Had he been there to see her?

Her aunt's reply sounded shocked. "What, not Colin Galloway?"

"The very one."

"That will never do. I could never see a member of my family married to that man."

"That man, as you put it, is a respected landowner. She could do much worse."

The pitch of her aunt's voice continued to rise. "He led our only son to death's door, Charles. And now you would see him united in marriage to your niece? Why, the idea!"

"You must let that notion go. I loved Freddie, do not doubt it, but he was a headstrong, obstinate sort. I do not believe that he would be swayed by Colin Galloway to do anything he set his mind against. Freddie joined the army of his own accord, of that I am sure."

She thought she heard a sob, and then her uncle's voice seemed to soften. "If not Galloway, who then?"

"Bradford?" her aunt responded. "Or Johnson from over in Dellton? I am not certain, but these things take time, especially without a dowry."

"We do not have time. Something must change. Now."

Isabel did not know if she should interrupt or wait until they were done, but within seconds she heard her uncle's heavy boots coming in her direction. Not wishing to be suspected of eavesdropping, she stepped back into the corridor until her uncle had exited and the sound of his footsteps faded away.

When she was certain enough time had passed, she stepped into the room as she had been bid.

She had visited the beautiful space every day since her arrival, not only to listen to her cousin's music, but to see the painting of her mother. By the light of day she noticed the pale pink wallpaper boasting tiny green vines, the polished wood floor, and the ornate carvings in the chimneypiece. Today the French doors opened onto a veranda, allowing a fragrant breeze to enter.

She expected news of a gown or instructions for dinner, but her face fell as she assessed her aunt's pinched expression and narrowed eyes.

Isabel stepped in slowly. Cautiously.

Something was wrong.

It was written in her aunt's tight lips and on Constance's sympathetic pout.

With a sharp rap of her cane on the floor, Aunt Margaret stood. "I assume that you had a perfectly logical reason for that display."

Isabel flashed her attention to Constance, whose eyes were wide and mouth was pressed shut. "What display?"

Her aunt's face reddened to an unbecoming shade, and her chin shook as she spoke. "You were speaking with a man, Isabel. Mr. Galloway, no less, in view of all. I saw you from this very window."

Horror sliced her. Isabel grasped for an excuse. "I . . . I only just happened to encounter him on my walk. I . . . I—"

"That is no justification. And of all the people with whom to converse!" The sharpness of her voice cut at Isabel. "I certainly did not think that you would require instruction on character, but apparently I was mistaken."

Isabel's head swung slowly from side to side, and she searched her memory, trying to identify what she had done that was so offensive. "I am sorry, Aunt. If I had known anything I did was offensive, I surely would have avoided it."

Mortification wound its way around her. She began to feel like a child who had been discovered doing something wrong. Except being reprimanded for a character flaw felt worse.

"I can see quite unmistakably that I was right about that school of yours." Aunt Margaret hurled the words. "It obviously taught you nothing about propriety."

"It was all quite innocent," protested Isabel, unblinking. "I was out for a walk and encountered Mr. Galloway on the path. That is all."

"To you that might seem like all. Do you not understand? Here, your reputation is unblemished. Perfect. Talking to men freely? Why, I never saw the like. What if someone had seen you two together?"

Isabel tried to understand. "But we were introduced that first night I was here. I thought that after an introduction it was proper to—"

"You may have been introduced to him, but that hardly makes him your equal. Mr. Galloway is precisely the sort of man who is nothing as he seems. Do I make myself clear?"

Isabel could only stare, dumbstruck. Her aunt spoke so harshly of Mr. Galloway, even though her uncle recommended him so highly. In her stubbornness, Isabel wanted to defend herself. But she knew better. It would never do to argue with her aunt.

At length, Constance rose from her seat by the pianoforte. "Mother, I do not think that Isabel meant any offense. Surely you can see for yourself that you are upsetting her."

Aunt Margaret ignored her daughter's intervention. "Do I have your word, Isabel, that you will use more discretion?"

Isabel could feel the tears welling up and emotion closing her throat. She wanted so badly to please her aunt. But how could she apologize when she was not exactly sure what she had done wrong?

She nodded.

Aunt Margaret stomped into the chamber, the sharp rapping of her cane matching her footsteps.

After several moments Constance crossed the room and embraced Isabel. After releasing her, Constance stepped back and held Isabel's hands at arm's length. "Take heart, Isabel. Mother only scolds you because she loves you. She has high hopes for you and only wants the best for you. We don't want to ruin any future opportunity through a simple act of ignorance."

Isabel stood still. There could be no doubt that Constance had heard the argument between her parents as well. Did she share her mother's opinions or her father's? Unsure of whom to trust, and still not entirely sure what she had done wrong, Isabel remained quiet.

Her cousin continued. "You will grow accustomed to Mother's tone, I promise. She is only temporarily upset. She is a smart woman, with a keen sense for what a young lady requires. Do not look so shocked! This is a good thing. She is only trying to ensure that you have the best possible chance at happiness, you and Elizabeth."

Isabel did not feel happier, but she smiled at her cousin's eager effort to console her.

Energy infused each step as Isabel walked toward the foundling home. She clutched Lizzie's hand in her own as the pair headed over the dusty, leaf-crusted path that ran along the Emberwilde Forest. Perhaps because of the sharp reprimand that she'd given Isabel, or perhaps because of the argument she'd had with her husband, Aunt Margaret had consented to their reading with the foundling children.

The enthusiasm in Lizzie's steps matched her own, for both were eager to be out from under their aunt's watchful eye.

"Do you have the books? All of them?" asked Lizzie as she bounced along beside Isabel.

Isabel tightened her hold on the small satchel in her hand. "I do."

"Even the one about the girl and the boat?" Lizzie asked, squinting up at Isabel.

Isabel smiled. "Yes, even the one about the girl and the boat."

Isabel had been pleasantly surprised at the selection of books in Emberwilde's library. There were two libraries in the large home, in fact—one for family use and one that served as Uncle Charles's private collection. Her uncle's library contained mostly books on history and foreign lands, but the family library had been designed for the children and boasted many books for younger readers.

After a short walk the sisters arrived at the school, and Mr. Bradford was ready to meet them. Isabel could only suppose that her aunt had sent word of their plans.

"Ladies!" he exclaimed, a smile of welcome on his face. He stepped from the home's front steps and into the late-morning sunshine and bowed. "I saw you approaching from the window. I am so glad you could join us."

Both Isabel and Lizzie returned a curtsy. Isabel was glad to see him. His easy smile and manner had an uncanny way of putting her at ease.

"Good day, Mr. Bradford. I hope our visit does not interrupt your day's schedule, but Lizzie has selected a few stories for the younger girls, and we would like to read to them."

"Any visit from the two of you could hardly be considered an interruption. In fact, your aunt sent word you were to visit us this morning, and so the younger girls have been assembled. It is quite a treat for them. They are in the garden, if you should like to visit them there."

Isabel and Lizzie followed Mr. Bradford around the home and through a gate. A sparse yet pleasant garden unfolded, and in the distance under a substantial oak tree was clustered a group of young girls. There were about eight of them, and they were seated around her, dressed in somber, unadorned blue linen gowns.

Isabel studied their faces as well as she could as they approached. The children appeared healthy, but even more striking was how curious they seemed to be about Lizzie and herself.

128

Mr. Bradford addressed the group. "Ladies, Miss Creston and Miss Elizabeth have come to spend time with you this morning."

The children's eyes brightened, and a wave of motion swept through the group as they wiggled in excitement.

"It is very kind of the Miss Crestons to come read to you this morning, and I trust you will be polite and attentive." Mr. Bradford turned to Isabel. "Miss Creston, this is where I leave you. Miss Trendle will be here should you have need of her. Can I be of any further service?"

Isabel shook her head. "I think we are well situated, Mr. Bradford. Thank you for allowing us to spend time with your charges."

"The pleasure is mine."

He left the gathering, and Isabel turned her full attention to the girls. How they reminded her of the girls she had left behind at Fellsworth, and how they tugged at her heart. These children were just like Lizzie. No mother. No father. In fact, if not for Isabel, Lizzie could very well be in a home like this, with a bleak future and few options. That very thought charged her resolve to do what she could to help prepare these girls for the future. While a story might not seem significant, she knew that just showing interest in the children would do them a world of good. Perhaps the more they read, the more knowledge they would amass, and by doing so be better prepared to face their futures head-on.

Mr. Bradford had the forethought to bring a chair out for her, so she sat, and Lizzie joined the girls.

She could not help the smile that formed when she saw their eager faces. "Now, I think introductions are in order, don't you? I would like to know each of your names, and I would like to know how old you are."

Jane.

Bessie.

Mary.

Tilly.

Each girl had a name, but more importantly, each girl had a unique story.

And Isabel was eager to learn each one.

Chapter Sixteen

*L*ater that night, Colin set out to meet McKinney at the gatepost near the village square.

A heavy rain pelted the landscape, and low-hanging, shifting clouds blocked out the moonlight. Colin would have liked nothing more than to turn left at the end of the Benton Bridge and return to his quiet, humble room, but instead he turned to the right, passed the haberdasher's and baker's silent shops, and headed out of town. Normally, no one would venture out into such elements, but he hoped the reward would justify the discomfort.

The boxing match McKinney had mentioned was scheduled for that night in a nearby field, and it would draw men from miles around. No doubt this would be as good a place as any to hear rumors of smuggling if any existed, for men from all walks of life would be represented.

McKinney was waiting for him, leaning against the designated gatepost, a caped greatcoat over his shoulders and a wide-brimmed hat covering his head. "What took you so long? Bored to tears out here."

Colin adjusted his own collar against the wind and stepped out from under the protection of the canopy of trees.

"Been busy. When did you say it started?"

"Oh, it's been going on for these two hours. But you know how they are—could go on all night. No doubt there's quite a crowd already. Folks coming from as far away as Maytown. Had to move it from Foster's Field, though. All this rain flooded it, and heard tell it's ankle deep. Moved the bout to the barn at Kenter's Peak."

Colin frowned as he shrugged his coat higher. "That barn's not very big. Not many will fit inside."

"You know how people are, especially when there's a spectacle. They'll be packed to the rafters." McKinney passed a bottle over to Colin. "Take a swig. It'll keep ya warm."

Colin shook his head. He reminded himself that he was not going to this match as a spectator. He needed every sense sharp. Men of all sorts gathered at these events, and he was going as the magistrate.

"Suit yourself." McKinney took another swig and tucked the bottle in the crook of his arm. "Any word from the excise officer?"

"Looks like we'll be proceeding on our own. Their workload is such that they cannot offer assistance at this time."

McKinney fell into step next to Colin. "What does Ellison have to say about all this?"

"Ever since he showed me the caverns, he's been quiet about it. He's trying to handle it quietly so as to prevent further disruptions."

"I said it before and I will say it again," McKinney said with a shake of his head. "The man's in trouble. Financial trouble. He's got bigger problems than whatever's going on in that forest. Heard he owes a hefty sum to Thomas Payne and will be selling part of Emberwilde to cover it."

Normally Colin would take information about Ellison from McKinney lightly. The McKinney family and the Ellison family had not been on good terms since McKinney's father was dismissed from the estate well over twenty years ago.

"Aye, you're correct. Ellison is in debt to Payne. And maybe he is going to sell some of the farming fields. But what would that have to do with smugglers?" Colin knew not to say too much on the matter, even to McKinney. He chose his words carefully. "Over the past week or so I've been monitoring the woods, and there is evidence of activity, but we keep missing it."

"Be patient. Keep your eyes open tonight. Town's not so big that anyone can keep a secret. And then, you'll have me to thank for it." McKinney's big feet splashed water with each step. "Two men came into the inn earlier this week. Talked about a load to London and a bridge being out. But their carriage was not marked, nor would they say whom they were working for. They are as good as any place to start, and they will both be here tonight."

The walk to Kenter's Peak was unpleasant. Rain fell in intermittent sheets, and sharp winds hurled frigid drops and whipped the long, wild meadow grasses at their feet.

He could hear the activity in the stable before he saw it. Shouts and cheers tumbled on the gusty winds. Yellow torch glow oozed through the open cracks in the barn's walls, making it appear as if the entire building was ablaze inside.

Despite the heavy rain, shadowy figures gathered outside, their forms black silhouettes against the structure.

As they approached, McKinney reached out to grab Colin's arm. "Keep your head down. No one here likes a lawman, no mistakin' about that."

Colin nodded. Boxing matches were common in the villages around Northrop, but he had not attended any since becoming magistrate. In fact, it was up to him to discourage such gatherings, not attend them.

Colin and McKinney passed the shadowy men guarding the door without incident, but Colin had a quick glance at their faces. Normally, local men would oversee local events. These men were strangers.

As he passed through the propped barn door, hot air and the scent of wet hay and the stench of too many men in one room rushed him, as if the air itself was trying to escape the confines. Rain dropped through the wide slats of the roof, adding to the room's already thick humidity. Large torches lined the perimeter, their flames dangerously close to the old wooden walls.

Once inside, McKinney laughed and rubbed his thick hands together. "Here we go."

Colin glimpsed the men boxing. They were bare-chested and bare-fisted. Blood intermingled with sweat trickled down both men's faces and dripped down their chests. This would go on for as long as the men could last. It might be hours.

Colin and McKinney situated themselves in a far corner of the room—a bit too far away to watch the fighting, but a much better vantage point to see those in attendance without being seen themselves. Colin left his coat and hat on despite the heat.

The room was full. Men dressed in shades of gray, brown, and black crushed the boxing square, their shouts rising and falling with every blow.

Colin scanned the crowd. He was not sure what—or whom—he was looking for. He leaned toward McKinney. "See the men from the inn?"

After several moments of browsing the faces, McKinney turned his back toward the crowd and kept his voice low. "That's the man we want, the one with the carriage service. The man over there by Bradford . . ." McKinney had more to say, but Colin did not hear anything past *Bradford*.

It was the last name he had expected to hear at this event. He followed the direction of McKinney's gaze, and sure enough, Bradford stood against a back wall with a small group of men. His height and square jaw were unmistakable, and his straight, controlled posture set him apart from those around him. Bradford was silent as the men around him cheered.

Colin could recall a different side of Bradford—the Bradford from before the days of the foundling home—the days that had given Colin his first impressions of the man's true nature. Sure, people could change and grow out of bad behavior. But an unattractive element to Bradford's character remained, a selfishness that had always put Colin on edge, even when they were boys.

McKinney shifted, crossing his thick arms over his barrel chest. "Wonder what he's doing with that lot."

"Hard to tell." Colin did not recognize a single soul. "Do you know them?"

"I've seen them at the inn from time to time. Not so much to stay the night, mind ye, but to change the horses and eat. Don't know their names."

As if on cue, Bradford turned. Through the smoke and the flickering light, he nodded a greeting at Colin.

Colin returned the nod and muttered under his breath to McKinney, "Let's go. I want to talk to Bradford."

McKinney shrugged, and his heavy footsteps fell in next to Colin's. They wove their way through the thick crowd of rowdy men and boys.

Bradford faced Colin as he approached. "Evening, Galloway. I'm surprised to see you here."

"I was just thinking the same thing about you." Colin emerged into the small clearing where Bradford stood with his companions.

"Really? Hmm. That's strange." The crowd cheered. Bradford looked toward the boxing square, then turned back to Colin. "I would think you would remember my fondness for such attractions."

Colin did remember. In their university days, Bradford had garnered quite the reputation for gambling and cavorting. Then his father died, and he no longer had access to funds.

Bradford looked toward McKinney, his words full of irony. "Now you, I'd expect to see here."

McKinney rocked on his heels. "Never miss one if I can help it."

Another punch landed in the makeshift arena, the sound of which reverberated above the cheering crowd.

The voices around them calmed, and Colin motioned to the other men. "Who are your friends?"

"This is Christopher Dent, and this is Marcus Stanway."

The two men nodded at Colin.

"Gentlemen," Bradford continued, directing his words to the pair. "This is Mr. Colin Galloway, Northrop solicitor and magistrate, and Mr. Robert McKinney, owner of the Pigeon's Rest Inn."

Dent nodded in recognition to McKinney, but then the men turned back to the bout.

Colin folded his arms across his chest as he watched the fight, then said to Bradford, "How's the baby?"

Bradford did not take his eyes from the men fighting. "Fine, I presume."

"You don't know how she is?"

"'Course not." Bradford shrugged. "Babies are sent to a wet nurse in the country. I am sure she is well, though. I've not heard otherwise."

The callous disconnect between Bradford and his work was surprising, for despite Bradford's flaws, he was particular about the foundling home. Which is why if there was any questionable activity in the forest, Bradford would certainly know about it.

"Anything ever come of those boys and the man they saw with the knife?"

Bradford huffed a laugh. "They were just boys being boys and telling tales."

"That may be the case, but I've been apprised of some illegal activity going on in the forest, and I wanted to make you aware, for safety's sake."

At this, Bradford turned. "What kind of activity?"

"Not sure exactly. We are going to get to the bottom of it, be sure of that, but I wanted to make you aware. We suspect there are strangers in the forest who could be engaged in foul play. Those boys of yours may not have been telling tales after all."

Bradford guffawed. "Those boys are all mischief and trouble, no doubt about it."

Colin cut his eyes toward Dent and Stanway. "With all of these newcomers to town, I urge you to err on the side of caution."

Bradford chuckled as if amused. "Very well. I have been warned."

The dull thud of a punch landing incited another cheer from the crowd.

Colin excused himself and spent at least an hour mingling and making discreet inquiries of the others gathered in the barn. But when he failed to gather useful information from anyone, he pulled McKinney aside. "I think I've seen everything I need to see here. I am going to return to Northrop. You coming?"

"No," responded McKinney, not taking his eyes from the fight. "I think I will stay around here for a bit longer."

"Very well. I'll stop by the Pigeon's Rest tomorrow."

Colin clamped his hand on McKinney's shoulder before weaving his way out of the barn and into the night air. The rain still fell, but the intensity had slackened, and now it drizzled down in a hazy film. He pulled his hat lower to guard against the moisture, wishing he had brought Sampson. But the thick mud would have been treacherous for the animal, and no doubt he could return just as quickly on foot.

As he made his way to the main road, he considered Bradford's presence at the match. Colin was not sure he had made any progress or learned anything he did not know before, but he could not deny his curiosity in why Bradford was there. He'd never known Bradford to show interest in such activities in recent years, and the company he was keeping had been curious.

He was trudging down the muddy lane when a strange cracking noise made him pause. No doubt the sound was a squirrel or fox in the nearby woods, but he slowed his steps. He should follow his own advice. Times were changing, and the people around town were changing. He did have a blade in his boot for protection, but more than likely, he was overreacting to typical noises of the night.

He walked for several more minutes, then similar sounds caused him to pause again. He turned and looked behind him, but saw nothing in the night's ample mist. But as he resumed his walk, someone grabbed him from the back. Before he knew what had happened, a thick arm wrapped around his neck.

Every muscle in Colin's body sprang to action. He jabbed his elbow back into his attacker's belly, affording himself just enough room to spin around. The arm around him slackened, but as it did, a fist slammed into the side of his face, causing white spots to dart across his vision. He stumbled back but did not lose balance.

The man before him had a large frame. He was dressed in dark garments and something was tied around his face. Colin wished he had grabbed his blade from his boot when he thought of it earlier, but it was too late now. The man lunged at him, and Colin thrust his fist forward, pummeling him in his side.

Colin's breath was now coming in gaspy huffs, and perspiration trickled down the sides of his face. He took another blow to his jaw and then his gut, but in a sudden burst of energy he slammed his own fist into the stranger's nose, sending him staggering backward. The man recovered quickly and sprang toward him, nearly knocking Colin's legs out from under him. Again he grabbed Colin and whirled him around, but this time he held a blade. He forced it up against Colin's throat.

Colin froze, realizing the seriousness of his situation. "What do you want?"

The man, who was now behind him, gave a grisly, unfamiliar

laugh. "You've been poking that nose of yours around where it doesn't belong, haven't you? You'd be wise to leave good enough alone, Galloway. Stay away from what doesn't belong to you, or next time, our meeting might not be so congenial."

And with a mighty shove, Colin was pushed forward. The force caused him to stumble and fall. He righted himself and spun around, determined to learn his attacker's identity, but no one was there. The man, whoever he was, had disappeared into the woodland on the side of the road.

Colin snatched his blade from his boot, but the effort was pointless. He was alone. He gasped for breath, his expelled air pluming into white puffs in the night's stillness. He jumped to his feet, blade still in hand, and cast another glance around him.

He would not be caught off guard again.

Chapter Seventeen

*A*s she sat in church, Isabel could feel eyes on her.

She felt like a pet on display.

The uncomfortable sensation that the people around her knew far more about her than she knew of them troubled her.

She straightened her shoulders and focused her eyes on the somber-faced clergyman.

One of her new gowns had arrived the previous day, just in time for the service and her first true introduction to Northrop. Pale green sprigged muslin adorned her frame. Netting covered the bodice, and tiny white flowers graced the hemline.

There was no denying the clothing's beauty, but even after a couple of days of new attire, Isabel still felt odd wearing something besides her black gown. Today she was in different petticoats. Different stays. She wore stockings made of elegant pink silk instead of rough gray cotton. Dainty—and wholly impractical—white satin slippers hugged her feet instead of the black boots she was accustomed to. Her hair was different too. Burns had spent the better part of an hour twisting, braiding, and pinning.

She lowered her gaze for a moment to Lizzie, who was seated beside her. Lizzie, too, was in a new gown of blue muslin, with tidy white stockings and matching blue slippers. Instead of a tight braid, her hair hung down her back nearly to her waist. She looked every bit the young lady.

Isabel tried to focus on the sermon, but curiosity surged through her. So many new faces were around her. But some seemed to draw her curiosity more than others.

She cast a cautious glance over her shoulder. In the pews near the back sat the foundling home children. She had visited the home twice since her initial visit to read to the younger ones, and both she and Lizzie had become acquainted with several of the younger girls. There were probably twenty children present, varying in age from roughly five years to fifteen. They were sitting quietly and still, a testament to their discipline, and in the pew in front of them, Mr. Bradford. During the quiet, still moments he had occupied her mind over the past several days.

Isabel stole another glance as discreetly as she could. Mr. Bradford's light eyes were straight ahead, and the collar of his coat of black wool rose high on his neck. A sliver of sunlight cut through the stained-glass window, painting him in a bluish light. His hair was neatly trimmed and close to his head, and his face was clean-shaven save for the side whiskers that framed his cheekbones.

A strange flutter danced within her. She had not known him long, but in her interactions with him he had proved kind and gentle. Observant and careful. The argument she overheard between her aunt and uncle regarding her future was never far from her thoughts. As little as a month ago she would have thought of marriage as an unattainable dream. But maybe. Just maybe . . .

As she turned around slowly, her eye landed on another man—Mr. Galloway. As she looked a little more closely, she noticed bruising under his eye. Had he been hit? Judging by their past inter-actions, he was more reserved and solemn than Mr. Bradford, but the discoloration marring his face made her think otherwise. He had seemed so kind when she met him in the garden. Could her uncle honestly mean for her to marry a man who was prone to phys-ical altercations?

He was a handsome man, to be sure. His features were much

darker than Mr. Bradford's, his expression more secretive. Her aunt's warning rang in her head: *Mr. Galloway is precisely the sort of man who is nothing as he seems.*

Mr. Galloway, she noted, was seated at the edge of a pew, and next to him sat a black-haired boy who was probably around Lizzie's age. On the other side of the boy sat a woman with black hair, pale skin, and charcoal eyes. She wondered who they were. For he clearly had no wife, otherwise his name would not have come up as a suitable partner. But what explanation could there be?

At the conclusion of the service, most everyone followed the rector as he exited the nave, pausing to greet him and thank him for the sermon.

Aunt Margaret placed her hand on Isabel's back and nudged her toward the older man. "It pleases me to introduce you to my niece, Miss Isabel Creston. Isabel is my sister's child."

At the mention of Isabel's mother, the rector's eyebrows rose. "Can there be any doubt of the relation? She is the very likeness of her mother, God rest her soul."

Isabel did not know why it should surprise her that others knew of her mother. "You knew her?"

"I did, indeed. I've been the rector here for a very long time. So long, in fact, that I remember your mother around your age. And who is this?" The rector bent down to look at Lizzie.

Isabel opened her mouth to respond, but her aunt beat her to it. "This is Miss Elizabeth Creston, Miss Creston's younger sister."

Lizzie pleased her aunt with a pretty little curtsy and a smile, just as she had been taught.

"Both these ladies will be staying at Emberwilde for the time being," added Aunt Margaret.

"Well, then, I am glad to greet you. Any relation of the Hayworth family is most welcome here."

Her aunt ushered them to a group of older ladies at the edge of the church's small cemetery, and Isabel prepared for yet another round of introductions.

She was ready to return to Emberwilde. Her new slippers were uncomfortable, and the dress, though elegantly and fashionably cut, prevented her from moving freely. The sun was growing warm, and its light poked through the delicately woven straw of her bonnet.

She wrapped her gloved fingers around Lizzie's, but the child was growing impatient. The service had been much longer than the ones they attended in Fellsworth. Isabel tried to pay attention to the conversation, but the child's tugging distracted her.

"Look at the ducklings! Look, Isabel!"

Isabel shushed her.

But Lizzie had no interest in being silenced.

"May I go see the ducklings? Oh, please!" Lizzie pointed at a wooden fence separating the drive from a nearby pasture.

Isabel wanted the child to stay close to her, but how long could she keep her calm? She herself was itching to be free.

Perhaps a few moments doing something such as looking at ducklings would help calm the child.

Aunt Margaret would never approve of such a childish distraction.

Then again, her aunt would never approve of a scene either.

"Yes, you may," Isabel consented, albeit against her better judgment. "Do not touch them, and mind the mud and the carriages. Your shoes are new. And do not run."

Isabel had managed to pack a number of instructions into a quick whisper, and she watched as Lizzie crossed the small path, her steps controlled and dainty.

Isabel wished she could escape these conversations too, but with a sigh she turned back to the group of ladies she was preparing to meet. She smiled and nodded and was as pleasant as she could be, and for several moments, all seemed to be going quite well. She turned to ask her aunt a question and noticed her aunt was no longer a part of the conversation.

Concerned, she looked around and spotted her aunt speaking with Mr. Bradford. Her aunt's gestures were rigid and quick, and her round face was flushed, as if she was angry. Mr. Bradford's arms were crossed over his chest, and he was scanning the remaining parishioners. Something seemed amiss. Were they arguing? Isabel glanced over her other shoulder, seeking her uncle. Yes, she had witnessed more than one argument between her aunt and uncle, but they loved each other, she was certain, and if there was a problem, Uncle Charles would no doubt rush to his wife's aid.

Then a commotion distracted her. A horse whinnied sharp and high, and then a squeal sliced the reverent silence.

Isabel whirled toward the panicked sound.

Horror shot through her as she beheld Lizzie lying flat on the ground next to a horse. Her heart squeezed and then seemed to stop at the sight, only to resume beating at a painfully fast pace.

Propriety forgotten, Isabel dropped her reticule, gathered her skirts, and ran over to her sister's still form as best she could in the thin slippers.

Mr. Galloway was also running to her from the opposite direction. He reached Lizzie first and dropped to his knees beside her.

Isabel pushed forward. Her feet simply would not move fast enough in the ridiculous slippers. Mr. Galloway was speaking to Lizzie. He touched her arm, bending it as if to see if it was broken.

By the time Isabel reached Lizzie, Lizzie was sitting up. Dirt marred her dress and stockings, but she was talking and even smiled.

Regret and relief ran rampant within Isabel. She should have made Lizzie stay closer. She should have made her stay by her side. At least she was moving.

Isabel knelt next to her sister.

"Are you all right? What happened?"

Lizzie sniffed. "That horse bumped into me, and it scared the ducklings away."

Isabel shot a glance over at the big brown animal, which now stood still, his hindquarters twitching and his tail swatting. She gave her head a sharp shake. "I told you to stay away from the carriages, I—"

"I just wanted to see the ducks," defended Lizzie, her big eyes wide.

"Are you injured? What hurts?" Isabel could not get her own thoughts out fast enough. She looked to Mr. Galloway, as if seeking answers. "Mr. Galloway. Did you see what happened?"

Still on bent knee, he met her gaze fully. "I did. A dog ran past and spooked the horse. He skittered, but I do not think he hurt her, only scared her. Then she fell."

Now that she was certain her sister was all right, Isabel became aware of the crowd that had gathered. Embarrassment began to run high. This was not the sort of introduction she had hoped for.

Aunt Margaret arrived, flustered, her face florid from the exertion. "Oh, my dears! How did this happen? Are you all right? Oh, look at the mud!"

Isabel looked up, her arm around Lizzie's shoulders. "She is fine. Just a little frightened, 'tis all."

"Oh, well, that is a relief." Her aunt looked around. "Well, this is a fine welcome to Northrop, I daresay. Whose horse is this?"

As her aunt continued expressing her outrage, Mr. Galloway straightened and extended his hand toward Isabel. It took Isabel a moment to realize he intended to help her to her feet.

Isabel looked at his gloved hand, and her aunt's words of warning rang loudly in her head. But this man had helped her and shown her no wrong. She looked up at his face, resisting the urge to wince as she beheld his eye, and placed her hand in his. It was firm and steady as she leaned on it for support.

She muttered a word of gratitude to Mr. Galloway and bent to help Lizzie, but then, almost out of nowhere, Mr. Bradford pushed through, the volume of his voice high. "Please. Allow me."

In a graceful movement, he knelt next to Lizzie, who was still seated on the ground. "There, there, child. All will be well." He scooped Lizzie into his arms and looked toward Mr. Galloway. "Thank you, Galloway, but we can take it from here."

Mr. Galloway pressed his lips together and nodded. Without a word, he stepped back.

Isabel wanted to thank him, but before she could, her aunt's voice commandeered her attention.

"This is unacceptable. I demand to know who the owner of that beast is."

Isabel caught Lizzie's eye. The child's expression had shifted from innocent defensiveness, and now her frown tugged downward. Her tiny chin trembled and she averted her eyes. Lizzie did not like the attention. Could Isabel blame her?

Constance stepped forward and looped her arm through Isabel's. She lowered her voice to just above a whisper. "Come now, Isabel. What an ordeal this has been! We'd best hurry before Mother has a fit. I no longer fear for Lizzie, for she is fine as can be, and Mr. Bradford will see her to the carriage. But Mother gets so upset at these things, so it is prudent to hurry."

Isabel allowed herself to be led to the carriage. As she did so, she shielded her eyes from the sun's brightness and looked around her. A few people remained, chatting, but most of the church attendees had dispersed. She turned her head toward the village and finally spotted him. Mr. Galloway. For even though she only saw him from the back, there could be no mistaking him.

He was speaking with Uncle Charles. The men looked back toward the scene. No doubt Uncle Charles had sought out Mr. Galloway to learn the details of the event. Isabel was struck by how much faith and confidence her uncle put in the man. It just didn't make sense. Why was her aunt so opposed to him? Was it truly because of Freddie, or was there something else she did not know?

Mr. Galloway's aunt took his arm. The boy and woman who had sat next to him in church were several feet away, and another man trailed behind in close proximity.

The sight pinched her. Why, she was uncertain.

All that she knew was that everything was changing, and it was changing entirely too fast.

Her aunt hurried to her side and wrapped her arm around Isabel's waist. Gone was any trace of vexation. Instead, she seemed almost pleased. "Thank goodness for Mr. Bradford!"

Isabel pivoted to look at the man who held Lizzie in his arms. Lizzie had wrapped her arm around his neck. The child's awkward discomfort was fading.

Mr. Bradford caught Isabel's eye, flashed a smile at her, and bowed as well as he could with the girl in his arms.

She did not respond. Only dipped a curtsy.

This was a world she did not understand.

Chapter Eighteen

*M*r. Bradford accompanied the Ellison family to Emberwilde.

He did not ride with the ladies in their carriage. Instead, he and Mr. Ellison decided to walk, for the distance was not far.

"I am so glad that Mr. Bradford has decided to join us this afternoon," chattered Constance as the carriage rumbled over the Benton Bridge. She scooted to the edge of the bench, leaning toward Isabel. "It was so kind of him to help Elizabeth!"

"You are right, Constance," Aunt Margaret added, a satisfied expression on her face, nestling Lizzie against her side. "The day would surely have been ruined if not for Mr. Bradford's thoughtfulness."

Isabel was not certain how Mr. Bradford's actions saved the day, but she remained silent on the subject. She was unaccustomed to speaking so freely about the actions of gentlemen. Instead, she shifted the focus to Lizzie.

"Are you sure you are all right, Lizzie? Nothing hurts?"

Lizzie lifted her knee and exposed the torn stocking and the bit of blood beneath. "This does."

Constance jumped in before Isabel could respond. "Oh, do not worry about that, dearest. Burns will be able to tend to that for you, and you will be good as new."

"Mr. Bradford is a natural with children," interjected Aunt Margaret, unwilling to allow the topic to drop. "Did you not see how he knew exactly what do to? Such selflessness is an attractive quality in any person."

Isabel shifted to the side as the carriage hit a rut in the road. It was not abnormal for her aunt to speak favorably of Mr. Bradford, but she seemed to be singing his praises even louder than normal, which confused her, especially after what appeared to be a heated conversation between them in the churchyard. She saw an opportunity to learn more about him, and took advantage of it. "And is Mr. Bradford from Northrop?"

Her aunt continued. "He is. The home he grew up in is within a short ride. He and Freddie were friends, and he was often at Emberwilde. He even attended university with Freddie. He comes from a noble family, one of sterling reputation, despite the fact that they fell on financial difficulties. You would never guess it by the way he carries himself."

Curious, Isabel tilted her head to the side. "Were his parents at church today?"

"No, they both died a few years back. He is all alone in the world, for he had no living brothers or sisters."

Isabel leaned to catch a glimpse of Mr. Bradford, but the carriage had turned and the men were now out of sight. "How did he become the head of the foundling home?"

"His mother was always active helping the less fortunate, and I can only surmise that he followed her example. He was in a bad way after his parents died, so from the moment he came to us and inquired about letting the guesthouse for a foundling home, I could not say no. Such a visionary and such a heart for the less fortunate! He would be a prize for any young lady."

Isabel's cheeks flamed at the directness of her aunt's words. She had wondered if and when her aunt would bring up the topic of marriage. Was this her way?

When they arrived at Emberwilde, Isabel saw to Lizzie's injury, then joined the family on the lawn, where the servants had set up large open-sided tents and tables with food and drink. By the time she came down, her uncle and Mr. Bradford had joined them.

It was one of the first fine afternoons after a week of inhospitable weather. The sun glittered gold and yellow in the crisp afternoon sky, hanging cheerfully above the carpet of greening grass.

As she sat admiring the scenery, a deep voice sounded from behind her. "Might I join you?"

The question caught her off guard, and she turned to face Mr. Bradford.

But goodness, the man was even more handsome up close. The gentle breeze caught his thick hair and blew it about in a careless manner. His skin was fair and contrasted attractively against the curling locks, and his light chocolate eyes were more entrancing without the shadow from his hat's brim.

A jolt raced through her as he sat next to her. Without her aunt and cousin nearby, she could relax a little, for whether by coincidence or by design, they were not standing over her shoulder to analyze every word. His manner was so carefree, his conversation so easy, that his natural calmness put her at ease.

She was admittedly awkward when it came to talking to men. She had watched Constance and noted a general grace about her conversation. How did she come to possess such an easy manner?

Mr. Bradford leaned forward and rested his hands on his knees. His eyes met hers directly. "I hope you do not think this an odd admission, but I have been hoping for an opportunity to speak with you alone."

Isabel's heart thumped in her chest. "Oh?"

"Yes. I wanted to see how the reading sessions have been going at the school?"

"Very well. The children seem to enjoy them very much."

"I am glad to hear it. The children sing your praises. And Miss

Elizabeth's, of course. So few people show them genuine kindness. Some of the children have had such difficult lives. Any bit of attention and care is appreciated by them."

"They are sweet children, eager to learn." She bit her lower lip, weighing the timing and wisdom of her words. "The home provides for them very well, but with just a few tweaks you could vastly improve their education, which would give them a great foundation for life once they enter the world."

She held her breath, waiting to see how he would react.

After several seconds, he nodded. "I could not agree with you more. You know of my acquaintance with Mr. Langsby, but hearing him speak on such a topic is much different than hearing it from a student's perspective. I hope you do not find my questions intrusive."

"Heavens, no," she exclaimed, feeling herself relax at his suggestion. "It is a topic I enjoy; however, my aunt and cousin prefer I not speak of it. They find it unsophisticated."

"I've no wish for you to engage in a conversation of which your aunt would not approve, but you are exactly the person who could understand my endeavors."

Finally, it seemed that someone understood her reasoning and why she felt compelled to read with the children. "I would be happy to help, Mr. Bradford."

His expression brightened with enthusiasm, and his words tumbled out quickly. "When I was with Mr. Langsby, he shared with me how Fellsworth itself started as a foundling home, and then he shared with me bits of the school's history. It was quite fascinating."

Isabel smiled, a flush rushing to her cheeks. Even if just for a moment, she felt as if she had a bit of home with her, and that someone valued her past.

"You are correct, Mr. Bradford. The school started out as a foundling home in London, but after purchasing land in Surrey, the owners transitioned the framework to teaching older children. I am impressed you know so much of it."

"Do not be impressed, Miss Creston. I am still a long way off from making such a transition, but I am learning. Your aunt and uncle have been especially supportive. We would not even have a foundling home if not for their generosity. And yet, it is an ambitious project. I am quite at the mercy of those generous souls, but I have hopes of making the home into much more than it is now."

She smiled. "I admire your vision, Mr. Bradford. And I must say, I fear I am at a disadvantage, for you seem to know more of me than I of you."

"Oh, Miss Creston," he breathed, as if amused. "I am afraid there is not much to tell."

In the pause between his words, she noted how she liked the sound of her name on his lips.

In an effort to hide the feelings beginning to well within her, she prompted him, finding herself genuinely interested in what he had to say. "I do hope the boys who saw that man in the woods are feeling calmer. I was quite concerned for them when we quitted the home the day of my first visit."

Mr. Bradford expelled a little laugh. "*Thought* they saw a man in the woods. I thank you for your concern, Miss Creston. But I assure you, all is well."

"Do you not believe them?"

"It is not that, Miss Creston. I am sure they saw something, or at least they think they did." He lowered his eyes and leaned forward, as if taking her into confidence. "Have you heard yet about the legends surrounding the forest?"

Isabel cut her eyes toward her aunt, who was engaged in conversation with her husband. "While my family has not made mention of it, I have heard the stories. A story, anyway."

He raised an eyebrow in amusement. "I am sure you have."

"Are any of the stories true? About the gypsies, I mean?"

He laughed a laugh so contagious she could not help but smile.

"Some are true, perhaps, but more likely they are myths and nothing more. I am sure you are well acquainted with that, especially since one of the legends surrounds your own mother."

Isabel sobered, then frowned. His statement seemed so odd, so out of place, that surely he had misspoken. "My own mother?"

He straightened, and the smile on his face waned. "Of course. Your mother."

He blinked at her and nodded, as if expecting her to understand his meaning. But as the two locked eyes, her heart began to race. She shook her head as if to shake off the confusion. "I'm sure I don't understand."

He rolled his lips together and drummed his long fingers on his knee. "Forgive me. I only said what I thought you knew, or would at least remember, the . . ." His voice faded. "I have misspoken."

She reached out her hand as if to calm a frightened child. "No, no." She cast a glance over at her aunt, whose eyes were fixed firmly on her. She lowered her voice.

"Please," she urged. "Tell me what you know of my mother. I have very few memories of her, and if you have news to share, I would be most interested and willing to hear it."

He stared at her, shocked. He spoke hesitantly, as if every word he uttered might overstep a boundary. "Perhaps I have it wrong, for I was but a boy when she died. But there was a rumor that your mother fell ill after spending the day riding in the forest. That is one of the stories, that the ghosts of the gypsies will cause illness and certain death to those who go into the forest. Not everyone, of course, just ones with . . . with . . ."

The strangest sensation pierced Isabel's heart. Could this man know something about her mother that she did not? But no, her father had been quite plain in his explanation of her mother's death.

153

She may not remember much about her father, but she did recall his explanation with great clarity.

"No, you are mistaken, sir. Quite mistaken. My mother died of a fever. In London." She said the words slowly, as if to test her memory and convince herself of the credibility thereof.

But what would have given him such a thought?

Heat crept up her bodice, flushing her face and quickening her pulse. She glanced at her aunt, whose expression was concerned.

He cleared his throat. "Yes. Forgive me. Clearly I was mistaken."

His smile was kind, and she expelled her breath with a forced smile. Yet even with his easy manner, she was not sure he believed her. He was appeasing her. She would get to the bottom of this, and it was not his fault. Besides, the last thing she wanted to do was make enemies with this kind young man who seemed so bent on getting to know her.

Chapter Nineteen

*A*fter the church service, Colin spent the afternoon at Lockert Cottage.

Over the years, it had become a tradition that every Sabbath both Colin and Henry would return to the family home for a meal. Sunday afternoon was the one time of the week his aunt's servants were given leave from their duties, so the meal usually was comprised of cold meats and cheeses and other previously prepared items. It was often simple fare, but that did not matter. It was still the best meal Colin would eat all week.

Despite Miranda's presence, it was also the one time of the week he could relax. He enjoyed his aunt's and cousin's company. It was a moment to slip back to a simpler time when he could laugh and feel at home.

But tonight he felt restless, for talk of Emberwilde and the Ellison family dominated the conversation.

It could not be helped, he supposed. Rumors had been circulating about Miss Creston since the day she arrived at Emberwilde, and today was the first day that many people, including his cousin and Miranda, had seen her.

Before returning to the boardinghouse, Colin had made it his habit to see to the stables and outbuildings to ensure everything was in good repair. His aunt's manservant was aging, and for peace of mind, Colin would assess any needs.

Tonight was no different.

He stepped out again into the cool, damp night and headed toward the small stable.

Water from the previous days' rain still pooled in the low areas of the yard. His aunt's dog ran to join him and nudged his bare hand with his wet nose.

Since his aunt lived so close to town, she did not keep a horse, but the stable was home to a cow and a handful of chickens and pigs.

The wooden structure appeared sound and the animals within it content, but wind had disrupted a pile of early hay, so he grabbed the broom to tidy up before he left.

But then movement at the stable entrance caught his attention.

His breath suspended.

Miranda.

She had been unusually quiet this evening, as if hesitant to take part in the discussions of their newcomer, but now she stood in the stable doorway, leaning against the rough casing. Her long, lustrous hair was loose over her shoulders, with the exception of the bits around her face that were tied back in a loose ribbon. She was a lovely woman, with soft eyes and gentle features.

But the expression in her eyes concerned him.

He always tried to avoid being alone with her. Their past was well known throughout the town, and he would not give the gossipmongers any fodder to latch onto. Their history was a book best left closed, despite how time had changed the circumstances.

He returned the broom to the side and prepared to leave. The task could be finished at another time.

"You shouldn't be out here," he said as she crossed the threshold. "You'll catch cold."

She shrugged, her shawl loose on her shoulders, and ignored his suggestion. "I was worried about you. Your eye looks awful. What happened?"

He knew he could not avoid questions about his bruised eye

forever. He kept his gaze averted and moved a stool out of the pathway to set it against the wall. "An accident. It will heal."

"An accident?" she said, a small laugh coloring her tone with disbelief. "Somehow I doubt that. More likely you are up to something, and I hope against hope that it is not dangerous." Her words grew hesitant. "There was a time you would tell me about all your day's activities."

Here, in the darkness, it would be easy to fall back into old habits, to allow himself to relax in her company and share the thoughts on his mind. But something within him that he did not fully understand prevented it. "It's nothing."

She took a few steps farther into the building, her expression as nonchalant as if they were discussing the weather. "It was nice to meet Miss Creston today. I did not speak with her today, but you did. What happened with the horse? You did not tell us the whole story."

Colin reached for his lantern and lifted it, then regretted doing so, for as the light fell on her, he was reminded of her beauty. Of past feelings for her. He forced his voice. "The horse was spooked and knocked the child over, but she is fine."

Miranda leaned against the stall wall, her head cocked to the side. "You know, Miss Creston is as lovely as I had heard. Your aunt tells me that you have been in her company already."

The statement seemed dangerous. As if he were being led down a path. It would be best for him to leave. He tipped his hat and began to walk past her. "I must go."

Her voice was soft. "Colin. Wait."

She reached out and grabbed his hand as he passed her, the very touch stopping him in his tracks.

The fact that she said his Christian name did not affect him so much as the manner in which she spoke it. The lilt that accented her voice—tender, hopeful—hinted that something much more intimate existed between them. And for how many years had he longed for the touch of her hand in his? At times since William's death she had been forward, yes. But never had she been so bold as to seek him out. Alone. At night.

Miranda inched closer, and shadows blurred the details of her features. Her eyes were fixed on him with an intensity that seemed to freeze him to his spot.

He raised his eyebrows in question.

"I made a mistake all those years ago. A terrible mistake," she blurted, her voice rising in both pitch and volume.

He drew a sharp breath, his mind immediately attempting to map out the best course. This was the first time she had so openly referenced their past relationship. She had never mentioned it out loud, even though its presence was as imposing as if it had been an actual human.

"All that is in the past," he said. "It is best forgotten."

"Forgotten? Have you never made a mistake, Colin?" Her words were more a plea than a question, a desperate appeal.

Colin shook his head. It would be impossible to count the mistakes he had made over the years of his life. But now, for the first time, she was admitting blame for what had happened between them. Her betrayal, and his response, forever changed the course of his life.

He could feel her gaze on him, expectant. A sensation that once warmed him and filled him with hope now ate at him, infusing him with dread.

He grew uncomfortable and withdrew his hand from hers. "I must go."

"Do not leave, Colin. Not yet. You did not answer my question."

He stopped and looked at her. He knew his words sounded cold, and he had no wish to hurt her. But he also did not wish to leave her with any false hope. "What would you have me say?"

"I want you to say that you understand why I did what I did. That you forgive me." She hesitated, then reached to touch the wool of his sleeve. "Aren't you lonely?"

Lonely? The years of living alone flashed before him. Even his one room at the boardinghouse. It was lonely. He did wish for a woman's touch and warmth to guard against the cold nights.

He did not care to see another human hurting, but he would not extend false hope. He could give in to her, and they probably could be happy together. But something in him was changing. Perhaps it was Ellison putting the idea in his head. Or perhaps it was the growing attraction he felt every time he encountered Miss Creston. His own feelings regarding the past and the future were changing. At length, he spoke. "You must know that time changes everything."

"But I have not changed, Colin," she protested. "Not really."

"You are right," he conceded. "Perhaps I am the one who has changed. Regardless, what is done is done. And in all actuality, it is probably all best left in the past."

She lifted her hand to calm her hair blowing about her face. "I don't believe that you think that."

They stared at each other in tense silence.

This was a conversation he had avoided for so long. And now that the words were being spoken, he did not know why it hadn't happened sooner.

He thought of Miss Creston. Even though they had spoken at a handful of formal meetings, his mind was creating new ideas, new dreams.

"I am sorry. I am," he said, taking a step back. "But there can be no going back."

Chapter Twenty

Isabel sat in the music room, staring into the leaping flames, which were all too animated for the lateness of the hour and the heaviness of her heart.

Mr. Bradford had said nothing indecent. But his words clung like a damp shawl about her shoulders, weighing down her every thought and suffocating her mood.

Her memories of her mother were murky, but she was not prepared for stories about Anna Creston that contradicted the ones she had been told. And it was unnerving to think that someone outside the family might know more than she about the truth.

Isabel looked up as Aunt Margaret and Constance crossed the room toward her. It was amazing, really. Her cousin always appeared cheerful and perfectly polished. Even at this late hour, when the owls could be heard hooting from the forest, her cheeks glowed pink and bright, and her gown of green silk looked as fresh as if it had just been donned.

"Did you have a nice time this afternoon?" Constance's perky voice penetrated the silence. "It appeared that you and Mr. Bradford had a lovely conversation."

"We did," Isabel responded, and then, feeling the need to elaborate, she added, "He seems to be quite passionate about his work."

Her aunt seated herself on the other side of the fireplace. "That is certain. He pours every bit of heart and soul into caring for those children."

"Indeed," Constance added. "I daresay he was taken with you

before he even met you, so often did he inquire after you in the days before his departure to Fellsworth. I fear Mr. Bradford will have a very difficult time shaking you from his thoughts."

Now was the moment for Isabel to ask her question. "He did say something to me that was quite odd, though."

"Oh? That is surprising," Aunt Margaret exclaimed, her hand flying to her chest as if in shock. "Mr. Bradford is quite skilled at the art of conversation."

"Something he mentioned about my mother that took me quite by surprise."

"How strange," her aunt said, straightening in her chair. "What would he have to say about Anna?"

"He said she died of a fever on this property."

A strange frown tugged at her aunt's lips. "Yes? And?"

Growing frustrated, Isabel shook her head. "But that is incorrect. My mother died of fever, yes. But in London."

Her aunt and cousin exchanged concerned glances before her aunt spoke again. "No, dear. Your mother died here, at Emberwilde. But surely you knew that."

Isabel could feel the tears threatening, their heat fueling her frustration. Why were the women lying to her?

"No, I am quite certain." Isabel could not control the gradual increase in the volume of her voice. "My father told me quite plainly that she died of a fever in London."

Her aunt stood, her embroidery falling to the side. "Dear, your father is wrong. For she was my sister. I saw her take her last breath."

"But I don't remember this at all. Surely I would."

"You were only five years of age at the time. Of course you do not remember."

Isabel scrambled to make sense of what she was hearing.

"I can imagine this must be a shock. Your mother was my dearest friend, despite the pain her decisions put our family through. I know you understand the bond of sisterhood, for I see it when you interact with your own sweet sister. I would not tell you a falsehood, especially not on a matter so important. For whatever reason, your father did—or at the very least, you remember his account differently. I am so very sorry."

Isabel drew a sharp breath. Her stays felt too tight. Fire rushed her cheeks, then quickly dissipated, leaving her head light and her lungs thin. "What happened?"

Aunt Margaret's expression was sympathetic. "She went for a ride in the morning, and by the afternoon she had fallen quite ill. Your mother loved to ride. She loved it more than anything. You will notice that in the painting she is wearing a riding habit."

Isabel looked more closely at the painting, hungry for the details she missed on her previous assessments of it. But her aunt was right. She could see a riding crop grasped in her mother's right hand.

"When she married your father, they had no funds for a horse of her own. Your father was busy at his occupation, and she brought you here for a visit in an attempt to mend the family relationship. Our father was still quite upset with her after her indiscretion, but of course, Mr. Ellison and I could not refuse her request. That is why she was a guest at Emberwilde and not Heddeston Park.

"One winter morning she left Emberwilde before dawn for a ride. She took one of the horses out, alone. She was out of the habit of riding, and the day was wet and dark. I will never forget it, not as long as I draw breath on this earth. She went riding in Emberwilde Forest."

"The Black Wood Forest," breathed Isabel, drawing the connection.

Her aunt's lip twitched at the name. "Yes, some do refer to it as Black Wood Forest."

"But why would my father lie?"

Her aunt crossed the room and sat next to Isabel on the settee.

She took Isabel's hand in hers. "Who knows why grieving people say what they do? For I believe your father did love her, at least I can give him that. Word was sent immediately. He arrived in the black of night, inconsolable. I've never seen a man, before or since, so wild with grief and anger. He blamed us for her death, of course."

Isabel looked at her hands. That, at least, was not a surprise. For even though she did not know her father well, she did know of his extreme emotions.

"He refused to allow her to be buried in the family plot. Instead, he had her transported for burial in London and took you with her. My father, your grandfather, pleaded with him to allow you to stay and be raised either at Heddeston Park or here at Emberwilde. But I have never seen a man so enraged. So indignant. Eventually, we lost contact altogether."

"Heddeston Park?" asked Isabel, not recognizing the name.

"Do you not recall? That was your grandfather's estate, the very place where your mother and I were raised. I should have fought harder, I suppose, to have you here."

Isabel could hold the question in no longer. "How did you come to find me at Fellsworth?"

At this question, her aunt looked down at her hands. She opened her mouth to speak, then snapped it shut again.

Fearing that her questions were beginning to upset her aunt, Isabel remained silent. But did she not have a right to know about her own history and her own mother?

As if sensing the mounting tension, Constance leaned forward and covered her mother's hand with her own. "Don't you remember, Mother? Just recently there were the questions about Heddeston Park after Grandfather's death. The solicitor was trying to locate Mr. Creston, and—"

"No, no. That business was all settled long ago. After several years, I gave up hope of finding you. But as time passed, I continued to seek you out, and our solicitor did attempt to contact Mr. Creston. Then, in a stroke of good fortune, my cousin wrote to me with the news he had just met a man who knew your father very well. I cannot remember his name, but he remembered you quite well. His knowledge eventually led us to you."

Isabel's throat constricted. She wanted to challenge her aunt, to convince her that nothing of the sort happened and that the facts were as she had always believed. But then she sobered. To what end? What would she be fighting for? To preserve a memory that wasn't true? How much better to know the truth, regardless of how she came to know it?

Her aunt's expression held genuine sympathy. "Oh, my dear. This does explain a great deal. I am sorry to be the one to tell you."

Isabel looked back to the painting. Sorrow pawed at her, as if she had lost her mother all over again.

Chapter Twenty-One

*I*sabel could not resist.

Emberwilde Forest.

The Black Wood Forest.

Whatever its true name, it called to her.

She tried to rest in the heat of the late-afternoon sun, as Constance and Aunt Margaret did. Even Lizzie had fallen asleep in a restful nap. No doubt the effects of the past several days were beginning to catch up with her.

But Isabel could not rest. Not yet.

Were the trees black, as Burns had said?

Was the forest truly to blame for her mother's death?

She stood at the gate at the forest's edge, peering into the menacing shadows.

She bit her lower lip and looked over both shoulders before wrapping her fingers around the gate's iron handle and stepping from the light into the forest's dimness. Thick greens and coarse bark surrounded her, and coolness rushed her skin. She pulled her shawl closer and assessed her surroundings. A narrow footpath jutted to her right. The hairs on her neck prickled as a winged creature swept from one of the upper branches of a nearby birch, screeching. She bit her lower lip and cast a glance back at the gate before plunging deeper.

The path before her appeared in choppy bits. At times it was as wide as a road, rough and muddy, and at times it narrowed to be barely wide enough for her to place one foot in front of the other without losing her balance.

Drawing her shawl even tighter around her, as if gathering armor against a foe, she continued. Her heart beat wildly against her ribs. Not wanting her bonnet to block her peripheral vision, she loosened the silk ties and let it hang down her back.

She had expected the forest to be frightening, but the longer she was there, the more the tension in her shoulders eased. The place held a mystical allure. A mist settled on the forest floor, and the aroma of damp earth and cool leaves encircled her. Eventually the path opened onto a still clearing and then diverged. She stood still for several moments, deciding which fork to take.

She chose the one on the left, which curved away from Emberwilde. She was hardly one to know much about tracking, but she did notice footprints in the soft mud and dirt. With a quick look around to make a memory of the surroundings and which way she would need to return, she lifted the hem of her gown to prevent it from dragging in the mud.

The farther she walked into the forest, the cooler her surroundings became. Shadows became murkier; sounds became sharper. She did not know what she was seeking. But this time alone was good for her soul.

A twig snapped. She stopped short. Mere seconds ago bravery had infused every thought, but at the sound, she recoiled. She'd heard the residents of Emberwilde speak of foxes and even deer in this forest. Surely that was the sound she heard.

She hurried from her spot and turned a bend. The sunlight grew fainter and fainter, and the forest grew quieter and quieter.

At the school, she had never been free to explore on her own. Students and teachers were confined within the school's gates. The idea of being completely alone excited her. It felt wild and rebellious in a world that was controlled and dignified. It brought to mind the fairy stories that the girls at Fellsworth would read before bedtime, tales of hidden worlds and strange animals.

A new sound stopped her short.

Were those voices?

She cocked her head, straining to hear.

Yes, voices!

She stood still, attempting to identify the origin.

Then the clop of hoofbeats thudded on the damp ground.

A laugh. A horse's snort.

Her voice sounded odd and foreign in the woodland setting as she called, "Who's there?"

"You shouldna be here."

With a gasp, Isabel whirled around. A man, tall and thin, stood a few feet from her. His hat fell low over his eyes, and his black coat cloaked his frame. Even though she had heard a horse, she did not see one.

Her voice cracked. "I . . . I was only out for a walk."

"It's no good for a woman to be out alone in these parts. Didn't your mama ever tell you that?"

Isabel took a step backward, and she jumped when something snapped underfoot.

She fixed her eyes on him, afraid that if she broke her stare he would lunge at her. Her gaze lowered slightly to his hands. He held no weapon, nothing at all, but it was then she noticed—his left hand was missing.

Voices reached her from somewhere behind the man, and he looked over his shoulder before fixing his eyes once again on Isabel. "You will not be mentioning this little meeting to anyone, will you, lass? I would hate to have to pay you or your sister a visit."

Isabel's mouth fell open. This man knew who she was. And he knew about Lizzie. She snapped her mouth shut. She nodded in emphatic agreement.

The man glared at her for what seemed like minutes, a queer, frightening smile cracking his dirt-smeared face. He tipped his ragged cap to her and stepped back into the shadows. She stood completely still until the sound of his footsteps faded, but the pounding of the blood through her ears was deafening.

How many others were with him? Could they see her? Did they see her now?

She lifted her skirt enough to step freely. At first she backed away, but as her breath came to her in gasps, and as her imagination began to weave every sort of dangerous idea, she turned and ran. Her heightened sense of alarm disoriented her. Switches and branches tugged at her, and she screamed as she felt one snatch her face. With every step on the damp floor, with every labored breath and beat of her heart, her desperation to be free increased.

At length, a yellow glow of sunlight began to bleed through the leaves. She ran toward it. She ignored the pinching of her slippers and the dampness of the ground. She ignored the mud she felt splash up on her arms and skirt. She winced as yet another branch snapped her cheek. Her lungs began to burn. She did not look back.

She fixed her eyes on the bright spot ahead and ran.

Isabel's heart beat wilder. Faster.

Never had she encountered such a sinister-looking man. Her mind's eye recalled his uneven teeth. His sunken eyes. His missing hand. Never before had she felt so threatened. Her blood ran cold in her veins.

Her hair, which had been pulled from its pins by a low-hanging branch, blew in front of her eyes.

Blindly, she lifted her hand to move it away, and before she knew what had happened, she ran into something.

A strong hand grabbed her arm.

She screamed, and when no harm came to her, she shook her hair out of her face and opened her eyes.

There stood Mr. Galloway. His hand was still on her arm, gentle yet steadying. His face was very near her own.

Through the fabric of her gown, heat radiated from his bare hand. That sensation alone frightened her nearly as much as the man himself.

Mortified, she scrambled backward. "Mr. Galloway! You frightened me."

"I frightened you?" he asked, a comforting lilt to his voice. He was leading his horse with his other hand, and he adjusted the reins in his hands. "More likely something else did, the way you were running. What on earth were you doing in there?"

She swallowed, trying to figure out a reasonable explanation. "I . . . I was exploring."

"Most people don't go exploring in the Black Wood Forest," he exclaimed, then his gaze lowered slightly to her cheek. "You're bleeding."

"Am I?" She touched the spot with her finger. Now that she was aware of the wound, it burned and stung.

He pulled a handkerchief from his pocket and extended it to her, nodding toward her injury.

She accepted it and pressed the clean square of linen to her cheek. It smelled of soap and sandalwood. Fresh and comforting. She grasped for something to say. "How clumsy of me."

Isabel mustered her courage and met Mr. Galloway's gaze. His full eyebrows were drawn together in concern; his blue eyes fixed on her with a discomfiting intensity.

"I just walked too close to that branch, I am afraid. It caught my hair." She gave a nervous laugh and tried to lighten the mood. "Or maybe it was the ghost of Black Wood Forest trying to keep me here."

He winced at her statement. "What made you think there were ghosts in here?"

She felt as if she had been caught saying something she should not have. "Oh, nothing, just something Burns said. You know the stories."

She looked up at the brilliant canopy. Part of her wanted to tell him what had happened, as if doing so would somehow expel her fear. After all, he was the magistrate. This was something he would be interested in, wasn't it?

But she recalled the man's threat and remained silent. She wondered if he knew Mr. Galloway.

Nevertheless, he was calm and still, and she shook like a leaf quivering in the wind. In the magistrate's presence she felt safer. More confident.

"I must advise you to stay clear of the forest, Miss Creston," he said, his voice rough and low. "It's a dangerous place, and not because of ghosts." His deep voice was strangely comforting. "Mr. Ellison's gamekeeper set traps again last night. One could become injured if not careful."

She nodded and remained silent as they approached the fence, where she cast a sideways glance at her escort.

His hat was pulled low over his eyes, and the wind had blown his dark hair in reckless disarray. A day's worth of stubble framed his strong, square jaw, and side whiskers set off the brightness of his eyes. He certainly was not as polished or refined as the fashionable Mr. Bradford, but Mr. Galloway was attractive in his own right. She had never encountered a man quite like him—rugged, strong . . . and slightly intimidating.

His steps slowed as they approached the gate. "I will escort you back to the house if you like."

"No, sir. That is not necessary." Her words were clipped, and as they left her mouth she regretted their curtness. In truth, she would like nothing more than to have Mr. Galloway remain by her side, but the memory of her aunt's harsh reprimand prompted her to err on the side of caution. "I've no wish to distract you from your task."

"Not at all, Miss Creston. I am happy to be of service."

"No, sir. I thank you, but it is not necessary."

He shifted his weight from one foot to the other, as if hesitant to leave, and looked toward Emberwilde before fixing his eyes once again on her. "Very well, but perhaps it would be best if you did not mention this encounter to your aunt."

His gaze was so direct, his expression so poignant, that she could not look away. "Of course not."

He offered a hint of a smile, then bowed. "Good day, Miss Creston."

She opened her mouth to offer her farewell, but he was already walking back into the forest, his broad shoulders bushing against wayward branches, his boots crushing bits of leaves and sticks.

It was an odd request for her not to mention their meeting to her aunt, but given Aunt Margaret's treatment of the man, it was not entirely surprising. Isabel would not say anything about her encounter with Mr. Galloway, more to protect her own indiscretion than to expose his.

Regardless, that did not answer the question burning within her.

If the Black Wood Forest was so dangerous, what was Mr. Galloway doing there?

Chapter Twenty-Two

Colin was distracted.

He recognized the panic in Isabel's eyes. Having once seen it, fear was easily recognizable.

He watched her walk toward Emberwilde. Even though her bonnet was tied around her neck, it hung down her back, bouncing slightly with each step. She walked over the grass, her movements dainty, her figure swaying slightly. Her unforgettably blonde hair— the fairest he had ever seen—blew in wisps about her.

Beautiful.

How distraught she had seemed. She had tears in her eyes. A scratch on her flawless cheek. Her skin had been impossibly pale, making him wonder what exactly had happened to her in the forest. How odd that she should be drawn there. Most people ran from it.

Colin did believe her story. What reason could she have to lie?

Miss Creston was becoming a mystery.

A mystery he wanted to solve.

He turned his attention back to Sampson and patted his neck. "Well, boy, what do you make of her?"

The dappled horse nudged at his coat, searching for sugar or oats.

He slackened the reins and started walking to Emberwilde's main gate, where he had planned to meet Henry and McKinney. He arrived first, the sun high above him, vibrant in a clear blue sky.

"You're late," Colin exclaimed when the two men finally came into view.

"Sorry, Cousin. Couldn't get away. Business, you know," Henry said with a shrug, hopping down from the cart they had used to get there.

Colin looked up at the sky. He wanted to take advantage of the daylight. "At least you are here now. We'd best be moving if we don't want to be in the forest when the sun starts to go down."

Once the men were both free from the cart and had secured the animal, Colin began. "This is the plan. We've been unsuccessful to this point in our efforts to gain any undeniable evidence, and yet the activity has continued. We will confiscate the casks and crates and take them to the jail for the time being. Either those responsible will retaliate, which I suspect will be the case, or they will abandon the project. Either way, we will make progress. We'll bring Sampson to help us clear the crates. Come on, we've got work to do."

"What about Ellison? Or the gamekeeper?" Henry adjusted his hat on his head. "I thought they were going to join us."

Colin looked back toward Emberwilde. Yes, he had thought that Ellison was going to join them as well, but as it turned out, he was nowhere to be found. The scenario was growing more and more odd. For a man so intent on finding the source of the problem, Ellison had been curiously absent. It was unlike the older man to be forgetful or unreliable. But then again, perhaps it was unfair to judge a man in the midst of a financial crisis.

McKinney's steps were slow as he fell in next to Colin. "I don't see how I get roped into these things. I told you I wouldn't step foot in this place."

"You're too old to believe in such fairy tales. Stop your complaining. And remember—there's fifty pounds at stake."

The reminder perked McKinney's waning energy. "And it's all mine, mind you, if these are the kind of antics I have to put up with."

The men stepped into the forest and followed the path that had been worn into the soft earth. They made no effort to hide the fact that they were there. Someone did not want them around and had been willing to attack Colin to prove a point. But he did not frighten that easily. And something had spooked Miss Creston, he was sure of it. At least their actions today would incite a reaction—what kind of reaction remained to be seen.

They arrived at the cavern. Colin handed Sampson's reins to Henry and retrieved his lantern from the saddle. He opened the small door and entered the space. The scents of damp earth and wet wood surrounded him.

He raised the lantern high. The size of the crates struck him as odd. They were too large to fit through the entrance. The crates could have been constructed inside the cavern, but that seemed unlikely.

The soles of his boots sank into the soft mud. He noted how loose the dirt seemed, as if it had been disturbed recently. He pried the lid off one of the crates. Inside, glass bottles rested on tightly packed straw.

He investigated the rest of the small cavern. Stones provided the walls, and thick vines formed a roof. A patch of dirt in the wall caught his eye, glaringly different from the rest of the surroundings.

His imagination leaped to life as possible scenarios rushed him. Smugglers were a clever lot. From false-bottom boxes to hidden chambers, he was constantly amazed at the lengths to which these men—and women—would go to transport and hide contraband.

With his gloved hand, he reached out and scratched at the wall. It crumbled before him, and bits of rock fell to his feet.

"McKinney!" he called as the wall gave way. "McKinney! Get in here!"

A shuffling behind him signaled McKinney's arrival. "Hold on, mate. I don't fit in here too well." After a great bit of shuffling, McKinney muttered, "Well, I'll be. What is it?"

"It's got to be another cavern or a tunnel of some sort."

Colin knocked the opening free of hanging vines, then stuck his lantern through. Old bricks formed an arched ceiling.

"Where do you think it leads?"

"Hard to tell. I'm about to find out, though. Stay here," Colin said. "You and Henry watch this entrance."

"Where you going?" McKinney demanded.

"To see where this leads."

"Not so sure that is a great idea," his colleague warned. "Why don't you wait and—"

"I'm just taking a look. Wait here for me. Signal if anything odd happens."

He ignored McKinney's grumbling protests and stepped through the opening. As he did, his boot sank in several inches of mud. He pitched forward, almost falling over. Once steady, Colin lifted his lantern and stretched his frame. The space was wide enough for several men, yet he could not stand up to his full height.

Bits of vines, crumbling stones, and the stench of stagnant water verified that this was not a new tunnel. Far from it. Crudely cut stones had fallen from their positions in the wall and were treacherous in the darkness.

He lifted his sleeve to his nose. An animal had no doubt met its fate in here. He paused, jerked his neck cloth free, then tied it around his mouth and nose to block the stench. He rounded the bend, and the faint light behind him disappeared. He forged ahead, following an intricate series of bends and turns until he was quite turned around.

How odd to have spent so much time in this forest as a youth and not even know this tunnel existed. For, judging by what he saw, this passageway predated him by many years. Could this be the handiwork of the gypsies who were the basis of the local folklore?

He lost sense of how long he'd been walking. His back was

beginning to ache from his hunched position, and he reprimanded himself for not counting his steps to track how far he'd traveled.

Just when he was about to give up and turn around, a faint, white light glimmered ahead. He headed toward the spot and stopped in surprise. The tunnel forked into two different directions. He squinted as he looked down the left branch. The ceiling had given away. Grass and trees filtered down into the empty space, clinging to the sides and blocking the path. The opening to the ground above was a small one, but if he tried, he could work his way through. By his lantern's light, he studied the space for signs of activity, but a couple of inches of water stood on the crude floor. The foliage and surrounding dirt appeared undisturbed.

He backtracked to the main tunnel and took the other path. He walked for what he guessed to be several hundred feet until the tunnel finally came to an end with a series of steps that led up to a door in the tunnel's ceiling.

At the sight, his heart picked up its pace, not only at the excitement of a discovery, but also at the uncertainty of what was behind the door.

He climbed the short, narrow stairs and assessed the latch. As he was doing so, he noticed the light from his lantern catching on something shiny at his feet. He bent and picked up the object and held it to the light. A pocket watch. It was crusted with mud, but when he clicked it open, it was keeping time, indicating it had been wound at some point in the not-too-distant past.

He closed it, tucked the watch into his pocket to study at another time, and returned his attention to the door. It was fashioned so that it would open upward. For several moments he remained still, uncertain how to proceed. This door would open somewhere. But where? He had no pistol. He didn't even have a knife on his person— he'd left it on his saddle.

He had two choices. He could either open the door and see where it led, or head back for a weapon.

He sat for several moments and listened. Sounds of muffled dripping water met his ear, but other than that, silence prevailed.

He studied the door more closely and noticed a knothole in the wood. He poked his finger through it and felt heavy fabric.

He pushed at it, and it moved.

After considering his options, he decided to lift the door. He could feel something on top of the door shift. He moved it less than an inch.

He waited. No noise. No response.

He pushed it up just a bit farther and lifted his head. He blinked at the sudden onslaught of light. He could see a rough wood floor. It was dusty and dirty, but all was quiet. Slowly, he lifted the door the rest of the way.

He was alone in what appeared to be a toolshed.

He managed to climb through the door, careful to stay below the shed's window. His boots were wet and muddy. He would not be able to move in the space without leaving marks. If this was indeed an entry point for the smuggling activity, someone would be back.

He looked around and craned his neck so he could see out of the shed's single window. And then he saw it.

The back of the foundling home.

It made sense. The foundling home was on Emberwilde property, just like the forest. But why would a tunnel emerge here, in a toolshed of all places?

He returned to the steps and descended into the tunnel, letting the door drop slowly, hoping the cloth atop it would fall back into place.

He was growing weary of the stench. The murky floor. The tight walls. Carefully, slowly, he made his way back, past the fork to the other tunnel, past the rocks. Relief rushed him when he beheld the opening to the cavern.

"Well, you're a sight for sore eyes," exclaimed McKinney as Colin stepped back through.

Colin did not respond. He went straight to the door leading to the forest and burst through. He set the lantern aside and stretched his burning muscles.

"Was about to go in after you, not sure where you had gotten to. But the smell was so foul I decided against it."

"Thanks a lot," muttered Colin, untying his neck cloth from his face and inhaling a deep breath of the fresh forest air.

"What'd you find?" Henry asked, taking the lantern from Colin.

Colin sat on a log and kicked his boot against the side to dislodge the mud clinging to it. "Goes back quite a way and then forks. One of them leads to the forest floor. The other leads to one of the garden sheds behind the foundling home."

"What?" both McKinney and Henry exclaimed.

"It's falling apart in there. Dangerous, actually. I'm sure they're using it somehow. How else would they get the crates in here? And I found this." Colin pulled the pocket watch from his pocket and clicked it open. By this light, he was able to examine the piece closer. It had a white face, and the chain had been broken. He extended it toward Henry.

Colin's cousin frowned as he took the piece, held it up, and popped it open. Then he held it to his ear. "Hmm. Nice timepiece. There doesn't appear to be a marking or inscription, though."

Henry handed it back to Colin.

"I'll show it to Ellison. Perhaps he will know something." Colin returned the watch to his pocket and rested his elbow on his knee, turning his face into the bit of breeze coming through the trees. "Been in this forest all my life, and I had no clue those tunnels were there."

"That's why I don't come here." McKinney shrugged, sitting on a nearby log. "There's something wrong with the place. Secrets and tunnels, mischief and magic, I'm sure of it."

Henry ignored McKinney's statement and extinguished the lantern. "I've never heard of the tunnels either, but then again, I didn't spend as much time here as you did, Colin."

"That tunnel appears to have been here for ages." Colin used his sleeve to wipe the perspiration from his brow. "Someone has to know about it."

"But who?" McKinney asked.

Colin wondered the exact same thing. His first thought was Bradford, since the tunnel emptied onto the school's property. But that seemed unlikely. Bradford wouldn't step foot in a shed, let alone go about exploring tunnels. Besides, he and Colin had played in these woods together as boys. If one of them knew about the tunnel, it only stood to reason that the other would.

Colin locked eyes with his cousin. Henry had a sharp mind, and his ability to read people was impeccable.

Henry handed Sampson's reins back over to Colin. "Ellison?"

Colin took the reins in his hands and stood. It was true—who else besides the property owner would know of such a tunnel? Him, or maybe someone who worked for him, like Harding. But if they were somehow involved, why would Ellison have reached out to him in the first place?

McKinney rubbed his hands together, a twinkle brightening his eye. "Told you there was something not right in this forest. It's evil, and evil things happen here. So what are you going to do about this?"

"Not sure yet. First things first, let's break down these crates and take the contents to the jail for safekeeping. Let's get every-thing out. Also, I need to share this news with Ellison." Colin took a deep breath. "But things just got a lot more interesting."

Chapter Twenty-Three

*I*sabel's final gown was delivered just in time for the dinner at the Atwell house—her first true social event in Northrop.

She had never been a guest at such a dinner before. At Fellsworth, she had always taken dinner in the same manner, at the teachers' dining table in a room full of girls. Even since her arrival at Emberwilde, she had dined only with the family.

Tonight her nerves took flight within her, swarming her self-consciousness and fanning her apprehension.

Burns adjusted the lacing at the back of her dress, gently pulling the satin ribbon until it was flat against Isabel's ribs.

Isabel tried not to stare at her reflection in the mirror. Even more so than she had in the dress she wore to church and in the days thus far, she looked *different*.

With new stays her entire shape evolved. Curves were more pronounced. The change of hue against her skin made every feature appear different. The cut of her bodice made her neck appear longer.

"Lovely, Isabel. Simply lovely." Constance sat primly on the edge of the chaise lounge, her hands folded pristinely on her lap, her expression proud, as if she had just created a masterpiece. "That color is exquisite."

Isabel had never worn a lavender gown, not that she could remember.

"You were right about it."

Constance laughed. "Never doubt me when it comes to color, Cousin."

Isabel sucked in a deep breath as she assessed herself. When Burns finished with the lace, Isabel lifted the intricate overlay, then let it fall back into place. The gown was cut lower on the bodice and wider on the shoulders than she was used to. She touched the bare skin with her hand, covering it. She pivoted so she could see the back of the dress.

"You are worried about the cut, are you not?" Constance stood and crossed the room to stand behind Isabel. She looked over Isabel's shoulder into the mirror. "I assure you, this gown is entirely appropriate for an event like the one we are attending. I would not let you make such a misstep. You look divine."

Isabel nodded in silent agreement. She had told herself that this gown was an extravagance, a frivolous waste. There were so many other things to spend time and money on. But now that she was in it, now that she felt the fine silk underclothes against her skin and beheld the transformation in front of her, she silenced the battle within her.

She knew this was just a dinner, but to her, it was a brand-new experience—a welcome to a new world.

She turned to Lizzie, who was seated on the chair. Her sister was slumped, her elbow resting on the arm and her chin propped in her palm.

"And what do you think of your sister's dress, Lizzie?" asked Constance.

Isabel winced as she regarded her sister. Even in her new gown of pink striped muslin, she looked sad.

After a long pause, Lizzie sighed and lowered her hand. "It is pretty."

"Just pretty?" Constance interjected, acting shocked at the child's lack of enthusiasm. "Child, this gown is stunning."

But Isabel knew her sister. The dejected countenance was not about the gown.

She lifted her skirt, stepped over a hatbox, and knelt next to her sister. "What is wrong, dearest?"

Lizzie cut her eyes to Constance before fixing her attention on Isabel. Her lip popped out in a pretty pout. "I want to go. Why can't I go?"

"You know why." Isabel rubbed her sister's arm. "Such dinners are for adults."

Lizzie's frown confirmed her displeasure with this idea. She draped her arms over the side of the chair and let her head droop toward them.

"Besides, I fear you would find it terribly boring," Isabel said. "There will be no children, and you would have to sit still. You will have much more fun here, you will see. Burns has promised to keep you company all evening." Her lady's maid flashed a smile at the little girl. "You will like that, will you not?"

Logically, Isabel knew her sister would be fine. In fact, she could make the argument that Lizzie's constitution was stronger than her own. She was a fearless child almost to the point of recklessness. Still, a nagging guilt tugged at Isabel. "I promise you, I will come in and see you when I get home."

"But I will still be alone at some point." Lizzie's lip trembled. "What if a ghost comes and grabs me?"

Isabel frowned. "What would make you think that there would be a ghost here?"

"Burns told me so. She said there are ghosts in the Black Wood Forest."

"Excuse me, miss," Burns said, making a convenient exit from the room without looking at Isabel.

Isabel followed her sister's gaze out the window. A shiver traveled her spine as she recounted her own experience in the Emberwilde

Forest. Outside, the day was darker than it should be given the hour. A heavy rain pelted the earth, and tumultuous clouds pushed out the day's light. Thunder grumbled low, and an intermittent flash of light brightened the room. There, framed by the window, was the Black Wood Forest, swaying and bending to the storm's demands.

Isabel turned back to her sister. "It is called the Emberwilde Forest, not the Black Wood Forest, and there are no ghosts."

She stood and kissed her sister's forehead just as her aunt appeared in the doorway.

"Burns tells me you are ready." Eagerness heightened the woman's voice, but her smile faded when she saw the child. "Merciful heavens, what is wrong, Elizabeth? You are not ill, are you?"

Isabel tapped a warning on Lizzie's leg and the child sat up straight, but her smile did not return. "No, ma'am."

"Well then, what is the matter?"

Everything her aunt said seemed to take the form of a demand. She was a woman obviously used to a model of behavior that Lizzie had not yet perfected.

Too many seconds passed before Lizzie responded, so Isabel quickly interjected, "She is quite well, Aunt."

"No, she is not," her aunt declared. "I can see that she is displeased about something. I do hope you are not prone to sulkiness, Elizabeth. That is a terrible trait to find in a young lady, and I will not encourage that sort of behavior in my own home."

A little shocked at the bluntness of her aunt's delivery, and eager to prevent a dramatic display, Isabel wrapped her arm around Lizzie. "It is nothing, Aunt. I promise you."

Her aunt turned her harsh gaze on Isabel. "You should not be so eager to defend her, Isabel. If she is to be a lady, the time to start such training is now." She looked back to Lizzie. "Tell me, child, why are you in such a gloomy state?"

Isabel braced herself for her sister's response.

Lizzie, always brave, always forthright, spoke. "I do not wish to be left alone tonight."

"Oh, is that all?" Aunt Margaret waved her hand in dismissive annoyance. "Oh, my dear, you are spoiled in such respects, I do believe. Do you not know that it is important for your sister to meet the people of Northrop? It is important for you to learn to be as content when you are alone as you are when surrounded by people. I would think that that school of yours would have impressed upon you as much."

The candid interaction between her aunt and her sister weighed heavily on Isabel's heart.

Lizzie looked to Isabel. "May I be excused?"

Isabel nodded and moved back to the dressing table.

At Fellsworth, she could not have imagined leaving her sister for the evening. It was just not the way things were done.

But here, it was. They both had to adjust to the idea. It was the price they were paying for security. A small price.

Burns returned to the room, and Isabel sat still to have her hair dressed. The lady's maid took great care in brushing her hair, braiding it, and weaving silver strands through the end. It was curled. Pinned. Fresh flowers were tucked in the comb, and Isabel found the scent of the blooms sickeningly sweet.

At length, her hair was done. She was not recognizable.

Constance stepped behind her and hooked a delicate silver necklace around her neck. On the jewelry hung an amethyst pendant.

Isabel had never worn silver, much less a jewel.

When Burns was out of earshot, Constance leaned close to Isabel. "Mr. Bradford will not be able to keep his eyes off you tonight."

Isabel knew the words were intended as a compliment, but they felt more like an omen.

Every care was taken to keep the ladies' gowns clean and dry on the way to the Atwells'. The velvet cape draped upon Isabel's shoulders was far too heavy for such a warm evening, but she wore it at her aunt's insistence, lest her gown become soiled.

She felt almost ill as the carriage rumbled over the Benton Bridge and through the village. Uncle Charles had stayed behind at Emberwilde with a sore throat, leaving the ladies to attend the event without him. Isabel felt his absence, for her uncle had a calming effect on his wife. Without him, her behavior could be unpredictable.

The damp heat, combined with the motion and her nerves, made it hard to breathe. And she knew why. Mr. Bradford was to be at the dinner tonight. Her family's expectations were becoming increasingly clear. Part of her was excited to see him again, but another part of her was cautious. For even though Mr. Bradford was charming, she found that her thoughts had been turning to Mr. Galloway as of late. Their interaction in the forest had been pressed into her memory and burned more brightly than any encounter she had shared with Mr. Bradford. She did not know if it was the solemn blueness of his eyes or the safe feeling of being in his presence, but as much as she tried to deny the fact, it was Mr. Galloway who had begun to capture her imagination during the quiet times of the day. She wondered if he would be present at the Atwells' dinner.

She tried to shift her thoughts and focus on the scenery flashing past—the church. A graveyard. A small row of cottages.

Constance spoke, breaking the silence. "The Atwells are one of the most influential families in the area."

Aunt Margaret added, "Their estate, Hetford Abbey, is not nearly as large as Emberwilde."

"Indeed not," agreed Constance. "But given the limited social opportunities for our situation, they will do, plus their daughter is a dear friend of mine. I am sure she will adore you, Isabel."

Isabel nodded and lifted the cape's hood away from her neck to allow some air in.

"Heddeston Park, the estate where our grandfather lived while he was alive, neighbors Hetford Abbey to the west," Constance said.

The reference to her grandfather piqued Isabel's attention. Only a few times during her stay at Emberwilde had she heard reference to her grandfather. She could not help but wonder what the members of her extended family had been like. Had they been fair-headed like she was, and had they been feisty like her mother? Or had they been more like Aunt Margaret, set in her traditional ways?

"Heddeston Park?" Isabel asked with a frown, trying to remember any details she may have heard about it since her arrival.

"Yes, you are correct. Mother mentioned it to you, do you recall? Where your mother's portrait hung all those years."

"'Tis a shame, for it's hardly worth mentioning now," said Aunt Margaret. She folded her hands in her lap and looked out the window. "Abandoned. A ruin."

"A ruin indeed!" Constance laughed. "Really, Mother. A bit neglected, perhaps, but not a ruin."

Isabel spied her opportunity to learn more. "Is that the home where you and my mother grew up?"

"It is, the very one."

"It is one of the oldest homes in the area," Constance added.

"And in terrible disrepair," Aunt Margaret repeated. "Worthless. It's nowhere near as large as Hetford Abbey. And Hetford doesn't begin to compare to Emberwilde."

"It is not as large," said Constance, "but it is beautiful, and it is home to Drannen Gardens, well known as one of the loveliest rose gardens in all of Surrey. The weather is far too unpleasant for you to see it tonight, but perhaps another day when the weather is fine we can show it to you."

Aunt Margaret frowned.

"I should like that very much." Isabel could feel her energy returning. "But it stands empty now?"

"Yes, which is such a pity," mourned Aunt Margaret. "My father's solicitor is in contact with the heir, but no one has lived there these many years."

Isabel struggled to keep her seat when the carriage hit a rut. "And who is the heir?"

"No one you know," said Aunt Margaret.

"A distant cousin," confirmed Constance. "You know how such estates are. They are very complicated."

Isabel remained quiet. No, she did not know how these things went. Not firsthand, anyway.

But she was curious. Her mother's home.

She felt as if she should see it.

"I wonder—" she began to ask.

"Isabel," Aunt Margaret said, much more loudly than necessary in the confines of the carriage, "I do think we should speak with Mrs. Atwell tonight about making a contribution to your efforts at the foundling home. I think she will be most interested in the efforts you and Mr. Bradford are planning, and surely she will want to support them."

Isabel blinked. "Y-yes, Aunt. If you think it best. Provided Mr. Bradford agrees."

Aunt Margaret pressed her lips into a firm line before speaking. "He need not agree."

Despite the rain and wind, Isabel and the Ellisons were dry when they arrived at Hetford Abbey. Large torches lit the gate, their flames lurching in the harsh elements.

At her aunt's bidding, Isabel returned her hood to her hair. Her excitement compounded as she saw other carriages line the drive.

"So many people!" she exclaimed, impressed by the grandeur.

"Oh, my dear, this is but a small gathering. I do wish we could limit this to only the people suitable for your acquaintance. But then again, it is not our gathering, is it? The Atwells are far too lenient, I believe, when it comes to their guest list."

Isabel looked at the house in awe. No, it was not nearly as large as Emberwilde, but it was elegant. Constructed of red brick, the home rose several stories high. Large windows blinked with warm light. A wide white portico supported by four evenly spaced columns welcomed guests, and a grand staircase ushered them inside.

For a moment, Isabel's amazement relieved some of her distress: her concerns for Lizzie, her loneliness for her friends at Fellsworth, her worries over her future. For at the moment, she felt excitement bubble up in her.

Isabel followed her aunt and cousin up the grand staircase. Torchlight flickered on the gathered carriages and footmen. She followed her cousin, taking great care to make sure her behaviors and actions matched Constance's.

"Merciful heavens, is this Miss Creston?"

Isabel resisted the urge to shrink back as a woman stepped forward and took her cheeks in her hands. "Oh, I would know you anywhere!"

Her aunt motioned toward Isabel. "Mrs. Atwell, may I present my niece, Miss Isabel Creston. Isabel, this is Mrs. Atwell."

Before Isabel could respond, the woman reached forward and embraced her. "You are the very image of your mother. Oh, how I do miss her! You are most welcome here, Miss Creston. Most welcome."

After the woman released her and more introductions were made, Isabel followed her cousin to the parlor. She met several people. The Wassons. The Tilden family. She met the Atwells' daughter, Anne, who was Constance's dear friend. Everything was sparkle and beauty, wealth and extravagance. But then, to her aunt's point, there were several guests in plainer clothing. Isabel felt at turns both out of place and at ease. All around her, people chatted and laughed, and her nerves swirled and danced within her.

When Mr. Bradford was announced, her heart fluttered as wildly as any schoolgirl's. Now that she was here, the nerves she had experienced in the carriage were shifting to feelings of anticipation. She allowed herself to get caught up in the evening's extravagance and excitement.

Mr. Bradford looked around the room as if searching. Heat rushed to her cheeks when his gaze landed on her, for she had been caught staring. But his reaction calmed her. A smile tugged at his lips, and he offered a bow, their eye contact never breaking.

He greeted Mrs. Atwell, then crossed the room to her.

He bowed to Isabel's aunt. "Mrs. Ellison." Then he turned to Constance and Isabel. "Miss Ellison, Miss Creston."

Her head swam with all of the expectations placed upon her. The glowing candles around her were making her warm, or maybe it was Mr. Bradford's proximity. She could feel his own warmth through her gown's gauzy sleeve. The heat in her cheeks would not dissipate.

It felt foreign to stand next to a man, yet pleasant. She tried to forget the thought she had of Mr. Galloway in the carriage ride over and focus on Mr. Bradford. After all, his manner was so easy, so effortless, so perfect. And he was so attentive to her.

Aunt Margaret and Constance excused themselves, feigning the need to speak with a lady across the room.

It was a contrived move clearly intended to leave Isabel and Mr. Bradford alone.

But it was not as awkward as she had thought it would be, for in truth, she was growing more comfortable in his company. How could she not? And since her family deemed him safe and appropriate, why shouldn't she?

"I fear I owe you an apology, Mr. Bradford."

"Oh? I cannot imagine you doing anything for which you would need to apologize."

"You are too kind, but I must." She fidgeted with the bracelet at her wrist. "For you see, you were right. About the Emberwilde Forest and my mother."

He seemed to sober at the mention of her mother. His smile faded, and he cleared his throat. He cast a glance over to her aunt before speaking. "You must believe me, had I known you were unaware of the situation, I would never have said a word."

She drew a deep breath and met his gaze. "No, you were well within your rights to bring it up. It is right that I should know the truth about my mother's passing."

"How is it that you had no knowledge of it?"

"I suppose my father thought it best to withhold the details."

"Regardless, I am still sorry to have been the one to tell you."

A loud laugh came from the foyer, and Isabel angled herself to see past Bradford.

Coming through the door was Mr. Colin Galloway. Her heart sank, though, when she noticed a beautiful, raven-haired woman on his arm.

And Mr. Bradford seemed to slip to the back of her mind.

Chapter Twenty-Four ————

$\mathcal{C}$olin stepped into Hetford Abbey's foyer, fully—and uncomfortably—aware of the possessive hold Miranda had on his arm.

He had arrived at this dinner with his aunt, Henry, and Miranda. As they exited the carriage, Henry assisted his aunt, and he assisted Miranda.

Ever since he arrived at Lockert Cottage earlier that evening, Miranda had acted as if their conversation in the stable never took place. Quite the opposite was true. She was bright and poised, and yes, he had offered her his arm to assist her, but she now clung to him with assertive confidence.

With a toss of his head he shook his hair from his face, and with his free hand he raked his fingers through the locks. He would not be rude to his cousin's widow, but until he more fully knew his heart, he would not give her reason to hope for more.

Within moments, however, one of Miranda's friends called her away, and he was left to observe the room on his own. Dinners at the Atwells' were always interesting, for the guest list never failed to include a wide range of people. Many familiar faces were in attendance, from landowners to tradesmen. It was a remarkable social mix, the sort of mix that he found most entertaining.

In truth, however, he had come to see just one person in particular.

Henry stepped next to him and folded his arms over his chest. "Sure is an improvement over the boardinghouse."

Colin could not disagree. He scanned the room as they moved from the foyer to the front parlor, seeking Ellison. He patted the found timepiece in his pocket and hoped to share it with Ellison that night, but the man was nowhere to be seen. Colin's growing suspicions about Ellison's potential involvement in the smuggling disturbed him. He knew a man's moral fiber could be tested when faced with true hardship, but he did not want to think his old friend had succumbed.

His attention shifted to a much more pleasant topic, Miss Creston. The blemish on her cheek seemed to be gone, and the smile had returned to her face. He had hoped to speak with her as well, but it would be trickier to have a conversation with her here than at the forest's edge.

His jaw clenched when he noticed who stood next to her.

Bradford.

Henry must have read Colin's mind, for he leaned closer and lowered his voice. "Seems Bradford is wasting no time. Word about town is that he is quite smitten with her."

Colin accepted a glass from a passing footman but did not drink from it. He turned away from the pair and surveyed the room. "Miss Creston is a beautiful woman. For all of Bradford's faults, he is not a dimwitted man."

Henry followed suit and turned away as well. "Miss Creston is charming, to say the very least, but from what I have heard she hasn't a farthing to her name. We both know Bradford is hardly a romantic. He would never marry a woman for her beauty alone. But if he is expecting her uncle to set her up with a dowry, he is sure to be disappointed."

Dinner was announced, and the guests began to shift. Henry's words echoed within Colin. He had not considered Bradford from Henry's perspective. He cast a suspicious glance back over his shoulder at Bradford, whose expression was light. Perhaps his intentions toward Miss Creston were honorable. Perhaps not. Time would tell.

Isabel was surprised by the number of guests at the Atwells' party.

She was even more surprised by the dinner's seating arrangements, for she was seated nowhere close to her aunt or cousin. No doubt the place settings had been carefully ordered so that family members could converse with other guests.

But she had never expected to be situated between Mr. Bradford and Mr. Galloway.

When her aunt had realized where her niece was to be sitting, she pulled Isabel aside. Her expression was severe, her tone direct. "Remember what we have discussed regarding these gentlemen, Isabel."

The words held a warning of sorts, but Isabel did her best to ignore her aunt's overbearing instructions and simply enjoy her evening.

She sipped from a crystal glass and assessed the faces around the table.

Just down the table from her was the young woman who had arrived on Mr. Galloway's arm. Her expression was pinched, and her lips were set in a fine line. Clearly, she was not happy about being seated so far from Mr. Galloway.

Isabel straightened and actually found herself quite comfortable. However, the man to her left affected her in a much different way than the man to her right. Mr. Bradford praised her. Flattered her. Spoke eloquently and of lofty ideals. Mr. Galloway, on the other hand, was quiet, and she found his solemn nature intriguing. Whereas there could be no doubt of Mr. Bradford's esteem for her, she was not certain of Mr. Galloway's opinion. After all, he had seen her running from the forest as if a banshee were at her heels. He had witnessed her fear over her sister riding a horse. He had endured her panic when she thought Lizzie injured.

Whereas Mr. Bradford prattled on about nothing of importance, Mr. Galloway was silent, tall and straight in his chair. He smelled of cedarwood and the outdoors. She cast a nervous glance around the table, for she knew her aunt watched her every move.

She studied the myriad of utensils surrounding her dishes. Normally, when faced with such an overwhelming ritual, she would simply follow her cousin's actions. But at the moment Constance sat on the opposite side of Mr. Galloway, which made it quite difficult to see what she was doing.

Isabel drew a breath and pitched forward slightly, attempting to nonchalantly peer past Mr. Galloway. The last thing she wanted to do was embarrass herself, not with a gentleman at each elbow, nor did she want to appear rude by not partaking.

So focused was she on her dilemma that she had not realized Mr. Galloway had ceased eating and leaned in toward her.

"Do you need something, Miss Creston?"

She froze. So Mr. Galloway had noticed her.

She could not help but laugh in spite of herself. How silly, a grown woman trying to imitate the actions of another. "I fear I am about to expose one of my many faults to you, Mr. Galloway."

"And why do you say that?"

She lowered her spoon. "You know I came from a very simple school. Dinners there were not nearly so complex. This silverware is lovely, do not misunderstand me, but I fear my education was geared more toward forming my moral convictions, and not so much which utensil to use when."

He smiled and lifted his napkin to the corner of his mouth. A good-natured chuckle emanated from him. "Is that all? If you are worried about what I think, then allow me to put your mind at ease. Believe me when I say the last thing I would notice about you is which utensil you are using."

She warmed under what she presumed was a compliment.

"Is that all?" she repeated, knowing full well that he would understand the playful nature in her voice. "You might not take it so lightly if you lacked such skills and worried what others might say of you."

"First of all, you are wrong on that account. I truly do not care. But in truth, my aunt made certain that my table manners would rival that of Freddie Ellison's at least. At one time the members of my family were frequent guests at Emberwilde, and my aunt made sure we knew what to do. Of course, we were children then, and took our meals in the nursery upstairs, but still, that's no excuse for poor manners. Or so I'm told."

The thought of Mr. Galloway as a child was amusing to Isabel, although she could not quite place her finger on why. He was such a controlled man, carefully guarded in his words and actions. How would a person like that act as a child?

Mr. Galloway took a drink and continued. "Of course, I credit my aunt for such knowledge. But my true education on such things did not come from home, as one might expect, but from the officer I served under in the army."

"The army?" she exclaimed. "How so?"

"My commander held the firm belief that even though we were at war, we were gentlemen, and a gentleman's manners must always be on display."

His tone suggested that he thought the idea ludicrous, but she sobered. She had heard of war conditions. She had read of them in the papers. The thought of Mr. Galloway in such a situation tugged at her compassion.

She checked to ensure that Mr. Bradford was engaged in another conversation, and convinced that he was not listening to her conversation with Mr. Galloway, she spoke. "I have heard that you and my cousin Freddie were friends," she said.

He leaned back from his plate and nodded. "Yes, we were very great friends. His fearless nature and my desire for adventure landed us in many exploits, I can tell you."

"Yes, Constance has told me that her brother was a bit reckless."

"That is one word for it, I suppose. But he did not act alone." Mr. Galloway smiled, as if reliving a memory. "We did have a number of escapades."

She felt brave. "In the Emberwilde Forest?"

He nodded. "Yes, in the Emberwilde Forest. A perfect place for exploring and hunting. We also spent a great deal of time at Heddeston Park. Have you been there yet?"

"My grandfather's estate? No, I have not."

"My property is on the far side of your grandfather's estate. It is called Darbenton Court. The main house was destroyed years ago, but the fact remains that your grandfather and I were at one time neighbors. There is a pond on my property, and we spent many afternoons fishing."

"It sounds lovely. I should like to have met my grandfather. I mean, I am told I met him when I was very little, but I do not remember."

She was aware of how intently his eyes were on her. "He was a good man. And a kind one. Your grandfather's steward served as steward for my property while I was still a boy, and he still assists with the tenants on my behalf."

"Do you have no wish to do that yourself? To live on your own property and manage your own estate?"

"Maybe one day. But for now, I work with my tenants, and I am kept quite busy with my work as solicitor and magistrate."

"How is it that you became magistrate, Mr. Galloway?"

"Well, it actually found me more than the other way around." He offered a warm smile. "A magistrate must be a landowner. Your uncle, Mr. Atwell, and others forwent the honor, and so that left me. I can hardly complain, though. There is always something new afoot. I rather enjoy the challenge."

She looked toward Mr. Bradford once again to make sure he was otherwise occupied before speaking. "Speaking of my uncle and my cousin, I understand that Freddie's death altered your family's relationship with my family's."

The question had crossed a line, she knew. But if she did not ask him, she would only know her aunt's side, a tale in which Mr. Galloway's reckless nature convinced her only son to sign his life away to the army.

At first she thought he was not going to answer, but at length, he lowered his napkin and leaned closer. "Freddie was my best friend, Miss Creston. His death continues to have a profound effect on me. It was not my idea to join the army, at least not initially. We were at university at a time of great patriotism, and Freddie, well, Freddie was insistent. He wanted to break free from archaic expectations, and I know he expressed as much to his father on several occasions. In hindsight, perhaps I should have discouraged his enthusiasm. After all, his family made their hopes very clear. But we both believed in the cause, we were both eager to be free from certain connections here in Northrop, and that idealism of youth is difficult to dampen."

"And you? Did you not have expectations placed upon you by your family?"

He wiped his mouth with his napkin. "Our situations were very different. I had already realized my inheritance. Looking back on it now, I should have stayed at Darbenton and taken my rightful role. I had a disappointment in my life that I did not handle well, and unfortunately, at the time I did not realize how significant a role the war should play in my future."

Isabel looked down at her napkin. She was unsure how to respond.

But then she lifted her head. He had a small smile and was looking at her. "I know your aunt and your cousin blame me for his death. I swear I would have given my life in a heartbeat to save his. But war doesn't always work out that way. I do not know what your opinion is, but I hope you do not judge as harshly."

They locked eyes for several moments, moments that seemed to bind her to him in some inexplicable way. In fact, in a moment of honesty she felt as if the rest of the room had somehow faded into the background, and her desire for a genuine conversation flamed within her. She wanted to share something of herself as well—to talk about the sorts of things that would certainly be discouraged.

Isabel felt movement at her elbow.

"You two seem very intent on your conversation," Mr. Bradford said. Isabel felt herself stiffen. His voice held its typically amused lilt. Normally that lilt was charming, but at the moment it irritated her. She turned to him.

"Do we?" Isabel asked, feeling a bit uncomfortable, as if caught doing something wrong.

A smile creased Mr. Bradford's face. "But then again, can I fault Galloway? You are such a charming partner, Miss Creston. I can see without a doubt why he would try to keep you from speaking with other gentlemen."

The thinly veiled insinuation made Isabel flush.

"Not at all," Mr. Galloway said. "I should hope that Miss Creston feels at liberty to speak with whomever she would like."

She settled uncomfortably between the two men, wishing there was anyone else with whom she could speak.

With every passing moment, questions began to rise concerning Mr. Bradford. He seemed unusually possessive, and not in a manner that made her feel appreciated or valued. Quite the opposite was true.

Chapter Twenty-Five

*D*inner passed quickly for Colin—in the best sense.

Miss Creston had completely captured his attention. Their conversation had been enjoyable. Hers was not the polished, practiced conversation of her cousin, but there was sincerity in it, an honesty that was refreshing. He could have spent the entire evening conversing with her and was sorry to see it come to an end.

After dinner she withdrew with the other ladies, leaving the men to their port. He was as far from her as he could physically be at the moment, and yet she remained on his mind.

Later in the evening, the gathering moved to the music room for the entertainment. Chairs had been placed around the elegant room. He was seated between his aunt and Miranda, and he found himself watching the mantel clock, eager for the next portion of the evening. The room was thick with ladies' perfumes—lily of the valley, rose, lavender, and every other floral scent. Several of the young ladies played and sang. Miss Creston did not.

Did she play the pianoforte? Sing? He watched her from the corner of his eye. She seemed to enjoy the performances, but when asked to sing, she politely declined.

Miss Atwell had played the pianoforte, and now Miss Ellison entertained them.

Miss Ellison had long been known throughout the area as the county beauty. It had not surprised him to learn that her mother had arranged for her to marry a wealthy banker. As the youngest Ellison daughter, she had been destined for such a match.

Miss Ellison began to sing. Her voice was strong. Elegant. Expertly trained.

His gaze shifted to Miss Creston. She was situated between Mrs. Ellison and Bradford. Miss Creston's attention was focused on her cousin's performance.

Miss Creston carried herself with a countenance far different from the other Ellison women. She surpassed them in beauty, but something beyond her fair features captured his imagination. She was unlike anyone he had ever met. At different points during their dinner conversation, she had shared with him about the time she had spent with the children at the foundling home, and her distress over the abandoned baby at the Holden farm had been sincere. He could not imagine one of the Ellison ladies, or even Miranda, for that matter, reading with the forgotten children of Northrop. Yes, the conversation stayed with him. Impressed him. He watched her, perhaps a bit too intently, but at an otherwise dull gathering she was as a breath of spring air.

His gaze shifted slightly to the man next to her. Bradford, as always, was dressed impeccably, with a bright white cravat, patterned waistcoat, and knee breeches. His posture was straight, but his chin was tilted toward Miss Creston. His eyes were on her instead of the performer.

When the music ceased, Bradford leaned toward Miss Creston and whispered. He smiled, a bit too familiarly.

Colin watched with interest for her reaction. He had hoped to see her pull away, but she sat still, and when he finished saying whatever it was he had to say, she smiled. A dimple pierced her flawless cheek.

He drew a sharp breath, already annoyed at Bradford's possessive ways. Colin had no right to have an opinion on this matter, he knew. But Miss Creston seemed so innocent, and Bradford was not.

Miranda's voice interrupted his thoughts. "She is a beauty, is she not?"

Colin snapped his head up, feigning distraction. "Hmm?"

The guests applauded Miss Ellison's performance. She stood from the bench and curtsied.

As Miranda clapped, she said, "You were staring. At Miss Creston."

He knew Miranda had been watching him. She had been displaying a quiet interest in Miss Creston since her arrival at Emberwilde, making only a few comments about the newcomer.

Colin did not respond. He only added his applause to the rest.

Under cover of the noisy applause, she said, "There was a time you looked at me in such a manner."

Colin stiffened.

She shifted toward him. Perhaps he had been wrong to resist Miranda in the stable the other night. Deep down, he knew that a part of him would always love her. She was entwined with his life, and she always had been. Aunt Lydia was supportive of the idea. Little Charles needed a father. Everything about the arrangement would make sense. He thought they had left things at an understood place in the stable that night, but her behavior was suggesting otherwise.

His hand could still feel the warmth of hers. It had been warm and soft, just as he remembered.

He sneaked one more glance at Miss Creston. If he were truthful, it was the idea of Miss Creston that prevented him from entertaining the idea of Miranda. Bradford said something to her, and again she smiled. Perhaps she was happy in her arrangement, but he could not be. Something in him had changed since meeting Miss Creston. True, their interactions had been limited to formal conversations and the occasional impromptu discussion. But her

Sarah E. Ladd

very presence had awakened the sorts of feelings he had long since buried.

As if reading the thoughts running through his mind, Miranda said, "If it is Miss Creston who is the object of your affection, I daresay you have competition."

Colin followed Miranda's gaze back to Bradford, whose head was thrown back in obnoxious laughter. He sat too closely to Miss Creston. He commanded her attention too possessively.

Miranda straightened as the small audience rose from their chairs and began to move about the chamber. "I notice Mrs. Ellison is offering no reprimand of his shocking display. But then again, she likely has little problem with this arrangement, for if she did, she would have the two of them separated so fast your head would spin. She's always had a soft spot for him, you remember."

Signaling the end of their conversation, Miranda stood and crossed the room to a group of ladies.

She was right. Mrs. Ellison had always favored Bradford. And now, judging by the interaction he was witnessing, Mrs. Ellison thought him a good match for her niece.

When the other young ladies approached Miss Creston, Bradford stood, bowed an exaggerated bow, and looked around for another conversation partner.

Bradford's watchful eyes landed on Galloway.

A pinch of annoyance turned Colin's stomach. He stood, realizing that he was too late to escape, for Bradford was headed his way.

He braced himself for an unpleasant conversation. On his way over, Bradford took a glass of brandy from a footman. Then he stood shoulder to shoulder with Colin, their backs to the wall, and scanned the activity in the room.

"Enjoying yourself, Galloway?"

Colin nodded.

"I heard about that nasty business after the boxing bout. You

202

look to be recovering all right, though. It's a sad sign of the times when a man must be wary walking to his home, is it not? But I don't suppose I have to tell you that, being the magistrate and all."

Colin bristled. Part of him wanted to ask Bradford how he knew about the attack and what he had heard. It was odd that the attacker had given him such a physical warning then failed to follow through after Colin so obviously disrupted the cavern.

Did Bradford know about the tunnel? He'd lived on the property for several years now, and Colin could not help but wonder.

At length, Bradford spoke, a wry grin curving his lips, his eyes fixed on Miss Creston. "She's a lovely addition to Northrop, is she not?"

Colin did not want to discuss Miss Creston with Bradford. The mere mention of her raised a defensive warning in his mind. He only responded, "She is."

Bradford gave a low, dry laugh. "You say that so unenthusiastically. There is not a doubt in my mind that you have noticed her."

Noticed her? Little else had occupied his mind since last seeing her in the forest. The very thought of her tugged at him. He could not forget the expression in her eyes. She was searching. Wandering.

And he could relate to that empty, desperate ache.

Colin cast a glance toward Bradford from the corner of his eye. The other man's expression was hungry too. But it was a lustful, selfish hunger.

Bradford continued. "She is beautiful. And charming. And her story is most interesting. I hope to be able to learn from her about her experiences at her school so that I might apply them to the foundling home. As I am sure you have heard, her help has become quite indispensable to me. Quite honestly, I don't know how we managed without her."

Bradford was attempting to incite jealousy, but Colin's concern for Miss Creston grew. The desire to protect her from Bradford's chameleon-like nature burned brightly within him.

He listened to Bradford praise her beauty. Her clever wit. Her keen sense of humor and attractive innocence. He remembered Bradford saying similar things about Miss Ellison before her engagement had been announced. Perhaps Bradford's interest in Miss Creston was genuine. Any man would likely be drawn to her, though Colin suspected it was the Ellison fortune, prestige, and net worth that Bradford found most alluring.

But then the topic took a turn.

"I hope you don't mind my saying so," Bradford started, the tone of his voice growing sober. "But I have seen you and McKinney in Emberwilde Forest, lurking around like you're stalking prey. What are you doing there? Playing hunters?"

Colin's jaw clenched at the snide joke, but he would not let Bradford get the upper hand. "Like I told you. There is suspicious activity in the forest, and we have been investigating."

Bradford's thick eyebrow rose in patronizing interest. "Oh? Are you still about that business?"

Colin shifted his weight from one foot to the other. There was no need to hide the fact the investigation was intensifying. Besides, it was in Bradford's backyard, a place where children played and learned. Now that he was aware of a possible threat, he owed it to the children to notify Bradford of foul play, even if it was only a suspicion. His only concern was regarding how much information he should share.

"We were investigating the forest the other day, and we discovered a tunnel."

Bradford's voice was rich with surprise. "What sort of tunnel?"

"An underground tunnel. It ends in a shed on the foundling home grounds."

"On our property?"

"Yes, a shed in the back garden. The door lifts up into the shed's floorboards. It has one window and is rather small."

Bradford frowned and shook his head. "I know it. I don't think anyone but the groundskeeper has been in the shed in years. I've never even been in it."

"Well, as I said, there is another entrance to the tunnel. But I thought you needed to be aware."

Bradford stiffened, but any trace of sincerity fled from his voice. "Thank you for letting me know."

"If you see anything of a curious nature, please notify me. I think we have the situation in hand, but any information is always helpful."

Colin was grateful to end the conversation on a business note as opposed to a discussion about Miss Creston. He stepped away, but he was far from comfortable—or relieved.

But then something made him stop. The memory of the pocket watch burned in his mind. Bradford was just the sort of well-dressed man who would be in possession of such a quality piece. He turned toward Bradford. "Do you by chance have the time?"

Bradford shrugged. "Sorry. I don't have a watch with me. I'm sure Wasson has his. He's right over there."

"Of course." Colin smiled in parting, but his mind was beginning to fit pieces together. Perhaps Bradford was not as ignorant as he proclaimed.

Chapter Twenty-Six

*L*ate that night, or perhaps very early the following morning, the rain stopped. The intermittent clouds cleared just enough to allow the white moonlight to stretch to the ground in fleeting glimpses. Isabel checked on Lizzie as soon as she returned from the Atwells and found her sister asleep in her chamber.

Her mind was alive with the evening's events as Burns helped her undress and unpin her hair. Burns stoked the fire before leaving, and Isabel moved next to the blaze to brush her hair, each movement slower and sleepier than the previous.

She indulged in a yawn and stretched in preparation to retire. A knock sounded at her door.

"Yes?"

Her chamber door cracked open, and Constance stepped inside. "Are you to bed yet?"

Isabel lowered her brush. "Not at all. Come in."

She rarely saw Constance with her hair down. If it were possible, her cousin was more beautiful now than ever. Instead of carefully controlled curls and elegant gowns, she was in a simple white sleeping gown. It was nice to see her cousin in an unpretentious state, one not overly manicured or primped. She seemed approachable, more vulnerable.

Constance hurried over to Isabel, drew a small ottoman closer, and sat down. "It is so nice to have another woman my age to talk to after such an evening! My sisters and I used to gather and talk about the night's details. But then, one by one, my sisters left, and I have been alone with no one to talk to. But now that you are here, I thought we could start our own tradition."

Isabel smiled in response. She understood the idea of camaraderie. The idea of starting a new tradition appealed to her. She returned her brush to the small table next to her and moved closer to her cousin, enthusiasm shaking off her sleepiness.

Constance stretched her fingers toward the fire and sighed. She slumped her shoulders in an uncharacteristic lack of decorum.

Isabel was happy she felt so comfortable around her as to shed her pristine manners.

Constance raised her eyebrows. "Did you have a pleasant time tonight?"

Isabel looked to the darkened ceiling as if to relive the evening's experience. "I did. It was unlike any dinner I had ever attended."

"Well, you might as well grow accustomed to such gatherings, for now that you are here you will find that we spend time with those families quite often. Some more than others, mind you, but it at least gives you an idea."

Isabel leaned her temple against the side of the chair and looked to the fire. There were parts of Emberwilde that were difficult to adjust to, but evenings such as this were intriguing.

"He is quite taken with you, you know." Constance toyed with the end of a long lock of hair.

Isabel knew to whom Constance referred. "He is just kind, I think."

"No, no. I have known Mr. Bradford a very long time. All of my life, in fact."

Isabel did not disagree, but something in her opinion of him had changed over the course of the evening. "I cannot help but wonder why he has not settled."

"Oh, some men are restless. I think he is of that sort. He has proven himself, and has done his bit for humanity in the way of the foundling home." Constance ducked her head down and to the side, as if to study Isabel more closely. "And yet, I sense that you are not convinced."

"I suppose the idea is still so very new. I know I should trust Aunt's guidance, but something about him seemed a bit different tonight. I can't quite put my finger on it."

"But you cannot judge a man by one night's interactions. Think of all that he has done in the past."

"There are just so many unanswered questions that linger in my mind about his character. Oh, I do not doubt his charms. He has those in abundance, but something about him seems amiss at times. At one point Aunt mentioned that he lost his family's estate. How did that happen?"

"It is a reasonable question." Constance's countenance sobered. "In the months following his father's death, he made poor choices regarding his finances. It was fortunate for him that Mother and Father believed in him enough to support his endeavors, otherwise who knows where he would be today. A loyalty was forged between the families that cannot be broken. A bond of sorts."

Isabel gave a nervous laugh. She did not know why she should, at this point, begin to question Mr. Bradford's reputation. "I am sorry if I sound mistrustful. You must know how new this sort of talk is to me."

Constance waved her hand. "Oh, Isabel, this sort of thing is all I have talked about since I was old enough to form words. My mother has been planning for my marriage for as long as I can remember."

Isabel wondered what it would be like to have someone fuss over her and plan with her. "I should like to meet your fiancé one day."

"I've no doubt you will meet him very soon."

Whether it was because she was tired or growing closer to her cousin, she could not help but ask, "Do you love him?"

Constance flinched, as if shocked by the question, and then her practiced smile returned. "I am very fond of him, which is important. But love is not always necessary for a desirable match."

The remark, which rang with an air of rehearsed exactness, did not sit well with Isabel. She had always thought that if she married at all, it would be for love.

An awkward silence ensued.

"I must say, you seem awfully quiet on the matter." Constance playfully arched an eyebrow in Isabel's direction.

An odd sense of self-consciousness washed over her.

When Isabel did not respond, Constance continued. "There were other young men in attendance tonight. Any one of them could be considered extremely handsome."

"Who do you mean?"

"Oh, I don't know, just thinking my thoughts aloud. You are lovely, and you naturally draw the attention of young men." She looked down and hesitated before speaking. "But Mr. Galloway was the most handsome, do you not agree?"

Isabel could feel the heat rushing to her face.

"Oh, you poor dear!" exclaimed Constance. "You are blushing, and I had no intention of embarrassing you. But as your cousin, it is my responsibility to keep an eye out for these sorts of things, and I watched him. I daresay that Mr. Bradford could well have competition."

The memory of her time spent in conversation with Mr. Galloway rushed her. She could almost smell the scent of leather that seemed to accompany him always. "I don't know what you mean."

Constance laughed. "You can pretend all you want that you do not know what I am talking about, but every woman, regardless of her upbringing, knows when a man is taken with her. Perhaps that is what has put doubts in your mind about Mr. Bradford."

Isabel bit her lower lip. The memory of Mr. Galloway's hand

on her arm and the warmth in his eyes affected her in a way that no interaction with Mr. Bradford would.

Instead of trying to understand it, she said, "But your aunt dislikes him so."

"That is true. Do not mistake me, my mother can make a match to rival anyone, but she is so set on a good financial match that she might overlook a match of the heart. Only you can know that." Constance stood from her ottoman and shook out her gown. She tilted her head to Isabel and smiled a sleepy smile. "As for me, I care only for your happiness and security. I must go to bed now. You should get some sleep too."

Constance turned to leave, but then she paused. She stepped to the small table next to Isabel's chair and lifted Mary's needlework. "What is this? Did you make it?"

Isabel stood and closed the space between them. "My friend Mary gave that to me when I left Fellsworth."

"What does it say?" Constance tucked her hair behind her ear and angled the linen toward the light to see. "What a beautiful little poem."

"It's a psalm," Isabel corrected, tracing the stitches with fondness.

Constance seemed satisfied with the answer and straightened. "Hmm. Very pretty. Well, I am exhausted. I am going to bed. Good night, dear Isabel."

Isabel stood in her chamber and waited for the door to close behind Constance. Linen still in hand, she crossed the room to the window. Her fire was beginning to wane, and the room had become quite dark. She pulled aside the heavy velvet curtain and saw that more of the moon was evident now, its bright white light crisp. Mere hours ago an angry rain pummeled the earth, but soon dawn would arrive, fresh and clean.

She leaned her forehead against the cool glass. How she wished the window would open. She could use some fresh air. Moonlight touched the edges of the Black Wood Forest.

Isabel read the second half of the psalm. *In the morning will I direct my prayer unto thee, and will look up.*

As if obeying, she lifted her eyes toward the sky. Dawn was still a few hours away, and the unsettling feeling that she was going to have to make more life-altering decisions in the not-so-distant future hung heavily on her heart. How she missed Mary and the advice she would give. Mary was always so confident and self-assured.

Of course, her aunt and cousin meant well, but they had a different way of seeing the world.

Isabel rubbed her finger over the smooth, perfect stitches once again, returned the needlework to the table, and climbed into bed in hopes of being swept away in sleep's solace.

Chapter Twenty-Seven

The night following the Atwell dinner, Colin and McKinney were returning from a nearby village. They'd met with a farmer who saw a child stealing a chicken from his yard.

It was a sad sign of the times, for such crimes were becoming all too common.

Darkness had fallen, and the men were taking the main road past Emberwilde on horseback. It was a chilly night, damp with gray fog. Silence surrounded them, and save for their horses' hooves on the soft road, all was quiet. Colin fixed his eyes on the woods as they rode past. The mist was shifting, and blackness shrouded all. It was easy to mistake the uneven shadows for moving people. His eyes were tired, but worse than that, his spirit was tired. Even Sampson seemed unusually slow and solemn.

"Long day," exclaimed McKinney, stretching a large arm over his head to release the kinks in his back. "I told Martha to keep the stew hot until we returned."

"Good thought," Colin added, but his mind was far from his stomach.

"Feels like old times, doesn't it, out and about? Been awhile since we've had so many things to tend to."

"You say that like it is a good thing." Some men did not mind the business. It could be quite lucrative if one was willing to walk both sides of the law. But Colin was not one of those men, and it made his job all the more difficult.

Their path took them by the foundling home.

How he wanted to go investigate the shed he had seen earlier. He doubted it was being used, for it had been very dusty.

The stone house stood tall in the night air. No lights winked from its windows. No foggy smoke puffed from the chimneys.

But it was not the windows that caught his attention, nor the lack of chimney smoke.

Two men were walking along the school's fence, near the forest.

Colin slowed his horse's pace and reached out to tap McKinney's arm. Once he had McKinney's attention, he nodded toward the two men.

As they drew closer, one of the profiles was startlingly clear. He recognized the pair as those who had been with Bradford at the boxing match.

Colin jerked his head in their direction to get McKinney to follow him.

They approached cautiously. The lack of light made it almost impossible to tell if the men were armed, but it was wise not to make assumptions. At least he and McKinney were on horseback—a distinct advantage.

"Awfully late to be out in this part of the town, don't you think, gentlemen?"

"Oh look! It's the magistrate," exclaimed Dent, almost amused.

McKinney leaned his arm on his leg and looked down at the men. "You two stayin' at my inn tonight?"

Dent looked to Stanway before answering. "Yeah. And?"

"Going to be locking up for the night shortly. I'd advise you to return before too much longer lest you be locked out. I'm not about to get out of my bed to let you in."

"Can't fault a man for taking an evening stroll, can you now?" Stanway asked.

"We don't often see strangers here in town this time of night,"

Colin stated, not breaking eye contact with the man. "There's nothing down this road that would concern you."

"Well now, that's not your place to say, is it?"

Stanway sniffed in amusement as his friend's cockiness, but then Dent lifted his hand. "Obviously these men are sensitive about something here. None of our business, is it, Stanway? Like I said, we're just two men out for a walk to get to know the village. We're here quite often now, so we might as well learn to make ourselves at home. Didn't think it was a problem for a man to go for a walk this time of night, but I guess you do things different here in Northrop."

Colin bristled. It was almost as if a threat was hidden within Dent's words, a challenge.

Dent shifted, and then Colin noticed an unusual attribute about the man. He was missing his hand.

"Good night to you, gentlemen," exclaimed Dent.

The two rough men resumed their walk toward the village, and Colin followed them with his eyes.

After the men were out of earshot, McKinney said, "I don't trust either one of 'em."

Colin urged Sampson forward. "I don't either."

The sky started to drizzle as they headed back to the inn, and Colin could not shake the sense that these men had a part to play in the odd events in Emberwilde Forest. But he still did not have any proof.

At that moment he thought of Miss Creston, and the fear in her eyes as she came running out of the forest a few days prior. Maybe she had seen something. Perhaps it was time to start broadening his search a bit more.

Chapter Twenty-Eight

*W*here was Lizzie?

About a week after her visit to the dinner at the Atwells', a gentle breeze wafted through the open window, gently lifting the lacy curtains around the canopy bed and teasing wisps of hair around Isabel's face.

She had asked her uncle about having the nails removed. He had no qualms about it, and only yesterday a footman had been up to take them out. The window, although a bit stuck, now was open. She surveyed the manicured lawns, the lush forests, the vibrant sky, and the puffy clouds.

When they first arrived, Lizzie had visited Isabel in her room each morning. But as she had grown more accustomed to Emberwilde, she became more adventurous and would often venture out before Isabel was even awake.

This was one of those mornings.

Isabel had waited for Lizzie to join her, but when her sister did not come, Isabel rang for Burns, who rose early and would often help Lizzie dress. Within moments the lady's maid arrived, a tray of tea balanced on her arm. She set it on the table.

"Good morning, Burns," Isabel said, stepping to the tray and helping herself to a cup of tea.

"Good morning, miss. I hope you slept well."

Burns stopped short when she noticed the window.

An uncomfortable silence hung in the room as Burns stared. At length, she spoke. "I see the window has been opened."

"Yes, I asked my uncle and he had the nails removed."

Burns stepped away from it, shaking her head as she did so. "Maybe you know what you are doing. But I've seen things, and I still don't think this is a good idea."

Isabel ignored the tremor of uncertainty that coursed through her at the older woman's words. She did not believe in ghosts or omens or any of the sort.

She quickly changed the subject. "Have you seen my sister this morning?"

"Miss Elizabeth was up with the crows. She had her breakfast in her room and went down to see the horses. Do not fret, miss. If you don't mind my saying, it is good for the child to be out in the fresh air. There is nothing quite so lovely as dawn at Emberwilde. Everyone says so."

Isabel could not disagree, for the delicious breeze dancing in the room and the vibrant garden out of the window called to her as true as any birdsong. If this was to be their home, it was only right that the child should be at ease. Isabel had not spoken to anyone about the Emberwilde Forest since her conversation with Mr. Galloway, but the topic ran wild in her mind. At first she thought to warn Lizzie to stay away from it, but she feared that would only pique her sister's curiosity. In all likelihood Lizzie was down at the stable. She'd become fast friends with Carter, adored Caesar, and was hard at work renaming every pony, horse, and cat.

Isabel swallowed the dread that rebuilt itself nearly every morning. Lizzie should move about freely and without fear. But one glance out of the windows and her heart clamped within her. The stranger's threat echoed in her mind.

Isabel grew restless as Burns helped her with her stays and took her time fastening the tedious buttons down the back of her gown. Each button seemed as if it were caging her in. She did not want to insult the maid, but her speed seemed impossibly slow, and by the time she reached the final button, Isabel felt about ready to burst from the confines of the gauzy fabric.

Once free, she stepped away. "Thank you, Burns, I can finish from here."

A frown pinned Burns's face. "But your hair, miss. I've not even touched it."

From the corner of her eye Isabel could see her unruly, light curls. She had never been out of her chamber with her hair in such disarray. At Fellsworth, she would have been punished for such an oversight.

Here, she would be reprimanded as well.

Begrudgingly, she returned to the chair and allowed Burns to draw a comb through the curly strands, wincing as the woman caught on a tangle. They sat in silence, Burns focused on her work and Isabel with her eyes fixed on the window facing the Emberwilde Forest.

She hurried Burns along. She wanted to keep a sharp eye on her sister.

Colin slowed his steps to match Ellison's more labored ones. Ellison had missed the Atwell party due to an illness, and today was the first day he had been well enough to meet with Colin to discuss the progress of their investigation. Even now, Ellison seemed unwell.

They had just returned from a walk in Emberwilde Forest, where Colin had shown Ellison the tunnels. The contraband was still being removed, and Ellison had placed two of his hired men to watch the forest. The effort seemed to curtail activity for the time being.

"It seems everything is secure, but for how long?" mused Ellison. "The Emberwilde Forest is a large one. Who knows where else they have these tunnels."

"We'll not give up. We will find them and stop it at the source. And I have been meaning to ask you, have you thought any more about the watch that we discovered?"

Ellison frowned as he lumbered down the cobbled path.

"This is where I leave you, unless you fancy a bit of a beverage."

"No, thank you. I am taking your advice, you will be happy to know. Later today I am meeting with some of my tenants who have fallen behind on rent. My goal is to arrange for them to clear the main estate lands in lieu of back rent. Hopefully we can reach an agreement with them on the terms. Like you said, there is no time like the present."

Ellison's face brightened at the news. "There now, that is good news indeed. Mark my words, you'll have that property up and running in no time."

Colin watched as the older man headed up the stairs. He had thought he was far too mature for such feelings, but it felt good to know the older man was proud of him. Since Colin's uncle died, Ellison had taken him under his wing and offered him a great deal of guidance—some of which he took, and some that he let be. But he respected the man's experience, and even despite his financial trouble, Colin trusted his advice.

Colin turned to take the path to visit Harding and McKinney to go over a few more details regarding the forest. As he did he soaked in his surroundings and drew a deep breath. There were worse things, he mused, than visiting the Emberwilde estate. The morning light bathed the green surroundings in a yellow glow that warmed his shoulders and back. The sun shone on wealth and power, security and privilege. This was what so many aspired to.

Yet for him, satisfaction could not be found in such things. He wanted justice, but more importantly, he craved freedom. And, to his surprise, companionship.

Every time he visited Emberwilde his attentions seemed to

wander, and at some point he would scan the landscape, looking for Miss Creston. Normally, she was nowhere to be seen, but today was different.

She was at quite a distance, but there could be no mistaking her for her cousin or one of the servants. But something seemed amiss. Her gait was unusually quick. She looked to be pacing. She stopped, stared in the direction of the forest, then turned back to the walled rose garden and entered it.

Curious, Colin resumed walking and guided his horse alongside him toward the garden by the fence that separated them from the woods. He arrived just as she was exiting.

Her hair whipped around her face in the morning wind, and she was alarmingly pale.

He stepped through the gate and gave a bow. "I hope I am not intruding. I saw you from across the lawn as I came through the gates."

She did not smile, nor did she greet him with the customary curtsy. "Good morning, Mr. Galloway. Did you by chance see Lizzie?"

Colin squinted in the morning sun and propped his hand on his hip, surveying the surrounding lawn. "I did not."

"It is very odd, for I cannot find her anywhere." Miss Creston knitted her fingers together. "When I awoke this morning she had already left her chamber."

Colin kept his voice calm, as if to counteract Miss Creston's rising anxiety. "I shall keep my eyes open and let you know if I see her."

At this, the slightest hint of a smile twitched the corner of her full lip. "I would be very grateful. I thought for certain she would be at the stable, but Carter says he has not seen her yet this morning."

"I would not worry. There is plenty to do to keep a child occupied on this property. I am sure you will find her in a garden or climbing a tree or something of the sort."

At this her shoulders lowered. "I think my aunt might frown upon that."

He leaned toward her and whispered, "Then perhaps it is best she doesn't know."

He thought he noticed a smile. She turned to leave, then stopped. "It is nice to see you, Mr. Galloway."

The soft sincerity in her voice touched him, the gentle sound breaking down wall after wall around his armored heart. "It is a pleasure to see you as well. And do not worry."

She looked out toward the woods again, almost like a lost child herself, fearful yet curious, cautious yet bold. She clutched the white fabric of her skirt in her hand, dropped a quick curtsy, then turned from him and walked in the opposite direction.

She left like a vapor, making him wonder if he had actually encountered her or merely imagined it.

Chapter Twenty-Nine

$\mathcal{C}$olin pulled his horse to a stop at the edge of Emberwilde Forest.

It was a shock of blue, bright blue—a color not normally found in the forest—that caught his eye.

He slid from the saddle and approached the blue item lying at the base of a tree. It was a doll. The toy's porcelain face was smeared with dirt and grime. He held it out before him, assessing it as if he had never seen one before.

Lizzie.

Who else could it belong to?

McKinney's voice cut the silence. "What's that?"

Colin looked back over his shoulder, having momentarily forgotten that McKinney was with him.

"It's a doll."

"I can see that." McKinney dismounted and snatched the doll from Colin's hands. "Those blackguards will smuggle anything into this country. Best take it with the rest of the contraband."

"Normally I'd agree with you, but there is a young girl staying at Emberwilde at the moment, do not forget," he stated, remembering Miss Creston's morning search for her younger sister. "'Tis far more likely that it belongs to her."

Colin moved to take the doll back, but a noise made him stop. Shuffling.

"Stay here," Colin ordered, and then he grabbed the doll away.

He looked down and saw small footprints in the soft ground. They led him to a giant yew tree surrounded by some brush, then disappeared through a small opening under one of the roots. A tiny scrap of lighter blue peeked out.

Colin knelt and popped his head in through the opening. He heard the child scrambling, but when their eyes met, she drew her knees up close to her chest.

He extended the doll, almost as a peace offering. "Does this belong to you?"

Lizzie eyed him, then angled her head as if to peer behind him. With a hesitant hand she reached out to take the doll, her eyes not leaving him. "Are they gone?"

A sinking feeling coursed through his stomach. "Is who gone?"

"The men with the black dog."

Colin reached into the brush and extended his hand to help the child out. She stared at it for several moments.

When she did not take his hand, he asked, "There were men in the forest?"

She nodded.

"Do you know who they were?"

She shook her head.

He had no wish to frighten her with an onslaught of questions, but he had to know. "Had you ever seen them before?"

She finally spoke, her small voice high and soft. "No."

She looked scared—legitimately scared. In his brief encounters with this child, she had seemed almost fearless, from her first pony ride to the mishap with the ducklings.

"Did they hurt you?" he asked, keeping his voice as gentle as possible.

She fixed her large eyes on him. "They did not know I was here. I hid when I saw them coming."

Colin offered a smile. "Smart girl."

Lizzie finally accepted his outstretched hand and he helped her to her feet.

She ran her hand down the front of her skirt. It was covered in dirt and dead leaves. If her aunt were to see her in such a state, she would be horrified. But Colin suspected something more unsettling than simply a dirty dress. He helped her from her hiding place.

"What are you doing out in the forest? Didn't your sister or aunt tell you it was not a good place to play?"

She looked to McKinney and ignored his question for several seconds. "Yes, Isabel, Aunt Margaret, and Burns all told me, but I wanted to see the fairies."

"Fairies?" he repeated, a bit amused. "What made you think there are fairies here?"

"The girls at the foundling home said that there are fairies and creatures in the forest. They said they see them sometimes. I wanted to see one too." She fixed her eyes on McKinney and leaned close to Colin. "Who's that?"

"That is Mr. McKinney. He is a friend of mine." He knelt next to her. "Your sister is looking for you. She will be happy to know that I have found you."

Lizzie wrinkled her nose. "Do you think she will be mad?"

"She is worried about you. She cares for you very much."

Lizzie frowned and looked to the ground. Her chin began to tremble.

"But there is nothing to be worried about. All is well, right? See here, I want to show you something."

It did not take him long to find one of the gamekeeper's traps half covered with leaves and forest debris. He knelt down on the ground not far from it and pointed. "See that piece of black metal over there?"

She nodded.

"That is a trap. It is what the gamekeeper uses to catch hares, and if you accidentally step on it, you can be hurt very, very badly. Do you understand?"

Again she nodded, and this time she swiped her hand across her face, smearing dirt.

He reached for his handkerchief. At the rate he was encountering Creston females in the forest, he was going to run out of handkerchiefs. He wiped away the dirt near her eye, then gave the cloth to her.

"You must promise me not to come into these woods alone again. If you want to come in, I am sure your uncle would bring you. But it isn't safe for young ladies alone."

She nodded, but he doubted she heard his warning, for she refused to let her chosen topic of conversation drop. "Have you ever seen the fairies, Mr. Galloway?"

"There is no such thing as a fairy."

"If you have never seen one, then how do you know?"

The corner of his mouth tugged. She was a clever little thing. "Just promise me you will not come back in here."

"Because of the ghosts?"

He shook his head. He was being bested by a child. "There is no such thing as a ghost either."

"But why would people talk about ghosts if they aren't there? Ellie said—"

"I do not know who Ellie is, but I can promise you as surely as I am standing here, there are no such things as ghosts. Now, I know you like horses. Would you like to ride on mine?" He did not want her walking in the forest at all. "His name is Sampson and he is very friendly."

She nodded eagerly.

Lizzie felt light as he lifted her up on his saddle and set her sideways on it. He lifted a chunk of mane and directed it to her. "You hold on tight to this. Do not let go, all right?"

She smiled and leaned over to look at the ground, a smile lightening her face. "I have never been on a horse this big before."

He cast a glance over at McKinney. "I am going to take her back to the house. You coming?"

McKinney jerked his head to the side. "No. I am going to head to the site."

"I will meet you there shortly. Just let me get her away from these traps."

Isabel had been pacing the property all morning, watching, waiting.

She'd alerted the staff to the fact that her sister was missing. The housekeeper stated she had seen Lizzie earlier that day and told her not to worry, that children would be children.

Isabel mentioned to her aunt that Lizzie was nowhere to be found, and her aunt simply replied that if given more discipline, Lizzie would show more respect for rules and regulations.

Aunt Margaret's jabs at her ability to care for her sister thrust deep, adding to the unspoken rift that had already seemed to form between the two women.

Mr. Galloway had been the only person to take her concern seriously, or at least he had seemed to.

Perhaps if her family was aware that there were strange men in the forest, as she was, they might feel differently. She now regretted her decision not to tell anyone, but was it too late?

She had been invited by Constance to visit Miss Atwell with her that morning, but she decided against it. She could enjoy no company until her sister was found.

Later in the afternoon, Constance returned and emerged through the music room doors and onto the broad veranda, bonnet in hand.

"If you are going to be out in this sun, you should at least put a bonnet on. The last thing you want to do is freckle. Your cheeks are already getting pink."

"You've returned," Isabel muttered as she turned and accepted the bonnet, but the last thing that concerned her was the shade of her complexion. Not when her sister was alone. Each passing hour Isabel's mind churned with the possible scenarios, but none echoed louder than the rough man's warning. But then Isabel saw a gray horse break the tree line, and on its back, a small figure in blue. Mr. Galloway led them.

With a sharp little cry Isabel let the bonnet fall to the veranda's stone floor, and she flew from the space. Throwing propriety aside, she quickened her steps to a jog, then slowed when she saw a smile on Lizzie's face.

She was safe.

With the knowledge that her sister was not in danger, anger began to flush through her. She'd gone into the forest! What had the child been thinking?

"Lizzie!" she exclaimed as her steps brought her closer to the horse, Mr. Galloway, and her sister. "Where in heaven's name have you been? I've been beside myself with worry!"

Lizzie's smile faded. Isabel noticed the mud smeared on her cheek and on her pinafore. She looked at Lizzie's face. Her smile had transformed to a frown, and her eyes were downcast.

Isabel immediately regretted the sharp bite to her words and looked to Mr. Galloway for clarification.

He cleared his throat before speaking. "I was tending to some business in the forest, and I found her there."

A fresh wave of panic washed over her. The words of the handless man echoed in her mind for the thousandth time. "What were you doing in the forest, Lizzie? You have been told not to go near it."

Mr. Galloway helped Lizzie down from the horse, the movement swift and effortless. His patience and tenderness struck Isabel like a sudden, unexpected light. He smiled at the child and held her steady until certain she had her footing. Lizzie looked so small next to him.

But what tugged at her heart the most was the manner in which Lizzie looked at him. Her smile was genuine, her expression trusting. Mr. Galloway held the horse's head low so Lizzie could brush the soft muzzle with her hand, then he straightened.

Without prompting or reminder, Lizzie offered an unbalanced curtsy to her rescuer and in her most grown-up voice said, "Thank you, Mr. Galloway."

Mr. Galloway returned Lizzie's address with a slight bow, but did not move.

Lizzie ran toward Isabel.

Isabel's heart flipped when she did. For how could she stay angry or upset? She was only happy that Lizzie was home. Safe.

Isabel knelt in the grass as her sister drew near and put her arm around Isabel's shoulder. Lizzie's pinafore was covered with mud. It marred her stockings. It was even in her hair.

Isabel brushed her sister's dirty cheek and softened her voice. "Lizzie, what were you thinking? What were you doing in the forest?"

Lizzie lowered her voice and whispered. "There were men, and I got scared."

Isabel forced a swallow. Her throat felt dry. Too narrow. She exchanged a somber glance with Mr. Galloway before returning her attention to the child. The thought of her small sister, alone and tiny in the presence of such men, unsettled her to her very core. "Tell me the truth, Lizzie, did they hurt you?"

The child shook her head, her damaged ribbon floating in the spring breeze, her tousled hair tangled and catching in the mud on her cheek. "No. They didn't see me at all. I hid, but they found my doll's blanket and took it. I want it back."

"Well, a blanket is a small price to pay. You could have been hurt very badly, do you understand?"

The child bit her lip and nodded.

"We need to get you cleaned up, and preferably before Aunt sees you." Isabel lifted her gaze to Mr. Galloway. He, too, was smeared with dirt. But at the sight, she felt relieved.

When no one else at Emberwilde would take her concerns seriously, he came to her aid.

"Run on in now and go to your chamber," she said to Lizzie. "Take the back stairs and ring for Burns. She will help you. Whatever you do, try to avoid Aunt, all right? I will be up in a few minutes."

She stood and watched as the child walked back to Emberwilde with very fast, very controlled steps.

She did not turn back to Mr. Galloway until she saw Constance escort her sister inside. "I can't thank you enough, Mr. Galloway. I don't know how long she would have stayed hidden if not for you. It seems you are developing quite a habit of assisting those who meet trouble in the forest."

She was about to turn and follow Lizzie when Mr. Galloway's words stopped her. "I do not wish to take much of your time, Miss Creston, but I was hoping for a moment."

Her instinct was to follow her sister, but the gratitude she felt toward him fixed her to the spot. "Of course, Mr. Galloway."

"That day when I encountered you leaving the forest. You were upset. Are you sure that nothing happened? That you encountered no one? I do not wish to pry, but in light of some recent discoveries, it is important that I know."

Isabel swallowed the lump of concern forming in her throat. It had been easy to pretend that the man who confronted her all those days ago was not real or a viable threat, but someone frightening her sister was another matter entirely.

It was time to share what she knew.

She looked up to meet Mr. Galloway's eyes. His gaze was gentle and patient, and something within her stirred under the directness of his attention. His quiet nature made her confident. Such a sharp contrast, she noted, to Mr. Bradford. Whereas Mr. Bradford always seemed to talk over her, or her aunt always seemed to be telling her how to act, Mr. Galloway genuinely wanted to know what she had to say. It was refreshing.

She drew a deep breath. "I did encounter a man in the forest that day."

Mr. Galloway's jaw tightened. "Did he hurt you?"

"No, no, but we spoke, and he did threaten that if I told anyone I saw him, he might harm Lizzie. And so I did as he bid and told no one."

Mr. Galloway adjusted his stance. "Did you by chance recognize the man?"

Isabel shook her head and bit her lower lip. "I'm not yet familiar with all the faces of Northrop, of course. The only thing I remember with accuracy about him is that he was missing one of his hands. His left one."

She studied his reaction to see if the description meant anything to him, but his expression remained stoic. He cast a glance toward the upper windows of Emberwilde, then fixed his gaze on her. "Thank you for letting me know, but please, do not worry."

They stood for several moments in silence in the late-afternoon sun. Somewhere a bird's call rang out, and a pleasant breeze swept through.

Now that Lizzie was safe, Isabel found that she did not want to leave Mr. Galloway's presence. He exuded quiet strength. Still patience. He probably wondered a dozen things, such as why she did not inform her uncle of such an event. "I hope this news is helpful and not a burden."

The corner of his mouth lifted in a kind, subtle smile. "You could never burden me, Miss Creston." He hesitated, then took another step toward her. "I do not think your aunt and cousin know about this investigation, and your uncle has asked to keep it that way. It is perhaps for the best to keep these events to yourself."

She nodded. "Of course."

He bowed and then mounted his horse. He nodded in her direction before looking to his left, and his profile cut a handsome line against the brilliant sky. Her pulse, which had been beating at am impossible rate, seemed to slow.

She had expected everything to change upon coming to Emberwilde, but she had not anticipated such alterations to her heart.

Chapter Thirty

*I*sabel walked back to Emberwilde, flooded with relief. She let her thoughts linger on Mr. Galloway. And she smiled.

She knew how she must look. Her hair was loose, dirt was on the hem of her new dress, and she did not know if it was smeared on her face or not. She needed to make sure that Lizzie had changed, but she needed to change as well.

She went through one of the servants' entrances and climbed the back stairwell. Before she went to her own chamber, she stopped at Lizzie's. She opened the door, fully expecting to see her sister inside, but as she stepped into the room, no sound met her ears.

Her sister was not here.

Isabel frowned and assessed the room. It looked as if the girl had not come upstairs at all. Isabel returned to her own chamber and rang for Burns.

But it was Constance, not Burns, who appeared in her doorway.

"Constance!" breathed Isabel. "Do you know where Lizzie is? I cannot keep up with that child today."

"She is down in the parlor with my mother."

Dread snipped at Isabel.

Constance looked a bit pale as she continued. "Mother has asked that you join them."

"Are you all right?" Isabel asked, brushing dirt from the side of her gown, noting the change in her cousin's complexion.

Constance offered a little laugh. "Of course. Speaking of spoiled gowns, you should change as well. Here, I will help you."

231

Isabel accepted Constance's assistance, and before long she was in a fresh cream-colored gown.

"Much better," exclaimed Constance, stepping back to assess Isabel.

Something still seemed amiss about her cousin's breathlessness. "Are you sure there is nothing wrong?"

"Absolutely positive."

Growing more concerned, Isabel followed Constance to the parlor.

Her aunt appeared in the doorway. "There you are, at last! I was beginning to fear you'd gotten lost, and I was about to send Beasley out in search of you. But here you are, so no harm done. Come in here. I've a surprise for you."

Isabel did not much care for surprises, so she wiped her cheek again with the back of her hand and stepped into the chamber, bracing herself for what might await.

Bright afternoon light filtered through the tall west windows, the leaded glass casting its skewed geometrical shadow on the carpets and furniture. The sound of Lizzie's laughter drew Isabel's attention to the back corner of the room. Her sister, still clad in the gown that displayed the forest's muck and mire, was seated next to a woman in gray.

Once they noticed her, the new woman stood, and Lizzie jumped up and ran to Isabel. "Isabel, look!"

But whereas Lizzie showed great enthusiasm, the woman, whom Isabel judged to be about ten years her senior, remained stone faced, her expression pinched and her eyes fixed.

"Isabel, this is Miss Smith. I've engaged Miss Smith to be Elizabeth's governess."

Isabel snapped her attention to Aunt Margaret. A wave of indignant energy rushed through her. Her words left her lips before she had the opportunity to check her tone or volume. "Governess? No, no. Lizzie does not need a governess."

Her aunt raised her hand. "If Elizabeth is to become a proper young lady, then we must see to her education. We've already lost much time."

"Lost much time?" she shot back. "I am not sure I follow your meaning."

Desperation washed over Isabel, inciting anger and frustration simultaneously. But it would never do to lose her composure. Her aunt seemed to feed on such lapses in control. Calm. Isabel knew she had to stay calm.

"I have been seeing to my sister's education, and we are quite content with that arrangement."

"But consider, your circumstances are different now."

"The circumstance has not changed. I am as capable of teaching her as anyone."

Her aunt stood and crossed the room. Isabel froze as the woman touched her back and whispered to her. "There is no need to cause a scene, Isabel. For can you see to Elizabeth's French and Italian? Her dancing and etiquette? You might be fine to teach the children from where you came. Indeed, you are well suited to educate the children of our foundling home, and I imagine the demands on your time will only increase. But as long as Elizabeth is under my roof, every care will be taken to ensure she becomes a lady, despite her past. All of these things I mentioned are necessary, but you, admittedly, cannot teach them to her. Elizabeth has a brilliant future ahead of her. And I've no doubt she will be a beauty, to be sure, but we must start preparing for her future now. Your efforts up until this point have been valiant, but Lizzie is already behind other young ladies of her same age. Time is of the essence."

The words stung far more than Isabel cared to admit. But

the source of the pain was deeper. Her aunt did not consider her enough of a lady to see to her sister's upbringing.

"I must protest, Aunt. You have been very generous to us, and we are grateful. But I never agreed to this. I never—"

Lizzie drew closer and tugged at Isabel's skirt. "Look at what Miss Smith gave me!"

Isabel looked at her sister. The pert nose, the inquisitive chocolate eyes. The smattering of freckles, a result of too much time in the sun without a bonnet. Her governess would surely remedy that habit.

As she looked at the child, Isabel saw glimpses of herself.

Once young and wild.

And it hurt her heart.

"Are you looking?" Lizzie demanded, dragging Isabel back to the present, waving the book close to her.

Isabel took the leather-bound volume in her hand and touched the embossed word. *Verses.*

Her aunt clicked her tongue. "This is my case in point. Speaking so demandingly to adults. The very idea! It is not to be borne. Miss Smith will break that horrid habit, mark my words."

Isabel's response rang strong and defensive, even to her own ears. "She only spoke in such a manner because she is excited."

"That is no excuse. In fact, it's exactly why she needs someone outside of the family to teach her the proper way. You are too lenient with her. Oh, I am not faulting you. She has a strong will, and she needs a firm governess with even a firmer stance to shape and mold that will."

Isabel decided to try another tactic, especially as she recalled her uncle's earlier words on economizing. "You have already done so much for us, Aunt Margaret. And we are so very grateful. But please, we cannot impose and ask you to incur an additional cost."

Aunt Margaret threw her head back as if amused. "Oh, my

dear, money is hardly an issue. I will not have a child in my house without a proper education, and you have other activities that require your attention."

Other things? The only thing that mattered to her was caring for her sister. It was all she had left. "What could be more important than Lizzie?"

"A dozen Lizzies! Or have you already forgotten that Mr. Bradford and I are relying on you for all those children at the foundling home?"

Isabel felt as if she had been struck. Yes, the children were important to her, and she did enjoy her time there. But her aunt had seemed to discourage such interaction before now, and nothing could be more important than her sister. She had tried to be useful, to bring some good to the children at the home, and now her aunt was using it against her in a demeaning fashion.

She looked toward Constance, hoping to find support. But Constance's eyes were fixed firmly on the floor.

She glanced at Miss Smith. The unadorned woman looked like the sort of person Isabel had worked all her life to be.

A tight chignon at the base of her neck.

A severely cut gray dress.

Isabel had, at one time, considered that life suitable, but now she was not sure.

Everything was changing, and control of her fate, which had always been so important to her, seemed to be slipping away.

Chapter Thirty-One

*I*sabel stomped from the parlor, caring little that her carriage was unladylike and her cheeks were flaming.

Normally, she could control her reactions, but this had gone far enough. Thoughts tumbled and rumbled in her head, each one battling for dominance.

She replayed the argument over and over in her mind. She knew she should be grateful for this opportunity to live at Emberwilde, for without it, Isabel at some point would be forced to accept a governess position. She might end up like the austere Miss Smith, and ultimately she and Lizzie would be separated. That she could not bear. Why then was this so difficult to accept?

Her ability to manage her temper had always been a source of pride for Isabel. She was rarely riled by anyone or anything. But now, heat radiated from her.

From the odd encounter in the woods to her sister's disappearance to the strict rules imposed by her aunt, even the air around her felt too heavy to bear.

She traced her way through the labyrinth of old walls and narrow corridors that whispered of centuries past.

She stepped into her chamber, its colored walls and gilded furniture welcoming her, and let the door close behind her. She wanted to be alone and to shut out the scary and unfamiliar things of the world.

She tossed her shawl onto the chair and folded her arms across her chest. Life here was to be easier—carefree and effortless—was that not what Mr. Langsby had said? And she supposed it was. She was not expected to do any work. Helping Mr. Bradford establish a school at the foundling home was considered an act of charity. And it seemed that her one responsibility, her sister, was being taken away from her only so she could learn the idle ways of this new world.

Deep down, Isabel understood that a lady's governess would be a positive change for Lizzie.

The girl would become a lady.

She would learn skills that Isabel never had the chance to learn, and therefore could never teach her.

She moved to her bed and sank onto the soft coverlet, then let herself fall backward. She stared at the silk canopy of pale blue above her, almost like a sky. Life was changing whether she wanted it to or not.

A tear slipped from her eye. Then another. She could not remember the last time she had lain in bed, crying. She'd never had the need. Her life had been simple but predictable, calm and stable. Now, nothing was as it seemed.

She shivered when she thought of the man in the forest, whose beady eyes and wicked scowl seemed to grow more villainous with each thought.

And then her aunt, whose actions were no doubt intended to be helpful but hurt and stung.

Of Constance, who took everything in stride, accepting and not questioning.

Of Mr. Bradford, who, if it were up to her aunt, would be her husband.

And ironically, of Mr. Galloway, whose kindness and gentleness were more attractive than money or prestige.

It was all too much.

The tiny sampler Mary had made her was just within her grasp on her side table. She reached for it, then held it in her hands and mouthed the words. How she missed Mary. And how she wished she had strength and faith like Mary to believe that everything would work out for good.

Chapter Thirty-Two

Isabel and Lizzie struggled to adjust to life with a governess. It was not easy. From the strict schedule to the difficult new subjects, Lizzie was frustrated and angry.

Isabel went so far as to wonder if the child would be better off back at Fellsworth. She had blossomed there, and here she seemed to flounder. But common sense always seemed to prevail. For they were preparing Lizzie for a life of advantage and security. Isabel could not deny her that. Lizzie would adjust. After all, she was still so very young.

If Aunt Margaret and Constance were aware of the child's struggles, they gave no indication. They forged ahead with their social schedules and dress fittings, and spent a week planning a dinner to welcome Constance's fiancé to Emberwilde for a few days.

As if that were not difficult enough, her aunt informed her that Mr. Bradford was on the guest list.

She was less bothered by the prospect of his attendance than by the manner in which her aunt spoke of him.

"Is it not wonderful? Mr. Bradford is such an agreeable person. And so handsome!" Aunt Margaret said as they sat in the music room one afternoon with their sewing, taking advantage of the room's wealth of light. "He is a pleasant addition to any gathering, large or small."

Isabel fixed her eyes on her needlework. She tried to focus on the fact that each day her needlework was improving. Her stitches straighter, her patterns daintier.

But her aunt was not about to allow her out of the conversation so easily.

"Do you not agree, Isabel?"

Isabel swallowed the discomfort rising within her but could not manage to make her eyes meet her aunt's. "Yes, Aunt."

"I should think so!" Her aunt's voice held more enthusiasm than judgment, and that put Isabel further on edge. "And it warms my heart to think of the real reason he so eagerly accepted the invitation."

At this, Isabel could no longer make her needle pierce the linen fabric on her hoop. She knew the not-so-subtle implication behind the seemingly innocent words.

Constance must have sensed Isabel's frustration at her mother's insinuation, for her response came quickly. "Come now, Mama. They have not known each other very long, in truth. I think it is too early to make such an assumption."

"These matters of the heart do not take long." Her aunt's words were colored with shock. "He is not nearly as wealthy as some, to be sure, but his breeding is sound. He may not have much of an inheritance, but he is clever, hardworking, and would no doubt set it to right."

Her aunt's response was clearly directed to Constance, as if Isabel were not in the room, and as if her opinion were not an integral component of this arrangement. Isabel had tried to ignore the increasing frequency with which her aunt incorporated Mr. Bradford into their daily conversations, and how she had found excuses to happen past the school frequently to "check on her investment."

Day by day her aunt's hopes and intentions regarding Isabel and Mr. Bradford had become more obvious, to the point that Isabel could not hear his name without her heart racing, not in anticipation of a future, but with anxiety.

The older woman hurried across the room, her lily-of-the-valley scent reaching Isabel before she did. She sat very close to

Isabel, so close that Isabel had to resist the urge to recoil. "You shall wear that green gown tonight. You've not worn it yet, if I am not mistaken. Mr. Bradford will not be able to take his gaze off you." Her aunt reached out and touched Isabel's cheek. "You've a gift, Isabel. Does she not have a gift, Constance? You are blessed with your mother's beauty."

"I do not think it is prudent to assume Mr. Bradford cares for me in such a manner," Isabel said. "He does not know me, not really."

"Oh, child. Will you not get that notion out of your head?"

"But do you not think this all very sudden? Too sudden?" Isabel lowered her needlework. "I've not even been at Emberwilde an entire summer, and I—"

"Listen to me." Her aunt's words clipped her own, and she looked Isabel square in the eyes. "Believe me when I say that this is the very best opportunity for you at the moment. You've no dowry, need I remind you. We just have to wait for him to make a move on the matter. Now this conversation is over."

Her aunt bustled from the room with more energy and enthusiasm than Isabel thought possible.

Once her aunt was gone, Isabel dropped back in the settee, pushing her forgotten needlework to the side.

Constance, who had been a quiet bystander to the interaction, leaned forward. "Do not be upset, Isabel. Please."

"I am not upset," lied Isabel. "It is just that I do not wish to disappoint her, and yet I do not know how it will be possible for me to make her happy."

"And what makes you think you will disappoint her? You are putting far too much pressure on yourself. Mr. Bradford will be fond of you. He *is* fond of you. How could he not be?"

"You misunderstand me." Isabel attempted to clarify. "I've no desire to marry right now, or anytime soon."

A little expression of amusement crossed Constance's face,

then when she realized her cousin was not joining in the joke, she sobered. "You cannot mean that."

Isabel fixed her eyes on her cousin. "No, I am in earnest."

"But why?"

"I do not even know Mr. Bradford. I only know what has been told to me."

"And is that not enough?" Constance rose to her feet. "It is true. If you do not have romantic feelings for Mr. Bradford, do not fret. They shall come. At times like this we must trust those who love us and have more experience than we do. Consider me. Left to my own devices, I would have accepted the first suitor who came along. But Mother had a much better perspective than I. I turned down the first suitor and now enjoy a much more advantageous match."

Isabel picked up her sewing again. She did not expect Constance to understand, for this was the very situation that Constance had been preparing for her entire life. To make a match. To marry. To grasp security.

When Isabel did not respond, her cousin spoke again. "At least promise this: do not close your heart to the idea of it. I do not mean to be cruel or inconsiderate, but it is the future we must think of, and the sooner we settle the details of our future, the better it will be."

"How can that be better?"

"Life is uncertain, Isabel. Our circumstances today may not be our circumstances tomorrow."

Isabel nodded. Did she not know that to be true? For just several months ago she never would have imagined herself away from the school and living in such luxury. But nor would she have imagined contemplating the idea of marrying a man she barely knew to secure her future.

"I know very little about Mr. Bradford," Isabel said. "I do not know if he prefers the color blue to the color green. If he takes sugar in his tea. I do not even know his age."

"None of these things are important."

"Not important?" Isabel almost choked on the words.

"I do not mean to be callous. But your situation is, well, tempestuous. You are, of course, secure at the moment. My family is your family. As long as they are living, you will never be alone. But that is just it. No one is promised tomorrow. Not a single one. So it is best that we live to protect ourselves. Have I upset you?"

"No, it is only that you must understand: I grew up fully intending to become a governess. That was my purpose, my goal. I would prefer to not be dependent upon anyone."

"We would all like to think that, I suspect, but the truth is that we are both dependent upon others." Her smile was kind. "Consider my Mr. Nichols, my own fiancé. He does love me, I think. At least I hope. And it is lovely that we enjoy each other's company. But even if I did not, I would still marry him. Mother worked very hard to secure a match that would provide for me through all my years on this earth. But I am not dull-witted. If something were to happen to my dowry—if the estate were to go bankrupt or if Father would pass away, for example—the relationship would likely be severed. It is the one source of my anxiety. How I wish the wedding date were already here so I could put all such concerns behind me."

An emotion streaked through Isabel. Was it sadness? Disbelief? She was not sure, but Constance, her confident, prepared cousin, seemed unusually vulnerable as the admission slipped from her lips.

Isabel was not sure what her response should be. Perhaps a lifetime with little had caused her to expect little. Few possessions or resources. Minimal help from those around her. The idea of marrying for survival was not new—it was imbedded in stories and newspapers. But her own cousin?

Constance spoke. "Just promise me that you will not do or say anything that will commit you permanently one way or the other."

"Very well. But then you must promise me you will not leave me alone with Mr. Bradford tonight."

Constance sobered. "That I cannot promise."

"Why?"

"Because I do not agree with you in this instance."

Chapter Thirty-Three

*T*he date of the dinner—along with the long-awaited Mr. Nichols—arrived.

As requested by her aunt, Isabel dressed in the green gown that glittered in the candlelight with her every movement. Even six months ago she would have coveted this dress and the small emerald drop necklace that encircled her neck, matching the emerald tiara that sat atop her hair.

Today she felt a little ridiculous when she considered the cost and extravagance of this dress. For not a mile away stood a modest foundling home where children were in need of books, clothes, and even food. Near her were women in such need that they would be willing to leave their babies on doorsteps, hoping that a stranger could provide for them better than they could themselves.

She frowned when she considered the number of things that could have been acquired with the funds used to purchase this gown.

As her thoughts turned to the needs of the children at the foundling home, she considered Mr. Bradford. It was impossible not to, for the two were bound together. He was always so impeccably dressed, with the finest waistcoats and most fashionable boots. But his wardrobe, stylish as it was, could not be inexpensive. Why would he choose to spend funds on such luxuries when so much was needed?

Lizzie reclined across the bed, watching as Burns finished dressing Isabel's hair.

"You look like a princess." Lizzie rolled to her belly and rested her chin in her hands.

If Miss Smith had been in the room, she would have reprimanded Lizzie for such unladylike posture. But Isabel enjoyed this rare moment with her sister.

"Can't I go? Please, I will be on my best behavior."

Isabel moved to the bed and sat next to Lizzie. "You know you can't."

Lizzie sighed in disgust and flopped to her back. "I know, I know. I will never be grown up enough to do anything fun."

Isabel smiled. "You will be an adult faster than you know. You are already becoming a young lady."

"But it is so boring here." Lizzie toyed with the hem of her pinafore. "Do you miss Fellsworth? I do."

Melancholy tugged. Yes, she did miss Fellsworth and the people there. But she could not verbalize that sentiment to Lizzie. "Perhaps you are forgetting how fortunate we are. Need I remind you of your beautiful new gowns? Of Caesar? We have so much to be thankful for."

"I know, but I miss my friends," lamented Lizzie. "I had fun playing with the girls at the foundling home, but now Aunt Margaret and Miss Smith will not let me go there anymore. It isn't fair."

Isabel smoothed her fingers along her sister's hair, which was splayed over the bed.

And then a shout echoed from the distance, followed by a high-pitched rant.

Isabel startled, and Lizzie jumped from the bed and ran to the door. The child flung the door open and stuck her head out in the hall.

Curious, Isabel followed her. "Wait here," she instructed Lizzie, and without giving her a chance to respond, she stepped down the corridor.

The tirade continued, but it was so muffled Isabel could not make out the words. She came around the corner, and there stood her aunt and uncle in the hall. Aunt Margaret was already dressed for the dinner in a gown of deep sapphire blue. Pearls encircled her neck, and her pale hair was swept atop her head.

As soon as they noticed her, they stopped arguing.

Feeling horribly intrusive, Isabel withdrew. "I-I'm sorry. I did not mean to interrupt. Is everything all right?"

"All right?" shrieked her aunt. "Of course it is not all right. For your uncle has invited the Galloway men to the party tonight. To *my* dinner!"

Isabel pressed her lips together and raised her eyebrows sympathetically in her uncle's direction. But his eyes were fixed on his wife.

At last her uncle spoke. "Now, Margaret, calm yourself. They have been assisting me with a project for a while now, and they have done me a great service. I spoke with Mr. Colin Galloway on the matter, and he was going to pass the invitation to his cousin. It is too late to send word otherwise. Besides, I enjoy their company."

"Enjoy their company!" Aunt Margaret shot back. "That man led your only son to the battlefield, and you say you enjoy his company?"

"That is not fair, Margaret," combatted Uncle Charles. "You know it."

A tear trickled down her aunt's cheek, and her red lips trembled. "I demand you retract the invitation."

Her uncle's voice was firm but unwavering. "I will not. I am master of Emberwilde, and if I would like to invite a guest to dinner, then I shall do so."

Isabel backed away. This was not her conversation, and she should not be listening to an argument between a husband and wife. But as she turned around to retreat, she could not deny the fluttering of her heart.

So Mr. Galloway was coming to the dinner.

She hated to see her aunt—or anyone, for that matter—so upset.

The arguing resumed, but as she returned to her chamber, the words grew muffled.

A gradual sense of optimism swelled within her. Perhaps this dinner would not be as unpleasant as she had thought. Her dread began to melt away, and a smile tugged her lips.

What a difference a few moments could make. For now, anticipation bloomed. She did not dread the dinner anymore.

No, she did not dread it at all.

When the hour for the meal arrived, Isabel took the servants' stairs down to the main floor. Guests were already starting to arrive, and sounds of laughter and chatter floated to meet her. As she rounded the corner, it became clear this was to be a gathering very different from the Atwells'. No farmers or tradesmen were in attendance, only those individuals and families deemed worthy by her aunt.

Even though Isabel looked the part in her smart new gown, she could not help but feel slightly out of place. Her confidence wavered as her slippers tapped each step. The guests had gathered in the drawing room, and as she approached, Isabel scanned the room for familiar faces. But something in the foyer caught her eye.

It was her aunt and Mr. Bradford.

Isabel cast a glance over her shoulder to ensure no one was watching her, and could not resist pausing in the hallway long enough to hear.

Her aunt and Mr. Bradford were leaning in toward one another, but they seemed to be arguing. It reminded her of the morning at church, when she had spotted them engaged in what appeared to be a quarrel.

She held her breath in an effort to hear above the conversations leaking from the drawing room.

She could barely make out her aunt's words above the chatter. "We are running out of time."

"But this is quite a diversion from the plan. I'm not sure I—"

She winced as his words were muffled. What could they possibly be running out of time for?

The next snippet of the conversation came from her aunt. "I know what I know, and I am not afraid to push the matter further. Our arrangement is such that—"

Again, the words were covered.

Isabel leaned forward and ever so slightly around the corner, hoping to get another glimpse of their faces. Perhaps by doing so she could either read their words or gauge their demeanors. But as she did, Mr. Bradford looked back, and his eyes landed on her.

His face was flushed, his eyebrows drawn together. It was the most frustrated she had ever seen him. But then, as he realized it was her, his jaw slackened, and he raked his fingers through his hair.

Isabel stood her ground, despite the fact that everything in her screamed to leave the space at once.

Mr. Bradford murmured something to Aunt Margaret and then approached Isabel with determined steps.

Something was wrong, she could feel it in her very core, but she forced a sweet smile to her face, covering her suspicions with the prettiest smile she could muster. "My goodness, Mr. Bradford. Is everything all right? You and Aunt Margaret seem to be engaged in quite the conversation."

Without a look back at Aunt Margaret, he flashed a smile at Isabel. "Oh, it is nothing that concerns you, Miss Creston."

He drew closer to her and offered his arm. "You know how your aunt can be at times. I have vexed her, I'm afraid. But do not fret. Her grievance with me will not last."

She placed her hand on his extended arm and allowed him to

lead her into the drawing room, pretending not to notice his altered demeanor.

Shortly before dinner, Isabel was introduced to Constance's Mr. Nichols. He arrived very late, to the irritation of both her cousin and aunt, but at least he arrived. He did not look at all like Isabel had expected. Constance spoke of him with such high praise, but he was a rather plain man who could be no taller than Constance herself. He was portly, with dark hair and eyes and a rather severe countenance. Two of his friends had unexpectedly accompanied him for the visit. To Constance's evident disappointment, Mr. Nichols seemed more interested in his companions than in her.

Once settled in the chair she was to occupy for dinner, Isabel sipped from a crystal glass. She was, not surprisingly, seated next to Mr. Bradford, but his mood seemed more somber than normal. She assessed the faces around the table.

The Atwells were seated across from her. The Wassons were in attendance, and the vicar and his wife. And of course, Colin and Henry Galloway were both present, to her aunt's chagrin. To Isabel's dismay, however, she was seated as far away from the Galloways as possible.

During dinner Mr. Bradford attempted to keep her engaged in conversation, but Isabel was distracted. She could not shake the heavy sensation that pressed upon her after seeing her aunt argue with Mr. Bradford, nor could she keep herself from watching her cousin. Constance was seated next to her intended. Isabel felt sad for her, for the beauty's cheeks were pale and she appeared a little frightened. Mr. Nichols talked with the friends who had accompanied him and paid little attention to his betrothed. Isabel thought of Constance's nonchalant words—her fiancé did not love her. Not yet.

She could not help but compare Mr. Nichols's actions to those of Mr. Bradford. At this point, her family considered Mr. Bradford a good match for her, and there could be little doubt that he was attracted to her. And whereas Mr. Nichols ignored his fiancé, Mr. Bradford was most attentive. But the more she was in his presence, and the more she observed how he interacted with others, the more doubts began to surface. Something about him seemed disingenuous.

She leaned forward and looked down the table. There, toward the end, was Mr. Galloway. Her breath seemed to catch in her throat when she realized that she would much prefer to sit next to the magistrate.

After dinner, the women retreated to the drawing room, but Isabel escaped to the Blue Parlor, a lesser-used room that was off her uncle's study. She was certain she would not be disturbed there, and she needed a few moments of breathing room.

It was dark in this chamber. Quiet. No fire blazed in the grate, nor had the servants lit any of the candles. She made her way to the settee on the far wall and sat down. Since she was alone, there was no need to keep her spine poker straight and her chin tilted elegantly into the air. She leaned against the supple cushions and relaxed as much as her stays would allow. The only care she took was to not wrinkle her gown, but she indulged in several deep breaths.

She had intended to stay only for a few moments, but she soon lost sense of the time that had passed. The sound of a voice made her bolt upright. Ready to retreat if necessary, she stood and listened for the source of the sound.

She soon realized it came from the other side of the door that connected the Blue Parlor to her uncle's library. She recognized the voices of her uncle and Mr. Galloway. She suspended her breath and listened.

"All the contraband has been removed from the tunnels. Every last cask."

"I am glad to hear it. It's good to finally be rid of it. I thank you for your assistance in this matter, Galloway."

"I am not sure it is quite time to thank me yet, Ellison."

"What do you mean?"

"When we were clearing the cavern, we came upon an abandoned wagon. Either we scared someone off, or it is being held there for future use."

Her uncle's whisper was strained. "Surely they would not be so daft as to continue to track through my land, knowing they've been discovered."

"It's not quite that simple. These smuggling rings can be powerful and complicated. In all honesty, they do not care about you or the possible ramifications of discovery. All they care about is selling their wares, and once their routes have been established, they do not give them up easily. McKinney has noted two men in particular who have been at the inn a great deal as of late. I myself encountered them several nights ago and have further reason to believe that they are involved. One of the men is quite recognizable. His left hand is missing. I am beginning to suspect that the foundling home is somehow involved as well."

Isabel's heart thudded in her chest. He was talking about the man who had threatened her! And the foundling home. She should not be listening. There were too many secrets going on within this house. Too many things she did not need to know; nay, did not want to know.

Mr. Galloway continued. "Also, this timepiece was found in one of the tunnels. I have not had the opportunity to share it with you until now. Does it look familiar to you at all?"

Isabel wanted to hear no more. She turned to leave, but as she did, her eyes landed on a large, black shadow.

She gave a little cry.

For there stood Mr. Bradford.

"You gave me a fright!" Isabel exclaimed, jumping back. Her heart beat wildly.

"I did not mean to frighten you. I just wondered where you escaped to. For that is what you were doing, was it not? Escaping?"

Her heart raced within her chest. She was escaping, yes. But not in the sense he meant.

She swallowed and finally, reluctantly, lifted her eyes to meet his.

His expression held such warmth, such intensity, that she silently reminded herself she may not be able to trust what she saw. It was her heart that sounded the first warning. Beating rapidly and hard, it alerted her senses to danger.

Most women could hardly consider Mr. Bradford a danger. For not only was he handsome, he was *good*. He dedicated his life to others. He helped the needy.

But then, Mr. Galloway had mentioned the foundling home in relation to the man without a hand. Her aunt and Mr. Bradford had been arguing. Something was wrong, she could feel it.

He stood between her and the door, his broad shoulders filling the frame. She parted her lips to draw breath, for regular breath was insufficient.

"If you will excuse me, Mr. Bradford, I am sure my aunt is wondering where I am."

She offered an awkward smile and attempted to brush past him to the safety of the corridor, but as she did, he blocked her path.

She glanced around quickly, looking for any escape. How foolish she had been to wander off alone. She should have gone to her room, or any room not so close to the gathering.

But he persisted. "You did not answer my question. Hiding or escaping?"

She had to force herself to look him in the eye. "Neither. Merely getting some air."

"That is a relief," he exclaimed. "For I hope I would not cause you to wish to escape."

The comment was innocent enough in nature, yet spoken with such an air of familiarity that Isabel stiffened. "Of course not, Mr. Bradford. I . . . I am just not used to such gatherings."

"Yes, I daresay events like this were uncommon at Fellsworth. I suppose that is one of the reasons I find your opinions on such things so important. You are intriguing, Miss Creston. I must admit that I find you a bit fascinating. Might I share a secret with you?"

She did not want to hear it.

But he continued anyway.

"I care little for these sorts of gatherings, other than the fact I enjoy the company of your dear aunt and cousin, and of course, you."

She could no longer meet his gaze. "I must return to my aunt."

He stepped closer, his breath barely above a whisper. "Do you not feel it, Miss Creston?"

She remained silent, unable to organize her thoughts quickly enough for a suitable response.

"Please, sir, I am not one to hear such things. I—"

"From the moment I first saw you, darling, beautiful Isabel, my mind has not been able to focus on any other idea. You consume my every thought, you are my every desire."

Her ears burned at the sound of her Christian name on his lips.

He stepped closer, and she shrank back against a table. She was trapped.

He reached out to touch her arm. She jerked it back, disrupting the contents of the table and sending a small figurine to the floor.

He did not seem to notice her discomfort. Instead, he pressed closer. "Oh, my Isabel. For I may call you that, may I not? I know you have felt it too. I see it in your expression. I flatter myself into thinking that by some glorious miracle you might return my adoration."

His voice crept to an intimate whisper, and he lifted a finger to brush her hair from her face. "I see no sense in delaying, do you? Say you will, dearest Isabel. Say you will become my wife."

The door to the library creaked open.

She drew a sharp breath. Discovery would either save her or condemn her.

The light from the library lit a man from behind, his broad shoulders strong and straight in the light.

"Mr. Galloway," she breathed. Rescued.

Again.

Mr. Bradford turned, and Isabel took advantage of his moment of distraction and ducked away from him.

Relief rushed her, but embarrassment soon replaced her fear.

She wanted the ground to swallow her.

She could feel Mr. Bradford's energy change. The warmth in his eyes had cooled, and they were fixed on Mr. Galloway.

"Forgive me. I've no wish to interrupt." Mr. Galloway's words were clipped, and iciness lingered unapologetically in his expression. He appeared almost angry as he assessed Mr. Bradford.

Isabel did not take the time to consider this too closely, for she found the opportunity to step toward the middle of the room and put distance between herself and Mr. Bradford.

"You are not interrupting at all, Mr. Galloway." She rushed toward him, perhaps a bit too eagerly. She felt her energy rise, her heart rate calm, her flushed face cool. "You are most welcome here. My aunt will be wondering where I've gotten to."

She cast a quick glance at Mr. Galloway as she passed him at the door. She whispered, "Thank you."

She did not linger. She had avoided what she feared would lead to something worse than an undesired proposal, and she did not look back.

Chapter Thirty-Four

*M*iss Creston flew past Colin, a vision of shimmering muslin and glistening eyes.

The two men stood locked in a dead stare for several seconds. Bradford's eyes hardened. "What do you want, Galloway?"

Colin folded his arms across his chest. He was not sure what he had interrupted, but he did not like what he saw. "I was just leaving the library after a talk with Ellison."

"Only the most poorly bred find themselves above knocking."

If Bradford meant the stab at his background to hurt, he chose the wrong ploy.

Bradford's face deepened to crimson, and he yanked at his cravat. He lifted his chin in the door's direction. "What did she say to you, on her way out?"

Colin forced his own expression to stay calm and vigilant. He ignored Bradford's question. "Consider yourself fortunate that it was me and not Ellison who happened upon this little rendezvous of yours."

"I did not ask for your opinion," spat Bradford. He stepped so close that Colin could smell the port on his breath. "I'm warning you, Galloway. Do not interfere."

"You are warning me?" Colin exclaimed, as if amused by the idea.

"I don't know what you are up to, but heed my words. Do not insert yourself between Isabel and me."

Why the sound of her Christian name should incite such fury, he did not know. But he could feel anger begin to bubble within him. Yes, he had stumbled upon Bradford in a compromising position. But Colin had another advantage, one that was far broader in scope and impact.

"I shall not interfere unless given a reason to," Colin said. "But are you sure this is only about Miss Creston?"

"What do you mean?"

Colin reached into his pocket, retrieved the pocket watch, and extended it toward Bradford. "If I am not mistaken, this is yours."

Bradford snatched the timepiece and turned it over in his hand. "Where did you get it?"

"Found it. In the Emberwilde Forest tunnels behind the foundling home. I can't help but wonder how it got there."

Bradford stuffed the watch in his pocket before muttering, "Obviously it was stolen."

"Really?" challenged Colin. "Stolen by whom? One of the children? Dent or Stanway?"

Bradford clenched his jaw before responding. "You are sorely mistaken if you are suggesting I am involved in whatever game you are playing."

Bradford stomped from the room like a spoiled boy, and his action brought their conversation to a screeching halt.

Once Bradford was gone, Colin stood in the room's silence for several moments.

He had heard Bradford confess that the timepiece was his. That should make him happy. He was one small step closer to figuring out this mess, for he highly doubted it was stolen, as Bradford suggested. And he had done a great job pretending the sight of Miss Creston and Mr. Bradford had no effect on him. But the silly grin on Mr. Bradford's face made his stomach turn. He had not seen Miss Creston's face, and he dared not linger on the thought.

He recalled Mr. Bradford's ways with ladies, his ability to manipulate a woman's good sense and mold it to his liking. He had no way of knowing whether Miss Creston was a willing participant or an innocent bystander in this rendezvous, but the idea of Bradford having her in his sights made him sick.

Colin was ready to quit Emberwilde for the evening.

He found his cousin in the billiards room. Henry was seated along the far wall under the window, glass of port in hand, watching a game between Wasson and Ellison. Bradford was not present.

He crossed the room and tapped his cousin's arm. "Let's go."

"What, leave? I'm not ready to leave." Henry huffed at the ridiculous notion and indulged in a long swig. "What's wrong with you? You look as sour as an old goat. Plus, you and I need to talk. You left the office so early today I haven't had a chance to keep you updated."

Colin did not wish to hear about the work that was waiting for him. "Can it not wait? This is hardly the place."

"I've never known us to need somewhere special to talk. Besides, no one here is interested in what either of us has to say, and I think you will find this interesting. Do you remember that day when the Holden girl brought the baby in? I told you I was heading out to Heddeston Park to assist the steward and solicitor in locating the official heir?"

Colin nodded but was distracted by the thoughts swirling in his head. "Yes. And?"

"To make a long and complicated story short, it turns out that our Miss Creston is not completely dependent upon her aunt and uncle, as we thought."

At the mention of Miss Creston's name, Colin jerked his attention back to his cousin. "What do you mean?"

His cousin leaned forward and cast a quick glance around the room to make sure no one was listening. "Earlier today I had another meeting with the solicitor assisting the steward at Heddeston Park."

Colin stiffened as the image of Mrs. Ellison's childhood home flashed before his mind's eye.

Henry continued. "The very one. After meeting with Heddeston's steward, who stayed on to sort out the estate after the late master's death, they had significant trouble finding the heir. It seems that after all this time, they have found her."

Colin raised his eyebrows. "Her?"

"Yes, *her.*" Henry pressed his lips together and nodded. "Mr. Hayworth left his estate to his eldest child's eldest child. Anna was his firstborn, and they searched for her daughter but could not locate her. As you know, there was a great scandal around the Crestons' marriage, and Mr. Hayworth made every effort to hide the details, even from his steward, which complicated matters. But his steward was diligent, and eventually tracked down Mr. Creston, only to learn that he had died. He almost gave up hope of finding their daughter but grew suspicious after Mrs. Ellison invited her niece to stay with them."

Colin shifted in his chair, not liking the direction this news was taking. "Surely Mrs. Ellison would know the details of the family inheritance and inform Miss Creston. I would imagine that to be common knowledge within the family."

"Too true, but this is where it gets interesting. Keep in mind that Mrs. Ellison is the *younger* of Mr. Hayworth's daughters. There was no other legal entailment to the property, and since their father was a self-made man, he could leave the estate to whomever he chose. His will was written specifically that the property should pass down through the oldest child's line. Since Anna Creston is dead, her offspring has until the age of twenty-one to lay claim to the inheritance, otherwise it will pass to the next child in line, which is Mrs. Margaret Ellison. So in short, the estate passes to Anna's offspring. And that is—"

"Miss Creston." Colin breathed the name.

"Exactly."

"If the solicitor knew that Mrs. Ellison had her niece in her home, why hasn't he spoken with them yet?"

"Apparently there were some questions surrounding Mr. Creston and whether Miss Isabel Creston was indeed the person they were looking for, but now he is quite certain she is."

"Does Miss Creston know this yet?" asked Colin.

"I don't know how she would, unless a member of the Ellison family has informed her." Henry shrugged. "I about fell out of my chair when the solicitor finally informed me of all the details. Somehow the Ellisons were able to get to Miss Creston before the solicitor." Henry cut his eyes to the billiards table, where the other men were fully engrossed in their game. "So to your question of whether Mrs. Ellison knew of the will . . ."

"Are you saying the Ellisons intentionally kept this information from Miss Creston so they could lay claim to the estate?"

"I do not wish to put words in another person's mouth. But if Isabel Creston does not claim the inheritance by age twenty-one, Heddeston Park will pass to Mrs. Ellison."

Understanding dawned over Colin. "And Mr. Ellison will control the assets."

"And all their financial troubles will vanish." Henry took a swig of the port.

Colin hardly dared to believe the Ellisons would deceive their own flesh and blood. Money—the pursuit of it, the possession of it, and the promise of it—could cause people to act without conscience.

"When is her twenty-first birthday, do you know?" Colin asked.

"According to the solicitor it is the twenty-third of August."

Colin's disgust turned to anger within him as he reviewed the story in his mind. Miss Creston needed to know the truth. And he would do whatever was in his power to make sure that no one, not even her own family, took advantage of her.

He stood and prepared to leave the room. "She must be told."

Henry laid a hand on his arm. "Wait a moment. If the Ellisons have brought her here for their own gain, consider that you might jeopardize her safety."

Colin yanked his arm free. "I will protect her."

He left the billiards room, intent upon finding a moment to speak privately with Miss Creston.

But for the rest of the night, she was nowhere to be found.

Chapter Thirty-Five ─────────────

*I*sabel lay curled in her bed, tears racing down her cheeks.

She had not returned to the party after the interlude with Bradford.

She was far too mortified.

Mr. Bradford had proposed to her, and she never gave an answer. Not really.

So that meant the question was out there, lingering in the shadows and hidden places of Emberwilde.

And what was worse, Mr. Galloway had witnessed their private interaction.

She wondered if her aunt would discover her offense. It seemed unlikely that a man would share information about a failed proposal, but the relationship between Mr. Bradley and her aunt was an odd one.

Seconds slipped into minutes. Minutes slipped into an hour.

She watched the moon outside of her window slide across the endless black sky and waited for the inevitable explosion that would occur when her aunt learned what had happened.

Isabel sighed and looked to the space where a fire normally glowed. There was no fire in her grate, no lit candle lamp.

How she wished for brightness and lightness. Everything felt heavy, shrouded in dismal melancholy. The dawn was still hours away.

At some point Isabel drifted off to sleep, but a sharp rapping at her chamber door jerked her awake.

Isabel straightened, still in her new gown, as Aunt Margaret burst into her chamber.

"What have you done?" Her aunt's shrill voice echoed off the chamber ceiling. "Of all the disrespect!"

Constance followed her mother into the chamber, a sympathetic expression on her tired face.

Isabel stood. She could pretend not to know what her aunt was angry about, but it would be a lie.

"After all we have done for you and your sister. You ungrateful, selfish child."

Isabel froze. Never had she been spoken to in such a manner.

"Mr. Bradford told me what has happened. How dare you run away like a spoiled child. Your future, Isabel! Your future! We cannot be responsible for you forever. He deserves the decency of an answer, and you will give one to him."

Isabel knew he deserved an answer, but she did not like her aunt's forceful tone. "I never asked you to be responsible for me forever."

Her aunt huffed. "And what are you going to do? A lady needs to be married and settled. You will be of age in just a few weeks, and what then? The world is a scary, uncertain place. Do not be so foolish to think that your training will be enough to protect you. Consider Miss Smith! Is that the life you would have for yourself?"

Isabel jutted her chin out. She felt like a reprimanded child. Well, she was not a child. She was a woman of sound mind and judgment. "Why yes, I think it far preferable to marrying a man I do not love."

"Do not fool yourself. You have no fortune, no dowry. Consider, Isabel!"

The words were hard to hear. Isabel shook her head, as if to dislodge them from her memory. "I am not afraid of work, Aunt."

And it was the truth. She was prepared, more prepared than

she thought she had imagined. It was this new life and these new expectations that she was not prepared for. "I do not understand this rush to marry."

Her aunt threw her hand in the air. "Are you daft? It is crucial because nothing is certain. Money is not certain. Futures are not certain. Engagements are not a guarantee."

Her aunt fixed a narrow gaze on Isabel. The whites of her eyes shone in the darkness. "Mr. Bradford is coming in the morning. And you will accept him. If you do not, you will no longer be welcome at Emberwilde."

The next morning at the appointed time, Isabel descended the stairs and walked into the music room. She felt as if she were en route to an inquisition—one in which the outcome was already fixed.

Isabel wondered if this was how her mother had felt when her family rejected her decision to marry.

Under the weight of injustice, she now felt an empowering bond with the mother she had never really known. Her mother had married her father for true love, and Isabel would not marry until she also had a true love of her own.

Mr. Bradford had not yet arrived. She had not seen her uncle yet, and the only word from her aunt was a message indicating which gown she should wear. Even Constance, whom she saw every morning, did not pay a visit to her chamber.

Nerves tightening, she sat alone on a settee in the music room, the very same seat she had taken on her first night at Emberwilde months ago. From where she sat she could see the Black Wood Forest. Its beauty was both alluring and dangerous. Despite her fear of what lingered within it, Isabel found herself wishing she were under that green canopy, far from this room.

Her empty stomach churned as she waited. She had not even been able to drink a cup of tea or hot chocolate. She jumped as the small mantel clock chimed the eleventh hour in a sharp tone. Did her aunt not say Mr. Bradford would be here at that time?

She rose and stepped to the picture of her mother, which still intrigued her. She now knew the piece by heart. She had memorized every wisp of hair, every shade of blue used in her eyes. She tried to draw courage from the woman who had already overcome her predetermined fate.

"If I did not know better, I would think that a portrait of you."

Mr. Bradford's voice scratched her ears.

Isabel turned slowly. He stood before her.

She winced as he pulled the door closed behind him. It was improper to be alone with a man anywhere, but behind a closed door was most distressing and reawakened her fears of the previous evening.

"Mr. Bradford." She remembered to curtsy.

Her heart pounded harder with every step he took toward her. His expression was far too intimate, as if he could read her thoughts.

The scent of sandalwood surrounded him. His shadow eclipsed her.

"Such a beautiful woman. And like I said, you are her very likeness."

She swallowed, but it did little to combat the ringing of her ears or the lightness of her head. "Thank you, Mr. Bradford."

"How I wish you would not call me that."

She looked back to the painting. "What would you like me to call you?"

"My name is Edmund."

She could think of no man whom she had called by his Christian name. But now that he had asked, could she refuse him? "Very well, Edmund."

The room grew warmer, and she felt him draw closer. His very presence suffocated her. She stepped away from the painting, drawing a deep breath.

He spoke at length. "I am sorry if I upset you last night."

"It is I who should apologize." This was what she was supposed to say. "It was impolite of me to run off as I did."

"On the contrary. It was a sensitive topic, and foolish me, I should have made sure we were alone. But we are alone now."

Isabel looked at him. She had not expected an apology. It was clear to her now that their engagement was a plan between him and her aunt, an agreement of sorts that had already been arranged. In all likelihood, this was what he had been discussing with her aunt so heatedly. Otherwise he never would have been so bold as to shut the door.

Again, panic began to bubble. "Let me call my aunt, Mr. Bradford. She will be sorry to have missed you."

"It is not your aunt I am here to see. I am here to see you."

The sinking feeling started again, but this time it was worse. He reached out and took her hand in his own. The warmth spread through her like a fire of dread.

She did not resist as he tugged her hand, silently imploring her to sit beside him.

Not knowing what else to do, she complied.

He did not let go of her hand. "I want to take care of you. I want my home to be your home."

There could be no mistaking his meaning.

"When you quitted the room last night, I cannot even describe my despair. You left, and I had no idea where you went. I feared my action caused you pain. I can no longer pretend that my feelings for you are not in earnest. I love you, Isabel."

"But, Mr. Brad—Edmund, there is much to consider. I—"

He ignored her protest and stroked the top of her hand with a long finger. "Oh, my dear Isabel, I know what I need to know. I know you are caring. Loving. And oh, my dear, so incredibly beautiful."

He reached out to touch her hair, and she instinctively shrank back. "Please, wait. I pray I have not given you the wrong impression or led you to believe that I return your feelings. While I am flattered, of course, I . . ." She paused.

He was smiling.

Why was he smiling?

"Isabel, I have sought your aunt's counsel on this. And she warned me you would say such things. You have done nothing wrong. I can assign no fault to you. But my heart is willing to wait."

"Wait? For what?"

"Poets oft speak of love at first sight, but I know precious few experience it as I have. I am one of those ill-fated souls. I also know that you do not return my regard. But I can only pray that you will learn to return my affection. For if you could return even a small percentage of the vast emotion I feel for you, then my heart will be full."

He leaned toward her, his handsome face beaming with unguarded emotion that appeared to be genuine.

She suddenly realized he meant to kiss her.

Panic pushed her to her feet. This was not at all how it was supposed to happen. This was not part of her agreement in coming to live here. She glimpsed the portrait of her mother.

Strong.

Headstrong.

Determined.

She had all those qualities flowing through her own veins.

Her decision was formed in that very second, as the noonday sun fell through the music room windows.

"I am sorry, Mr. Bradford. But I cannot marry you."

His eyebrows drew together, and his eyes narrowed. "Why not?"

He deserved the truth, at the very least. Whatever his reason for proposing, he deserved at least that.

"Because I don't trust you."

"Give me the opportunity to earn your trust."

"I am sorry. But my answer is no."

Chapter Thirty-Six

With one refusal, Isabel thrust herself and her sister into a life of uncertainty.

Moment by moment she questioned her decision. Not only had she turned her back on a secure future, she had wrested a lady's life away from Lizzie.

Had that been fair? Selfish?

On the same day, a fair day in July, Aunt Margaret made good on her promise. Despite Constance's pleading, the Creston sisters were no longer welcome at Emberwilde.

Isabel had thought returning to Fellsworth would be a natural transition, but that was far from the truth. Her teaching position was no longer available and her bed had been reassigned. Mr. Langsby did take pity on them and allowed Isabel to stay in an unused chamber at the school, and Lizzie rejoined her classmates. Otherwise, nothing was as she remembered.

During her months at Emberwilde, her life had been more relaxed. Less structured. She'd become used to the luxuries, and returning to life at Fellsworth was proving difficult. Even Lizzie struggled, for now she had a fancy for riding. Of French and Italian. Her experiences already stretched beyond what many of the other girls would experience in their lifetimes.

One moment Isabel felt confident in her decision.

The next moment she regretted it.

But then she recalled the awkward, sickening feeling as Mr.

Bradford leaned to kiss her, and she found peace with her decision once more.

Once again she rose at dawn. It would not be long before the mornings held autumn's crisp chill, but for now, the early hours were warm. Since she and Mary no longer shared a room, they went for walks in the garden before the rest of the school would awaken. During their time together, Isabel shared the details of her time at Emberwilde, but more specifically, the reason for her departure.

"I wish I could have seen Emberwilde," Mary mused, a far-off expression in her light eyes. "It sounds absolutely lovely. I do wish, for your sake, it could have ended differently."

"I must say that I am surprised to be back," Isabel said as she walked down the wooded path. "It is definitely not how I imagined it to end, that is certain, but I could not have wed him, Mary. I just couldn't have."

Mary spoke softly. "Why is that?"

It was an innocent enough question, one for which Isabel should have had a good answer. After all, by marrying Mr. Bradford she would have security. He was handsome. Doting. She would have remained close to family. Most importantly, Lizzie would have had the future she deserved. Isabel considered her words carefully. "It was a feeling that prevented it, Mary—a sense that something about him was not as it seemed. I cannot put it into words, exactly."

"Then maybe you do not need to try." They walked in silence for several moments before Mary asked, "Was it because maybe there was someone else? You did mention another young man you met while at Emberwilde."

At the question, Isabel's steps slowed. She'd be lying if she said that Mr. Galloway had not been on her mind and that she hadn't thought about their encounters several times since she left Emberwilde. The thought that she would not see him again haunted her. She had not even had the opportunity to bid him farewell.

A sigh escaped her lips. There was nothing to be done about it. Besides, it was unlikely that she meant anything to him or that her failure to bid him farewell saddened him in some way. Her attraction to him was a silly infatuation, surely.

Mary waited for an answer, so she drew a deep breath. There could be no point in lying to her friend—not someone who knew her as well as Mary did.

"Yes," Isabel said slowly. "I don't even know how it happened, how I allowed my feelings for him to change. It was a silly inclination on my part to leave my heart unguarded in such a fashion. But how could I accept Mr. Bradford when I had feelings for someone else? That is something I did not want to do."

"Then I think you made the right decision," responded Mary, looping her arm through Isabel's. "And selfishly, I am glad."

Isabel smiled. "I am too. At least I will not be married to a man I do not love."

"Well, perhaps your time at Emberwilde was not meant to be your great adventure. I wonder what will be."

Isabel wished she could share her friend's optimism. "I think my time of adventure is over."

"Oh, I don't know about that. The important thing to remember is that no experience is ever wasted. It is being used to fashion you into the person you are meant to be, and to move you to the place where you are supposed to go."

"Be that as it may, what comes next frightens me." Isabel looked toward the neighboring trees, which reminded her so much of the Emberwilde Forest. A strange, unexpected pang of homesickness struck her. "Mr. Langsby said that there is a governess position open just to the north of London, and he has recommended me for it. He is waiting to hear back from the household. If they accept me, I fear I will have no choice but to go, and if I do, Lizzie will have to stay here. Being apart from her is my worst fear."

Mary's steps slowed. "That does seem so far away."

"Now there is nothing to do but wait."

Regret began to wind its way into her heart, and Isabel squeezed her eyes shut to keep the dread at bay. She had to accept the consequences of her decision, for there could be no turning back.

Colin rode to Emberwilde. Miss Creston needed to know the truth. It could not wait another day, and he would make sure she knew.

He handed Sampson to one of the stable boys who came around as he approached, and with determination he mounted the stone steps to the front entrance. This was not a visit for which he would take the tradesmen's entrance, for he was not here for Ellison. No, he was here for another person entirely.

Mrs. Ellison must have seen him approach. She was in the foyer before he could even hand his hat to the footman waiting to receive it.

"Mr. Galloway," she said, surprise draining her already pale complexion of color. "What are you doing here? If it is Mr. Ellison you seek, you should find him in his study, like always."

"I am not here for Mr. Ellison," he stated. "Is Miss Creston at home?"

Her hand flew to her neck. "Why, the nerve, calling so openly on a young lady! You should be ashamed."

Colin did not even flinch. He'd expected to receive at least a handful of attacks on his character. This was nothing new. "This is not a social call, Mrs. Ellison. I need to speak with Miss Creston on a legal matter."

Mrs. Ellison lowered her hand and drew a deep breath. Could it be that she was summoning courage? For a moment, her gray eyebrows drew together in concern, but the expression quickly passed, and she thrust her chin into the air. "She is not here."

Her response caught him off guard. "What do you mean, she is not here?"

Mrs. Ellison toyed with the long chain about her neck. "She and her sister have returned to Fellsworth. It seems she was not suited for life at Emberwilde."

Colin was not sure he could believe what he had just heard. The muscles in his jaw began to tense. "Fellsworth? Why would she be at Fellsworth?"

Mrs. Ellison's lips formed a hard line before she opened her mouth to speak. "You might as well know. No doubt everyone will know soon enough. Miss Creston has disrespected our family in the vilest of manner. She is no longer welcome in our home."

Colin could only stare at Mrs. Ellison for several seconds as her words took hold in his mind. Anger crept in, slowly choking out disbelief. "No longer welcome? Why? What has she done?"

Mrs. Ellison raised her eyebrows, as if to suggest that the conversation was beneath her. "I owe you no information or answers. This is a family matter."

Colin struggled to keep his voice controlled. "Like I told you when I arrived, I am not here on a social call. I have information that needs to be discussed with her immediately."

"And what could be so important? She is gone now, and she will not be coming back."

"I would not be so sure on that regard. But perhaps you have not heard. Miss Creston has been named the heiress of Heddeston Park."

Colin waited for her response. Her expression remained as stone, unflinching. Unchanging. Had she already known?

At length she spoke. "Leave it to my father to distribute our family's fortune to such an undeserving, ungrateful wench."

Of course she would speak of her own niece so unkindly. Colin was quickly realizing the older lady's tactics. "Think of her what you will, but her character has no bearing on the situation. She has until her twenty-first birthday to claim the property, otherwise it shall pass to you." He watched her closely for any reaction before adding, "But I am sure you already knew of that."

"And how would I know what was in my father's will? It was not public!"

True, old Mr. Hayworth was a private man, but in Colin's experience, family members knew where a fortune was going. "So you had no knowledge of your father's plans for the property? I know the steward has spoken with you on several occasions regarding the heir. You never thought to mention Miss Creston to him? Even after you went on a quest to find her and bring her here?"

"I hid nothing, Mr. Galloway. I knew nothing. And I owe you no answers."

What she did not say spoke much louder than the words that came from her mouth.

"How is it that you were conveniently able to locate her before the steward even knew her name?" he demanded.

"As I have said before, my cousin wrote to me after coming into contact with a colleague of Isabel's late father. My cousin, of course, knew of the relation and made the fortunate connection."

"That is most convenient, is it not?" Colin could not prevent accusation from coloring every word. "And when she arrived, did you not put the pieces together? Or did you plan to keep it from her, so her birthday would come and go without mention?"

"You should not speak of things that do not concern you, Mr. Galloway. Again, I did not know the details of my father's estate. My father was very secretive with his will and his intentions. I am hardly on trial here. I offered my niece kindness, and in the end she offered betrayal. If anyone is to be blamed for the current state of affairs, it is she."

"And what constitutes betrayal?" He should stop talking. He should turn and leave. For he was no longer speaking as a magistrate or solicitor. He was speaking as a man whose feelings were hopelessly intertwined with the situation.

He did not expect her to respond, but she did. "A match was made for her. She encouraged a gentleman's affections and then refused his offer. That sort of loose behavior is not to be borne, especially under my roof."

"Ah. I see." The pieces were becoming very clear. Colin began to pace. "The gentleman you speak of—that is, of course, Mr. Bradford?"

"Who else?" Her round face was growing red now, and the area around her eyes was turning pink. "She made him believe she had affection for him, and he proposed, and she denied him. I cannot have a woman with such questionable morals in my house."

"And that would be most convenient, would it not?"

"What does that mean?"

"Even if the connections were made, and Miss Creston did inherit, the property and all of its resources would undoubtedly slip into her husband's control. And Mr. Bradford is an ally of yours, is he not? Having him in control of Heddeston Park would be the next best thing to controlling it yourself."

He'd stepped too far, and yet everything was making sense, falling into place like a completed puzzle.

Her jaw trembled. "You need to leave now."

The volume of his voice rose as his confidence increased. "I will leave, Mrs. Ellison, but rest assured, I have full intentions of informing Miss Creston of her inheritance. I cannot stand by and watch an innocent young woman be taken advantage of and deceived in such a manner."

He turned to leave, but the high pitch of her voice stopped him. "You are fooling no one, Mr. Galloway. You speak of acting nobly, and yet are your own intentions truly honorable? My niece will be quite the catch once her fortune is made known. I have no doubt you see your opportunity to marry for money to right your own estate. You should be ashamed of yourself, and I would, quite honestly, expect no less."

Colin knew she was looking for any opportunity to take the focus off herself. He would not play that game. He bowed a low, formal bow. "Good day, Mrs. Ellison."

He spun to leave, and as he did, he caught sight of Mr. Ellison standing in the corridor that led back to his study. His graying head was stooped, his posture sagged, but his eyes were fixed firmly on Colin.

Colin wondered how long the man had been listening. "I did not see you there, Ellison."

Mrs. Ellison chimed in cold tones, "Mr. Galloway was just leaving."

Ellison ignored his wife and nodded toward the door. "I will see you out."

Mrs. Ellison huffed as they were leaving, but Colin did not care. Anger pumped through him, fueling his demand for justice. He did not want to speak anymore to an Ellison; he had heard enough. But as they stepped into the cool of the morning, the older man's words were soft and controlled.

"I know what you are thinking, Galloway. I would be thinking the same thing."

Colin doubted very much that Ellison knew what he was thinking. "And that is?"

"You are thinking that I had some part in this."

The men stepped down onto the lawn, where the dew still clung to the grass.

"And would I be right?" Colin challenged.

The farther they stepped away from the house, the more Ellison had to say. "I heard a great deal of what you said to my wife, son. It is no secret that Emberwilde is in trouble. Adding funds such as what Heddeston Park would afford to us would certainly help set us to right. But you must know that I had no part in it. Truth be told, I returned home from visiting a tenant to find my nieces out of the house. But what can be done? My financial burdens at present are so heavy that I cannot pretend it is not a positive thing. Did I not even try to convince you to consider marriage? I had no idea my wife would take things this far."

To Colin, Ellison's explanation seemed thin and weak. "It is not too late to set things right."

"No, it is not. I heard you say that you will travel to Fellsworth to inform Isabel personally."

"I will."

"Then travel with my blessing. Not that you need it."

The men fell silent as they walked the familiar path. Colin wanted to believe Ellison. The man had been almost like a father to him since his uncle passed. He had taught him a great deal about managing an estate, information he would find beneficial in the coming months as he turned his sights more fully to transforming his own property. But money—and want or need of it—could cause men to act out of character.

Colin did, in this instance, feel a bit sorry for the older man. More than likely he was telling the truth. 'Twas no secret Mrs. Ellison had the propensity to act selfishly. How many times had she acted thus when making marriage arrangements for her daughters? And would she not act in the same manner to secure her own future?

But Colin's questions and concerns loomed. There was another matter to discuss. "And Bradford? What say you on that account?"

At the mention of Bradford's name, Ellison looked toward the sky. "Bradford is an eager pup, perhaps a bit too eager. He has my wife's ear, and for good reason. Without our support, I am not sure what would happen to the foundling home. It is the one charitable institution we have been unwilling to cease supporting. Mr. Bradford is a savvy man. He knows where his opportunities lie; he always has. Perhaps his intentions toward my niece were honest, but more than likely my wife had designs to keep her close, and away from a union with someone outside of her control. The irony of that situation is that, in light of recent circumstances, if Bradford were to marry Isabel and gain Heddeston Park's assets, he would be much better off than we are at Emberwilde. He would not need us anymore." Ellison shrugged. "I cannot pretend to understand this mess fully."

"There's hardly time to plan a wedding in advance of Miss Creston's birthday," Colin said.

"True. So perhaps Bradford was merely a convenient distraction. But as it stands, the future of the foundling home is in jeopardy, for I have had a letter just yesterday from someone interested in buying the building. It has access to the main road and is closely situated to town. As much as I would hate to break up the property, I may have to sell it."

Such news was upsetting but hardly unexpected.

"Well, Henry and I are to meet with the solicitor one last time to get all of the paperwork in order and ready, and then I will travel to Fellsworth as soon as possible to inform Miss Creston. I understand she will turn twenty-one years of age shortly, so time is a factor."

"Good luck, son. Keep me posted on what you learn. I should be anxious to hear it."

Colin left Emberwilde with a heavy countenance. He should feel better about the situation than he did. After all, Miss Creston was to inherit, and she would most likely return to the area. But despite his complicated relationship with the Ellisons, he did not want to see them in a predicament like the one they were about to endure.

Chapter Thirty-Seven

Isabel had been back at Fellsworth only a couple of days when she was summoned to Mr. Langsby's office.

The request had a strange sense of familiarity. Memories of the morning when he had informed her of Aunt Margaret's request rushed her.

But today there could be no doubt that he was summoning her to announce whether he knew of a governess position.

Like that morning several months ago, she was clad in her gown of black. Her hair had been slicked back into her Fellsworth chignon. This time she was not nearly so careless about how her hair was dressed, nor did she care whether her gown was embellished with fresh blooms. She followed every rule.

She forced a smile to her lips and brightness to her expression. She lifted her hand to Mr. Langsby's door and knocked.

His voice was muffled. "Enter."

She stepped into the office. It looked the same as ever. Crystal clear windows. Faded maps on the wall. Dusty books on the shelf. Tall, thin Mr. Langsby was seated behind his desk.

But nothing could have prepared her for the man who joined him there.

Mr. Galloway!

She drew a sharp breath at the sight of him.

The corner of his mouth curved upward as she entered. At the sight, her stomach flipped within her.

Mr. Galloway offered a bow. "Miss Creston."

Remembering her manners, she curtsied in return.

Mr. Langsby, who did not get up from his desk, leaned forward on his elbow. "Miss Creston, I trust you are familiar with Mr. Galloway."

"I am," she responded, forcing her eyes toward the superintendent and hoping the men could not hear the pounding of her heart.

"Then you know that Mr. Galloway is the magistrate for Northrop. He claims to be here on legal business."

Isabel's heart fell slightly. It was childish, but a part of her had hoped he had come for a more romantic reason. "Of course."

Mr. Galloway stepped forward. The light slanted through the window, highlighting his dark brown hair and broad shoulders. "As I explained to Mr. Langsby, I have a message for you to be delivered in private. It has been prepared by the solicitor of your grandfather's estate. It is of a sensitive nature, to be delivered personally."

His words sounded serious. Isabel wrung her hands as his words registered. "My grandfather's estate? You are worrying me, Mr. Galloway."

Before Mr. Galloway could respond, Mr. Langsby stood. "You do understand, Mr. Galloway, that I am hesitant to leave one of our ladies alone in the presence of a man we do not know."

"He is not a stranger, Mr. Langsby," interjected Isabel. "I assure you I will be quite safe."

Mr. Langsby studied Mr. Galloway for several seconds. "Very well. I will be right outside in the hall, but I shall leave the door open. Just a few minutes, mind you."

Isabel had not realized she had been holding her breath until Mr. Langsby passed through the door. She turned to Mr. Galloway.

Once they were alone, a full smile brightened his face. "It is good to see you, Miss Creston."

She could barely control her own smile. "It is good to see you as well."

He shifted his weight. "I hope this is not too forward, but I have just learned about what happened with you and your aunt. And Mr. Bradford. And I am sorry for it."

His voice held no malice, no judgment, and his expression was soft with sympathy.

"I suppose only time will tell if my decision was prudent." She shrugged and forced a little smile. "But it seems I am right back where I started now."

He stepped closer and fidgeted with his hat in his hands. "Like I said, I am sorry for it, but if I am not too bold, I must say that I think you made the right decision."

Her breathing seemed to slow at his words, and yet her pulse seemed to race. The fact that he had an opinion about her personal life touched her. "What do you mean?"

When he hesitated, she prompted, "Please, I would like to know."

He drew a deep breath and fixed his gaze on the plaster ceiling for several moments, as if trying to find the right words. "I do not mean to speak ill of anyone, mind you. But I have known Bradford all my life. And I will only say that he may not be exactly the man he seems to be."

A little wave of relief swept over her. He was not going to scold her for turning down the proposal. Her words rushed from her lips. "I value your opinion, Mr. Galloway. Thank you for sharing it with me."

"You are well?" The concern in his voice warmed her.

"I am, thank you."

"You look very—"

"Different?" she offered with a laugh, not giving him time to finish his sentence. With a nervous pat she smoothed down her hair, certain that she was no longer beautiful. Gone were the gowns of muslin and silk. Gone were the lovely feminine colors. Gone were the intricate curls of her hair and the expert styling. She wore no jewelry. No embellishments.

He hesitated, as if a bit surprised by her interjection, then abruptly extended a letter. "Here is the promised news. From Heddeston Park."

She took the missive from him and frowned as she slid her finger beneath the wax seal, popping it free from the paper. She opened the letter and began to read. "What is this?"

Without giving her the opportunity to finish reading the letter's contents, he responded, "Heddeston Park was left to you. In its entirety."

She lowered the letter and met his gaze. "Why, that cannot be. Constance said it was left to a distant cousin."

He shrugged. "Well, she was misinformed. It belongs to you now. You need only claim it before your twenty-first birthday. You see, there was no entailment with the estate, and so your grandfather was free to leave it in whatever manner he chose. His will was written so that the estate passes to his oldest child, and thereafter, to his oldest child's oldest child. And that is you. If you have a child, your child will inherit, and so on, thus keeping Heddeston in your direct family line."

"But that cannot be!" she repeated, shocked. Disbelief shook her voice. She attempted to read the letter, but her hands began to tremble with the surprise. "I thought my grandfather was furious with my mother for marrying my father."

Despite her nervousness, Mr. Galloway remained calm. "He must have changed his mind at some point and reconsidered his opinions of your mother, for it was all left to her. As you know, your grandparents and the Ellisons lost contact with your father after your mother died. When your grandfather died, they resumed the search for you, but by then your father had died and you were quite hard to trace."

"But my aunt was able to locate me eventually." Isabel lowered the letter. "Was she aware of this inheritance?"

Mr. Galloway shrugged. She sensed hesitation in his voice. "That I cannot say."

Isabel struggled to put the pieces together in her mind. "But if she knew, surely she would have said so."

Mr. Galloway fidgeted with the hem of his waistcoat and cleared his throat before speaking. "From what I understand, if you fail to claim your inheritance by your twenty-first birthday, the property will pass to her."

The truth was becoming clear. "So she intentionally kept this from me so she could inherit."

"Far be it from me to pry, but I assume you are aware that Emberwilde is facing financial troubles. I believe your aunt saw the opportunity, and, well . . ."

Isabel caught his full meaning.

Suddenly, the past several months made sense. Everything fell into line. Emberwilde was in financial trouble—the sort of trouble fixed by the sum of money of an inheritance. Her aunt was frightened of being without money—it was evident in her every lavish expense. And Mr. Bradford was a pawn—a way for the Ellisons to simultaneously keep tabs on her and be rid of her.

As comprehension intensified, so did her anger. She had been bested by those acting as family.

"I believe Miss Ellison did not know," Mr. Galloway offered, as if reading her mind.

Isabel sank down into a chair. The room felt hot. She looked up to Mr. Galloway. His lips pressed together in sympathetic understanding.

"And how is the estate being cared for now? Aunt Margaret said it was in ruins."

"Not at all. It's in excellent condition. Your grandfather established a trust to see to the care of the estate for five years."

Mr. Galloway approached her, the first time he had moved since he had been here. He sat in the chair beside hers and rested his hat on his knee. He carried with him a scent of the outdoors and horses, of a long ride. And yet, the realization that he had accompanied the letter instead of allowing the solicitor to send it warmed her.

"This is a great deal to take in, but I thought it best that you hear it from someone you know."

"Yes." She nodded, surprised by the tears blurring her vision. "I am grateful to you for delivering the message personally."

He gave a little chuckle. "You look so very sad. This is a wonderful thing, Miss Creston. In fact, I think congratulations are in order. Heddeston Park is a desirable home with a healthy income in its own right. You and Lizzie will be set for a very, very long time."

She offered a smile. She was torn between the thrill of excitement and the sting of her family's betrayal.

"I've no doubt this will take some time to sink in. It is a great deal of news. Good news, I might add."

She appreciated his effort to lighten the moment. "Yes, you are right."

His voice lowered, as if taking her into confidence. "It is not my place to say, but as your friend, I might offer a bit of advice, if you should like to hear it."

She found herself hungry for safe counsel from someone who genuinely cared for her. How rare it was to find, she realized, in the world outside of Fellsworth. She nodded.

"I do not pretend to know what you yourself must do. But there is no need to rush anything, Miss Creston. Be cautious."

She nodded.

"You have a few options that I would like to share with you. The solicitor will continue to see to the day-to-day management of the estate. You may go and live at the estate immediately, or you may choose to stay in your current circumstance. There is no need for you to rush a decision. And I can recommend the steward, Driscoll. He served your grandfather faithfully and is a fine man. From here I will travel on to London, but with your permission I will stop back at Fellsworth in two days' time. If you decide you would like to travel to the estate then, I would be happy to escort you and your sister. If that is agreeable."

Unable to find her voice, she nodded her agreement. She sensed he was preparing to depart. Her heart sank within her at the thought.

He stood and straightened his cravat, a playful grin on his lips. "I will be on my way. I do not wish to worry your superintendent."

Isabel stood and refolded the letter that had announced her change of fortune. She wanted to plead with him to stay. She had so many more questions, so many more things she wanted to hear him say. But all she could utter was, "Thank you, Mr. Galloway."

He turned to face her. "Oh, and I wasn't going to say *different*."

"Hmm?"

"Earlier, when I commented on your appearance."

She ran a hand down the front of her dress. "I . . . I . . ."

"I meant you look beautiful."

He locked eyes with her. Her arms suddenly felt heavy, her legs unable to support her. She was both frozen and impossibly light at the same time.

But before she could respond, Lizzie burst into the room.

"Mr. Galloway!" she cried, running to him with childlike vigor and jumping at him.

Isabel marveled at the sight. Never had she seen her sister so affectionate toward anyone.

Mr. Galloway laughed and swept her up in his arms. The sight of unrestrained happiness tugged at something deep inside of her, the secret part of her that longed for a genuine home.

"Have you missed me?" Lizzie demanded, placing her arm around his shoulder.

"I have," he responded, amusement brightening his eyes. "Very much."

"Good." She settled and turned to face him more fully. "Do ponies have memories?"

"I can honestly say that I do not know." He smiled at the question. "I am sure they do. Why do you ask?"

"Because I have been thinking about Caesar. I miss him ever so much. Do you think he misses me?"

"Oh, I've no doubt he does. Who else would be riding him?"

"That is what worries me," she said, shaking her head, her lips forming a pretty pout. "Nobody else is small enough. Nobody except for me. What if he is lonely or sad?"

"Mr. Carter is with him. Do you think Caesar does not enjoy his company?"

"I suppose so, but Mr. Carter does not always give him the sugar that he likes. He thinks he knows which is Caesar's favorite, but he doesn't."

Mr. Galloway shifted Lizzie in his arms. "If it will make you feel better, I shall take some sugar to Caesar on my next visit to Emberwilde. How's that?"

Lizzie furrowed her brow, as if contemplating the offer. "When will you go next?"

"Well, from here I must go to London, but I should be back in Northrop within the week."

"I suppose that will have to do," she said. "I do not know if I will ever go back to Emberwilde. Isabel says she does not know if we will ever go there again."

Mr. Galloway looked up at Isabel before responding. "Well, I've no doubt that your sister knows what is best for you."

"I do," Isabel said, joy unfurling in the bottom of her heart. "And what's best for you, Lizzie, is neither at Emberwilde nor here."

Chapter Thirty-Eight ————————

*W*hen Mr. Galloway returned with a carriage two days later, Lizzie and Isabel were prepared.

Several months ago they had left Fellsworth with very little.

Recently they had made their way back with little more.

And now they each clutched only one valise but possessed something far more valuable: security.

Mary, who was standing to Isabel's left, squeezed her hand as the carriage rumbled to a stop. "How cruel it is to have to bid farewell to you twice!"

Isabel turned and hugged her friend, who had been with her through so many of life's ups and downs. "I will send for you, Mary. You have my word. As soon as I am settled, you are coming to live with us."

Mary's eyes filled with tears. "I should like that very much."

Isabel squeezed her in a tight embrace. Then, with Lizzie's hand tucked in her own, she stepped toward the carriage. A small crowd of students had gathered, as they usually did whenever a carriage arrived, and Isabel searched the faces for Mr. Galloway.

Her heart leaped at the sight of him. He was head and shoulders above the rest of those gathered, and he was speaking with Mr. Langsby.

Isabel told herself not to allow her mind to run away with her, not to get lost in the questions and the hurts of what had transpired at Emberwilde. There would be time to sort those feelings. But now it seemed as if she had been given a gift: The gift of having lived with plenty and with little. The gift of having seen the true versions of herself and Lizzie in both circumstances. It was an experience she would never forget. She hoped Lizzie never would either.

The carriage jostled them away from Fellsworth for the second time, and it rumbled across the back roads and through the Surrey countryside. Sunlight peeked through the clouds. Isabel leaned to look out the window, and from where she sat she could see Mr. Galloway through the window, riding Sampson alongside the carriage.

She recalled seeing him for the very first time through the carriage window when they had arrived at Emberwilde. Her heart swelled as she thought of how her opinions of him had deepened into a strong and unfamiliar affection.

Lizzie, who had curled up on the bench beside her, now rested her head on Isabel's lap. How her sister could sleep on these rides Isabel would never know, but at least the child seemed to find peace.

Isabel took Mr. Galloway's hand as she stepped down from the carriage. The breeze carried with it sweet scents of roses and earth. She pushed down her insecurities, her fears of everything she still had to learn, and enjoyed the moment. Her foot landed solidly, squarely on the ground. A shiver of connectedness surged through her, as if she had finally arrived home, as if she had finally found the place she was meant to be.

Mr. Galloway squeezed her hand, then turned to help Lizzie down from the carriage.

"Welcome home, ladies. Welcome home."

Isabel's breath caught in her throat as she beheld Heddeston Park. Even though Mr. Galloway had assured her the house was in excellent condition, she still had her aunt's words in her mind and expected the home to be in ill repair. But the home before her was beyond her wildest dreams.

The redbrick house adorned with stone quoins at every corner rose three stories into the afternoon sky. It was capped by a hipped slate roof, and four symmetrical chimney stacks seemed to touch the wispy clouds. Tall sash windows complete with glazing bars were evenly spaced on each level. A white, cheery door served as the main entrance, and a fanlight positioned over it seemed to welcome her. Behind it, trees stood at attention, dressed in their full summer splendor.

A handful of neatly dressed servants were on hand to greet them as formally as any at Emberwilde ever would. Isabel's time at Emberwilde had prepared her for such a day, and despite the pain associated with her recent time there, she was grateful. Mary was right—every step of her journey had prepared her in some way for the next.

She was sad to see Mr. Galloway depart shortly after their arrival, but he promised to return soon, and she was eager to explore the house and grounds with Lizzie. But her happiness was short-lived, for several hours after their arrival one of the servants brought her a letter.

"What's this?" Isabel asked as the young girl approached her.

"A boy just came by the servants' entrance and said I should give it to you right away."

Isabel took the letter, dismissed the servant, and retreated to the drawing room, where she sat on one of the west-facing window seats in the sun's warmth to read the letter. The handwriting was vaguely familiar, which both intrigued her and concerned her, for who would already know that she was here? She broke the seal with her finger and unfolded the paper. Her eyes skimmed quickly the signature: Edmund Bradford.

Her hand flew to her mouth. It was highly improper for a man to send her any manner of correspondence, especially without being engaged to her. And she had made her feelings on the matter perfectly clear. Confused yet curious why he should be writing her, she angled the words to the sunlight.

My dear Miss Creston,

Allow me to be among the first to offer my sincerest congratulations on your new endeavor. Heddeston Park is a splendid home, and it pleases me to think of you there.

My apologies on disrupting you when you have so recently returned, but I am writing with news that I think will be of concern to you. One of our young girls, Jane, has fallen quite ill. She has asked about you several times, and knowing your kind nature, I thought you would like to know that your presence has been requested.

It pains me to think of how things were left between us, but that does not change the fact that I always did admire your willingness to assist. I do hope that what has conspired between us does not affect your affection for the children. If you are agreeable, please come at your earliest convenience. I know she would be most grateful for your visit.

Yours respectfully,
Edmund Bradford

Chapter Thirty-Nine ————————

Colin's body was weary from the days of travel, but satisfaction spread through him. Miss Creston and her sister were safe, and not only in the sanctity of their new home. There was no need for them to fear or to worry who would provide for them.

Despite his personal desire to remain in Miss Creston's presence, Colin had not lingered at Heddeston Park any longer than necessary. The day had been overwhelming for his charges, and they needed to be settled.

He spent the afternoon on his own land. Work had begun on clearing the space where the original manor once was, and he found himself actually excited for the estate's future. His injured heart had always been closed to the land, unwilling to revive it to its former glory. But something in him seemed to change today. Maybe it was frustration with his current role. Maybe it was a dissatisfaction within him that urged him to settle down. But whatever the reason, his attitude toward his birthright was changing.

Colin was eager to catch up with McKinney on the town's happenings while he was away, but one task remained before he could visit his friend to recap the week's events. While in London on business, he had retrieved a package for his aunt, and he aimed to deliver it before day's end. By the time Colin returned his personal items to his room at the boardinghouse, twilight's purple had given way to a misty night. A tentative rain drizzled down, cloaking the earth in a chilly dampness.

When he arrived at the cottage, however, he was surprised

to learn that his aunt had already retired for the evening. Lockert Cottage was dark, save for the main fire and the candles winking from the front window. It was Miranda who greeted him. His nephew and the few servants were nowhere in sight.

Colin had not spoken privately with Miranda since their conversation at the dinner at the Atwells. Whether by design or coincidence, she had kept her distance. Now she leaned against the doorframe in the shadow of night, as she had so many other times. If she was reluctant to see him, she gave no indication. He reminded himself that there was no reason why he should feel uncomfortable.

After explaining his reason for being there, he handed the package wrapped in brown paper to Miranda. "I am sorry I missed her. If you could tell her I will be by tomorrow, I would appreciate it."

Given her recent behavior, he expected the conversation to end then and there. But she said, "Will you not come in? It is quite cold out, and the fire is still strong. It would not take any time at all to heat a meal for you."

There was hope in her voice, and an eagerness he could not deny. "I thank you for the offer, but I am due to speak with McKinney before the night is out."

He tipped his hat and turned to leave, but she reached out to detain him, her hand just short of brushing his sleeve. "I have heard that Miss Creston is the heiress of Heddeston Park and that you've brought her back with you."

"News does travel fast, does it not?"

"I suppose so, but Henry told me the real reason for your trip not long after you left." She toyed with the hem of her work apron. "I suppose your willingness to travel on your cousin's behalf had less to do with the inheritance at hand than with the personal endeavor involved."

Colin drew a deep breath. *Personal endeavor.* He could pretend that was not the case, but the truth was winding its way around him. Each interaction with Miss Creston bound him to her tighter and tighter. Even if he wished it to be otherwise, he doubted he could change the course of his attitude toward her. And apparently, his attempts to hide the true nature of his feelings were insufficient to trick those who knew him best.

"I did what needed to be done, under the law."

She laughed. "Come now, Colin. We are not children, and I am not blind. It does not do for you to hide from the truth. For as you know, all truth eventually comes to light, does it not? I wonder when the Ellisons will learn of her return."

"Henry was to send a message informing them that the estate has been settled. If they do not already know, they will very soon."

"I see." She folded her arms over her chest, a coy smile on her face. "I cannot help but wonder if Mr. Bradford has also heard the news. His anguish at her refusal is well known throughout Northrop. He has not been at church since Miss Creston left, and he is rumored to be quite heartbroken. But I daresay one man's pain is another man's gain." Miranda continued. "Does she return your regard?"

This topic was highly improper, yet he did not reprimand her. For the question lingered in his own mind—it was one he had wrestled with since he learned she had been sent from Emberwilde. "I can only hope that she does."

He looked at Miranda, really looked at her. He could see the longing in her eyes, just as he did nearly every time he encountered her. He did not want to see her hurt.

Now was the moment to set things right, once and for all. "Our paths diverged a long time ago, Miranda, and you must know that it was never my intention for you to feel any discomfort or pain because of me. But I do think things are best the way they are."

It was not the first time he had spoken such words to her, but as they left his mouth, something felt different. Perhaps it was the expression on her face as she received them. Perhaps it was because he believed them himself this time. Perhaps it was because he knew his heart was no longer his to give.

"I do beg your forgiveness if I have caused any pain," he continued, taking note of the manner in which she averted her gaze to the ground. "If there is anything I can do to make things easier, please know I am at your service. But my heart belongs to another."

After leaving Miranda, Colin approached the Pigeon's Rest Inn. Two torches blazed outside the tavern's main entrance. As he stepped over the cobbled stone to the door, it was flung open from the other side. On the threshold stood none other than Bradford.

Colin had only seen Bradford once or twice since interrupting him and Miss Creston that evening in Emberwilde's Blue Parlor, and they had not spoken since that night. But he was surprised to encounter Bradford here, for he was not one to frequent the Pigeon's Rest Inn.

Bradford ducked to step through the low-beamed doorway. By the torches' light Colin could not deny the fact that Bradford appeared much altered. A shadowy beard masked his normally clean-shaven jaw, and his hair hung disheveled beneath his hat. Dark shadows cupped his eyes as one deprived of sleep. If Colin had not heard the rumors of Bradford's broken heart, he would have judged the man to be ill.

He expected Bradford to pass by him without a word. Instead, Bradford blocked the way, preventing Colin from advancing.

"Galloway. Just the man I have been waiting to see."

Colin stopped, bracing himself, unsure of what to expect. "What can I do for you?"

"Heard you made a delivery to Heddeston Park today."

Bradford's words held a challenge. Colin cleared his throat. "If you are referring to Miss Creston and her sister, then yes. They have been safely delivered and are, no doubt, settling into their new home as we speak."

Bradford laughed and looked to the distance, but the expression on his face was anything but amused. Within moments, his tone once again sobered, and all trace of laughter dissipated. "I imagine she believes you rode in and saved the day. Quite the hero."

Colin brushed off the sarcasm in an attempt to end the conversation as soon as possible. He thought of the conversation he had with the Ellisons, and the role that Bradford played in using Miss Creston for financial gain, and he bristled. "You forget my cousin is a solicitor involved in finding the heiress, and I work for my cousin."

Bradford snorted. "You visited Miss Creston on behalf of your cousin? Come now, Galloway. Despite what the rumor of the day may be, I am not a fool. Your interest in her is hardly a secret. Let me ask you this. Do you think it better for her to be attached to someone like you instead of someone more established? Her family approved the match. I believe she did as well. Until you filled her head with other ideas. Accusations against me."

Colin bit back his words, for the very family that had approved the match had also attempted to take advantage of her situation. Both were unforgivable. "I made no attempt to sway her."

"So you deny it," Bradford accused. "You deny that you knew full well her aunt's intentions—"

"Were you aware?" Colin challenged. "Did you know that Margaret Ellison's intentions were to prevent Miss Creston from laying claim to Heddeston Park?"

Bradford sighed and looked out at the drizzling sky. The anger left his voice. "I did not. Whatever you may think of me, my affection for her was sincere."

The signs of his grief inclined Colin to believe him, and yet something in him resisted. For even though Miss Creston had not a farthing to her name when she arrived, she now had an impressive fortune, and any man who married her would be wealthy indeed. Even with this knowledge, Colin thought he could muster some compassion for the man, until Bradford said, "You were the manipulative one."

With each word that Bradford uttered, Colin found it increasingly difficult to keep his own temper in check. "Miss Creston, regardless of what you may think, is hardly a puppet to be manipulated. She has every right to make up her own mind, especially regarding her future. I had no part in her decision to refuse you."

"Did you not?" A sly smile curled Bradford's lip. "I am sure that once you learned of her inheritance you thought you could bend her situation to your advantage."

Colin shrugged. "She could inherit thousands of pounds and it would make no difference to me. But what about you? Now that she has fallen out of favor with the Ellisons, is your love still strong enough to chase her? Or can you not afford the cost of Mrs. Ellison's fury?"

Bradford's face twisted in anger, and he pushed past Colin into the dark of night.

Colin looked back to the inn to see McKinney's thick build filling the doorframe. Warmth and light tumbled from the door, and the sounds of clanking pewter and laughing patrons met his ears.

He wondered how long McKinney had been standing there, and if he had heard Bradford's insinuation of his interest in Miss Creston. But McKinney only shook his shaggy head, looking out toward Bradford's retreating form.

"Wondered when you would get here."

"Would have been here sooner, but I just had a little conversation with Bradford."

"Nothing will mess with a man's senses quite like a woman."

Colin followed McKinney's gaze and watched as Bradford turned the corner to the main bridge and disappeared into the night's shadows. He was not sure how to respond. Perhaps the man's heart was broken, but if so, Colin doubted it was from unrequited love. More like an unrealized fortune.

He turned back to McKinney. "Something is not right."

"About what?"

"About a great number of things."

"He plays a convincing role."

Colin nodded. "That he does. But that's just it. He plays the role too well. We need to keep our eye on him, McKinney. Like I said, something is not right."

Chapter Forty

"So I take it you brought the ladies back with you?" asked McKinney as he led Colin toward a table near the fire, where they were seated.

Colin nodded and drummed his fingers on the table. "Yes, Miss Creston and Miss Lizzie are now at Heddeston Park."

McKinney clicked his tongue. "Serves those Ellisons right. Never did like them, this is just one more reason why. Bet Miss Creston is none too happy living so close to them."

"Oh, I don't know," Colin replied, allowing his thoughts to rest on her for several moments. "She does not seem like one to hold a grudge. After all, she's not as cantankerous as you."

McKinney threw his head back in laughter. "Well, this is true. Besides, at least the story has a happy ending. Look at that new home of hers. I'd gladly endure a bit of betrayal if in the end I was to walk away with a dwelling like that."

Colin sobered and glanced around the room at the dozens of faces. "You have quite the guest list tonight. Anything interesting happen while I was gone?"

McKinney sobered. "There was a man found battered and beat up along the Black Wood Forest yesterday. He's fine now but wouldn't say who touched him."

Heaviness pressed against Colin's chest. That was the way it was in the smuggling world. No one would dare speak out against the ring for fear of retribution. "Who was it?"

McKinney shrugged. "I'd never seen him before."

"Where's the man now?"

"He stayed here one night and was gone the next day. A new trading company has come through and increased traffic even more. To that point, our friend is back."

Colin frowned. "Who's that?"

"Dent."

McKinney nodded toward the corner Dent frequented.

Colin lifted his gaze, and at the sight, he went on alert. After all, not only was Dent one of the main suspects for the smuggling, but he was the one-handed man who had threatened Miss Creston.

The thin man huddled in the corner, alone. He bent his head over his meal, his shaggy hair hanging in his face, seemingly oblivious to anyone around him.

Colin returned his attention to McKinney. "Thought he hadn't been seen in a while."

McKinney stretched out his long legs. "You know how these traders are. Some come through regular, and others are a bit more unpredictable. He's just come through a few days ago, and now he's on his way back."

Just as Colin was about to respond, the door flung open to reveal a youth—one of the youths Colin had encountered that morning many weeks ago in Mr. Bradford's study. His small chest heaved and his eyes were wide. He scanned the room.

The boy's panicked expression alarmed Colin, so he stood and went to him. "You look like you've seen a ghost."

The boy gasped for air. "Is Mr. Bradford here?"

Colin sensed McKinney approaching from behind. "No, you just missed him. Did you not pass him on the road?"

The boy shook his head. "No, sir."

"Is something wrong?"

The boy gasped for air. "We saw a man sneaking around on the home grounds. He tried to get in, Mr. Galloway. Some of the boys scared him off, but I got out to find Mr. Bradford."

Colin looked over his shoulder to make eye contact with McKinney and gauge his opinion, but as he did, he noticed something else.

Dent had disappeared.

Every muscle tensed and Colin gripped the boy's shoulders. "You stay here. I will go check it out."

"But I can't stay here," the youth protested. "I must—"

Colin looked directly at the boy. "Stay here until I come back for you, is that clear?"

McKinney was now just behind him. His usually jovial expression was darkened.

Colin directed his words toward McKinney. "Where did Dent go?"

"I don't know." McKinney shrugged. "I looked up and he was gone."

Colin looked at the boy. "You stay here, all right?"

The boy nodded.

McKinney adjusted his coat. "Where are you going?"

"I'm going to find Dent." Colin pulled his hat low over his eyes.

"What, now?" McKinney gaped.

Colin gave a sharp nod. "Yep. And you are coming with me. Go get your weapon and I will find my cousin," he said. "Meet me back here."

McKinney lowered his voice to just barely above a whisper. "What's the plan?"

"Not sure yet. But the boy should have met Bradford on the road."

"Unless Bradford was not headed home."

"And now Dent has seemed to evaporate. If Dent is connected somehow to the activity at the foundling home and he heard the boy's words, then perhaps he went to secure something. Or warn someone. I suspect if we can find Dent, we will be that much closer to figuring this out."

By the time Colin had returned to the boardinghouse, informed Henry of the night's happenings, and returned to the alley by the Pigeon's Rest Inn, McKinney was waiting for them. Drizzle fell in uneven mists, and a haze blanketed Northrop.

"Where's the boy?" Colin asked.

"He's inside with Martha. She gave him some tarts and suddenly he wasn't so concerned about getting back to the home anymore."

"Good." Colin said the word aloud, but in fact nothing was good at all. There were many other children in harm's way at the moment.

The men decided to take a back road through the Black Wood Forest to the foundling home, avoiding Benton Bridge and the other main roads.

Colin had expected Dent to retreat to the forest, where he could hide in the shadows and mist. But by the time they reached the home, there was no sign of him. No noise, no activity, only stillness.

The trio settled in a low-lying spot at the forest's edge, one where they could easily keep an eye on the foundling home and the toolshed where one of the tunnels emerged. The home rose up majestically to meet the pewter-tinged clouds. But tonight the structure seemed to cast eerie, foreboding shadows. An occasional shadow would pass across one of the foundling home windows, but otherwise, all seemed normal.

"Don't think we are going to see anything here," growled McKinney, shifting his weight. "Think we ought to go check on the children?"

Colin was about to agree when he thought he saw movement along the tree line. How this reminded him of another time so very long ago, when he hunched in battle waiting for an enemy to burst forth.

He adjusted his grip on his pistol and fixed his eyes on the spot as if daring it to move again.

An owl's cry broke the silence, and Colin squinted into the shadows.

And then they saw him.

A figure, thin and wiry, crept out from the foliage. He was near the small shed, the one that marked the tunnel's entrance. Colin's heart raced.

"Think that's Dent?" asked Henry.

Colin looked to the man's hands, but darkness covered all. "Not sure."

McKinney kept his voice low. "I'd be willing to bet that wherever Dent is, Stanway is near. Stanway wasn't with him at the inn, but from what I've observed, where one is, the other is close behind."

Colin nodded. It would be foolish to assume that Dent was doing anything alone, and now he wondered if Stanway might be the man the children saw earlier.

McKinney jerked his head toward the forest. "What are you wanting to do? Follow him?"

Colin licked his lips, forcing his mind to stay calm. He wanted this business to be done, for as long as there was smuggling going on, the safety of the village was in jeopardy.

As Colin was weighing the best course of action, the man crept back out from the shadows, like an animal in slow retreat. He hunched as if dragging something behind him.

McKinney leaned close. "What's he doing?"

Colin strained his eyes to watch the man. He appeared to be headed toward one of the home's side doors. Alarm rushed him.

Colin had assumed that any criminal activity was confined to the tunnels.

"Is he going into the foundling home?" whispered Henry.

The very question sent a chill through Colin. There were children in that building. Young, innocent children. And as far as they knew, Bradford may or may not be there to protect them.

"I don't know, but I am going to find out. McKinney, you go check the shed where the tunnel leads. Do you know the one I am talking about?"

McKinney nodded his understanding.

"Henry, you take the far side of that fence. The other tunnel comes up just on the other side of the gate. See what you can find. But be careful. Signal with an owl's call if you need any help." Colin pressed his finger to his lips to remind the men to be quiet, left his comrades, and made his way along the forest's edge, just as the mystery man had done.

Once he was closer, he got a better view of the situation at hand. The side door to the yard where the children played was slightly ajar. A faint yellow glow flickered from the space.

He held his breath in sickened disbelief as the shifty man made his way to the open door, dragging something behind him as he did.

Colin had not been in the rooms beyond Bradford's office, and he was not completely familiar with the home's layout, but he noticed the same flickering light coming from Bradford's study.

The man had closed the door behind him, and Colin took advantage of this cover to hurry over to the window.

He lifted his head just enough to see over the window's ledge. He saw Dent and Stanway inside, standing before an open door in Bradford's office.

Anger flared and his chest tightened painfully. In that instant, all the lines connected. Every bit of evidence thus far made sense. Bradford was a part of this, and far from oblivious to what was happening in his own backyard. True, Bradford's timepiece had been found at the scene, and that could, he supposed, have been an accident of sorts. But now, with the two main suspects in Bradford's study, there could be no denying it.

Colin turned his attention back to the men in the study. They stood at an open door he had never noticed before on the opposite side of the desk. The door appeared to be built into the wall paneling, undoubtedly to disguise it. Through the opening, it looked as if a staircase led to a lower level, and the walls seemed to be made of a familiar brick—the same brick that lined the tunnels. Suddenly, it made sense. The disguised doors. The hidden tunnels. They were all connected.

Colin watched the men for several moments, then shifted his gaze to the other side of the room. Where was Bradford? If he had been coming back here from the inn, he should have arrived by now. Colin cast a glance over his shoulder to the road, as if he expected to see the man walking up it. But all was shrouded in hovering mist.

He would not allow this opportunity to slide. He assessed the men for weapons. Their weapons might be concealed, but a pistol sat on Bradford's desk in plain view. He saw nothing else.

He was about to straighten when a sharp jab to his spine stopped him.

"You just can't leave well enough alone, can you, Galloway?"

Colin stiffened at the familiar voice. *Bradford.*

Bradford continued. "Just go ahead and toss that pistol on the ground there."

At that moment, Stanway opened a side garden door, saw Colin, and leveled a knife at his head. It would be fruitless to attempt to fight them off, not with a pistol behind him and a blade before him.

Colin obeyed and tossed his weapon on the ground. He locked eyes with Stanway and kept his voice sharp. "Seems I've been out-played, is that not right, Bradford?"

"You'll be coming with me." Bradford's motions grew rougher by the moment. "Let's just say I'll not be underestimating you again, Galloway."

Again.

Colin fixed his feet firmly to keep his balance as Bradford pushed him forward. "Walk."

Colin complied, not taking his eyes off of Stanway. He stumbled over the uneven ground. He could only hope that McKinney or Henry had observed what happened, but he could not be sure. And he had his blade in his boot, just as he always did. It was not an inconceivable idea that he could wrest away from these men, even while they were armed, but he needed to be smart about how to proceed. He clenched his jaw as Bradford shoved him into the house.

Chapter Forty-One

*O*nce inside Bradford's stifling study, the image Colin had glimpsed through the window was much clearer. There was indeed a door that he had never noticed before. In fact, Colin realized, the entire wall was a line of paneled doors that might be closets or entries to other tunnels. A second panel was slightly ajar.

"So you knew of the tunnels the entire time, did you?" Colin said more as a statement than a question as he fixed his eyes on Bradford.

"They've been around longer than you or I. I'm surprised, actually, that someone so observant as yourself never noticed."

Bradford's dripping sarcasm irked Colin. Bradford's coat sat askew on his shoulders, and his neck cloth had come untied. He moved past Colin, and the scent of spirits hung heavy in the air. Colin soaked in all the details he could before Bradford's heavy hand pushed him down into a chair.

Dent stepped in through the tunnel door's opening and caught sight of Colin. His face twisted in question. "What's he doing here?"

Bradford cut his eyes toward the smaller man, accusation stiffening each word. "Thought you weren't followed."

Dent dropped a crate on the ground. "Didn't think I was."

Bradford gave Dent a warning glance and motioned for Stanway to continue lowering crates into the tunnel. "Go find me a length of rope to secure him. Quickly. Then get back to work."

Bradford cocked his pistol, blew something off of it, and returned his attention to Colin. "Congratulations, Magistrate Galloway. I had a nasty hunch that you were going to figure this out sooner or later. You were always clever. After all, the simple-tons surrounding us may believe in ghosts and spirits and fairies, but you? Surely not."

Colin ignored the sarcasm. "So are you going to let me in on your little secret?"

Bradford shrugged, no doubt in an attempt to appear untrou-bled, but the tightening of his jaw betrayed him. "What does it look like to you?"

Perspiration trickled down the side of Colin's face. His waist-coat felt too tight, his neck cloth restrictive. The gravity of his situation pressed heavily on him. But he could not let his nerves show. "Come now, Bradford. I'd expect you to be above smuggling."

"Would you?" Bradford asked. "And I never took you to be so naïve."

"There are children near," reasoned Colin. "Innocent children whom you have vowed to protect. Think on it, Bradford. The pres-ence of these men puts them in danger."

"The children are in no danger," Bradford shot back through clenched teeth.

"Really?" huffed Colin in pointed disbelief and fixed his eyes on the pistol still poised in Bradford's hands. Light from the dying fire reflected on the shiny metal. "I don't know about that."

He was poking Bradford, he knew. But Colin was not one to back down.

Colin continued to stare at the reflection, and the sad reality became clear. All these years everyone had believed Bradford's deter-mination to run the foundling home had been in earnest. All this time, had he only been interested in the building itself, for the tun-nels and secrets it hid? Colin could only guess there was much more to the circumstances than met the eye. For all the stories that had come out of the forest of ghosts and people disappearing and folklore suddenly made sense. This building had to be tied to it in some way.

Bradford sat atop his desk, half watching the man in the tunnel and half watching Colin. His foot tapped an erratic rhythm on the wood floor, the sound magnified in the quiet space.

From the looks of things, Bradford was getting desperate. If Colin knew anything about desperate men, it was that they were capable of anything. He wondered how long it would take McKinney and Henry to figure out what had happened. Hopefully not much longer. If only he could get to the blade in his boot and not be detected.

Colin considered Miss Creston. How easily things could have taken a much darker path had Bradford lured her into this world. Either he loved her, as he claimed, or he knew of her inheritance and the wealth that would accompany such a union.

He needed to formulate a plan and quickly. He scanned the room for exits. The door between Bradford's study and the foyer was closed. The front windows were latched. That left the door to the home's halls and the series of secret paneled doors that seemed to line the room. He focused his attention on another paneled door that was ajar.

Was it just his imagination, or did he see a flash of movement in the opening?

Colin bit his lip and watched as closely as he could without giving the impression that he was staring.

He noticed another movement. It was long, dark fabric, like that of a gown. And then he saw the toe of a narrow boot. Someone else was in this room. A woman.

Colin shifted his eyes back to Bradford so the captor would not grow suspicious.

Bradford turned his attention once again to Colin. "We had such a lovely arrangement all these years, did we not? Pity you had to ruin it."

Colin unclenched his jaw. "It will all catch up with you sooner or later, do you not know that?"

Bradford snorted. "Well, for that to be true, this would all need to be reported, and you are the only one who knows of our little arrangement. And there are ways to prevent you from sharing what you know."

Colin took the moment to assess his captors. Bradford held a weapon. Stanway had a blade tucked in his waistband. Dent was still finding a rope.

He rubbed his cheek against the shoulder of his coat to wipe away the perspiration.

With pistol still in hand, Bradford leaned over one of the crates, pried it open, and lifted a bottle of wine.

Colin fixed his attention on the pistol. Yes, it was in Bradford's hand, but Bradford was distracted.

Colin glanced toward the open door.

The fabric was dark, like the gowns the other foundling home workers wore, or perhaps a child.

But then another thought crossed his mind. The black fabric was the same hue that Miss Creston had been wearing when he delivered her to Heddeston Park.

The thought nearly stopped his heart.

Surely not. Surely the person inside was not Miss Creston.

But what had he told himself all along?

Desperate men were capable of anything.

Bradford lifted another bottle and assessed it. The nearby candlelight flickered on the bottle's glass.

Something had angered Bradford, for he reached toward Stanway and grabbed his arm and ordered to know something about the crate. As a result, Stanway returned to the tunnel.

Colin pressed his eyes shut and drew a deep breath. He could handle this situation. He did not want a woman or a child harmed. He flexed his hands.

Now was the time to take advantage of the break in Bradford's concentration.

Colin moved to stand, and as he did, the chair scooted across the wood floor, the sound shrill in the silence. Bradford whirled and his expression flamed into anger. He aimed his pistol at the same moment Colin jumped toward it and gripped Bradford's wrist tightly with both hands.

Bradford sprang into action.

Colin attempted to wrestle the pistol from Bradford, but a fist slammed into his ribs. Colin doubled over. With every ounce of energy he had, he rammed his body into Bradford, forcing him to stumble backward against the broad desk. The pistol flew from his hand.

Stanway emerged from the tunnel, grabbed Colin's collar, and pulled him off of Bradford, but Colin jabbed his elbow into Stanway's belly and twisted from his grip. Gasping for air, Colin did not like his odds. Both men were larger than he. He gave a quick scan of the room. Dent's figure was retreating into the corridor that led to the other rooms of the home.

He swung around and punched Stanway's jaw, sending the black-guard staggering backward. The man fell to the floor, unconscious. But for how long? And how long before Dent returned? Colin drew a deep breath.

He turned back to Bradford, who by this time had regained control of the pistol. It was pointed directly at him.

Chest heaving, Colin had no choice but to raise his hands in defeat.

"I will achieve my ends, Galloway. And you will not stand in the way." Perspiration now dripped to Bradford's coat, leaving dark spots on the fabric. He cocked the pistol.

Seeing the moment to distract him, Colin spoke. "Who is behind that door?"

Bradford twitched. His eyes flashed to the door and back to Colin.

"There is someone in there. Who is it?" demanded Colin. Despite the gun pointed at his chest, he felt a strange surge of confidence. As he spoke, he calculated how many steps it would take to retrieve the blade at his ankle and reach Bradford.

Whoever was behind the door moved just enough to make the door creak outward, as if she wanted her presence to be made known.

Bradford looked. Colin snatched his blade and lunged, slapping the gun from Bradford's hand and sending it clattering to the floor.

Bradford was a match for Colin. The men were of similar build. But Bradford swiftly ran out of air and energy. Colin wrapped his left arm around his opponent and squeezed and held the blade at his throat with his right hand, preventing Bradford from moving.

At that moment, McKinney and Henry burst in through the back entrance. Colin had never been so relieved to see the two men in his life. Henry gripped Dent's arms, which were bound behind him, and McKinney had his own pistol pointed at Bradford.

McKinney adjusted his aim, and his voice slid through gritted teeth. "What's going on in here? Looks like a bunch of nonsense to me."

Bradford expelled the air from his mouth. His shoulders slumped. He was trapped and outnumbered, and he knew it.

McKinney kicked the pistol that had been knocked to the floor to Colin, then secured Stanway, who was still collapsed on the ground.

Colin motioned for McKinney and his cousin to lead the men out to the lawn.

McKinney carried the unresponsive Stanway outside and then returned to help with the other two. Colin followed, and once on the lawn, the men bound the three captives and sat them on the grass. Both McKinney and Henry fixed their pistols on them.

"There is someone tied inside," Colin said. "I'll be right back."

Confident the smugglers were secure, Colin ran back inside to the slightly open door. He flung it open.

His fear was confirmed.

Miss Creston, bound and gagged, huddled in the corner of the tiny closet.

Tears stained her face, and her hair was hanging loosely over her shoulders. She was trembling as he reached inside to help her to her feet. Her legs were unsteady.

He opened the panel, but this one led not to a tunnel but to a closet of sorts. She stumbled as she stepped from the tiny space, and with her hands bound behind her back, she lost her balance. He caught her as she began to fall.

He quickly released the cloth around her mouth, and she coughed.

"What happened? Tell me immediately." His words were harsh, he knew. But seeing her in such a state sent fresh anger through him. He forced himself to wait for her answer before running to the lawn and taking his frustration out on Bradford. "Did he hurt you?"

She sniffed and shook her head, regaining her balance enough to turn so he could cut her ropes with his blade. Once her hands were free, the rope fell to the ground and she rubbed her wrists.

He returned his blade to his boot and took her wrists in his own rough hands. Her skin was flaming red, and he gently rubbed a finger over the injuries. A million questions ran through his mind. He pulled her into his embrace tightly. Desperately. He never could have guessed that Bradford would mean to harm her, and it wasn't until that moment that he realized the full extent of his own feelings.

He pressed his lips to the top of her head. She leaned more fully into him. Her shoulders shook. A sob escaped and she buried her face against his chest.

At length, she lifted her head from his chest. He leaned down to hear her, and her face was very near his. Her voice was raspy as she spoke. "I received a letter that one of the children was very ill and had asked for me. I did not want to disappoint the child, so I left Lizzie in the care of the servants and arrived here as soon as I could. But when I got here, the scenario was not at all what Mr. Bradford had described. He beckoned me into his office, and he was quite distraught. He spoke of time running out, and he told me how he loved me and wanted to marry me right away and how it would ruin everything if my aunt and uncle lost control of the foundling home. It made no sense. He seemed desperate, almost crazed. Of course, I refused his offer, and he grew angry and refused to let me leave. I thought he had gone mad, truly I did, and then he bound me and put me behind that door. I have never been so glad to hear a voice as I was to hear yours."

Her words wound their way around his soul. Around his heart. He drew a deep breath and tightened his arms around her, and she did not pull away. He inhaled the scent of her hair and reveled in the warmth of her in his arms. She nestled even closer. He could lose himself in this moment very quickly, if he had not three men to deal with on the lawn.

He tilted her chin up to see her eyes. He never wanted to see them glisten with tears again. With his thumb he brushed away a tear track. "I must go see to these men. I would not leave you for the world, but I cannot rest until I know the man who did this to you is securely restrained."

She nodded her agreement.

He could scarcely leave her. His boots wanted to stay fixed to the floor.

Colin took a deep breath. "I will never forgive myself for

allowing him to harm you." He brushed her hair away from her face. "I swear to you, with your permission, I will spend the rest of my days keeping you safe."

Her smile was all the encouragement he needed. He lowered his lips to hers, and she did not pull away. Instead, she wrapped her trembling arms around his neck.

She was what he had been waiting for, and now he knew what he had to do. He took her hand in his own and squeezed it. "Stay here with the children until I come back for you."

Miss Creston nodded and slipped out of the study.

The night air was cool as he stepped outside, but anger warmed him. He looked back to the building and saw the children watching from the windows, their innocent, curious faces somber at the scene. Many offenses could be overlooked, but those that threatened the safety of women and children could not.

Colin stood over Bradford, who stared defiantly back at him.

"If it takes me until my last breath, I will see that you pay for what you have done, you have my word on that," Colin said.

McKinney began to jerk the criminals to their feet, and Henry handed Colin a pistol. With a push, McKinney forced the men to start walking.

Colin did not take his eye off Bradford's back until they reached Northrop's small holding cell. He could not change what Bradford had done, nor could he change the fact that it took him awhile to put all of the pieces together. But he drew a satisfied breath. He had brought about some justice.

But what warmed him even more was to know that Miss Creston—his Isabel—was waiting for his return.

Chapter Forty-Two

*A*s Colin approached Heddeston Park, a stable boy came to take his horse.

He was eager to check on Isabel after the previous night's activity. She had seemed well enough when he had returned her to her home. He hoped sleep had found her and she was able to rest.

Stephenson, the butler, greeted him.

"Pleasure to see you again, Stephenson," Colin said as he handed the man his hat. Once his hands were free, Colin brushed off the dust that had gathered on his coat on the ride over. "How is Miss Creston this morning? Is she taking visitors?"

"I shall let her know you are here."

Stephenson showed him to the parlor, then went to notify his mistress.

While he waited, Colin assessed the room. The house was not nearly so fine as Emberwilde, but lovely in its own right. The air still smelled a bit stale, as it had been shut up for so very long. Sheets still covered furniture and paintings. The wood floors beneath his feet were highly polished and looked to be freshly cleaned. Windows stretched to the high ceiling and looked out over the Trace Lake, where Colin had spent hours fishing with Isabel's grandfather so many years ago. Two fireplaces graced the room, one on the north wall and one on the south, and paintings of all shapes and sizes hung on the striped wallpaper.

He was studying one such painting when the door opened. He turned, and there was Isabel.

His breath suspended. The memory of their moments alone the previous night rushed him. He could only pray that her feelings were still the same as they had been in Bradford's study.

He had grown comfortable in her company, and yet the very sight of her dislodged his sense of time and space. He felt nervous, and he never felt nervous. She smiled in his direction, and for a moment he forgot why he was here and what he was supposed to do.

She stepped into the room. She was clad in her Fellsworth gown of black, and her hair was gathered at her neck. She had never looked lovelier. Her expression was happy, her complexion dewy.

"Mr. Galloway!" she exclaimed. "I am so happy to see you."

"I wanted to check on you and make sure you were all right. I hope I am not intruding."

She drew a deep breath, her smile warm and intoxicating. "You could never intrude. I don't know what I would have done if you had not come when you did."

The door closed behind the butler, and when all was silent, Colin took several steps toward her. She did not retreat. Instead, her lovely eyes brightened, and he drew so close he could smell the scent of lavender on her skin.

Words failed him. He could barely concentrate on what to say over the wild beating of his heart. Instead, he gently reached out and took her hands in his. "And your wrists? How are they?"

"I shall recover just fine."

There were so many things he wished to say to her, so many things he wanted to ask her, but his words seemed unorganized in her presence. "How are you settling in here?"

"It is a dream. I look around and can hardly believe this is all true."

He smiled. She seemed genuinely happy, and her countenance seemed unaffected by the previous night's events. He thought of her at Emberwilde, during the moments when she was distressed, as when Lizzie was lost or when she had been caught alone with Bradford in the Blue Parlor. But now she practically glowed in her new freedom.

"You can believe it," he said, "for it is all very true, very legal. No one can take this from you."

She drew a long, satisfied breath. "I am so glad you have come to visit, for I am not sure I have adequately expressed how grateful I am for all you have done for Lizzie and me."

He grew uncomfortable under the praise. He released her hands. "There is no need for that."

She stepped closer, her fingers knitted together in front of her. "Yes, there is. For you have done so much for us, both while we were at Emberwilde and also at Fellsworth, and then again last night. We are very grateful. I . . . I am very grateful."

He did not feel worthy of her thanks. "There are no words to express my anger at what happened last night. I can only hope the incident was not too upsetting for you."

She lifted her fair eyebrows in question. "What will happen next? To Mr. Bradford and the others, I mean?"

"They will face trial for their crimes."

"And the foundling home? The children?"

Colin shrugged. "For now the head nurse has been given control, but a new superintendent will need to be hired. The board that governs the home will lead the search."

Miss Creston shook her head. "This will be so very difficult for my aunt."

Colin cleared his throat. "I have news on that front. News that I am afraid may be difficult to hear."

Isabel's eyebrows drew together in concern. "Oh?"

"Bradford shared a bit more information last night when we took him to the cell. He could very well be trying to shift the blame, but since you were involved, you need to know the truth."

Her face paled, and she sank onto the sofa. "What is it?"

He sat down next to her, his hand so very close to hers. "Apparently, your aunt was aware of the smuggling activity. She was not involved, but she knew of it. From what I gathered, she had arrived at the school when Bradford was meeting with the men and overheard the scheme. Instead of going to the authorities, she decided to use it to her advantage."

Isabel drew a sharp breath but remained silent, her pale eyes fixed firmly on him.

He looked down to her hand before continuing. "She did know the details of the Heddeston inheritance long before the solicitors were able to locate you. She enlisted Bradford's help to get you to Emberwilde. She threatened him. If he refused to help her, she would have notified her husband and the authorities of his activities. So he complied. She wanted to keep you where she could keep an eye on you, to prevent you from finding out about the inheritance."

"Why, that is absurd!" She gave a shaky laugh of disbelief. "Surely I would have found out about it sooner or later."

"That is true, but she was betting on the fact that you would reach the age of twenty-one before that happened."

Isabel's lips formed a firm line.

He continued. "She began to fear that you would marry swiftly, and so she enlisted Bradford's help to distract you. She promised him a tidy sum if he kept you occupied until your twenty-first birthday, but then Mrs. Ellison grew nervous, because she thought someone else was beginning to develop feelings for you."

"Who was she worried about?"

"Me."

Her face flushed the most becoming pink, and she lowered her eyes.

He moved his hand so that it brushed hers ever so gently

before taking her fingers in his own. Fire ignited at the simplest touch. "She was right. By that time, you had captivated me. All that prompted Bradford to propose. Your refusal, combined with the fact that we were so close to figuring out the smuggling operation, sent their plans crumbling. When your uncle shared that he was considering selling the school property, that was the final straw for Bradford."

Isabel shook her head slowly. "I can't believe it. My own aunt."

"Your aunt bears some blame, but not all. Bradford always has been a master at manipulating the opinions and feelings of others, and I suppose he saw Mrs. Ellison as an easy target. Bradford knew about the tunnels, and if I had to guess, I would say that he targeted that building years ago, knowing it would be perfect for the smuggling operation. The home was a cover, I am afraid."

"Those poor children," Miss Creston whispered.

"They will be far better off now."

"But what if Uncle sells the property?" Miss Creston shook her head.

"In light of the recent realizations about the tunnels, I do not think your uncle will be selling that piece of land anytime soon, or at least not until this is all figured out."

He studied the toes of his boots before once again meeting Isabel's eyes. He softened his tone. "I am sorry, Isabel, for the injustices you experienced, not only at Bradford's hand, but also while at the Ellisons'. Had I known, had I even suspected, I would have intervened."

She pressed her lips together, no doubt at the memories. "It is no one's fault but my own. Nothing is without a price. But I did learn a great many lessons while there, Colin, so I do not regret it, not in the least."

The sound of his Christian name on her lips spread warmth within him.

She tilted her head to the side. "May I ask you something?"

"Anything."

"While in Mr. Langsby's office, you offered me guidance. You said to be careful."

"I did."

She paused. "What did you mean by that?"

"I only meant that this world, the world of estates and tenants and properties, can be a difficult one. You have a capable steward and butler, and you can trust them to get you started on the right foot. But many others will ask for your trust who do not deserve it."

A sigh escaped her lips. "Yes, I have learned that lesson."

She studied her fingers, still wrapped in his, for several moments before looking back to him. "I appreciate your willingness to offer your counsel, Colin. Your guidance is very important to me."

Her words lingered in his mind. They hung in the air, thick, like a mist that settled in the forest after the rain. By all accounts her words were positive, agreeable in their connotations and meaning. But kind as they were, they did not accurately match the emotions he had developed for her.

He feared overstepping his bounds. He had just cautioned her against those who would impose upon her trust and take advantage of her trusting nature. Was he any better than those he described? But he cared little for the estate, or the wealth, the house, or anything that went along with it. He cared only for her.

He did not know what to say now that silence had fallen, but he knew he could not let this moment pass. For as life resumed, he might never have another opportunity.

"Isabel," he began, "it has been my pleasure to offer whatever assistance I could, but after all this time, and after all that has transpired, I would like to offer you more than merely guidance."

Her eyebrows drew together in question. Bravery infused him. His fingers tightened around hers.

She looked down at their hands and did not pull away. He was so close that he could feel her warmth, her energy.

She drew a deep breath, and her blue eyes flicked boldly to his. She showed no distress. Instead, he thought he noticed a tremble in her chin. Moisture in her eyes. She looked at him fully. Trusting him.

He leaned toward her. "I have watched you for so long. I have witnessed your betrayal. I have seen you endure injustice and handle it with grace. I have nothing but admiration for you, and somehow you have become a part of my daily thoughts. When I heard you had been sent away, I could not rest until I knew you were safe. Say the word and I will speak no more on the matter, on that you have my word, but I cannot leave this room without telling you how much you have captivated me."

At this, a tear slipped from her eye and slid down her smooth cheek, but her gaze did not waver. He reached out his hand, slowly, and brushed the tear away with his thumb. He could not pull his hand away. He cupped her cheek with a gentle caress. She tipped her head into his palm. At her response, he could not prevent the grin spreading across his face. "I have just spoken to you of being cautious, but I cannot let this moment pass without offering you my love and everything I am. If you allow me, Isabel, I will dedicate every moment of my life to making sure you feel not an ounce of pain or heartbreak."

She drew a shaky breath, and at length, a smile formed on her face. He stood and, taking both of her hands in his, helped her to her feet. She stood so close to him. He moved his hands to her arms, then brushed the hair from her face, just as he had imagined doing a dozen times.

Her breath was still shaky, her eyes still fixed on him. "I . . . I can't imagine doing anything, or being anywhere, without you."

Her words filled him with courage. He stepped even closer, so that the fabric of her skirt brushed his legs. He drew her close and she did not resist. Quite the opposite—she leaned into him, resting her head on his shoulder.

At long last, for the first time since he could remember, love and adoration replaced the empty restlessness that had so occupied his soul. He held her for several moments, relishing the feeling of her so near to him, knowing that she trusted him. Cared for him.

He tilted her chin up to look at her. A smile, pure and genuine, curved her full lips. How beautiful she was. "Oh, Isabel, my Isabel," he breathed as he looked from the top of her golden curls to her eyes to her lips. "I could never bear to be separated from you. Never again. Marry me."

Tears fell freely from her eyes, but he was not alarmed. For the light in her eyes, the smile on her lips confirmed tears of joy.

Before she responded, he added, "I want to take care of you. And Lizzie. Today and every day hereafter."

She drew a deep breath and nodded, and with every second that passed, her smile intensified. "Yes, Colin. Yes!"

He drew her close. He doubted his own ability to stand when she wrapped her arms around his neck. His lips found hers, naturally and fully, and he very soon found himself lost in the wonder of her kiss.

He had found the place his soul had yearned for. After searching for home, he had finally found it—with her.

Chapter Forty-Three

*M*rs. Isabel Galloway sat at the breakfast table next to her husband. His hand was resting on the table, and she reached out and covered it with her own.

He looked up from his paper with an expectant smile, waiting to hear what she had to say.

She lifted the letter that had been delivered that morning. "I have news. Mary has accepted our invitation and will be here in three days' time. Are you sure you do not mind if she stays with us?"

He lowered the paper. "If it makes you happy, then I am fine with it."

She beamed under his words. "She is my dearest friend, and I cannot bear the thought of her alone. It is my hope that we can give her the opportunity for a new future and outcome."

"I think it is a fine idea. And you mention she is unattached? Hmm. Henry is unattached. That might be a project for you, my dear."

She gave a little shrug of excitement and lowered the letter to the table. "May I confess I thought the very same thing? Wouldn't that be something?"

Isabel returned her attention to the letter. In the time since their wedding, she and Colin had settled into a new routine. They'd had no contact with Emberwilde, and Bradford was in a cell, awaiting his trial. Her aunt, because of her status and the fact she was not directly involved in the smuggling, had escaped any sort of reprimand. Colin had resigned as magistrate and was busy assisting in the search for a new superintendent for the foundling home. He was usually gone by that time of day to see to the duties of both his family's estate and Heddeston's, but today he had stayed behind in anticipation of a very special delivery.

Lizzie, who sat across from them, bounced in her seat, barely able to contain her excitement. "But when will he get here?"

Colin smiled at the girl. "He should arrive at any time, but we must be patient."

"But that is impossible!" she cried, her dark eyes bright. "I've been waiting for days and days."

"Then a few more hours should not hurt," Colin teased.

Isabel watched the scene with satisfied happiness. Lizzie was blossoming here at Heddeston, and her relationship with Colin had deepened.

"Can we go to the stable now? I need to check his stall again."

Isabel could not help but smile at her sister's enthusiasm, for today she was to get a pony of her own.

Colin, as usual, was unable to resist the little girl's wide eyes. "Ah, all right. I will go with you." He squeezed Isabel's hand and pressed a kiss to the top of her head as he brushed past her. She smiled at the touch, still giddy at his attentions. She feared she would always be.

Lizzie raced around the room, prancing next to Colin. She tucked her hand in his as they left the house.

Isabel stood and moved to the window to watch them walk to the stable, but she stopped short when she saw a carriage in the drive. It bore the Ellison crest on the door—the very carriage that had retrieved Lizzie and her from Fellsworth so long ago.

Panic began to rise within her. She had had no contact with her family since her arrival at Heddeston Park. She had not refrained from visiting the friends she had made, nor had she neglected dinner invitations, but it was as if the Ellisons had disappeared after the scandal. Isabel had written Constance but received no response. She had resigned herself to accepting that the relationship was severed.

She lifted her eyes to the path that led to the stable. Colin had seen the carriage too. She could see him looking toward her, but then Lizzie tugged his hand. Isabel waved at him to continue on. Whoever was in that carriage, and whatever conversation awaited, she could handle it on her own.

It was Constance who emerged, beautifully dressed in a striking gown of pink and gold. Isabel watched as she was received by Stephenson, then hurried from the breakfast room, taking a few moments to pat her hair into place. Enthusiasm to see her cousin trumped all hurts.

Constance stepped into the foyer, and Isabel hurried to her. Unable to resist, she hugged her cousin tightly. "Oh, Constance! What a day this is. I am so happy to see you!"

When she stepped back, Isabel found tears in Constance's eyes and sadness tugging at her lips.

"Whatever is wrong? Come, come with me to the parlor. We can talk there."

She took her cousin by the hand and led her like a child to the settee. She sat down and motioned for Constance to join her. Constance took a seat, slowly, and looked around the room.

"Your home is beautiful."

"Thank you," Isabel responded.

"It is just as I remembered it when we used to visit Grandfather."

Isabel bit her lower lip. A million questions raced through her mind, and dozens of things that she wanted to say waited to be said. But she gave her cousin a moment to collect herself.

At length, Constance spoke. "Mother does not know I am here."

Isabel thought it a strange way to start the conversation, but she remained silent.

"I am leaving Northrop on Monday. Mr. Nichols and I will be married soon, and I do not know when I will return to Emberwilde. But I could not leave, not with you here, not like this."

Emotion tightened Isabel's throat as she watched her cousin struggle with the words.

"I don't even know where to begin," Constance said. "There are so many things I need to say to you. So many explanations you are owed. I am sure they seem overwhelming, for if I were in your shoes, I should feel that way. But all I can do now is to ask for your forgiveness. I swear to you, Isabel, I knew nothing of what Mother had planned. Nothing. I do hope you believe me. I am shocked and embarrassed. I had my concerns about Mr. Bradford, and I should have been more forthcoming. Please, please forgive me."

Isabel took her cousin's hands. "I know you did nothing wrong. You are my cousin and dear friend." Isabel took several breaths to summon the courage for what she was about to ask. "And what about your mother? How is she?"

"To this day she can barely leave the house for the shame. She has become quite frightened that she will be accused of participating in the illegal activity, but I think she is safe from that. Her crime was one of greed. I am worried about her, actually. But my frustration and anger lie mostly with Mr. Bradford. He is at the crux of this, and he will have to answer for his actions."

Isabel frowned in sympathy. She had witnessed firsthand Mr. Bradford's persuasive ability to manipulate others.

"Let me put your mind at ease, Constance. You have my full forgiveness." Isabel reached out and squeezed her cousin's hand. "I must say, I have been wondering how our family was holding up."

"I suppose you have heard the rumors, then."

Isabel looked down to her hands, for it was true. She had heard the servants whispering, and even Colin's own family had shared news with her. "I have heard that Uncle sold the west farmlands to

Mr. Atwell, and I have also heard that Emberwilde itself may have to be sold."

"It is a sad thing to think of, that is for sure. But perhaps it will be a positive thing, for a heaviness seems to hang over all." Constance shook her head. "But what pains me the most is that I tried to press you into an arrangement with Mr. Bradford. If I had known anything of his true character—"

Isabel raised her hand to silence her cousin. "Please, do not think about it. We are each on our own journey, and nothing is by accident. I have found my happiness, and that is what matters, is it not?"

For the first time, a hint of a smile tugged at Constance's lips. "I have brought you something." She stood and signaled to the carriage driver from the window. Isabel watched as he brought in a large item draped in a sheet and placed it against the wall. Constance removed the cloth.

Tears filled Isabel's eyes as her gaze landed on the portrait of her mother. Her heart warmed at the sight of the soft strokes that so carefully portrayed the woman she could barely remember but truly understood. Her lips trembled with the effort to keep her tears at bay.

"This belongs here," explained Constance. "It belongs with you."

Isabel touched the gilded frame and let her sight linger on the image that she had tried to re-create in her mind so many times. "I . . . I thought I would never see it again. Is your mother all right to part with it?"

"I told Mother I intended to give it to you, and she did not protest." Constance lowered her gaze. "I do not mind sharing with you that I was concerned my betrothed would not honor our arrangement in light of the scandal, but since my dowry is unaffected, he has agreed to continue as planned. You must know I am eager to be free from the shadows surrounding Emberwilde."

Pain pricked Isabel. She had hoped that her cousin would find a match made of love, like she had, but it appeared that Constance intended to proceed with her plans for marriage. Isabel forced a smile to her face, despite the twinges of sadness that tugged at her.

Constance's expression brightened. "I am so pleased for you. Please accept my congratulations on your marriage and your new home. I understand from Father that Mr. Galloway has ceased his employment and now dedicates himself full-time to the care of your estates."

"Yes, now that the properties are joined, it only makes sense. There is much to do and much to oversee. I confess it makes my head spin. I had no idea what such a position entailed. Fortunately, Mr. Galloway seems to enjoy the challenge of restoring both estates to their former glory."

"Father says that this union makes your combined lands the largest estate in the area. I am so thrilled for you, Isabel."

Isabel reached out and squeezed her cousin's hand. "Thank you for coming, Constance. You cannot believe what a joy this is for me."

The cousins embraced, and the moment was a bittersweet one for Isabel. She was happy to be reunited with her cousin, her first true friend outside of Fellsworth, but she also knew she was bidding her friend farewell.

Later that evening, after night had fallen and Lizzie was in bed, Isabel and Colin stood in the parlor, preparing to hang the portrait of her mother.

The painting above the fireplace had been removed, yielding the place of honor to the painting that meant more to Isabel than any other.

Their staff was still meager, and Stephenson was far too old to be climbing on ladders, so Colin did the task.

"Is this centered?" he called, looking over his shoulder at her.

Isabel could barely breathe, so full was her heart. Colin, so handsome, so loving. She almost forgot to respond.

"Isabel?" he prompted.

"Oh, yes," she hastened. "Yes, that is perfect."

He secured the painting and climbed down the ladder and joined her in the center of the room. He stood with her, shoulder to shoulder, as they assessed the portrait.

"She was beautiful, was she not?" Isabel breathed.

Colin wrapped his arm around her, drew her close, and kissed her forehead.

"I do wish I could have known her," she said.

"I know. But at least you are here now, in her home, and there is part of her here."

Isabel allowed Colin to enfold her in an embrace. The light from the fire cast a warm glow onto his face, and she closed her eyes, relishing his touch.

She had found it—home. She found it within these walls, but more so, she found it within Colin's arms. Past betrayals were now distant memories, and their future spread before them in vivid detail.

"I love you, Colin." She tilted her chin up to meet his kiss.

"And I love you, Mrs. Galloway." He smiled, and once again, she surrendered to his kiss.

Acknowledgments

Writing a novel is never a solitary endeavor. So many people have encouraged me as I wrote this book, and I feel blessed by each one.

To my family—thank you for inspiring me to tell stories and for supporting me through the process. Your cheers, encouragement, and advice mean more to me than you will ever know.

To my first readers—thank you for brainstorming with me and helping me get the story just right!

To my agent, Tamela Hancock Murray—thank you for your guidance and friendship. I can't wait to see what the future has in store!

To my fabulous editor, Becky Monds—thank you for believing in my story and working alongside me to make it the best it can be.

To the rest of the team at HarperCollins Christian Publishing—I am constantly amazed by each one of you and by the work that you do!

And last but not least, to my writing friends—thanks to each and every one of you for sharing this journey. To my accountability partners Carrie, Julie, and Melanie—thank you for keeping me on track! And to Kim—thank you for all the support you give me. To the "Grove Girls"—I am inspired by your willingness to share your gifts and inspire others.

Discussion Questions

1. Isabel thought she knew what her next steps in life would be, but with one letter, her entire future changed. Have you ever had a life-changing moment? If so, how did that make you a different person?
2. Who is your favorite character in the novel? Why? Who is your least favorite character in the novel? Why?
3. If you could give Isabel one piece of advice at the beginning of the story, what would it be? If you could give her one piece of advice at the end of the novel, what would that be?
4. During this time in history, it was the goal of most women to marry—after all, marriage meant security. Do you think Isabel was wise for refusing Mr. Bradford when she did, especially considering that Lizzie was depending upon her?
5. Do you think that Colin ever really loved Miranda? Why or why not?
6. How would you describe Constance? Do you think she was a good friend and cousin to Isabel? How did their relationship change throughout the course of the story?
7. In what ways does Isabel change throughout the course of the novel?
8. It's your turn! What comes next for Isabel and Colin? What comes next for Lizzie? If you could write the rest of their story, what would it be like?

WHISPERS ON THE MOORS

JOIN AMELIA, PATIENCE, AND CECILY ON THEIR ADVENTURES IN REGENCY ENGLAND.

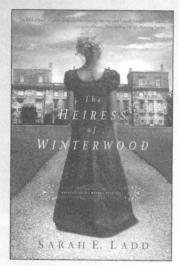

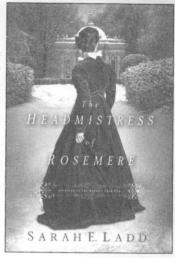

"Ladd proves yet again she's a superior novelist, creating unforgettable characters and sympathetically portraying their merits, flaws and all-too-human struggles with doubt, hope and faith."

—*Romantic Times*,
4-STAR REVIEW OF
A Lady at Willowgrove Hall

CAMILLE IVERNESS CAN TAKE CARE OF HERSELF. SHE'S done so since the day her mother abandoned the family and left Camille to run their shabby curiosity shop. But when a violent betrayal leaves her injured with no place to hide, Camille must allow a mysterious stranger to come to her aid.

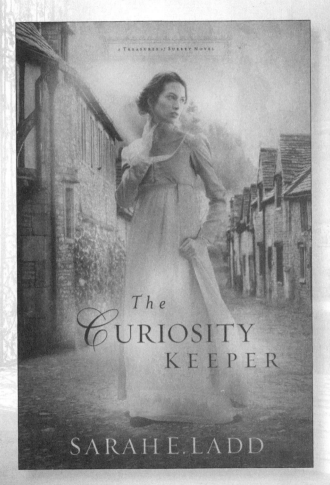

AN EXCERPT FROM
THE CURIOSITY KEEPER

Chapter One ————————————————————

IVERNESS CURIOSITY SHOP, LONDON, ENGLAND, 1812

Camille Iverness met the big man's gaze.

Bravely.

Boldly.

She would not be bullied or manipulated. Not in her own shop.

Camille recognized the expression in the man's eye. He did not want to speak with her, a mere woman. Not when the owner of the shop was James Iverness.

But James Iverness—her father—was not present.

She was.

She jutted her chin out in a show of confidence, refusing to even blink as he pinned her with a steely stare.

"As I already told you, Mr. Turner, I have no money to give you," she repeated, louder this time. "Any dealings you made with my father you will need to take up with him. I've no knowledge of the transaction you described. You had best return at another time."

"I've seen you here, day in, day out." His voice rose in both volume and gruffness. "How do you expect me to believe you know nothing about it?" The wooden planks beneath his feet groaned as he shifted his considerable weight, making little attempt to mask his effort to look around her into the store's back room. "Is he in there? So help me, if he is and—"

"Sir, no one besides myself is present, with the exception of my father's dog."

It was in moments like this that she wished she were taller, for even as she stood on the platform behind the counter, the top of her head barely reached his shoulder. "If you would like, I will wake the animal, but if you have seen me here often, as you claim, then no doubt you have also seen Tevy and know he does not take kindly to strangers. You decide. Shall I go fetch him?"

Mr. Turner's gaze snapped back to her. No doubt he knew of the dog. Everyone on Blinkett Street knew about James Iverness's dog. His whiskered lip twitched.

A warm sense of satisfaction spread through her, for finally she had said something to sway the determined man.

Mr. Turner's face deepened to crimson, and he pointed a thick finger in Camille's direction, his voice matching the intensity of his eyes. "Tell your father I've a mind to speak with him. And tell him I want my money and won't take kindly to his antics. Next time I am here I will not be so willing to leave."

He muttered beneath his breath and stomped from the store, slamming the door behind him with such force that the glass canisters on the near shelf trembled.

A shudder rushed through her as she watched him lumber away, and she did not let her posture relax until the back flap of his gray coat passed the window and was out of sight. How she despised such interactions. As of late, Papa seemed to be angering more patrons than he obliged, and he always managed to be conveniently absent when they came to confront him.

She needed to speak with Papa, and soon. Awkward conversations like the one with Mr. Turner needed to stop.

Camille tucked a long, wayward lock of hair behind her ear and drew a deep breath. Once again her father's dog had come to her rescue, and he was not even in the room.

"Come, Tevy," she called. In a matter of moments the massive brown animal was through the door and at her side, tail wagging enthusiastically.

"Pay heed!" she laughed as he nudged her hand, forcing her to pet him. "That tail of yours is likely to knock every vase off that shelf if you're not careful, and then Papa will blame—"

The door to the shop pushed open, jingling the bell hung just above it. She drew a sharp breath, preparing to deal with yet another customer, but it was her father who appeared in the doorway.

He was a short man, not much taller than she herself, but that was where their physical similarities ended. His green eyes made up in intensity what he lacked in stature. His hair, which in her youth had been the color of sand, was now the color of stone, and years spent on a ship's deck had left his complexion ruddy. His threadbare frock coat, dingy neckcloth, and whiskered cheeks made him appear more like a vagabond than a shopkeeper, and despite his privileged upbringing, he often acted and spoke like an inhabitant of the docks where he did much of his trading.

"Good day, Papa."

He ignored her welcome and bent to scratch Tevy's ears. After pulling out a bit of dried meat and handing it to the dog, he reached back into his coat. "This came for you."

He stretched out his hand, rough and worn. Between his thick fingers he pinched a letter.

Camille stared at it for several moments, shocked. Clearly she could make out her name—in her mother's handwriting. The edge of the paper was torn. She could not recall the last letter she had received from Mama.

He thrust the letter toward her. "Don't just stand there gawking, girl. Take it."

Camille fumbled with the missive to keep it from falling to the planked floor below, but for once, she found herself unable to find words. Unprepared—and unwilling—to deal with the onset of emotions incited by the letter, she blinked back moisture and shoved it into the front pocket of her work apron.

"Are you not going to read it?" Her father nodded toward her apron.

Of course he expected her to read it, for he himself devoured every one of his wife's scarce communications the moment they arrived. Though they both felt her absence keenly, they reacted to it very differently—and they never, ever discussed it. Over time, Camille had made the topic off-limits in her own mind, and a letter crafted by the very person who was the source of the pain was unwelcome.

"I'll read it later. There is far too much to do at the moment." She sniffed and gestured toward the curtain that separated the shop from the back room. "There was a crate delivered to you by cart in the alley, but it was too heavy for me to lift."

She was a little surprised at the quickness with which her father let the topic of the letter drop. "Why did you not have the men delivering it bring it in?"

"I tried, but they refused—said it was not their duty. They left it in the courtyard out back."

"When are you going to learn that such things are your responsibility? You should have persuaded them to bring it in." Her father shifted through the papers on the counter, not pausing to look up. "Had you been a boy, this would not be an issue."

Camille folded her arms across her chest. "Well, I was not born a boy, and there is precious little I can do about that. So if you will fetch the delivery in for me, I shall tend to it. Or it can spend the night hours where it sits. But the sky looks like it holds rain, so whatever is inside that box will just sit there and soak."

After much grumbling, Papa disappeared through the back and returned dragging a large, awkward crate. Camille helped him bring it close to the counter, then pried the lid off and reached for one of the linen-wrapped items inside. Laying it on the counter, she carefully pulled back the fabric and revealed a canvas. Strokes of emerald and moss depicted a countryside set below a brilliant sapphire sky. She flipped through the next canvas, then the next. All boasted lush pastoral landscapes.

She clicked her tongue as she assessed the cargo. "They are all paintings. Why did you buy these?"

"I didn't buy them," he muttered. "I traded for them."

"That is the same thing, Father. Paintings do not sell well. You know that. They will sit on the shelves for months, I fear. And we haven't the space as it is."

"When will you learn not to question my ways? Sometimes such deals must be made to clinch future arrangements. You mind the counter and leave the dealings to me."

She ignored him and lifted another canvas out of the crate. "Speaking of dealings, Mr. Turner was just in looking for you."

At this he raised his head. "Did he make a purchase?"

"No, quite the opposite. He said you owe him money."

"You didn't give him any, did you?"

"Of course not."

Her father returned to his stack of papers. "Turner is a fool."

"Do you owe him money?" She leaned her hip against the counter. When her father did not respond, she continued. "If you insist upon doing these business dealings on the side, that is fine, but you must understand that you have put me in some very awkward situations. Mr. Turner was quite angry."

Her father disappeared through the doorway, signaling he was finished with the conversation. She sighed and lifted another canvas, assessing the delicate brushstrokes with a practiced eye. A lovely piece, expertly done. In another shop it might fetch a pretty penny. But not here. Their patrons wanted the unusual, the wildly exotic—unique treasures from far beyond England's shore, not calm renditions of their own British countryside.

But Camille's practical side could not quiet the beating of her heart as she took in the tranquil meadow and vivid flora depicted by the artist's strokes. Memories of her time in such a setting rushed her. She remembered running through the waving grasses, wading in the trickling streams, breathing air so fresh and clean it practically sparkled.

So long ago . . .

When she was small, Camille and her mother had lived on her paternal grandfather's country estate. At that time her father had been endlessly absent, either away on business or incessantly traveling the world to quench his thirst for the rare and mysterious. But after her grandfather's death, the lavish estate had been sold. Her father, the sole heir, had invested the proceeds into this shop. And life as Camille knew it had changed forever.

She longed to flee from the dirty confines of Blinkett Street and return to the countryside, to once more breathe fresh air and to bask in the golden sunshine that bathed the meadows. But Grandfather was dead, and Mama was far away, and Papa begrudged even her necessary outings to the greengrocer and the butcher.

She sighed as the door's bell signaled another customer.

Camille had not left London since she first came to the city eleven years earlier.

She was beginning to wonder if she would ever leave London again.

The story continues in *The Curiosity Keeper* by Sarah E. Ladd.

About the Author

Sarah E. Ladd received the 2011 Genesis Award in historical romance for *The Heiress of Winterwood*. She is a graduate of Ball State University and has more than ten years of marketing experience. Sarah lives in Indiana with her amazing family and spunky golden retriever.

Visit Sarah online at www.sarahladd.com
Facebook: SarahLaddAuthor
Twitter: @SarahLaddAuthor